PODRIC MOON
AND THE CORSICAN TYRANT

About the Author

Photo: Matthew Usher with kind permission, Archant

Barney Broom is a screenwriter and director with many years' experience in the film industry. Barney has worked in the USA, Europe and the far east including China.

His varied work includes music videos, commercials, corporate and educational films and documentaries for the History and Discovery channels.

Barney's theatrical short film *Knights Electric* is catalogued by the British Film Institute as an iconic musical memoir of 1980s Britain.

Barney Broom is a member of BAFTA and the Directors Guild of Great Britain.

He lives in London and North Norfolk.

Also by Barney Broom

HAUTE CUISINE

MOON RIVER
Podric Moon's Adventures in the American Civil War

PODRIC MOON

AND THE CORSICAN TYRANT

BARNEY BROOM

Podric Moon Ltd
London

PODRIC MOON and the Corsican Tyrant

Podric Moon Ltd
30 Sherwood Court
Chatfield Road
London SW11 3UY UK

First Published by The Book Guild 2018
Second edition published in the United Kingdom 2020

British Library Cataloguing-in-Publication Data.
A catalogue record for this book is available from the British Library.

ISBN 978-1-8380460-2-6

www.podricmoon.com

In memory of my mother and father without whom there would be no reality – ultimate, alternative or otherwise.

Origins of the name PODRIC

[B]Padraig is, of course, pronounced "Porrick" on BallyK; but the Irish golfer Padraig Harrington is called "Podrick" by all the commentators, including the Irish. Furthermore, the Irish patriot, Padraic Pearse's name is pronounced "Podrick" by the Clancy Brothers and Tommy Makem.

Google

Part 1

Discovery of Ultimate
Alternative Reality

Prologue

I t was the trip of a lifetime.

His dad having organised him a ride in a Typhoon, Podric Moon sat in the instructor's seat. The aeroplane pulling four and a half G banked hard over the coast and levelled out low over the grey North Sea below.

Not only was he flying in the type of fast jet his father flew – a T3, but in his dad's *actual plane* and on his *actual seat!* It was blowing his mind.

The pilot of ZA119, Squadron Leader Ian Shawcross was both younger and junior to Podric's father, Wing Commander Sean Moon, but the two men had been complicit in getting Podric his ride. It was his prize for the boy's latest victory in computer games.

At a recent competition in London, Podric, nearly seventeen, had won the title of 'Best under twenty-one player' in Europe. In fact, he had played and beaten several of the top adult contestants in the world. Both Sean Moon and Shawcross were avid computer games aficionados and their interest in virtual reality formed a special bond between them and Sean's son.

The flight – which was a regular training sortie, had been all too simple to organise and now as they climbed, bursting out through the clouds into brilliant sunshine, Podric knew this was what he wanted to do for the rest of his life. One day he'd be in the front seat flying with his dad in this same jet.

"Want to feel the controls Podric? They just about match the new '*Fastjet!*' game console."

Podric could barely speak, he was so excited. Shawcross's voice was calm, controlled and very RAF.

"I know you know what to do. You have control, Moon."

*   *   *

The screen flickered into life and Sean Moon's face appeared. The webcam image showed him dressed in his RAF flying kit, his helmet with its spotless visor, visible beside him.

"Hi son. Going up in a few minutes, I've been thinking about our virtual reality chat. Technology's going to fly-."

Sean laughed.

"Sorry. And lives are going to be oh so different. You know I'm the techiest geek around. It's why I love your playing computer games. They're smarter than some of the kit we use."

Sean fidgeted in his chair.

"It fascinates me - all the stuff that's going to be happening. Won't be long now before we're all tagged - shared information. It's the coming world. I'll be obsolete. You know the weakest link in the aeroplane I fly? Me. Terrifying, huh? On board kit can outthink me and my body can't cope with the strains the aircraft can."

He sat back slightly.

"As for the ideas we've had for developing an alternative re-ality, you won't need to move matter. It's all in the mind. Never forget Podric, whatever the future holds, it's important to have an understanding of the past. Winston Churchill had a good line on it like he did most things the cocky bugger. It ran something like, 'if a man doesn't have an understanding of history, he can't begin to reckon with the present let alone have any grasp on the future'. It's true I think. And where we're going in this crazy old world, a person will need all the sense of perspective they can get to help see them through."

The ops room speaker system emitted some jarring squawk.

"Got to go son. You know what it's like here - duty calls! Love you all and catch you later."

Sean's hand reached forward to click off the webcam and for a second, his face filled the frame.

"This world and our virtual one Podric - adventures are to be lived! Never forget that. Bye now."

Just before the screen went blank, Sean winked.

Chapter 1

The Loss

"He wouldn't have known a thing. Death was instantaneous." It was only a few weeks after Podric's trip and now his father was dead. The RAF Station Commander, a woman Flight Lieutenant and a man from the Ministry of Defence sat on the patterned sofa in the Moon's living room. For several seconds, there was silence; grave concern on the service people's part, disbelief on the woman's.

"Your children - there'll be counselling - for yourself too." The Flight Lieutenant was solicitous.

"Thank you."

Barbara Moon heard her voice strange and far away.

"Amy and...Podric is it? I know your daughters at the junior school here, but your son's away I believe - at school in Ireland."

The MOD man was sombre.

"At his father's old alma mater - Kilkenny College I think it is..."

Group Captain Malinson's utterance was sad.

"Sean wanted Podric to go there - he loved it so."

The afternoon was getting to a point where no one quite knew what to say; the effect of commiserations ran deep.

"I believe Podric wants to join the service." The MOD man looked around distractedly.

"I was with a girlfriend, painting in Ireland. We were in Kerry. Sean had started at Cranwell, but his mother being ill, he'd got home to Tralee for a long weekend. Into my landscape walks this beautiful trainee pilot. Kenmare Bay on a perfect summer evening is the most romantic place in the world..."

"Are you Irish, Barbara?" Flight Lieutenant Maureen Carpenter tried to keep her voice light.

"Me? No. I'm from Bradford!"

Minutes later they were gone. And Barbara Moon howled. Then she went numb. Then she howled some more. An hour or so later, a car pulled up outside and a young woman and a little girl got out. Running into the house, nine-year-old Amy Moon clutched some daubed paper. The youthful artwork was vibrant in its choice of colours.

"Mummy, mummy, Miss Smythe brought me home as a treat. Her cars got heated seats and videos in the back."

Jenny Smythe stood hesitantly in the doorway. She was a new teacher, attractive and slim.

"Would you like me to stay?"

Barbara thanked her but declined.

"If there's anything I can do – any help you need..."

For once Barbara was grateful she was in a service environment. The RAF station school was very good and while the tragedy that had befallen her was not common, it did happen occasionally. Barbara also knew there would be an infrastructure to support her for the short term at least; the service was proud of looking after its own.

It wasn't till several days later that Barbara could travel to County Kilkenny and see her son. Podric obviously had to be told and this sad task fell on his headmaster, Mr. O'Connell. A striking man with a shock of unruly red hair, Bryan O'Connell was a popular head. He'd invited Podric to his study, and coffee and biscuits were brought in.

Podric Moon had a willowy physique but was tougher than his rangy frame suggested. Fair haired, a mop of his own shaggy locks frequently fell across his eyes causing him to push them back behind an ear. Without waiting for O'Connell to open his mouth, Podric said, "I know sir."

O'Connell looked uncertain.

"You...know?"

"It was online and I've heard from someone on the base."

"You've spoken to your mother then?"

Podric shook his head. The headmaster looked at his pupil.

"She's coming over."

Podric didn't respond. Drinking coffee and eating biscuits, they spoke desultorily.

"You're a computer games champion, aren't you?"

"I've...won some things..."

"A bit more than that I believe Podric. Didn't I hear you were the best under twenty-one player in Europe?"

"I'm joining the air force."

"I know you're down for it."

O'Connell adjusted his blotter.

"There's little I can say. It was a freak accident I believe."

Whilst details were still unclear, what little was known suggested that the Typhoon was on an extremely low flying exercise and had collided with a light aircraft which had somehow penetrated military airspace. The weather had been bad, but for the moment Podric intended keeping his counsel as to the collisions exact cause to himself. He finished his coffee.

"If there's nothing else sir..."

For once the charismatic headmaster was caught off-guard.

"No, well if you want to talk again Podric – if there's anything I can do..."

They both stood up and shook hands.

Two days later his mother arrived, accompanied by an Air attaché from the British embassy in Dublin. Barbara had made the decision to bury Sean in his home country, and Podric would leave with her to attend his father's funeral. As the term was nearly over, he was also granted an exemption for its remaining duration, travelling to England and their home on the RAF base for the school holidays.

On getting back to Coningsby, Podric went to see Ian Shawcross. The Squadron Leader recently discharged from hospital, was on leave recovering from his injuries. Sitting in the Shawcross's conservatory, rays of wintry sunlight casting late afternoon shadows over the Lincolnshire countryside, Podric studied the man who was his father's closest service friend. Adjusting his body in a wheelchair, the normally exuberant Shawcross was withdrawn. Although only in his late thirties, he had aged visibly since the accident. His wife, Wendy brought in tea.

"I hope your mother wasn't upset I called you, but I found your text on Ian's phone."

"She didn't mention it but it's okay you did."

"You still want to fly?" Shawcross's croaking voice cut across the conversation. Podric nodded.

"Even now that Sean's gone?"

The Squadron Leader's vocal cords had been damaged in the crash and his rasping tone was bitter. Podric studied one of the two men he'd idolised more than any other in the world.

"You should stick to bloody computer games; more your sort of thing. Winning competitions and little trophies."

These hurtful words caused Shawcross to start a spasm of coughing, and a short while later, Podric left. Wendy Shawcross was apologetic.

"He doesn't mean it Podric, but...well, he blames himself for the accident."

"It wasn't his fault."

"The preliminary findings at least suggest not."

"It wasn't his fault," Podric was firm.

"Well no, but...you seem very certain?"

"I am. Dad told me."

*   *   *

In the weeks that followed, Podric didn't do much. Even virtual reality games didn't hold any appeal. He just seemed to shut down.

His sister, Amy, was seven years his junior and to Podric, an irritating person. At first, she was hysterical when she learned about the loss of her dad, but after several days of uncontrollable emotion, Amy appeared to adjust, and returned to being the sunny child she was. It was difficult to predict what her long-term reaction might be but for Podric, things ran deep. Such was the intense bond he had with Sean, the loss of his aviator father left the boy bereft.

For their mother, the challenges she faced were even greater if that were possible. Not only was she trying to come to terms with her own grief but she also had to make decisions which would affect her children's lives. It was horrifying to realise how this tragic event caused such profound familial dislocation. Whilst the RAF were considerate, as the weeks went by, the matter of their accommodation inevitably came to the fore and Barbara Moon decided that she must move from their service home. It was at this point Podric announced that he had no intention of returning to his school in Ireland.

Though the ramifications of leaving Kilkenny at such a critical juncture in his schooling weren't lost on Barbara, this decision didn't displease her as much as might have been expected. After mulling things over, she decided it would be sensible to move somewhere in the vicinity of her parents. However, this decision was arrived at with considerable misgiving.

Being a north-country couple, it was a mystery why Barbara's mum and dad, Gerald and Oona Fosdyke, had retired to rural Hampshire. But then it was strange Oona, the love child of artist Rempray McFarland, had ever married market gardener Gerald in the first place. Her husband buying himself a pet's home, 'The Fosdyke Pet Emporium,' only added to the contrariness of their existence.

After driving around her parent's neighbourhood, usually accompanied by Amy, Barbara chose the village of Drinkwell some ten miles away. A pretty hamlet of historic significance, the Moons couldn't afford any of the grander properties, but Briony Close which had been built on the outskirts, would become their home.

Barbara's next task was to find schools for her children and a job for herself. Podric's refusal to return to his private academy in Ireland was in some ways a blessing. The monetary saving was not inconsiderable and his mother hoped that his being around would be company for her. Wendbury High provided the educational answer – Amy being enrolled in the junior school and Podric, the senior.

As to a job, sitting in Briony Close one evening surrounded by unopened packing cases, Barbara was sipping coffee whilst flicking through a free community newspaper, when she spied an advertisement offering the position of PA to the managing director of a local business. The painter in Barbara had been hoping for something more artistic. When married, she'd had several exhibitions but money earned from her work was erratic and only occasionally supplemented Sean's RAF pay. But in her new situation beggars couldn't be choosers and the following morning Barbara called Tweeney's Waste Disposal. After a few minutes conversation with the man himself, Ralph Tweeney suggested she came by for an interview and an appointment was duly made. The meeting was successful, and Barbara was hired to start work the following Monday.

The Sunday morning after they'd moved Barbara went into Wendbury shopping, leaving Podric and Amy supposedly asleep. It wasn't long before the little girl came down and started watching a Shrek DVD. A drip dropping onto the doll she was dressing, Amy looked up to see a wet patch appearing on the ceiling and water running down the light cable. With surprising composure, she ran upstairs and opened the bathroom door. A plug left in the sink and a tap not properly turned off had caused the overflow. Amy managed to pull the plug out and water gurgled away. But the bathroom floor was flooded and grabbing some towels, she threw them on the floor.

"Podric."

Amy's call meeting with no response, she banged on her brother's bedroom door.

"Podric!"

Amy tried the handle, but was unable to open it. The door was jammed.

"God you're irritating. The bathroom's flooded. Your help is needed and if you won't open up, I'll break that mug you always use."

There was no response.

"And that picture of dad's plane in mum's bedroom."

That did it.

"Touch it and I'll kill you."

Amy went back to the bathroom and seconds later, Podric appeared. His hair a sight, he wore a Kilkenny rugger shirt and tracksuit bottoms.

"Hand down some more towels, will you?"

Amy nodded towards the airing cupboard and Podric's lanky

form obliged.

"I wonder about mum."

Having mopped up the water, Podric disappeared back to his room and Amy went downstairs to resume her viewing. A few minutes later, Podric showed up in their sitting room carrying two mugs of tea. Brother and sister sat together watching the film when Amy suddenly said.

"Are you going to go to this school?"

"I quit school."

"That's dumb Podric. If you do that, you won't get grades and if you don't get grades, you won't get into the RAF."

"I don't want to get into the RAF now."

"Yes, you do."

Amy finished her tea.

"Okay kid – you know more than I do."

"You've got to go to school Pod. You can't let dad down."

Podric didn't reply. He stared at the television.

A little while later, Barbara's battered VW came up the drive. There was some family communication about the flooded bathroom, after which Podric headed for his bedroom.

"Don't go hiding Pod."

Amy looked at her elder brother with all her nine-year-old gravitas.

"Mum and I will leave you alone, but don't go hiding."

"At least with her new job, they should have good plumbers."

The rest of the day Barbara was distracted. Though not usually the worrying kind, her son's behaviour troubled her and that night she went to bed preoccupied.

The following morning getting ready for her own first day at work, Barbara dressed in her eccentric clothes. Wearing multi-coloured leg warmers and a scarlet Mexican poncho – despite having lost her husband she was an original character and her free spirit wasn't going to change.

"Got everything?"

Amy stood in the kitchen and presented a painting. An interesting composition, it depicted the whirling's of a sinks' waste disposal with the words 'pull the plug and see the flow!' inscribed in its spiral waters.

"Good luck mum. Come on Podric, we'll miss the bus!"

Watching her daughter skip out of the door, Barbara barely glimpsed her son, just catching sight of his gawky figure loping down their short driveway after his sister. Podric carried no bag and seemed totally unprepared for attending school. He really was an enigma – someone she didn't truly know, yet loved so completely.

At the bus stop, a youth of Podric's age stood waiting. Beside him, a stout middle-aged woman sat on a bench. A large scarlet macaw hopped around beside her. Loosely tethered by a string, it flapped its considerable wingspan and squawking loudly, made Amy uneasy.

"Whoa Eamon, calm down."

Spoken by the other boy, Billy Johnson also seemed nervous.

"Dad says you shouldn't have him out like that Mrs. B; 'Bird like that could hurt someone."

"My Eamon wouldn't harm a flea...would'ya, yer big softy?"

Eamon squawked some more and flapped harder. The school bus arrived.

Driver Claude Linklater released the electric doors which opened just in time to let Eamon fly in. Chaos ensued. The bus was in pandemonium as the macaw flailed its way amongst the alarmed school children. Linklater not taking command of the situation, Podric spied a piece of old sack lying in the hedge. Grabbing it, he jumped aboard and managed to throw the rotting hessian over Eamon's head. Another boy, Miles Willoughby, caught the string and together the two lads extricated Eamon from the vehicle. As the flapping macaw was brought out, Billy took hold of the lanyard and led Eamon back to Ivy Bickerstaff.

"I'm going to report you." A panicky Linklater yelled from the bus at the relieved Ivy.

"That bird's a liability!"

Giving the string to Ivy, Billy said, "You'd better take him home Mrs. Bickerstaff. You really shouldn't have him out."

The youthful bus passengers still excited, several of its occupants were yelling the old 'Pieces of eight' pirate cry. Amy confronted Mr Linklater.

"Shouldn't we be on our way?"

"Are you one of the new kids?"

"Me and my brother."

Claude checked the list.

"Amy Moon and Podric is it? Podric Moon. Rum name."

"He's good with escaped birds."

The three newcomers climbed aboard. Claude slung his clip-board on the dashboard and closed the electric doors.

"Daft old girl. I'm definitely gonna report her. Could have hurt someone...that bloody squawking parrot."

"It's not a parrot, it's a macaw."

Two identical twins, Maurice and Clive Jenkins, spoke in unison. Impeccably dressed, they were precise types.

"I don't care if it's Polly, the chirping budgerigar, she's still goin' to get reported."

The coach lurched off.

"So, we have a new hero then."

The school bully, Barney Sturridge, sat with two of his cohorts, 'Plug' and 'Gnome', several rows back from Podric. The former thug acolyte was a ringer for the *Beano*'s Bash Street Kids character, and Gnome's nomenclature perfectly matched his size. But Barney was different. Big for his age, he had a presence and was smarter than his arrogant attitude suggested. Slouching in his seat, he wore earplugs and hummed sporadically.

"Quite the Birdman of Alcatraz... But this does not mean much to either the dwarfed or aurally challenged!"

Speaking loudly due to the music playing in his ears, Barney's gaze moved from Gnome to Plug, as he twisted one of Plug's large auditory protuberances.

"I love Dry Bone Sister - a band after me own heart. And you friend with the skin and blister. A man of birds then - shiver me timbers if he ain't. Get that P and G? Shiver!"

His two confederates grinned stupidly.

"God..."

Releasing Plug's ear, Barney sat back tapping along to the track on his mobile.

"What's yer name?"

This question directed at Podric, the new boy fiddled with his iPhone. Podric's fingers darted across its display. He adjusted settings not applied by most users.

"I said, what's yer name?"

"Leave him alone Barney."

Billy Johnson spoke up.

"Oh? A voice from the milk round. Getting in on the act are you gold top?"

Barney leaned forward aggressively, drawing back his fist.

Podric turned and pressed something on his device.

"I said – aaagh!!"

All of a sudden, the bully ripped the earphones from his head, and clutched his ears in pain.

"My name is for my friends."

Snapping off his iPhone, Podric briefly caught his sister's eye.

Barney was still moaning in agony as the coach pulled up outside Wendbury High.

"I'm deaf. I can't hear, I'm deaf!"

Getting off the bus with his friend Miles Willoughby, Billy Johnson, turned to Podric.

"Well cool – but you'll need to watch out."

Barney clutched his head and while barging through them, blindly tripped over Amy's bag.

"You don't want to mess with my brother. He'll zap you off the face of the earth. See you Pod."

Giving Barney the *Krimon Avenger* fingers, Amy skipped off towards the junior school. Barney punched Gnome's bag. Looking at their leader, the two associates yelled, "Shiver!"

"Don't shout – aagh!"

Barney kicked one and shoved the other.

Miles Willoughby tugged Podric's sleeve.

"Make an enemy of him at your peril Podric – he's not one to cross."

Chapter 2

An Accident

That morning being the start of a new term, Podric Moon was welcomed into his class. Their teacher, Miss Mullins, was a fit young woman - bright, intelligent and capable. Podric found the ambiance of his co-educational form very different to the public school he'd attended in Ireland. Advised of the family's recent tragedy, Miss Mullins asked Podric to wait behind when they broke for lunch.

"I was very sorry to hear of your tragic loss, Podric."

Standing near her desk at the front of the empty classroom, Podric didn't reply.

"I believe you want to go into the air force - do what your dad did."

"Yuh."

"I don't have to tell you what a big year this is academically. You'll need good grades."

Podric remained silent.

"Well, if there's anything I can do to help, any work you need assistance with - you just have to ask."

The teacher and pupil looked at each other.

"It must have been very difficult for you."

"Miss Mullins - I don't really want to talk about it if you don't mind."

Denise Mullins studied the boy. Podric's slightly diffident manner intrigued her.

"Thanks for your consideration, though."

They parted.

It was during the afternoon, Barney Sturridge made his retaliatory move. Although in the same year, he was in a different stream to Podric. Barney was in general and Podric, science. Neither did they attend the same practical classes. These were divided into three sections. The subject options being metalwork, woodwork or domestic science, Podric had selected metal and Barney ostensibly, woodwork.

Late for the metalwork class, Norris Widget spied Barney and two other henchmen turning into the corridor. Diving into Mr Micklediver's metal work room, 'The Widge' as he was known, just had time to slip by Podric whispering "Big Barn – coming now" before the bully appeared.

Micklediver overseeing a weld on a giant dolphin Billy was making didn't notice Barney enter.

"Alright, Mr. Mike?"

Wielding a welder's torch, his vision focused on the job in front of him, Micklediver couldn't react. Barney picked up a metal rod and passing along a far bench, thwacked Podric on the leg.

"That's for this morning Moon – just a beginning."

The attack was swift. Podric reeled in pain. Barney pressed his face into Podric's.

"Reckoned you were smart, did you, Podric Moon?"

Barney pushed Podric hard.

"Bollock stupid name. Bollock stupid twat. No one, repeat no one gets anything over Barney Sturridge. Got it?"

Barney hit Podric's other leg with the rod which sent Podric to the floor.

"Ha. Guess you know who runs things now, geek. So long."

"Hey. Sturridge? What are you doing here? You're with Mr Czvnik aren't you?"

Micklediver had raised his visor and shut down his welding torch.

"I am sir – though he's not really my type. Just having a little discussion with Moon here. Carry on class."

With that Barney promptly tripped over some rods that had mysteriously moved across his path. A voice said, 'Glad your hearing's better Sturridge' followed by the whole form murmuring "S-h-i-v-e-r."

It was the end of the day. Barney wasn't aboard the bus that night, his father having collected him from school in a large Jaguar. On the journey home, Podric didn't let on to Amy what had happened.

"What do you reckon about school Pod - irrecreemingly boring?"

Her brother smiled grimly at his sister's incorrect choice of word. She was always doing that - trying to use words that were a bit beyond her nine years.

*   *   *

Life at school settled down. Podric and Amy fell into a rhythm as did their mother.

Because the Moon's finances were limited (Sean's pension was just sufficient to live on but it was necessary Barbara worked at Tweeney's adding to it) Podric decided to take a paper round at Godiver's local shop making early morning deliveries. This had the double benefit of receiving praise from his mother along with the more tangible advantage of earning money for himself. It also led him to something that changed his life though the creation of this invention began in an unfortunate way.

On the morning in question, Podric was delayed in starting his round because Mr Godiver didn't have his papers ready. By the time Podric had completed his deliveries, he was seriously late and in order to get home, drop off his bike and make the school bus, he began peddling through the village at a frantic rate.

Cycling through the more affluent part of Drinkwell, Podric turned a bend, when a car travelling too fast came up behind him. Podric heard it a second before it hit him. He swerved his bike up the hedge and nearly escaped, but the car just clipped his rear wheel which caused him to lose control. Over the handlebars he went taking a bloody tumble. The car didn't stop.

It was Billy Johnson and his father, Arthur who found Podric. Their milk float pulled up beside the concussed boy.

"It's Podric!"

Billy's concerned face swam unfocused into his new friend's orbit.

"Pod. Pod! You okay?"

Podric grunted.

"Nasty cut he's got on his leg – and his head... Right mess."

"Maybe we shouldn't move him? What do you think, Dad?"

Arthur gently felt Podric's neck, torso and legs.

"Doesn't feel like there's anything broken. Better get him into a house. Do you know who lives there?"

Arthur looked at the nearby property. Its driveway lead to a substantial residence. Billy shook his head.

"Who cares? He needs help."

Podric murmured pathetically. Father and son Johnson helped him up and together carried him down the drive towards the front porch of the house. Billy pressed the bell. An intercom system emitted an electronic voice enquiring who was calling.

"It's me mate, missus. He's had an accident."

Looking at the scene on the CCTV system, housekeeper Alannah Brodie took in the situation at once. An enormous Irish wolfhound began barking. Irritated at the animal getting in her way, Alannah went to the front door.

"Oh dear. What happened?"

"A car – hit and run madam."

"Can we bring him in and call for help."

"Of course."

Following the housekeeper, the milkman and his son brought Podric inside. Crossing a Victorian hall which featured double doors with stained glass panels – they walked through a futuristic high-tech kitchen and entered a small study. Laying his friend down on a chaise longue, Billy couldn't help letting out an exclamation.

"Wow! Be alright here Pod. Oh, er, sorry missus."

Billy was impressed.

"Better get back to the float. Can't leave it where it is."

Arthur moved to leave. Alannah said, "The accident should be reported."

"I'll do that. Can I give the address here?"

"Of course. I'll give you the details."

Alannah went into the kitchen followed by Arthur. Billy turned to Podric.

"How are you feeling Pod?"

"Great."

Alannah re-entered. Billy looked around at her.

"I've got to get to school, but I don't think he can."

"Not with that gash."

The housekeeper seemed very capable. Billy noticed she was smart and spoke with an Irish lilt.

"Where does he live?"

"Briony Close."

"The new estate?"

Billy nodded. Podric tried to raise himself.

"Hey, hey – you just lie back. I'll get the first aid kit and ring the doctor."

Concerned, Alannah looked at Billy.

"Your dad's reporting the incident and I've given him the number here."

The housekeeper plumped up a cushion for Podric. Billy headed for the door.

"Is it okay if I get his bike off the road?"

"Sure. Leave it by the porch. I'll make sure the police look at it."

"See you Pod. I'll come by your place later."

Podric Moon lay back and took in his surroundings. The small library was traditional and overlooked a lawn. A stream ran along its perimeter. It was an idyllic scene. Podric became aware of something wet nuzzling him and looked round to see the giant dog trying to lick him. Nudging the animal away, the boy spied a PlayStation on a side table. Reaching across, he picked up the controls and pressed 'Start'. Immediately a TV monitor activated, but the unit was locked and requested a passcode. Podric toyed with the handset. Alannah returned carrying a first aid kit and a drink.

"I brought you some coke."

Preoccupied, Podric muttered thanks.

"Like the computers, do you?"

Still fiddling with the device, Podric nodded. The housekeeper began to clean his cut. The enormous hound did its best to obstruct her.

"Get out of it Dog – wretched animal. Did I hear your friend call you 'Pod'?"

"Uhuh." Podric nodded.

"What'll that be short for then? Would it be Podric by any chance?"

The boy winced as the housekeeper applied some disinfectant.

"That's deep and nasty."

Alannah continued with her work.

"Are you part of the family I heard about, the one that recently moved here?"

For the first time, Podric looked up.

"If you mean we've come here 'cos my dad was killed in an RAF flying accident, then yes."

He sipped his coke.

"I was sorry to hear it. You'll be Podric Moon then?"

An electronic voice came to life. 'You are inside the world of Krimon. Welcome to the game.'

"Did you just get into that?"

Podric nodded.

"But it's barred. Locked."

Surprised, Alannah took out a plaster.

"It's an okay game *Krimon*. Anyway, getting in wasn't too difficult."

Alannah smiled.

"Guess you don't know whose house you're in, young man? The person whose coke you're drinking invented that game."

Podric didn't reply.

"Aren't you impressed?"

"Well...it's not bad, but the latest *Death Raider's* better."

Dog licked Podric.

"You've made a friend."

The phone rang and Alannah turned around to pick up an extension on the desk. For several seconds, she listened intently.

"I don't think that'll be necessary."

There was a pause.

"Alright then, see you shortly. You have the address."

Alannah replaced the receiver.

"It's the police. They're on their way. When the garda's finished with you, I'm going to call the doctor. We'd also better speak to your mum. You should have been back from your round by now."

Sergeant Paxman was attentive. In truth, Podric couldn't really describe the accident in detail. He'd been peddling fast and the car had come up behind him. Reacting instinctively, he'd gone up the bank, but the vehicle, which was quite big (Podric thought it was a dark colour, blue or black) clipped his rear wheel.

"You were lucky. Another few inches and you could have been a goner." Sergeant Paxman stood up.

"We'll have to take your bike with us – do some paint tests. Probably not much chance of finding the driver, but we'll check the camera at the Wendbury intersection. It might turn up something. You never know."

After the police had gone, Alannah checked Podric's mobility. With his leg and head dressed, he didn't look too bright but he could move.

"I think we can get you to the surgery."

On their way to the housekeeper's car, an electronic voice barked from an intercom. Dog howled.

"Brodie, what's going on? Police. Blasted interruptions!" Alannah spoke into the device. "A lad met with a hit and run – came off his bike. He's cut and bruised, I'm taking him to the doctor."

"You know I need an overnight."

"It'll be ready. You're not leaving till six."

"Make sure it is."

With these petulantly disembodied words, the speaker rang off. Archie Light looked down at his housekeeper helping a limping youth into her car. His studio vantage point located on top of a gothic Victorian tower, he had spied the whole scenario from Podric's arrival to the police visit, via the internal closed-circuit television system.

In his late forties and good looking, Light had lived in Drinkwell for five years and had never quite figured out why he'd gone there. It wasn't near anywhere relevant to his life – London or the coast – but in some particular way, he'd fallen for the place – not least because of where he now stood. The turret being linked to the main house by a glass bridge, it was this unique feature that had influenced him when deciding to buy. He sat there for hours. It was in this lab that he'd created *Marvin the Destroyer* and *Guns of Orion*, both smash hits in the video games market in their time.

Archie had largely been the brains behind the computer giant Secorni's position in games entertainment – attacking Pasaro and other leading suppliers with innovative and challenging products. *Krimon and the Undersea Invaders* had left all rivals standing, as did *Petra's Universe*. These two games when launched, won a large percentage of the global business. British and American management had often deferred to him in their boardrooms – both in London and New York. He'd even been entertained in Hollywood when Secorni signed a movie deal for *Knights of the Avenger*.

The head of Paramount Studios told him that the game was bigger than the movie and was a taste of things to come. But that was three years ago and Archie hadn't had a major hit since. In fact, the company hadn't marketed any of his recent efforts, and there were rumours that 'the old man' had lost his touch. Now, clad in his silk dressing gown, looking down at the stream running through his garden below, Archie reflected on the shortness of people's memories. Those games had been so successful they'd netted Secorni millions, but the company having made its money, rapidly forgot how it happened or who had created them. Short term thinking in a selfish world.

Chapter 3

Mind Dreams

Barbara Moon met Alannah Brodie and Podric at Drinkwell's surgery. The local GP advised that because of Podric's head injury, he should have a brain scan, 'It's run of the mill Mrs. Moon, but it is recommended just to be on the safe side'. A couple of hours later, Barbara took her son to Wendbury hospital where he was admitted as an out-patient at the MRI unit.

Whilst Barbara was concerned about the procedure Podric was to experience, the boy himself wasn't afraid of going into the tube. To Podric, it was more a feeling of complete relaxation. As he lay there staring at monitors, out of the corner of his eye he could see angles of his brain on screens, the neuro-imaged patterns moving as the computed axial tomography recorded the activity of his various lobes and cerebellum. This sent Podric into a dream-like state, the patterns of data having a mesmeric effect on him.

His mother was on the phone when Podric entered Dr. Martens' consulting room after the scan. A bandage wrapped round his head, he sat quietly as the doctor played back the recorded images, explaining various sequences.

'Your head tooking a knock, we look for any sign of cognitive impairment - headaches, concussion or clotting between the skull and subdural haematoma."

The doctor indicated one of the screens beside him.

"And, we ensure that there is no subarachnoid haemorrhage - er, bleeding in and around the brain."

"What are those?" Podric pointed to a particular image and data.

"The precuneus, posterior parietal, frontoparietal, occipital and dorsolateral prefrontal regions - in other words, your imagination."

Dr. Martens eyed Podric.

"If there's anything unusual in your scan, it's the level of activity."
Martens paused.

"Yours is heightened to a remarkable degree young man."

Podric studied the image.

"So these regions control my creative thoughts."

Martens nodded.

"Does it interest you?"

Podric didn't reply immediately.

"I was just thinking...instead of my thoughts controlling me, what if I could manipulate them?"

Martens laughed.

"Ha! You mean...live the dream. Then you really would be revolutionising 'studio in cerebro'."

Barbara completed her call and entered the doctor's consulting room.

"Sorry about that. Is he alright?"

Martens smiled.

"He's certainly alright." The doctor glanced back at a screen.

"Do I need to check on anything else, any follow-up?"

"Just keep an eye on him. Make sure he's calm. There's plenty going on in that brain of his...huh, Podric?"

Martens smiled and tapped some information into his computer.

"I'll print a full report for you."

The consultation concluded, the doctor, patient and his mother stood up.

"That idea of yours Podric – dissimulating one's imagination..." Dr. Martens removed several sheets of paper from his printer " ...a pamphlet was published a while back talking about adjusting the synapse."

Clipping the printed sheets together, he slipped them into a file.

"Pretty off the wall stuff, it theorised about somehow reversing the process and creating a kind of receptive gateway."

Seeing the doctor might be going down some transcendental alley and unsure where it might lead, Barbara took the file from him.

"Thanks for everything doctor. Your professional assistance is very much appreciated."

Barbara smiled at Martens.

"You may have noticed, my son has a particular intelligence and an inquiring mind."

She put the file in her bag.

"You wouldn't be the first to fall victim to his innovative ideas."

A twinkle in his eye, Dr. Martens opened the door and the patient and his mother departed. For a moment Martens remained where he was. A buzzer on his desk advised him of his next patient.

"Receptive Gateway. Mind dreams..."

*   *   *

Leaving Wendbury, Podric was a little pale as he sat beside his mum in her battered Beetle. She'd called Tweeney's and told them she wouldn't be in that day because of her son's accident and now they were headed for home.

"I'm only so glad you were taken to that house. Alannah whatever her name is was very sensible. She's coming by later. Wants to know how you are."

Barbara and Alannah got along famously. Before either could say 'four-leafed clover,' an affinity between Podric's mother, the Emerald Isle and her guest's Irish origins gave flood to a babble of conversation. At least an hour went by before the two women stopped to draw breath. Alannah asked about Podric's talent for computer games. His mother burst out laughing.

"Forgive me...talent? Does Podric have talent with computer games? Is the pope a catholic?"

"Well, they say he might be."

Walking into the living room from the conservatory where they'd been talking, Barbara went to check on Podric. Seeing him asleep, she adjusted the quilt covering him and tiptoed away. Indicating to Alannah to follow her upstairs, Barbara led the way to her son's bedroom.

"Don't touch anything – it's his domain."

She opened the door to reveal an unusually tidy, but cramped bedroom. The walls were covered with pictures of planes – each featuring his father, either in flight or standing beside an aircraft. Thirty or so trophies were crammed on top of a dressing table. Other bigger and more ornate ones stood on the floor beside some virtual reality visors.

"My G-!"

"He's won more competitions than you can shake a stick at. At the last event he took part in just before Sean died, he beat the adult European champion. It was out of competition, but he's brilliant."

"Wait till I tell... My boss, the family I work for – he's a games creator. He's really successful – or was, but recently the ideas he's produced haven't been so good and between you and me, Secorni are thinking of dropping him."

"Well, I'm not sure what Podric could do, but he has a lot of experience and he knows every game there is."

"He's also young, Barbara – he'll have his finger on the pulse. The type of games that would sell – what people want."

Moving into the room, Alannah took a closer look at the trophies.

"It really is amazing. Podric might just be the answer. Would you have any objection if I set up a meeting between him and Doctor Light?"

"Doctor?"

"Engineering, electronics. He's a clever man."

"No, well, I'm sure that's fine. Be good for Podric; he's taken the loss of his dad very hard."

Emerging from Podric's bedroom, Alannah's mood changed.

"Hmm... It's only fair to tell you that the doctor's also taken the rejection of his recent efforts badly. His failures coincided with his wife leaving him. He's become petulant. Right now, he's on something of a downward spiral."

"Drinking?"

"And other stuff. Maybe my idea's not such a good one..."

"Does he have kids?

"One. Cosima – the most spoilt young madam you ever laid eyes on."

"How old is she?"

"Seventeen going on twenty-three. She's away at school most of the time but comes home on sufferance in the holidays. Sometimes. She runs rings around her father who idolises her."

Barbara looked at her new friend.

"Sean and I have never been overprotective of Podric and I wouldn't want to start being now. Sean wouldn't thank me for that. If I keep an eye out my end and you yours, I can't see much harm coming from it. Who knows...maybe it'll be mutually beneficial –for the doctor of computers and my young games whizz!"

*   *   *

"You say he just got into it?"

Standing in the Lighthouse (the name Archie gave to his loft space), Brodie hung her boss's travel-hanging cover on the back of a chair.

"Yup. I'd only been gone a minute or two."

"Could have been a fluke..."

"You said it was secure to me – not that it matters. I don't play games."

"Huh. And he didn't think much of '*Krimon*' you say?"

"Well, he wasn't entirely dismissive but he said it wasn't very difficult."

"Little upstart."

"I'd say he's far from that. To be the best in your age group three years in a row and beating the adult European champion hardly suggests a lack of skill."

"Out of competition doesn't count."

Archie dropped the document he was reading on the table and walked over to a bookcase full of files.

"You should meet him."

"Why on earth would I want to do that?"

"Two reasons – because he's a computer games champion and because he's young."

Alannah dusted a leather designer swing chair.

"This having what bearing?"

"Isn't it obvious? Your last three submissions haven't been picked up and the latest one's just been rejected. Podric's the right age; his finger is on the pulse. He knows which games have appeal and why."

"And I don't?"

The two looked at each other then resumed their tasks.

"I think it was fate that brought him here."

"Unfortunate for him then."

Alannah looked around at Archie, who studied some papers.

"Came a cropper on his bike, didn't he?"

"The victim of a hit and run!"

The housekeeper was vehement. Approaching her boss, she spoke to him directly.

"You should do yourself a favour and see Podric. Even if you think it's a waste of time, what's half an hour? It might actually help you."

"Podric? What kind of a name is that?

"An Irish one!"

Leaving the room, Alannah was cross.

A couple of hours later, watching Archie's vintage Facel Vega coupé head down the driveway, Alannah picked up a note lying on the kitchen counter. 'Ar mhaithe le do temperament Éireannach – Will see the boy 5.00pm Wednesday.' Knowing his housekeeper's love for her native tongue, Archie often used Gaelic when communicating with her.

"I'll give him the sake of my temperament – it's his bloody future for heavens sake!"

Chapter 4

The First Step

Being off school for a week to recover from his accident, it was during Podric's convalescence that the fateful encounter between the games creator and young champion took place. Walking up the stairs in Archie's house, Podric couldn't help noticing a large black and white photograph of a young woman. The housekeeper caught his glance.

"Beautiful, isn't she Podric? She's the doctor's daughter. I don't do the tarot but I've always felt there's danger there for whoever is chosen. We go this way."

They walked along the gallery with its glass-covered walkway. About thirty feet from the ground, it crossed part of the garden and connected to the tall gothic tower which was otherwise completely separated from the main house. At the far end, Alannah pushed open a door into the lobby and pressed the lift button.

"You'll find him either in his den or the lab. I've put some coke in the fridge."

Podric entered the glass panelled elevator.

"Have fun and er, don't let his rudeness put you off. It just hides his inadequacies."

Podric began to ascend. Arriving at the top of the building, the lift door slid back and he stepped into Archie Light's study. Podric looked about. No one appeared to be around, and glancing at some awards on the mantelpiece, he noticed an arch at the end of the room, leading to a spiral staircase.

Walking down a floor, the room configuration on this level was different. A little kitchen had been created and two other rooms were positioned either side of the lift shaft. Peering into one, the room seemed to be a mini-computer museum. The equivalent of a personalised Smithsonian Institute's history of the computer, it contained a model of every key development type in the products' evolution. Podric looked at some of the antiquated styles and sizes – was anything ever that big?

"I wasn't aware we were meeting in here."

Dr. Light stood in the doorway.

"Couldn't see anyone around."

Ignoring Podric's reply, Light walked past him.

"Know when the first game was invented? The nineteen fifties – *Tennis for Two*. This one's the only model of its type in private ownership. Then there was '*Spacewar!*' in the seventies. Those were the days – Atari, Mario and..."

Light inspected a unit.

"Mine. The first game on that console to reach a million sales worldwide."

The computer games inventor turned.

"Seeing as you presumptuously entered my private domain, we may as well go to my inner sanctum."

Without further ado, Archie walked out. Podric shrugged and followed him. *Weird guy...this Dr. Light.*

Crossing a corridor, the other room was Light's laboratory. High-tech, a clinical work counter ran its length, behind which electronic equipment had been bolted into a rack. Several PCs and lap tops were on the bench. Other computer paraphernalia included an array of hard drives, virtual reality kit, and several pairs of Google glasses – all neatly stored in designer built trays.

Light handed Podric a similar PlayStation control to Brodie's. For a second or two, the boy admired its design.

"Not on the market yet...it'll be out next year. My housekeeper tells me you got into it."

Podric activated the handset and only took a few seconds to overcome its security block. A wall-mounted plasma screen activated, and he spooled through the half dozen game options available before putting the controls down on the bench. Although apparently paying minimal attention to Podric's activities, Light was in fact surreptitiously watching him.

"What sort of games level do you play?"

"Championship."

"Ah."

For no logical reason, Light sounded condescending.

"I gather you don't appreciate the finer points of one of mine – *Krimon*."

"It's all right. 'Bit outdated."

"In what way?"

"Graphics, Options…it's not very difficult."

Light was annoyed at Podric's casual dismissiveness.

"The record for level 10 is thirty-four minutes twenty-eight seconds."

"Yuh, officially. It's not on the current circuit now, but I used to quite often get home in under half an hour."

In years to come Archie Light would reflect that this was a defining moment in their relationship – the boy almost nonchalant, himself acutely agitated.

"I take it you have no objection to my putting you to the test."

Podric didn't say anything but picked up the device.

Defeating the Sentinels with ease at early levels, Podric rapidly began moving up the tiered ranks of challenges and within fourteen minutes, was at the games highest grade. In spite of himself, Archie's attention increased as he watched Podric overcome the more difficult obstacles and guide Krimon to total victory in twenty-seven minutes thirteen seconds. 'Player Wins!' flashed onto the screen along with a fanfare of trumpets. Some text appeared 'Sentinels outta here – easier meat cookin' in a galaxy near you!' Podric put down the PlayStation controls.

"The thing is computer games suck."

Podric's statement met with an ominous silence.

"Doctor, Podric – your mum needs to be going soon."

Brodie's voice called down from the den. Light slammed the door shut.

"Go on."

"Though they say they're making them more difficult, they're not and there's nothing new."

Archie looked at Podric for several seconds. The boy had relaxed and was walking over to some other trial stations, idly turning them over.

"My dad was a pilot in the RAF. He was brilliant and took me to the Air Force Training Centre where they test pilots on simulators. It was great. It was so great that dad got me into virtual reality and I played games all the time. That's when I got good. I started winning things – won my first VR headset."

Podric put down a unit and picked up a docking component.

"I played and played every game I could find. So many games. Crazy. Competitions. Championships… But now there's nothing out there to excite me, which is why I've been thinking about another dimension."

Hitting a key, Podric activated a monitor. It revealed a lot of codex information. 'The Arch Twister' was a device Archie was working on which would raise a game's challenges much more quickly.

"Neat idea."

He closed the screen.

"When I was playing at the highest VR levels, pushing anything a game could do – sometimes I could almost feel lost inside it and I've been thinking how cool it would be to create that. I don't just mean virtual reality – I mean a player becoming a *part* of the game, *part* of the action. It would make any adventure *real*. That would be something else."

"Podric, darling we've got to go."

His mother opened the lab door.

Archie Light was a man with varied talents not infrequently using them to throw others off balance and someone used to getting his own way. Not only with her son had he met his match but also the boy's mother who gave a squeal of delight at seeing two pictures of Facel Vegas on the wall.

"Oh, the FV4 and the Excellence. They only made six types, didn't they?"

Barbara's eyes were bright. Archie's jaw dropped, then gathering himself, he looked at this lively woman.

"Mrs. Moon. Your son and I have only just begun our conversation."

"Well, you'll have to continue it another time."

With that, she took Podric's arm.

"I'm sure we can arrange something."

Barbara smiled and she and Podric made to leave.

"Your family is...!"

Barbara turned back.

"Fabulous. You should have known Sean. We flew!"

She took another glance at Archie's Facel Vega pictures.

"Pity they had trouble with the Faciella - real beauty."

Arriving back at Briony Close that evening, Podric and Barbara were greeted by Amy who had just come in from school. Mother and daughter quickly immersed in the events of the little girl's day, Podric wandered across their small lawn to the garden shed.

Left by previous owners, nothing much had been done to it. Barbara deposited the few garden implements the family possessed in a corner when they moved in, but what attracted Podric to the hut was the work bench left behind. The vice was a bit wonky but that could be fixed. If he put up some shelves the place would make an ideal workshop for the project evolving in his mind.

Although experiencing deep depression since the loss of his father, Podric hadn't been so dysfunctional that his brain had stopped working. What he'd said to Archie Light that afternoon had reignited thoughts buried deep in his subconscious these past months.

Activating his mobile, Podric watched Sean's last communication that he'd saved. His dad's exuberance was so engaging, it inspired him. In other conversations they'd had about the subject, Wing Commander Moon hadn't dismissed his son's apparently crazy idea out of hand.

"You'd be getting into wormholes on that one Podric. Capture that and I'll retire!"

Quizzing his father who had been away serving abroad at the time, Podric received a text with a website referral directing him to the Einstein-Rosen Bridge theory – the moving of matter. If he conquered something scientists had never been able to, it would be some accomplishment. But was he really trying to transport himself bodily?

What Podric wanted was the ability to be able to experience life inside the game. But a game being a fantasy, he sought to encounter adventures as a participant to *Krimon* and the countless other games' characters he'd met as a player. It was the *feeling* of an alternative reality he was after, the sensation – something he could go into and return from at will.

*   *   *

For the rest of the week Podric locked himself away in the Moon's garden shed, transforming it into a proper workshop.

The vice was strengthened and a soldering iron installed along with an array of XBoxes, PlayStations and an old PC, complete with hard drives and memory boards. Working long hours, Podric carefully dismantled one of his virtual reality visors and a PlayStation, exploring their contents. He also took a game he knew, *Tokyo Joe*, activating and deactivating it, following each step carefully as it loaded up.

For three days, Podric worked solidly – playing *TJ* and experimenting at altering the PlayStation's controls. Sometimes this caused the game to malfunction or not work at all, but the more he monitored, played and tried to link himself to *Tokyo Joe* analysing how its programme was written, the more he realized the complexity of what he was attempting to achieve. It was one thing to talk about immersing yourself in a computer world via some kind of mind path state, but surely quite another to bring that about, if indeed it could be.

On Saturday morning, Podric woke to discover that he'd slept at his bench (his mother had put a blanket around him late the previous evening). Going to the kitchen and making himself some coffee, he returned to his workshop, and sat back to ponder the problems facing him.

The previous night he had tried re-configuring some of the *Tokyo Joe* software. Considering the practicalities of linking the game to his own thought process, Podric felt that it might work if he placed tiny microchips in the frames of his virtual reality headset, syncing his synapse pulse to that of the game. He knew this was technologically crude, but it was all he could think of at the moment. Setting about the task with a vengeance, neither his mother nor his sister would see anything of him that weekend.

It was one of Barbara Moon's qualities that whilst she loved her children, she never smothered them. Barbara offered them her non-conformist support unconditionally, which enabled Podric and Amy to develop their own free spirits. Although at times her friends viewed this as rather a freewheeling way to bring up a family, it allowed her children to develop individualistically. The fact that Podric spent forty-eight solid hours working on his idea in the garden shed didn't overly concern his mother or bother his sister.

Amy had made a new friend, Lilian Bekes. A local girl whose mother claimed Romany blood, Lilian certainly had a Mediterranean temperament; 'do anything with my Taser gun, I'll have yer eyes!' The gypsy lass was surprised by Amy's reply that her version upped the voltage to render 'total wipe out!' But their strange, apparently fearless bond, seemed to unite them.

Barbara spent the weekend working on some marketing ideas for the brothers Tweeney. Her lively input having been recognised, MD Ralph Tweeney had requested that she take over their advertising and B to B trade publicity. Truthfully, this was less grand than it sounded. Technical head, Don T had no interest in that aspect of the business at all and Ralph's idea of a sophisticated strategy featured the tagline 'guaranteed to dispose the indisposable'. It was into this reservoir of originality that Barbara had to operate, and she quickly realised she had a challenge on her hands. Ideas for 'expending vortex' and 'waste whirlpool' advertisements flitted through her visually creative mind, as she struggled with the task.

By Sunday night Podric was all in. His mother, still preoccupied with flying detritus engulfed in a swirl of subterranean blades, suggested that he take a break and have some supper with them, resting up for his return to school the following morning. Feeling that in spite of all his efforts he was no nearer to achieving his goal, Podric went over to the house and slumped down in the living room.

"No joy, Pod?" Sitting cross-legged on a sofa opposite flicking cards into an old bowler hat, his sister was her usual idiosyncratic self.

"You don't know what I'm doing."

"Trying to make games have another life."

Too tired to argue, Podric took the glass of red wine his mother offered him.

"Supper in five minutes!"

Barbara sat down beside her son.

"Any nearer to your discovery, darling?"

Podric shook his head.

"You can help me come up with some waste disposal slogans. So far, I've only got 'Tweeney's twister – whirlpools of waste wiped in a vortex of vapor,' but I don't think that's quite right."

Podric sipped his wine.

"Waste disposal sucks."

Not thinking anything of his comment, a second or two later Podric was surprised to see his mother in paroxysms of laughter.

"That's it – that's the tagline! Waste disposal sucks. Brilliant darling, I'll use it."

Although he slept well that night, Podric woke early. Being a bright sunny morning, he was out of the shower and dressed before his mother and sister were up. Making his customary mug of coffee, Podric walked over to his workshop and sipping the steaming liquid, looked at the jumble of wired clutter lying on the bench.

Picking up his adapted virtual reality headset, Podric didn't think he'd done a bad job fitting the sensor pads with their encoded microchips into its sides. Looking at the unit, one could barely discern its alterations. Preoccupied with making yet more adjustments, he turned on the PlayStation and activated the tiny new switch.

Some very odd things started to happen. Wearing the visor, Podric was able to view the real world through virtual reality. This was strangely interesting. Looking out of the shed window at the garden, he could also watch a sequence of *Tokyo Joe* – villains on the run from Japan's finest attempting to take refuge in a zoo – a kind of double vision. Reality and game.

Part of their efforts to evade capture involved the criminals running through enclosures of dangerous animals, Joe and cohorts in hot pursuit. The hero cornered by a lion whose jaws started to open, coincided with Podric seeing his sister open the shed door. The king of the beasts was about to devour her and Joe. Podric fired Joe's stun gun and the animal fell back.

"Come on Podric. We'll be late for school!"

Japanese hoods apparently turning on Amy, Podric picked off games villains in rapid succession.

"You and your games... I'm off!"

Podric was so transfixed by the activity within *Tokyo Joe* that he completely ignored his sister.

"Far Ou-."

"Podric?"

The shed door opened again.

Inside the game, things were proceeding at a crazy rate. His mother appeared in his strange vision. Her dressing gown was gathered about her and her hair was in curlers. Yakuza members had commandeered a zoo truck containing some caged gorillas, and headed straight towards her. Using the PlayStation's controls to operate Joe's stun gun, Podric took careful aim at the driver. Zapping the guy, the gorilla crates flew off the truck as it rolled over crashing into a snake pit.

"Podric you must go now darling – Amy's already left."

Closing down the game, Podric's last vision was his mother in her night attire surrounded by deranged primates taking over Tokyo Zoo!

At the bus stop, his sister stood slightly away from the few other pupils waiting for the school coach.

"Success then, mein bruder?"

Podric shrugged. The bus arrived. Amy looked at her brother mischievously.

"I know you did something."

The bus stopped and they joined the little queue. Whatever it was that Podric had done wasn't exactly what he'd had in mind, but it was an interesting interim step along the road to formulating his idea for an alternative reality.

Chapter 5

Outside-in Reality

For Podric Moon, the next few days passed in a strange calm. Having accidentally created a new dimension to computer games – viewing the outside world in tandem with a virtual reality one, he had the opportunity to entertain himself with it morning, noon and night. But that wasn't the case. In fact, Podric didn't even go into his garden workshop. It was as if having accomplished what he had, he temporarily needed a break to regroup his thoughts. The stimulus to return to his fantastic computer developments was a jarring one.

Several days after Podric's return to school, Sergeant Paxman arrived to interview him. The sergeant reported that they had a possible trace on the car that hit him. Their chat prompted an unwelcome reminder of the incident and was compounded that afternoon by Barney Sturridge's aggressive behaviour.

"Pity it didn't nail you for good Moon – techno jerk."

For reasons best known to the Sturridge family, Barney's father had started dropping his son at school, so at least the bus run was spared the thug's loutish behaviour. But since he'd been attending Wendbury High, it hadn't escaped Podric's notice that Barney's bully boy tactics stretched far and wide. A number of pupils' younger than Podric were fearful of Barney's threats and more than a few in his own year, equally so. The lad was a menace.

Podric began turning his thoughts towards teaching the thug a lesson he wouldn't forget, something that would put him in his place once and for all. Any idea that he might have of entering physical combat with Barney was obviously problematic, the bully being much stronger than he was. No, he would have to outwit him using his brains.

Making a return to his workshop that evening, Podric idly spooled through *Tokyo Joe* with its 'Outside-in Reality' dimension. Slipping off the device, he thought about what he could do to incapacitate Barney – create maximum embarrassment, but make the bully realise he could be vulnerable and force him to back off from his thuggish behaviour.

Aware of the Inter Vth football challenge and knowing Barney would be playing, several people in Podric's class had expressed concern about the upcoming clash. Currently exempt from games himself due to his accident, an idea began to form in Podric's mind.

*   *   *

Sitting in his den going through his mail, Archie Light put aside bills and circulars, and opened a letter from Secorni. The company rejected his latest game, advising that *Andromeda Volcanism* was 'too derivative' and 'insufficiently original or challenging'. Secorni also indicated that they were looking to review the financial terms of his contract, offering several dates for a meeting. Archie reached for the phone and angrily hit a memory number. A couple of rings and the cool Californian voice of Carla Logan answered.

"Archie?"

"Carla put me on to Prendergast."

"I'll check if he's available."

"Put him on Carla!"

There was a pause before the voice of Secorni's vice president, Europe, Saul Prendergast came on the line.

"Archibald? To what do I owe the pleasure?"

"Don't give me that crap Saul; what the hell do you mean Andromeda's derivative and unchallenging? There's never been anything like it."

"That's not the view of our marketing people."

"Well, they can..."

"And I agree with them."

"Oh? Look here, Saul. I've made your company a fortune – so don't tell me my game sucks. I *know* games. I created the biggest seller of all time, or don't you remember?"

"Yeah, I remember Archie. I also remember that was five years ago. Things have moved on since then and I'm afraid you haven't."

"What do you mean?"

"It means that we'll be re-negotiating your contract – *if* we renew it."

"Yeah?"

Archie's voice was a snarl.

"Does Cy know about this?"

"Sure does. In fact, it was his idea."

"You b-!"

"There's thanks... Actually, I did try for you, but I guess from your tone, it's best you hear from our legal people. Goodbye Archie – and thank you."

The line went dead and with it Archie's career at Secorni.

Like a precocious child, Archie spent the next hour walking around his eyrie cursing. Then he went downstairs to his gym and worked out. After that he took a swim in his pool and lying on his back in the water, began to calm down. He calculated that whilst he hadn't saved as much as he should have, if he lived sensibly he wouldn't starve. Of course, he couldn't buy that other Facel Vega he'd had his eye on (a rare FV was coming on the market – damn the woman!). Equally, he'd have to watch his running costs. The house, his housekeeper and there was Cosima's education. It was his daughter who stirred Archie from his reverie, her svelte form emerging from one of the changing cubicles.

"Up early?"

"Ha."

Cosima languidly slid into the water, her body barely making a ripple as she began swimming effortlessly up the pool in an easy stroke. Archie got out.

After completing several lengths, the girl stopped at the far end, resting against its side.

"Louisa called. You know her ma's invited me to South Carolina, but she wants me to go with her to Gstaad."

"Bit late in the season, isn't it?"

"Not really. Anyway, not sticking around here for the hols."

Cosima dropped below the surface and began a length underwater.

Walking to his changing room, Archie experienced another bout of resentment, feeling that all he'd worked for was taken for granted. Did his daughter have any idea what it cost to keep her in the style to which she was accustomed? Yet he found he couldn't stop spoiling her. Was it a guilt thing? Whilst he hadn't always been faithful, his estranged wife - the honourable Charlotte, had behaved with consistent infidelity only months after they'd been married. But still his conscience nagged away - the perverse need to make up for something with his only child - as though whatever he did was never quite enough for her. This invariably seemed to involve spending large amounts of money.

The end of the morning saw the computer games creator back in his den, still restless and demoralised. He looked through another games idea he'd been developing and for the umpteenth time scanned *Andromeda Volcanism*. They just didn't know what they were talking about. He wrote a violent email to Secorni and was about to press 'Send' but then saved it as a draft.

Odd individual that he was, Archie Light had always been extremely disciplined. It was one of the reasons he'd done so brilliantly in his career. Now though, he went to the drinks cabinet and poured himself a large scotch. Despite his massive ego, Archie was hurt and he didn't like it. What was the point? What had been the point? The answer to that was money and the success that went with it. But what was he going to do? He actually felt like crying, then smashing up his lab, followed by totalling one of his Facel Vegas - but he couldn't do either. *Things must be bad!*

Standing at the table, Archie noticed a file with a Post-it from Brodie - 'for your benefit'. He flicked open the folder. Inside were several appraisals of Podric Moon.

His initial reaction was to consign them to the bin. Putting down his drink, Archie began flicking through the pages - in spite of him-

self, with increased interest. The kid had contacts. What was this –
Secorni's boss, Cy Zaentz raving about him? And Pasaro – the largest
games company in the world; their boss Fred Schepesi reckoned he
was a genius. The world was mad. But these were movers and shakers
in the industry, people who rated the kid and were actually asking his
opinion about games. For all Archie knew, Podric might have been a
consultant Cy had checking out *Andromeda!*

Walking over to the window he took in the view and thought
about his daughter and his housekeeper. The first was indolent, precocious and someone he loved. The second, a contrary Irish leprechaun, but a person who he knew had his best interests at heart.
Maybe he should see the boy again? Arrogant little bastard. What
had he been on? Some other reality trip... Nuts. But for all Archie's
conceit, he couldn't help acknowledge Podric's computer games brilliance. Well, as Brodie was so obviously keen to set up the meeting,
she'd know where to find the lad.

*   *   *

Podric's last lesson before lunch wasn't held in his classroom but
needing some books for his first period in the afternoon, he went
by to collect them. His teacher, Miss Mullins was talking to two
girls –Jane Cartwright and Carol Jenson. Podric didn't know
much about them, except that they were both sporty types.

"Podric, I believe you're exempt from games at the moment."

Gathering up her teaching materials, Denise Mullins fell into
step with her new pupil.

"Will you be on the touch line or are you attending one of the
clubs?"

Podric knew Natural History was an option having been told
by Clive and Maurice Jenkins they'd long ago opted out of sport in
favour of studying the organic world.

"Discovering the meaning of life, Podric... It's so much more interesting than running around, kicking a ball."

Clive sniffed.

"And as for that mud – oh!"

Twin brother, Maurice was dismissive. Breaking into Podric's thoughts, Miss Mullins smiled.

"Or perhaps you'd like to make a start on your French essay..?"

With a twinkle in her eye, the teacher noticed Jane and Carol leaning against the corridor wall, apparently glued to their phones. Walking a little behind his teacher, Podric passed the girls when Jane said, "Podric, we need a favour..." Jane was friendly. "Which involves computers."

The two girls eyed each other, then Podric.

"Got ten minutes after lunch? I'm sure with your skills it won't take longer."

Podric shrugged. Barney Sturridge materialised with a couple of gang members, Dwight and Darlene. The girl was quite as threatening as either of the two boys. A brass ring hanging from her nose along with facial and body tattoos added to her startling appearance.

"The man in the Moon hanging out with the mademoiselles, las señoritas."

Barney leered up.

"Not wasting your time on him, are you ladies?"

He looked at Jane and Carol.

"Mine's alright Moonface but yours... The pitch in an hour Dark Side. Looking forward to landing one on you right where it hurts. Ha!"

Reeling about, Barney and his two cohorts went on their abusive way.

"That bastard ought to be taught a lesson, bloody thug."

Carol's unfeigned distaste for the brutish Sturridge evident Podric turned to the girls.

"Okay, whatever it is you want help with, I need you to do something for me payback."

He briefly outlined his plan.

"No worries Pod, we'll sort that."

"But you get what you've got to do. One of these..."

Podric held up a small microchip.

"Put into his boots under the sole lining."

He replaced the microchip in the sachet with the other.

"Shouldn't take more than a few seconds."

"Looks like the double act Carty – form over function."

"Toss for it."

"Nah, you flirt, I'll do it. You'll love playing the come on with that prick and seeing him get his comeuppance."

"All in the phraseology, Carol."

Towards the end of their school dinner, Jane appeared across the table from Podric. She carried a hockey stick.

"Okay?"

Podric pushed his half-eaten plate of burger and fries to one side. Billy turned to Podric.

"Didn't know you played hockey Pod?"

"It's not his sporting skills we need."

Carol stood beside her friend.

"Ah, computer stuff huh? Not your irresistible personality then."

"Or his body!"

Carol swung her Grays 7000 Ultrabow.

"Come on. Let's make a move."

The two girls led Podric to a single storey building behind the senior school which linked it to the junior. Entering through a side door, Jane tapped a code into a digital combination lock and opened the janitor's boiler room. Podric looked on bemused.

"We use this to change – it's the warmest."

He had to admire their logic. Carol immediately dropped her sports bag on a trestle seat and began changing into her hockey kit. Jane walked over to a metal storage cabinet. Also code locked, she deactivated it. Inside were bundles of pornographic magazines along with an iPad.

"We've known for a while Braxby's a dirty old git, but the stuff on this is way wrong."

She put the iPad down on the janitor's table.

"There's shit there that could get him fired and more."

"But we had a little thinky and we thought before we got him exposed, we'd scare him…" Carol appeared in bra and jogging bottoms. The casualness of the girls amazed Podric but he was determined not to react "…which might just sort him. We thought if you planted a virus – maybe gave him the idea he's diverted to some police tracking system, that could haul him in line. Of course if it doesn't, then he'll get what's coming."

"Why don't you want him to get fired?"

"We have our reasons. It suits us to have him around...but we have to do something about this."

Podric didn't push his question and assumed the school caretaker had some knowledge of escapades Jane and Carol might have been up to. Beginning to strip off herself, Jane looked at Podric.

"So...you can help us?"

Podric turned the iPad over in his hands.

"We've already got his pass details."

Taking the device from him, she activated it.

"Come on Podric – you've got the techno crap to scare the shit out of the old perv."

Now wearing her hockey shirt, Carol leaned forward and kissed him.

"You can do it games whizz. We're relying on you."

In reply, Podric handed Carol a small bag.

"One good turn..."

Carol smiled.

"I can't wait. Come on Carty, we've got work to do."

Jane emerged adjusting her hockey skirt.

"Very funny! You okay Podric?"

She also gave him a kiss. Although on his hair, it was more intimate than her friend's peck.

"By the way, you won't be disturbed; Thursday afternoons are Braxelrod's origami class at the oldies home in Wendbury."

Podric looked up.

"I know – whacky. He makes some great stuff."

About to close the cabinet, Jane pulled out a box containing several exquisite paper items – flowers, birds and even a dinosaur!

"Not all bad see. But he still shouldn't do so much of that crap."

She nodded at the iPad Podric was working on and replaced the box in the metal cupboard.

"When you're done, just put it back on the shelf and close it.

Same with the main door on your way out. They both self lock."

Though he heard what she said, Podric didn't look up. Jane and Carol were ready.

"Now the beast... Sure it's going to work?"

"Which - your flirting or the insertions?"

Jane smiled.

"Fair enough!"

The boys changing rooms being out of bounds to girls, Jane's hockey stick slipping from her fingers causing Barney to trip over on his way there, meant she not only had to placate the bully but also ply her feminine whiles. Barney not fancying her, things would have been foreshortened had it not been for Plug and Gnome, who at that moment chose to repeat their S-h-i-v-e-r mantra. This sent Barney into apoplexy. Temporarily forgetting his bag, he grabbed one of Plug's ears twisting it ferociously, then stuffed Gnome's spotty head through the neck of his sweater.

"It's rapidly becoming a dubious pleasure to even bother abusing you two retards."

"Not the coolest gang members are they Barney? Brrr..."

Barney looked up to see Carol pretending to shiver and holding her hockey stick ready for combat. Putting his head back, he laughed.

"Okay duck face - anytime."

Carol kicked his sports bag over to him.

"Alright with me."

The two girls walked away with impressive casualness.

"Sorted?"

"Only one boot; the lining was stuck in the other."

"Single chip then?"

"Nah. Put 'em both in."

"Will that be okay?"

"How do I know?"

"Shouldn't we tell Podric?"

"If you want... He'll find out soon enough anyway."

Minutes after the girls left, Podric finished creating an artificial police warning. This meant that when Braxby booted up his device, it looked as though it was directly linked to the boys in blue with a notification that he was under their surveillance for his pornographic activities and liable for prosecution. Putting the iPad away and closing the cupboard doors, Podric returned to the table and opened his backpack.

His brilliance with computer games meant companies came to Podric with trial equipment, providing him with the latest technology. He owned special models of both Xbox and PlayStations, but possessing the skills and technological abilities he did, Podric decided it would attract less attention if he sunc up one of the games control units programmed for his plan to his iPhone.

The lock sounded and the door partially opened. Hearing the caretaker talking to someone in the corridor, Podric grabbed his things and quickly hid behind the boiler. A second or two later Braxby entered. Walking over to the metal cabinet, he opened it and took out the box of origami. Whilst Jane may have been correct about the caretaker's activities that afternoon, her knowledge of his timing was obviously awry. The janitor closed the cabinet and departed. Waiting a few seconds, Podric went to the door and slipped out into the corridor.

Arriving at the playing fields, Jane managed to tell Podric that Carol had only been able to insert chips into Barney's right boot and that she'd stuck both of them in it. This didn't bother Podric unduly, but just how effectively they would work remained to be seen.

Standing near the touchline, he watched the teams warm up. Miles Willoughby ran by looking even skinnier in his football shirt – his body skeletal and white knobbly knees knocking with cold; Billy was at his side.

"Fun afternoon this'll be. Sturridge and his mob'll slaughter us."

Billy limbered up.

"Reckon you're well out of this one, Pod."

Miles and Billy began passing a ball back and forth as Barney and several gang members came onto the field. Activating his iPhone, Podric moved his thumb across its face as if checking apps.

"You'll need more than a call for help Moony. Just 'cos you're on the touchline, don't think that'll save you."

The bully won the toss and elected to kick off, but there was only one person who was going to have first touch! Approaching the ball, Barney's foot suddenly seemed to veer away and he missed connecting, the ball rolling towards the feet of Miles Willoughby, who made a good pass.

As the game progressed, things only got worse for Barney. Every time the ball came to him, his right foot suddenly appeared to have a mind of its own and repeatedly failed to make contact. His efforts became more and more frenzied as the half wore on, other team members ignoring him which drove him crazy. So frustrated did Barney become, he barged past one of his own side and attempted an enormous kick near the goal mouth. Yet again missing the ball, the velocity of his effort was such, it caused him to smash into one of the goal posts and stun himself! Seeing Barney carried off the field concussed, Podric switched off his phone.

With Barney out of the match, his side's threat largely collapsed. Mr. Fantoni, the games master and referee, struggled to maintain some sort of order but things descended into chaos. A lucky pass from V Arts Jackie O'Hara flicked the ball to an out of position Billy Johnson who scored. Podric's friend went on to put the ball in the net for another later in the match. At the final whistle V G were defeated 2-nil.

His friends celebrating their victory, Podric strolled away from the touchline and fell into step with Jane who had just completed her game.

"Bit of a result then. Brain over brawn; hope we do as well with Braxby."

Podric smiled.

"He came back and collected his box of paper models."

"Did he see you?"

Jane was concerned. Podric shook his head. The girl sighed.

"If that was the only pastime he kept to."

Podric met his kid sister at the school gate. Parked outside was the smoothest car Podric had ever seen. Sitting inside the open topped coupé, Dr. Light tapped the steering wheel.

"Hop in."

"What do you mean?"

"Is English difficult for you or don't you want a lift home?"

"We're not going home." This from Amy. "And don't you know you can be in trouble for waiting outside school gates."

She could be a winner with dialogue could Amy. Archie's expression changed. His Facel Vega and their conversation were already attracting interest – largely favourable from female pupils, more jealously from boys.

"We're meeting our mum at her office in Wendbury tonight."

"Want a lift there then?"

"No, it's okay. It's not far."

Podric smiled. Archie didn't.

"Do you want another meeting?"

"If you call our last one that."

Archie fiddled with the gear stick.

"I thought we might, though your young minder doesn't seem keen."

"I'll come over at the weekend if you want."

Archie mused on this for a second.

"Midday Saturday – don't be late."

He started his car and roared away.

"I don't like that man. He's very rude."

Amy's face was a picture of hostility.

"But with one sharp set of wheels."

Billy was outright admiring. Podric betrayed no emotion at all.

Chapter 6

The Meeting

Barbara having announced she would take them for a pizza that evening, the two young Moons walked through Wendbury to their mother's office.

"Something worked then."

Amy's comment broke into her brother's thoughts. Podric didn't reply.

"I saw you on the playing field. Whatever you did got at Barney the thug."

"If you say so."

"He was moaning in matron's with a bashed head."

"You seem to know plenty."

"Eyes and ears Podric, eyes and ears."

In spite of himself, Podric had to smile.

"How do you know it wasn't self-inflicted?"

"Missing a ball twenty times? It's like he had a funny right boot and couldn't control it."

Amy was her particular self.

"All those apps you were checking. Good job you're on a deal with your phone."

Amy Moon could be very astute on occasion where her brother was concerned.

Tweeney's Waste Disposal premises were typical of their type. Located on an industrial estate on the outskirts of town, the building was bland and to Podric's mind, acutely dull.

Ralph Tweeney was a sleazy middle-aged bloke with thinning, greasy hair. Not only did he lack any kind of 21st century male awareness, he didn't even possess any 20th century male attributes. Indeed,

Ralph Tweeney could have been plucked from the imaginatively descriptive pages of a Dickensian novel. It was a complete anathema to Podric - not only that his mother could tolerate such a man, but that she might actually *like* him. To her son, Don was the more interesting brother, he being barking mad.

Walking into the engineering workshop (a partitioned section of the warehouse where Don slaved over refinements to the Tweeney system), Podric found the Technical Head of R&D working on an ever more powerful suction device 'guaranteed to dispose the indisposable'.

"Nothing that can't handle. Anything from an avocado stone to a marlin spike."

"Is it safe?"

"Safe? 'See the guard on the non-return valve? Take your grandmother's nuts to penetrate that."

Podric didn't want to think what his grandmother's nuts might look like.

"What about someone small getting to it?"

"You mean a kids' hand?"

"Yeah."

"Hahaha. That's where Tweeney's clever see. Have to unlock it separately. Think of everything we do. See it. Feel it. Dispose the indisposable. That's Tweeney's."

Barbara and Amy appeared.

"Ready darling?"

Brightly dressed in her colourful attire, Barbara was all smiles.

"You'll have those notes sorted for tomorrow, won't you Babs?"

Aghast at Ralph's name for his mother, Podric adjusted his backpack.

"'Fraid not till midmorning; I'm taking the children out tonight."

"Celebration?"

"Of our family."

Barbara's mood subtly changed.

"Though I grant taking one's children for a pizza is hardly the height of revelry. See you tomorrow."

And with that she turned on her heel, and headed for her car.

Amy and Podric followed.

"He's a sleaze bag mum."

"Yes, but a harmless sleaze."

"That's two we've met in the last hour."

"Oh?"

"That light bulb bloke turned up at school wanting Podric."

Barbara looked quizzical.

"Games stuff?"

"Expect so, unless he's a molester."

Amy skipped up to her mother's car.

"Do you want to meet him again darling? He was rather rude the last time."

Podric didn't reply. Barbara unlocked her car and Amy got in.

"That Ralph's got stuff on his collar."

"I might buy him some Head and Shoulders."

"They're funny too."

Barbara sighed and turned on the ignition.

"Well, Tweeney's are paying for supper and that Napolitano Romana's the most expensive on the menu."

"Three of those then!"

Arriving home after their Italian feast, a message awaited Barbara on the answer phone. Left by Alannah, she requested Barbara call her. The two chatting for a long time, ostensibly the conversation confirmed Podric's next meeting with Archie, but both Podric and Amy had long since disappeared to their rooms by the time their mother put down the phone!

*   *   *

At school next day, Podric was coming out of his classroom when he collided with a harassed caretaker. Sweating, Braxby was jumpy and nervous.

"Watch where you're going, can't you?"

Managing to hold on to his books, Podric stared at the janitor who ran up the corridor.

"What's happened to him? Plague of rats in the science lab perhaps?"

Podric turned to see the class's premier pupil, Catherine Halliday standing beside him. She was also the most attractive girl in their year, much fancied by one and all.

"You're the computer wunderkind people are talking about, aren't you? Podric Moon – the guy who gets collected in a snazzy car."

Podric smiled. How quickly word got around.

"Unusual name. I've got a problem with one of my maths games."

The games champion shrugged.

"I use them to help me work."

"Huh?"

"Maths isn't my favourite and computer games help. Take out any auto facility, they make things more interesting."

"I must try it. Top's not a bad slot."

Catherine smiled.

"Doesn't mean I like the subject."

"Got the game with you?"

"I've got it as an app on my phone."

An explosion shook the building.

"What the hell was that?"

Sally Frost appeared. A big girl with wiry hair, she was Catherine's best friend. The school's fire alarm went off and people began running hither and thither.

Disobeying school rules Podric, Catherine and Sally headed towards the action. Crossing a couple of corridors, Podric realised they were approaching the boiler room building. Turning a corner, they saw that its entire roof section had been blown off.

With sounds of the emergency services in the distance and staff blocking pupils getting any closer to the scene of devastation, Carol Jenson wandered by.

"Methane gas blowback from the boiler extractor."

Carol was matter of fact. Podric and the others watched as Braxby – face blackened, and overalls in tatters, was carried to safety by staff members. Jane Cartwright materialised at Podric's side.

"Reckon Mr. B will have other things on his mind than the activities we were worried about, poor sod."

*   *   *

Though he'd agreed to meet Archie Light, Podric Moon was out of sorts on Saturday morning and not in the mood to rendezvous with the games creator. Since meeting Catherine Halliday he'd thought of little else and was already looking forward to helping her with her maths game on Monday.

It was his sister who suggested he took his computer kit with him for the meeting with Dr. Light.

"Put it in your bag Pod and blow him way!"

For once Podric heeded her advice and slung the equipment in his backpack.

The one stipulation Archie had made about their meeting was that it should not be interrupted. Amy had gone to see her friend Romany Mad Lilian, and Barbara and Alannah decided they would go into Wendbury to see a film. Mother and son arriving at The Lighthouse, Podric reached across the rear seat and picked up his backpack.

"He must be clever, Podric."

"So?"

"Maybe he's got a project or something..."

"So?"

"Okay, okay – well if you want to cut it short, call me."

"You're seeing a movie."

"Text then; I can be back in twenty minutes."

Barbara's phone rang. Leaving his mother, Podric walked up to the front door and Alannah let him in.

"Thank you for coming, Podric. I've left food in the fridge over there."

The housekeeper paused.

"You're doing him a favour even if he doesn't realise it."

She stopped again, thoughtful. Then just said,

"I think you know where to go – or would you like me to take you?"

Podric replied that he was happy to find his own way and set off through the empty house. Walking up the stairs, he was again struck by the beauty of the girl in the photograph. Making his way across the glass bridge, he took the lift to the top floor and as before, the place seemed to be empty.

His phone vibrated. Podric sat down in the den and checked his messages. He was surprised to see one from Catherine Halliday, complete with a picture of her on a quad bike up to her eyes in mud. The message read 'My Saturday. What are you up to?' Podric's heart beat faster. He replied 'Guess. How did you get my number?' She instantly answered 'Not difficult. Why?'

"So, you got clearance from below."

Powering off his phone, Podric didn't understand Archie's sentence.

"Sorry?"

"Your junior – she accepted our meeting."

"You wanted to see me."

Podric adjusted his bag strap.

"In a hurry, are you? Got another meeting?"

Archie sat down on the sofa opposite. His behaviour suggested he was slightly drunk. Podric's phone vibrated again. Not answering it, he reached for his bag.

"Oh, don't be so touchy."

"Why did you want to see me again?"

Archie sipped some coffee.

"My housekeeper thought it was a good idea."

Not having a ready reply, Podric didn't make one. For several seconds, neither man nor boy spoke.

"She thought that with your interests, my skills might help you."

"How?"

As he'd experienced with the Moon's previously – although Archie was a smooth operator, he found Podric's directness disconcerting. This time Podric did speak.

"I can't help you with *Andromeda*."

Archie nearly dropped his mug.

"What do you know about that?"

"Secorni have passed on it."

"But..."

Putting down his coffee, Archie was speechless and it took him several seconds to pull himself together.

"How? Why?"

It was Archie's turn to be abrupt.

"They contacted me."

"They what?"

"They contacted me – wanted an opinion."

"Secorni contacted you?"

"Yuh. Mr. Zaentz."

"Cy Zaentz called you personally."

"Yuh – he does sometimes. They give me stuff to test, try out."

"I suppose you also have Fred Schepesi on the line."

"More. Pasaro is bigger."

Archie couldn't get his head round this.

"You're telling me you get calls from the CEOs of the two largest games companies in the world."

Podric nodded.

"Prove it."

Podric may have only been a couple of months' shy of seventeen but he'd had enough.

"Look Mr. Light."

"Doctor."

"Doctor Light. You wanted to see me again, but I don't understand why."

"You can't, can you?"

Archie's aggressiveness implied it wasn't really a question.

"Prove it."

Undoing his bag, Podric removed his futuristic glasses, uniquely modified PlayStation, and the controls. Rifling through the depths of his kit, he found a crumpled envelope and opening it, pulled out a 'From the Desk of' card. The brief note read 'To Podric whose skills are unequalled. Thanks again for the assistance – my company owes you. With all good wishes, Fred Schepesi' and on the back was scrawled 'Over in L-Town soon, will arrange a meet. FS'.

Standing, Podric left the note and games items on the sofa. Without another word, he walked out of the room.

Taking the stairs, on his way down Podric checked his iPhone. There was another message from Catherine 'Not heard from you. Want to meet up?' This was amazing from the best-looking girl at Wendbury High! Walking back to the house across the glass span, Podric came face to face with Cosima Light. The girl stood on the landing. She drank white wine and a slight smile played on her face.

To Podric Moon, her image was spellbinding.

"Ah. The computer boy, come to save daddy."

Transfixed by Cosima's beauty, Podric somehow pulled himself together.

"Doubt that."

For a second Cosima looked at Podric then burst out laughing.

"Beyond it is he, the dinosaur?"

She turned and walked towards her bedroom. Entering it, Cosima closed the door behind her.

Walking through Drinkwell, Podric's mind was in a whirl. Catherine contacting him was great, but Cosima Light was something else. She was - well she was something else!

"Hi, Pod. How's it going?"

Billy appeared on his bike.

"You okay?' 'Look a bit out of it."

Podric smiled.

"Sort Jane and Carol's little problem, did you?"

"'Reckon, though more likely other forces will have."

"Your computer stuff has its advantages."

Podric laughed. Billy pedalled slowly as Podric walked along beside him.

"What happened to Braxby? Rum that explosion; some gas – methane discharge they said. Amazed the school system runs off it."

"Good value. You know cows fart the stuff."

"You're not serious?"

"Blow flames from their arse."

"What?"

"Check it out on *YouTube*."

"God Pod, you're a mind of information. Milk, methane and

flaming cows - wow! I'd better go. Collecting round money. Right sweat getting it in from some of these big houses. Dad reckons deliveries aren't worth it. Maybe I should threaten 'em with explosive milk? They'd get their tenner's out quick enough then!"

Chapter 7

Another Mishap

U nlocking the front door of Number 5 Briony Close and letting himself into the house, Podric's mind was still in turmoil. Hearing the phone ring and going to answerphone, no message was left. Almost immediately his mobile vibrated. Not a number he recognised, Podric let it go to messaging – 'This is an emergency message for Mr. Podric Moon. Please call 01264 900300 – Officer Leslie Jenner. It's about your mother, Podric.'

"Hello."

Podric's voice cut in before Officer Jenner had completed her message.

"Podric?"

"Yes."

"This is Officer Leslie Jenner of the Hampshire police. I just need to check a couple of details. Your address, please?"

"How do I know you are who you say?"

There was a pause.

"Your mobile doesn't advise location."

This was said slightly accusatively (Podric had deactivated the facility on his phone).

"We've just called your house. If you'd prefer, we can call you on that number."

"No. It's alright." Podric gave his address.

"Is your sister Amy with you?"

"She's not home. I've just walked in."

"Podric, I've some serious news. Your mother's been involved in an incident and has been taken to hospital."

"What happened?"

Podric's voice sounded hollow. There was another slight pause.

"She and her friend Alannah met with an assault."

"What does that mean?"

"It means that your mother is hurt, but she's stable."

"How did it happen?"

There was squawk and radio communication from the police.

"Sorry, Podric. A car will be arriving outside your house in about five minutes. Can you locate your sister?"

"I'll try. How did it happen?"

The boy was coldly emphatic.

"We're still getting details but indications suggest your mother and Ms. Brodie were attacked."

It was Podric's turn to be silent.

"Podric?"

"Yes."

"Please contact your sister if you can. The car will be with you shortly."

The call terminated. Podric tried Amy but she didn't answer.

Minutes later he was speaking to a police officer who arrived in a patrol car. Amy and Lilian turned into the drive but seeing the police, Lilian took off. Breaking the news to Amy, whose cheeks were covered in blue face paint, his sister got into the car. Officer Ravilious looked at Podric.

"Let's go then. Locked the house?"

"Yuh."

"Mortice?"

Podric went back and double locked the front door as Officer Ravilious reversed onto the road.

"Can you drive fast?"

Amy was her usual direct self.

"You'll see."

Podric got into the police car beside his sister.

"How badly is mum hurt?"

"Don't know. Bad enough to be in hospital."

"Step on it then, smokey!"

Although concerned for the children's plight, Ravilious couldn't prevent a brief smile. Either the girl had a lively imagination or she'd been watching too many American cop shows. Whatever, the blue light went on and the car shot forward.

*   *   *

Sitting in his den, Archie's self-pity was pathetic. Helping himself to another dollop of scotch, he mooched moodily about his eyrie. Dog appeared. The wolfhound had a strange relationship with its master. The more Light disregarded the animal, the more Dog seemed to worship him.

Looking at Fred Schepesi's note to Podric again, Archie scrunched it up and threw it in a corner. Then he picked up the virtual reality glasses, and twiddled with them. Inspecting the adapted PlayStation unit and firing it up, Archie put on the weird specs. The slide switch Podric had fitted still showed Active. *Tokyo Joe* was already loaded and as the games creator began to operate the controls, his interest increased; realising he was both watching the game and reality, it was a strange experience. Gorillas on the rampage in Tokyo Zoo seemed about to attack Dog, who stood in front of him wagging his giant tail.

Operating the PlayStation's controls, Archie fired Joe's stun gun at an enormous male primate; the Silverback rolled away as Dog tried to lick his master. The game increased in pace, Dog in and out of view chased by both zoo creatures and Sino hoods. And what was this? His daughter appearing and a Japanese bad boy about to decapitate her using a samurai sword. This had to be dealt with!

"You're such a jerk."

Taking off the VR visor, Archie shook his head as if to clear it.

"I'm sorry?"

"Too late for that."

Walking away, Cosima was dismissive.

"I meant, I didn't hear what you said."

"I said you're such a jerk. So wrapped up with your silly little games, you didn't even hear the phone."

"That's what you think isn't it, silly little games, but I've seen the future."

"Whoopee. Reckon where you're concerned, that doesn't look so good."

Moving towards the door, Cosima turned back.

"Anyway, interrupting your childish play, you've got to call our housekeeper. She's been involved in some attack. Computer geek's mum's in hospital."

Although furious at his daughter's attitude, Archie quickly banished his emotions.

"What about Brodie?"

"Alright, she says."

"What happened?"

"'Didn't say much. She'd been trying to call you, but you were playing with your petit jouet."

Standing, Archie came over to his daughter.

"What is it with you? What did I do that you so despise me so much?"

Her face petulant, Cosima didn't look at her father. He took hold of her face. That got a reaction.

"Get your hands off me!"

Cosima's fire was up.

"Because you're a nobody; because you've got no class and mum was right to dump you."

An hour ago, Archie would have gone berserk but something had happened to the games creator during that time, something long overdue igniting within him. When he spoke, his voice was controlled.

"Is that so? Your honourable mother I'm afraid my dear, is a slut of the first order. I'm further afraid that as your father, I'm hardly perfect in that department but I'm whiter than the driven snow by comparison. I subsequently discovered that even at the time of our engagement she was involved with a variety of partners, including sidesmen chosen by her as 'friends' at our wedding. Let's leave out a bridesmaid or two for the moment, shall we?"

Cosima seemed unaffected.

"You'll be suggesting she had the page next!"

Archie looked at his daughter archly. In her mood, Cosima didn't catch it and went on.

"Ha! But mums got the one thing you'll never have – class. She knows the right people, not the rubbish geeky freaks you run around with."

Walking a little away, Archie actually appeared relaxed.

"Is that what you think breeding is – an honourable title? I know steel workers with more class than your mother – when we had some."

Archie picked up his mobile.

"That education I've paid for has been a profound waste of my hard-earned money – achieved from those silly little toys as you call them. And the geeky freaks you mention are the future. It's you who's the dinosaur and you're less than half my age!"

Cosima began to leave the room but Archie intercepted her.

"Get out of my way!"

"You've got no idea, have you? No idea about anything really and it's partly my fault. I apologise for that. You really are the poor little rich girl."

"You think we're rich? The sort of money I'm interested in wouldn't buy you a seat at the bottom end of the table. When I go out with my friends, I'm the poor one. You're right about not understanding *my* reality, the world *I* intend to inhabit."

Her words triggered something in Archie's mind and momentarily distracted him. What had Podric said about reality? Some other form of reality..? That's what he must have done with this game. That's what he was on about – but didn't he want something more?

"Let's face it Pa, you're a failure, both socially and professionally. You're even failing at those stupid games you were once so proud of! You're washed up; you're done!"

Archie slapped his daughter hard across the face and then immediately turned on his heel and walked off. Cosima was so shocked, she didn't yell or scream, but when she spoke her words were cold.

"You'll be sorry you ever did that, you pathetic plebeian bastard!"

Reaching the lift, Archie turned back.

"You're wrong Cosima. I should have done it years ago. I'm not turning you out of my house, but until you grow up and get some balance in your life, you'll do nothing, you'll achieve nothing – either in my eyes or anyone else's."

Archie studied his daughter.

"I may not have been much of a father, but I've always loved you. I've made mistakes and I expect I'll make some more, but if nothing else I hope you learn one thing – that life's a two-way street. You win, you lose – but if you want to achieve anything, you graft and not behave like the spoilt brat *you* are. I'm going to the hospital now to see the one person who performs a reality check on this little household. Coming?"

"I wouldn't go anywhere with you and when you get back, I'll be gone."

"Well that would be a shame – certainly for me. You're a month off eighteen, but the law's strange about young people's rights these days and I expect if I looked into trying to restrict you, they'd probably tell me I was out of order."

Opening the lift gate, Archie hesitated.

"Beware though, child. You think you know everything but in fact, you know so very little."

"That's it, isn't it? Losing your little girl. I'm not a child you can control anymore and your ego can't bear it."

His expression sad, Archie looked at his daughter once more and pressed Descend.

*   *   *

When later they tried to come to terms with the numbing events experienced that Saturday afternoon in Wendbury, Barbara Moon and Alannah Brodie always found the terrifying details got mired in disbelief.

Parking Barbara's car in the multi-storey car park, the two women made their way to a multiplex cinema. Their route involved a couple of lanes, one that ran past the back of a pub. Returning from the film, it was here they were set upon by three men.

In sight of a department store on the high street, two of the rapists attacked Barbara with such suddenness that she had no time to save herself. Dragged into a tiny alley yelling and screaming, she clawed one of the men's faces. The man spat out an oath. Brodie had a split second to react as the other villain came at her. That moment saved them both. Kicking the attacker, Alannah grabbed an anti-rape device from her bag and pulled its tag.

When the 'Rape Stopper' went off, the villain in the act of raping Barbara – who in spite of her biting and struggling, already had her jeans yanked halfway down her legs – was the angriest. His fellow ravager tried to pull him off the prostrated woman, but the rapist had a knife out.

"Bitch!"

Seeing the blade coming towards her, Barbara somehow managed to twist her body away from the worst of the thrust, smashing her head into her assailant's face. Before passing out, the last thing Barbara heard was the wail of a police siren.

Sitting in a corridor at the local hospital, Alannah worked her mobile phone. She sported a large plaster on her forehead and a bruised black eye. At the sight of her employer coming out of the lift, the housekeeper attempted a smile.

"Yes, to doing everything in my power to see that those bastards are caught...and yes, I'm alright."

Archie sat down beside her.

"Thank God for that. Mrs. Moon?"

"Barbara. She's much more seriously injured that I am I'm afraid. Broken ribs, they've been checking her for internal bleeding."

Archie looked around.

"She's in a side room. They've let Amy and Podric in to see her. A police woman's with them."

Brodie put her phone in her bag.

"Would it be okay if I went to Briony Close for a few days? Barbara won't be home for a little while."

"Sure...or would they like to stay at The Lighthouse?"

Brodie looked at her boss, sharply. *Was this really Dr. Light?*

"What about..? How would that go down with-?"

"Cosima? By now Brodie, Cosima has left Drinkwell and on her way to who knows where?"

Alannah looked at Archie. After a second or two, he went on.

"We had a fallout. I slapped her. It was ten years too late, but the spoilt brat has an attitude that's at the least, awry."

Archie flicked a speck of imaginary dust off his trousers.

"Some of it's my fault, some's her mother's and the crowd she runs around with. Indulged with too much money, she'll never amount to anything till she's experienced some of life's knocks – if that ever happens."

Had Alannah not just experienced so much horror, she would have been in shock of a different kind listening to her employer. As it was, for several seconds she just gawped at him.

A door opened and Podric and Amy appeared with Officer Jenner and a Staff Nurse.

"Mrs. Moon has been given a sedative. She's stable now, but needs to rest."

"Would you like me to ring your grandparents?" Officer Jenner was attentive to Podric and Amy.

"No!" replied the little girl.

"They drive us nuts. I can look after Podric."

Amy Moon was a chip off her mother's block and although traumatised by the afternoon's events, her nine-year old vehemence was respected. It was Alannah's turn to address the children.

"Dr. Light has invited you to The Lighthouse. Would that work for you?"

Amy looked at Podric and this time it was her brother who spoke.

"No."

Podric was less forceful than his sister, but no less firm.

"Podric, could I have a word with you?"

Not responding to Archie's question, Podric stared at the door of his mother's room.

"In private."

Podric still didn't respond, forcing Archie to continue.

"I want to apologise."

"Then you can."

"But it's more than that. Now is not the time nor the place, but it would be good to have you to stay – both of you – and we won't do computers."

With her instinctive intuition, Amy said nothing, and waited for her brother's response.

"That's a kind offer." Officer Jenner eyed both children.

"If you wish to decline, we'll have to contact your relatives."

"I'm nearly seventeen."

"But Amy isn't and you're too young to drive."

"So?"

"You'll want to visit your mum."

It was decided that the housekeeper would go to Briony Close for a few days and take care of Amy and Podric. Leaving the hospital, the police drove Alannah and the young Moons to fetch their mother's car. Still in Wendbury's multi-storey car park, the journey was sombre.

Chapter 8

Agrolution

"Hi, Podric."

Crossing the school playground, the computer champion awoke from his reverie. "Hi, er..."

"I was sorry to hear about your mum."

Catherine Halliday's concern was sincere but not burdening.

"Thanks."

"How's she getting on?"

"Hmm – so so. Early days.."

"I'm sorry. It must have been terrible"

"Didn't you want me to look at that maths app?"

Catherine was surprised by Podric's abrupt change of topic.

"You won't want to be doing that just now."

"Why not?

"Well, er, well..."

"Shouldn't take long."

Catherine fished out her mobile.

"No one else has ever touched my phone."

Podric looked at her. With extreme reluctance, Catherine handed it to him. Podric glanced at the android.

"Okay if I get into it?"

"It's locked."

Catherine raised an eyebrow.

"Go on then."

Podric started working on Catherine's cell phone. Reflecting it in the light, within no time at all, she heard her phone activate. Catherine looked askance.

"How?"

"Six digits – you can tell from the nonporous surface smudge."

Catherine was seriously impressed. Podric flicked through her icons. Finding the Maths Я Us Squared app, he activated it, made the required adjustments and handed the unit back.

"Doors to manual. Think you'll still come top?"

The school bell rang. Not thinking he'd done anything very clever, Podric headed for the entrance. Catherine's friend Sally Frost arrived. The girls followed Podric into school, and Sally noticed the look on Catherine's face was more than simply admiring.

A couple of days after Saturday's unimaginable events, Alannah was coming back from Wendbury with Podric and Amy after visiting Barbara, and turning into The Lighthouse driveway, explained she had a couple of things to do there. Suddenly, the garage door slid up and Archie emerged. Clad in overalls, the bonnet of one of his Facel Vegas was up; his hands were greasy from working underneath the engine.

He and Podric looked at each other.

"Saying I should apologise – what you've done is incredible. I tried your kit...astounding dimension. Makes everything else obsolete."

"But it doesn't take me where I want to go."

The words were out of Podric's mouth before he realised he'd spoken them.

"Hell of a thing, though. Amazing. I wouldn't have believed it's possible. Anyway, you'll want your gear back."

Podric did want it back.

"Oh, er..."

Leaving the garage door open, Archie wiped his hands and began walking towards his house. Podric was torn. He could call after the games creator saying his equipment could be dropped back another time, but he was here now. It wouldn't do any harm to collect it.

Going upstairs, Archie caught Podric glancing at the large black and white photograph of Cosima.

"She's gone."

Forcing his eyes away from the lovely image, Podric looked at her father.

"We had a row. She's a spoilt bitch and needs to grow up. Likely she'll reappear when she needs some money, but harsh words were spoken. Long overdue I'm afraid."

The man and boy walked across the gallery to the tower. Archie pressed the lift button and they began to ascend.

"Great view, isn't it? Only reason I bought the place."

Podric gazed out at the countryside below. The lift arrived at the top floor. Podric's virtual reality glasses, portable PlayStation, and controls were on the table.

"I've got a problem."

Archie turned to face Podric.

"You know Secorni rejected *Andromeda Volcanism* which you, er... advised on..."

This admission was obviously still uncomfortable for the games man to reconcile.

"But I've had a wake-up call."

Archie walked across to the far window.

"When you were talking about what you'd played, your successes and later, your apathy about how uninspired you felt games were, I didn't really take on board your skills and just what a talent you are."

Taking a couple of beers from the small built in fridge, Archie opened one and shunted the other across the table to Podric.

"I've been successful in my time but I need a new game to re-establish myself; a game that companies want, a game they get desperate for. And you, with this alternative reality idea you've got, I just couldn't believe what you've created."

Archie picked up Podric's virtual reality kit.

"Incredible."

He handed the gear back to Podric who put it in his bag.

"I was wondering if you'd help me write a game – one that you reckon would hit the spot. Obviously I'd ensure that rights wise you were credited and paid accordingly, and as part of the deal, I'm sure it could help you to have unlimited access to the lab here – use any of the equipment. You can come and go as you please and work on your project..."

"After I've made you a game..."

"'*We*' Podric. I do have some ability and I also have some money, which might be needed for your reality concept as much as anything else."

They were both silent for several seconds before Archie said.

"Will you help me?"

"I'd want at least shared copyright and minimum equal royalties."

Archie laughed.

"Not backward in your business skills either Podric. Got any thoughts for a game?"

"About six."

"Yuh? And how long would it take you to write one of these?"

"A week - maybe less. A couple are half written."

The internal phone rang. Archie picked up the receiver.

There was a pause.

"He can come down whenever you want."

Not bothering to cover the receiver, Archie turned to Podric.

"Food. Summoned by her who must be obeyed."

Podric picked up his bag.

"He'll be down shortly."

Archie replaced the receiver.

"I looked at your modified visor. Plan on developing the frame further?"

"Outside-in Reality was just a beginning, but having to wear something won't work."

"Agree. Interesting spin-off though. It's like you're half way there."

Archie sipped his beer.

"Anyway, I've been thinking about this, and I reckon you need to see it through the eye and then be absorbed into the world of the game, which I think is your intention."

Podric nodded.

"When I had the brain scan after my bike accident - talking to the doc, he told me about mind pathways, and creating a kind of receptive gateway."

"For real? That's pretty whacky stuff."

"Yeah, but the idea of being able to adjust one's imagination so that you control it and not the other way round, could help getting absorbed into a games world."

"Hmm. Okay, it's practicalities then."

Archie tossed his empty beer can in the bin.

"As you're going down, just come with me for a minute."

He led the way to the stairs. Descending a floor to the computer laboratory, Archie opened a cabinet. Full of components, he removed a tray. Taking out a small packet, he turned on a microscope light and placed a tiny object underneath it.

"Take a look."

Podric did so and viewed the minuscule object.

"A microchip so small that it can be taken orally as a pill."

Podric stood back. Archie turned off the light.

"Pre-encoded, it enters the body and sets a magnetic pulse to the brains' synapse, activated when a player programmes their PlayStation or Xbox using a corresponding code."

"That's sort of the technical side of what the doctor was saying."

"So you needed two doctors!"

Clearly impressed by Archie's idea, Podric was thoughtful,

"And to get out?"

"Exactly. To make this happen could require a bit of money – certainly likely to take a lot of time."

"Which if I work on it, will reduce costs."

"Or, I could take it to Secorni."

"No!"

Surprised by Podric's intensity, Archie was conciliatory.

"Pasaro, if you'd rather."

"Again negative. That's not what this is all about."

It was Podric's turn to pace around.

"This has nothing to do with money. I'm not interested in anyone else having it. I want alternative reality because I want the experience. It'll be unique; it'll be mind blowing."

"No doubt. But if we got – what is it? Outside-in Reality going commercially and this other form up and running later, it could make a packet of money."

"I'll make us a packet of money from the game I write."

Archie chuckled.

"As you seem disinterested in any input from me, when can I expect this masterpiece?"

"I'll have a first codex ready by the end of the week. I'll leave it raw, while you're doing the paperwork."

The games creator looked quizzical.

"Legal stuff."

Archie laughed at this.

"Trusting so and so, aren't you?"

"No."

"Okay then, I'll have my people talk to your people."

"There's a lawyer Mr. Schepesi put me on to for my consultancy contracts. He's pretty hot."

Podric walked to the door. Archie suddenly looked more concerned.

"Hang on Podric."

The boy turned back to him.

"You want a game. You want a game to make millions. That's what you're about Archie - money. I understand that. It's just I want something else. I want adventure - the ultimate adventure!"

*   *   *

Three days later, Alannah Brodie collected Barbara Moon from hospital. Still battered and bruised, Barbara returned home to a sizeable floral tribute from Tweeney's. Its message 'Our thoughts are with you at this time' scrawled on the waste disposal company's comp slip, boldly featured the printed slogan 'Tweeney's - waste not, want not!'

While visits from the local district nurse monitored Barbara's recovery, Alannah continued to help out as much as she could, and both Amy and Podric were actively involved in taking care of their mother. It was, therefore, remarkable that true to his word, Podric delivered much more than the structure of *Agrolution* within the time span he'd promised Archie.

The concept featured a player challenging urban violence in an

attempt to reach a world of utopian thrills. Not only would this satis-
fy the more militantly demanding participant, but also suit a games
company salving its social conscience by answering the market's bel-
licose demands for a 'better life' conclusion. The moral high ground
was something both the main computer games company's loved.
More importantly from a player's perspective, *Agrolution* combined
state of the art CGI work with extreme demands on a player's high-
speed skills. Podric had even incorporated Archie's override engine
into the code.

The game more developed than he'd expected to receive, Archie
couldn't deny *Agrolution* was both innovative and challenging. Given
his experience, he could smell its potential as being a winner.

Keen to see his young partner and discuss things, Archie dropped
by Briony Close at the end of the day. This happened to be at a time
Barbara was having a bad turn. The mental fallout from the attack
was, in many ways, worse than its physical effects. Barbara would appear normal for a day or so, then suddenly go into spasm – sweating
and distressed. At the Moon's when Archie made his unannounced
visit, Alannah quickly took him aside.

"Her body's healing okay but her mental state's becoming more
of an issue. I'm worried about her – what it's done to her mind."

"Can she travel? I mean to see someone."

"What do you mean?"

"A psychiatrist."

"Privately?"

"Yuh – get an appraisal."

Alannah thought for a moment.

"When are you suggesting?"

"Don't know. I just ask the question."

"I'm not sure financially…?"

"Did anyone mention finance?"

Alannah hesitated.

"I don't think it would work with you just taking her."

"You mean it's better with you?"

"Yes."

"But she'd be okay if I was driving and you were with her."

"I think so."

"Good. Then we have a plan. I may have to go to town in a few days' time. If you think she's up to it, we could take her to Harley Street. Where's Podric?"

"In his garden workshop."

"Through there?"

Archie indicated the conservatory which led to the garden.

Going outside, he approached the shed and tapped on its door. Podric opened it.

"Thought you were coming to the lab."

"Can't right now."

"No... I understand."

Archie looked around. The place Podric had made into his computer workshop looked pretty Heath Robinson.

"So, this is where it all happens?"

Podric didn't reply.

"Great work by the way – I particularly like the reaction speed element."

"Had to incorporate something of yours."

Archie laughed. Podric continued, "Going to take it to Secorni?"

"Thought I might."

"Would you like me to call Mr. Zaentz?"

"Er, no Podric. I think I'd like to go see them myself if it's all the same to you?"

Podric shrugged.

"Your shout."

As he left, Archie passed Brodie taking a cup of tea to Barbara.

"I'll give you the details of someone I know."

"Did you tell Podric?"

"No."

                    *   *   *

Friday morning saw Archie dressed in expensive smart casual – cashmere jacket, Italian trousers and loafers. Arriving promptly at Briony Close to collect Barbara and his housekeeper for their trip to London in one of his Facel Vegas, he'd had little or no communication with his new business partner since Podric produced

the structure for *Agrolution*. The games wunderkind hadn't put in
an appearance at Light's laboratory thus far, but Archie reckoned
he'd be seeing more of him when the anticipated deal was completed. In spite of concern for Barbara Moon, Archie's spirits were
high as they set off for town.

"These really are lovely cars."

Barbara looked out at the countryside. The Facel Vega Excellence
purred along.

"Do you like cars Barbara?"

Alannah was also enjoying the ride.

"Sean did. They were his passion – except for flying."

A few days ago, the housekeeper might have added 'and you' but
not now.

"And Podric's cleverness, of course."

"Did your husband like computer games...?"

For Archie, this was a hesitant comment.

"Crazy about them, but then he was crazy about anything Podric
did."

"Close, were they?" Alannah adjusted herself in her seat.

"Not in an obvious way. Sean was much more outgoing than
Podric, who as you have seen, can be quite retiring."

"It's attractive."

Alannah meant it. Archie checked his rear-view mirror but his
housekeeper was looking out of the window.

"How did your son get into games?"

Again, Archie was casual.

"Because Sean was so keen right from the early ones – they were
just around the place. I've always thought it was like being in proximity to a musical instrument. The games were lying there and Podric
just picked them up. It seemed to come naturally to him – not just
playing them well, but brilliantly – with almost no apparent effort.
That's why all these games companies consult him and want his advice."

"The computer companies rate him then?"

The question coming from Alannah, Archie checked his rear-
view mirror again, and discovered his housekeeper was looking

directly into it - and him.

"Oh yes. They've been on about his going to America, making a career over there for some time, but his real interest was flying with his dad. That's all he ever wanted to do. Now, of course...we'll see..."

By the time they reached London, Archie's mood had changed. For some reason, he was feeling dissatisfied with himself. Dropping Barbara and Alannah outside Dr. Liebermann's consulting rooms in Harley Street, Archie was disarmed when getting out of the car, Barbara looked him in the face.

"Dr. Light I'm aware I owe this to your kindness. Thank you."

Putting out a hand, she shook his. Unused to such manners, for a second Archie was taken aback. Alannah got out and it being necessary to move, Archie managed to mutter an appropriate reply. As he pulled away, Alannah called after him.

"Doctor - four o'clock, as arranged."

Heading over Grosvenor Place into St James's, Archie parked in his club's underground car park. At its reception, he notified the desk of the two women's arrival that afternoon. Then, attaché case in hand, he walked round the corner into Mayfair and Secorni's European headquarters. Strolling into the building, Archie was crossing the lobby towards the lifts when the receptionist called out to him.

"Sir?"

Archie stopped.

"Can I help you?"

"Doubt it. I was going up to see Saul."

"I see. What time's your appointment with Mr. Prendergast?"

Archie looked down at the young receptionist and smiled.

"You ever play *Captain Krimon?*"

The girl looked at him blankly. Archie continued.

"*Marvin the Destroyer?*"

This didn't seem to register either.

"*Guns of Orion, Knights of the Avenger, Undersea Invaders?* No?"

Archie was quite light hearted.

"Do you play any games?"

"Not really my thing."

Archie chuckled.

"What if I told you those games paid for the lease on this building and the salaries of everyone in this company."

"I'd call you a damned liar."

Saul Prendergast and a young aide emerged from an elevator and
now stood behind the man who masterminded those products. Archie turned to Secorni's European president.

"Then Master Saul you would be a bigger fool than I took you
for. Indeed, I happen to know the revenue from just one of them
kept this company afloat when it bombed in just about every other
operation for an entire year. Want to argue that?"

"I'm not arguing anything with you, Archie. Your contract is terminated, remember?"

"I've got a new game Saul and it's going to be big."

"Then go sell it to someone."

"I'm not talking about the one you've just passed on – this is an
entirely new game – different, ultra-high-speed challenges; it'll blow
you away."

"Like *Andromeda* didn't? We were waiting a year for your Volcanic
masterpiece."

Archie stood in front of Prendergast. It wasn't threatening but
feelings ran high.

"Listen, Saul – I urge you – look at what I've got."

"Well, I urge you to get out of here."

Prendergast smiled a hard North American smile.

"Now!"

His eyes darting about, Archie was aware of security people beginning to move. Such was his recent change of character, he managed to keep his cool.

"You've just made the biggest mistake of your business career."

Archie turned away, then looked back.

"When they make you Assistant Vice President of Maintenance
in Palookaville, remember this day Saul – the day you screwed the
deal of your life."

Addressing the whole reception, Archie made a mock dramatic
bow.

"Ciao all – and young lady – look up those games. They're actually fun!"

With that, Dr. Archibald Light left Secorni - and this time it really would be forever.

"Damned pseud, I'll give him deal of my life!"

Heading for the door with Prendergast, his young assistant looked more thoughtful than impressed by the way his boss had handled the situation.

Outside on the street, Archie's bravado crumbled. Turning into Davies Street, he bumped into his solicitor, Monty Limmerson. Monty was accompanied by a stunning looking woman.

"Archie. In town. You haven't just been where I think you have."

"Stupid goddamn idiots."

"The papers to sever your contract arrived on my desk this morning."

"We'll sue."

"We'll go to lunch. This is Kaliska my new head of Corporate. Come along. You like fish, don't you?"

In Blair's, an exclusive Mayfair fish restaurant, the ambiance was smart chic. There was a quiet hum of diners enjoying their food. Monty explained his additional guest to the maître'd and a larger table was quickly found. Menus were produced and studied.

"May I recommend the Sea Bass? The Gilt Head Bream in beurre blanc is a specialty, and the Gurnard Bercy, award winning. You're probably more a snapper man, though!"

Monty chuckled at what he considered his witticism. The waiter returned and Monty ordered an expensive bottle of Pouilly-Fumé. For his meal he chose caviar followed by gurnard. Kaliska and Archie both went for oysters, then Kaliska opted for the brill as her main and Archie, monkfish.

"Feeling in need of monastic flagellation? Surely things aren't that bad."

Kaliska and Archie ignored Limmerson's comment.

"So, Doctor Light, you have issues with Secorni."

Kaliska Monroe's voice was deeper than Archie imagined –huskier, with a slight lilt. The wine arrived. Monty approved it, and glasses were poured.

"Good health. Archie's got issues with everyone, haven't you Archie?"

Monty turned to Kaliska.

"Briefly, writing computer games he made a fortune for Secorni – and himself, but they passed on his latest effort and now wish to discontinue their links with the great creator."

"I know."

Kaliska looked Archie straight in the face and smiled.

"That's what you've been doing, staying at the office late."

Devouring a spoonful of caviar, Monty seemed mildly disgruntled. Archie sampled his wine.

"Presumably, Zaentz wishing to terminate my contract, I'm now free to go where I like."

"Hmm. I've only scanned the papers. They'll maintain rights to previous work, though we'll laugh at the five years they want. My advice is two, tops."

"But new material?"

"They'll try and inhibit. Sort of 'we don't want him you can't have him' stuff. You made some powerful enemies Archie."

"How come you upset them so much?"

Sitting back, Kaliska toyed with an oyster.

"Because I haven't written a good game in three years and they think I'm an arrogant son of a bitch."

"Are you?"

Monty laughed.

"When I last looked."

Archie smiled.

"Probably some. It's to hide my inadequacies."

Monty spluttered.

"This is a good lunch. I'm almost glad we bumped into you."

Having some more wine, Archie looked at Kaliska.

"I don't like anything second rate. And...in the last few years, my stuff hasn't been what I wanted it to be. Somehow, I couldn't create. They said I'd lost touch, but it wasn't that. The ideas just weren't there."

He turned to Monty.

"I was going to talk to you about another matter – albeit related. I may need your assistance in drawing up a contract with a developing partner."

"You do or you don't need my assistance? 'May' doesn't come into it."

"I'd forgotten what it's like talking to you. The thing is, it's – he's – the partner's still a minor."

"Got a parent?"

"Yup. Mother."

"Shouldn't be a problem then. What's his name?"

"Podric. Podric Moon."

"Podric Moon? What sort of a name is that?"

"It's a great name – wow."

Kaliska seemed animated.

With the arrival of the main course, the diners began eating. Archie drank more and the waiter refilled his glass.

"We've worked on this game. The kid's a computer champion. Won awards all over."

"And you're going into business with him. Surely you don't want a partnership with a kid?"

"Why not? Sounds like a smart move." Kaliska sipped her wine.

"The doctor's hit a dip and this young man Podric, is a games maven. His finger's going to be on the pulse – or rather 'Play' button – he'll know what the markets want."

Monty was thoughtful.

"Well, I don't know – I suppose he must have some talent."

"He does."

Archie sat back.

"If his mother and I had a company, the game could be launched via that association and not me personally – yuh?"

"Tricky. If you plan to do anything with it – could have other ramifications."

"Such as?"

"What I said earlier about your contract. You take the game elsewhere and your name is on it..."

"What if we were represented?"

Noting his client's concerns, Monty looked at Kaliska.

"The only really safe way is to have a holding company, but not in any way be part of the operating one."

Archie had some more Pouilly-Fumé.

"I presume you'd like another bottle."

It wasn't really a question.

"Not driving anywhere in one of your exotic cars I trust."

Masticating a mouthful of food, Archie didn't reply.

"What do you drive?"

"Some funny French sounding name. He's got several of them."

"Facel Vega."

"Wow – they are beautiful."

"Interested in cars, are you?"

"Kind of, but Facel Vegas are something else."

The second bottle of Pouilly-Fumé arrived and Archie was poured a glass. Picking it up aggressively, the look on his face wasn't one of pleasure.

"Don't see many of them around, I'll give you that."

Archie drank before continuing.

"What about a name?"

"For your partnership? I've been thinking about that. There's only one – MoonLight."

Monty laughed at Kaliska's suggestion.

"Very good – Moonlighting it is then!"

Forty-five minutes later, they parted. Amicable enough, Archie appeared preoccupied. Standing on the pavement, Kaliska proffered her hand.

"It was good to meet you. I'll send over some draft papers – the sort of contract where a parent or guardian is involved."

Archie muttered acknowledgment and managed to thank Monty for lunch. The legal people heading up South Audley Street, Limmerson said, "So, the problem child."

"He didn't say that."

Monty laughed.

"I don't mean Podmoon or whatever he's called – I'm talking about our client. There's always been a dark side to Archie Light.

He's got the most beautiful wife. Titled, she's treated him badly and he can't really handle it."

"Any family?"

Kaliska's voice was neutral.

"A daughter – Cosima. An exotic creature, stunning and spoilt, I believe she's also known to be contemptuous of her father. Such is the human condition. Clever, possibly brilliant but demons torture that man or my name isn't Montgomery Limmerson."

Walking away in the opposite direction, Archie experienced conflicting emotions. Angry at the treatment he'd received at Secorni and irritated at his solicitor's attitude, he was attracted to Monty's new head of business development.

Striding into his club, Archie went straight to the bar, where Alannah and Barbara found him an hour later.

"Ah, the Witches of Eastwick."

Leaning heavily against the counter, all thoughts of sensitivity had left Light.

"Potions and brews a-bubbling..."

Brodie studied her boss with a cold eye.

"What are you looking at me like that for?"

"You've obviously had a good day."

Alannah was hard.

"Where did this piece of inaccurate perception come from?"

"Doctor, presuming things haven't gone well, drowning your sorrows won't help."

Barbara's voice was polite.

"Oh, thank you for the homespun advice. What pray, gives you the right to comment on my behaviour?"

"Every, if you're to do business with my son."

"Oh yes? Is that so? Well, I have news for you. I've decided not to go ahead with his little game, so he can go and stuff it!"

"Very well Doctor Light, that is your decision."

Bright-faced, Barbara looked at Alannah.

"I guess I'd better make other plans for getting home."

"What do you mean?" Light cut in.

"Well, you're in no fit state to get behind the wheel."

"Really? I'll decide that."

"I don't think so."

"What are you going to do, report me?"

"I could drive you back if you like?"

"You've got to be kidding."

"Well it's either that or Barbara and I take a train."

Alannah was firm.

"I don't let anyone drive my FVs. Anyway, I bet you couldn't."

"You're on. What are the stakes?"

Archie laughed.

"Dr. Light, you might be surprised what some of us women can do these days. Having helped my husband with his pilot's exams, I can recite the exact rate of climb for a Typhoon T3 variant aircraft as per the RAF manual chapter and verse. Like to hear it? 'With full throttle and ailerons at inverted position...'"

"Oh God, you'll be telling me about the double wishbone suspension on my cars next."

Archie quaffed the last of his whisky. Barbara shrugged.

"Well, engine wise it's a good job that Chrysler V8 replaced the troublesome DeSoto."

She picked up a club mint from the counter and popped it in her mouth.

"I'm an advanced motorist Doctor Light, and driving an Excellence or Faciella doesn't pose any particular challenge." Forty minutes later seeing her swing the Facel Vega through London's streets and out into the country, Archie had to confess even if only to himself, that it clearly didn't.

Chapter 9

Alternative Reality

Arriving back at The Lighthouse that evening, Archie had sobered up sufficiently during the drive home and was able to acknowledge what an excellent driver Barbara Moon was. Having enjoyed herself behind the wheel, Barbara was in high spirits as she guided the car through the gates, bringing the Facel Vega to a stop outside the house.

"That was fantastic Barbara – you're a born Michael Schumacher."

"I hope not Brodie."

Archie was subdued.

"Ha. A light on in the Tower."

"Didn't you say Podric could use it?"

"He hasn't been."

"Well, maybe he is now."

They got out of the car.

"You'll want to be getting the key back from him if you're not running with the game."

Taking the garden path to his citadel, Archie didn't reply. The housekeeper and Podric's mother eyed each other briefly. Alannah unlocked the front door of the house and switched off the alarm. Dog leaped up to greet them.

Finding the Tower door locked, Archie was puzzled. There were no signs of a break in; he speed dialled Podric's number and half a minute later, the boy appeared.

"So, you decided to avail yourself of my facilities."

"You mean use your lab? You offered."

Walking to the lift, they climbed in. Neither spoke. Approaching the top, Archie said.

"You didn't ask how my meeting went."

The games creator and champion looked at each other. The lift came to a stop.

"Well, how did it go?"

Not replying, Archie pushed open the glass door and entered his den. Heading for the drinks cabinet, he poured himself a large scotch.

"Bastards."

"Ah. Want me to call Pasaro?"

"No, I do not want you to call Pasaro."

"Who then?"

"I don't want to pursue the game."

Podric appeared to accept Archie's decision with sangfroid.

"You won't mind if I continue with it?"

"Do what you like."

As Podric returned to the lab to collect his things, the lift began to descend. A few seconds later it came back up carrying Barbara Moon. Stepping into the den, she found Archie slouched in a reclining chair.

"Podric not here?"

Flicking through a magazine, Archie grunted and nodded towards the stair door. Seeing the glass of whisky beside him, Barbara's expression was surprisingly sympathetic.

"Doctor Light, I want to thank you again for organising my consultation today. It was very considerate though whether it was quite so beneficial as driving your fabulous car, is perhaps open to debate."

His mood dark, Archie grimaced.

"I'm also sorry you had issues with your games company. I'm sure the project you and Podric are developing will clean up. As I've said, he's been contacted by several other organisations and one of them is certain to take it."

"You obviously didn't hear me earlier Mrs. Moon. I'm not interested in this game and I'm not pursuing it."

"Oh, but you are doctor, and you will be."

Hearing his mother talking to Archie, Podric appeared. His back pack was on his shoulder.

"It's alright mum – really."

Ignoring her son, Barbara continued.

"You know you don't mean what you've just said and besides, you need the success."

"Oh really? You certainly have some creative theories."

Archie leaped up, angry.

"For your information, I do not need to write any new game. I do not *need* to do anything, so you and your oh so clever son can get out of my house now! Is that clear enough for you?!"

"We'll be making a move in a moment."

Barbara eyed the doctor coolly.

"Complicated man that you are, your saving grace is you're highly intelligent and when you calm down, you'll realise how stupidly you're behaving."

At this point, Archie looked apoplectic.

"My son is gifted but he needs you to help him. He needs your brilliance and he needs you as a man – more than ever now. Together, I think there are few boundaries you can't overcome so on Saturday, Podric will come back here and you can get on with the work and develop what needs to be done."

She turned to her son then turned back to Light.

"I believe he's told you he's been recommended a lawyer who will be needed to draw up any contracts."

Barbara took Podric's hand.

"Thank you again for your kindness and please don't let me down – or yourself."

With that, the Moons left. Doctor Light appeared to struggle with the reality of what he'd just heard.

The remarkable thing was that Podric Moon did return to Archie Light's laboratory the following Saturday afternoon, creator and champion working side by side as if nothing had happened. Both were sitting in front of large computer screens when Podric hit the return button and got up from his stool to stretch.

"Problems?"

Not taking his eyes off his screen, Archie was absorbed.

"I'm happy about the story structure, but the overall gameplay needs improving. Gamers like to be challenged – make it winnable, but difficult."

"These graphics packages are amazing. When I think back…"

"Still a lot to do; apart from being fun to play, a section needs to be pretty much done, so Fred gets the feel of how the whole thing's going to look."

"When are you seeing your best friend?"

"Wednesday evening."

"After school? Are they sending a car?"

Podric nodded. Archie sat back. He'd had a lot to deal with internally since nearly blowing their deal apart and even now experienced some difficulty accepting Podric's intimacy with the head of the largest computer games company in the world.

After his disastrous time in London and subsequent problematic behaviour, Archie finally made up his mind that if he was to proceed and get his barely started new business venture back on track, the first person he should visit was Podric's mother. Still at home on sick leave, he'd called her and she had agreed to meet him.

Arriving at Briony Close, the two had a full and frank discussion. Given Secorni's rejection of anything to do with him, the one stipulation Light made was that he and Podric should be represented by the same legal firm and he suggested Monty Limmerson. Archie also explained that given Podric's age and the controversy surrounding himself, it would make sense if Barbara and Alannah were the directors of Agrolution. In addition, a holding company involving Archie and Barbara could be set up, being a private arrangement far removed from prying eyes. Barbara accepted this.

During the intervening few days, Archie was busy sorting out paperwork and working on the business end of the arrangement. His mind more balanced now, the inherent respect he had for Podric had begun to return.

"They were going to come and see me, but I'd prefer it was there. They'll want to run checks."

"Obviously they hold you in high esteem."

"Huh. Just so long as they take the game."

Podric sat down in one of the leather reclining chairs.

"I've been doing some more work on alternative reality."

"Uhuh. Interesting what you were saying about realigning the imaginary process."

Saving his work, Archie got up and headed for the fridge.

"Still planning on developing it from your O-in R mechanism?"

"As you said, it was partly there but looking at the programmed microchip - I don't think it should be taken, but inserted - a tag in the wrist synced to the game via the eyes."

"Woah - that's getting surgical."

The games creator took out a couple of beers and handed one to Podric.

"The wrist's not a problem. A chip can be positioned under the skin quite easily."

Archie had a swig of beer.

"What about the eye?"

"Longer term a retinal implant, but for the moment it would have to be external. I'm thinking of something that fits in the ear, but can also be activated optically."

"An aural and visual experience."

Having a sip of ale, Podric looked at Archie.

"Yeah - existing within the adventure."

"You really think it's possible?"

"You got off on Outside-in. Full immersions got to be the next stage."

"Why the wrist then? Couldn't it be control activated with a touch to the head?"

"Potentially. One step at a time."

Putting down his beer, Podric stood up and acted out his concept.

"I'm thinking the right index finger positioned over the chipped left wrist to activate. A person's print being unique, it would be a perfect sync-up."

"And getting out?"

"Got to get in first, but working on an exit strategy, that would be another code."

"Crudely then, one in, two out!"

Podric laughed.

"Something like that."

Finishing his can, Archie reached over to the counter and took another.

"All this is making me thirsty." Ripping the tag, Archie had a long pull.

"I'm beginning to see why you want this. The way I feel sometimes, an alternate life definitely has appeal..."

*   *   *

Whilst Podric was preoccupied working on *Agrolution* and his alternative reality concept, he had been unaware of other difficulties Archie was experiencing. Worried about Cosima, the day Podric was being collected for his evening meeting with Pasaro, Archie received an early morning call from Davina Petrovna, the wealthy mother of one of his daughter's school friends. Demanding he come and collect his wayward offspring, the Russian's house was in Holland Park, only a mile or two away from Pasaro's West London offices.

"I tried to get hold of her mother, but Lady Charlotte's out of the country. That girl of yours is quite beyond control. After you've collected Cosima, I'm forbidding Arachine from seeing her again." The call perfunctorily terminated, Archie had little choice but to head up the road to London and fetch his daughter.

Wednesday at school was a bit of a let-down. Podric and Amy leaving the house as their mother was getting ready for work (she'd just returned to Tweeneys), Barbara wished him well but didn't make a big thing of it. Amy was more wackily upbeat having made her brother a card 'Revolution, Convolution, Resolution, Evolution AGROLUTION!' Touched, and knowing her preoccupation for making up words, Podric asked if she knew what any of them meant.

"Just the last one Pod and that's going to be a winner!"

Although he'd only mentioned in passing to Billy that 'some game stuff was coming up,' news somehow got around that Podric had a big meeting in London that evening. Before long, the school was abuzz with the usual mates ribbing – their games champion being 'multimillion Moon' and 'Moon the moneybags'. Passing Catherine Halliday in the corridor, she wished Podric well and asked about his mother.

"Her paintings look interesting on her website. Do you paint as well?"

"Not like she does."

Catherine smiled.

"Guess your images are more computer generated – 3D high res."

For a second Podric looked far away.

"More than that. Mine are real – or will be." Finding him increasingly attractive, Podric's enigmatic character only added to his allure for Catherine.

As it turned out, in the eyes of his friends, leaving school for his meeting was something of an anticlimax. The car sent by Pasaro wasn't as exotic as Archie's Facel Vega, even though it was a Mercedes limousine!

Earlier in the day, driving his Faciella, the games creator had arrived at the Petrovna house in Holland Park. Electric gates swung open and he parked in the driveway. A male secretary appeared at the front door followed by Cosima pulling an overhead carry-on case. Seconds later, the door was closed. Father and daughter returned to his car, Archie furious at the insult.

"What did you do – blow the safe?"

Sullen, Cosima didn't reply. Archie started the Faciella and they moved out of the driveway, 'Exit' gates opening automatically. Motoring along in silence, it was several minutes before Archie spoke.

"Good of you to tell me where you were."

Looking stoned, Cosima stared out of the car window.

"Back for long or will I be driving to Zermatt next time?"

"Shut up."

No one else on the planet could speak to Archie in such a way; his face was livid. Passing Pasaro's office block driving out of London, the computer man's mind switched to the gravity of the meeting Podric would be having there later that evening.

"Give me strength."

*   *   *

Considering he was the divisional head of a multi-national con-
glomerate, the office Fred Schepesi used when in the UK was not
overly ostentatious. A chrome and glass affair, it was uncluttered
and bordered on sparse. Two large sofas were separated by a low
coffee table, and the only personal items in the room were several
photographs positioned on a cabinet behind Schepesi's desk. Of
these, one featured the CEO with Podric Moon proudly holding
his award.

"Here he is, man of the moment."

Shown into Fred's office, Podric was still wearing his school
sweatshirt. Physically small, Fred Schepesi more than made up for
his lack of stature with a big personality. Taking Podric's hand, he
shook it firmly.

"How yer doin' Podric?"

Podric smiled. There was something about Mr. Schepesi he
couldn't help but like.

"Look, I er...don't want to say too much, but I heard about your
dad – tragic."

Schepesi appeared genuinely saddened.

"I can only add if there's anything, anything we can do at all –
help in any way – you've only to ask."

Podric refrained from saying 'take the game,' but thanking
Schepesi, smiled.

"So whattaya got fella?"

Unslinging his backpack, Podric sat down.

"It's called *Agrolution*. It...er, it's about street gang violence, but
when you win you get out of it and go to a magical place that lets you
travel through time and space anywhere you want to be. That's the
reward."

"So yer get out of hell and go to heaven, huh?"

"And it's difficult."

Schepesi chuckled.

"'Say that again!"

Schepesi looked at Podric.

"The NDA from..."

Schepesi adjusted a couple of papers on his desk.

"Some outfit – Limmerson somebody. Never heard of them, but it's signed and gone back."

Podric knew this, his mother having received such advice from Kaliska Monroe of Limmerson Bart & Co.

"I gather your company's called MoonLight; good name. Wish I could persuade you to come and work for us, Podric."

"Maybe I will – one day."

Schepesi clicked his fingers.

"You know what a lousy player I am. There's a young guy I'm in town with. One of our chief developers on the coast. Mind if I bring him in?"

Podric shook his head and opening his bag, took out the travel Xbox Pasaro had made him, along with its handset. Schepesi flicked a phone switch on the table.

"Kelly, have Michael come in, would you?"

Michael Allardyce was the classic Californian cyberpunk. Crew necked sweater, jeans and round 'Lennon' shaped glasses; his manner towards Schepesi was confident, but not arrogant. After introducing Podric, Pasaro's Chief Executive excused himself and left them to it. Michael and Podric began talking computer speak. During the course of their dialogue, the American wifi'd the game to a large monitor.

The action began. Playing *Agrolution*, Michael Allardyce quickly pushed its challenges to tougher levels, his facial muscles hardly moving as his fingers operated the controls. Occasionally, Michael fired a question at Podric who would look up from a Pasaro games magazine and reply with equal taciturnity. Michael finally put down the handset.

"I really like the 'leap' move. Cool. You know it was my game you broke?"

"Um. No."

"That's why Fred wanted me to try this."

He got up and left Podric reading his magazine. A short while later Schepesi reappeared.

"Let's go get something to eat before we run you back."

Outside by the lift, the two stood waiting.

"Guess I'll have my people talk to your people."

Fred Schepesi smiled.

"I was thinking – the Light in your company name. I knew a guy called Archie Light once – not well, he was an arrogant SOB. Pretty successful in the business though, wrote some good stuff, but we never worked with him. A Secorni man through and through. Gather he recently fell out with them."

The lift arrived.

"MoonLight and *Agrolution*. Maybe you might just start one."

Chapter 10

The Culprit

On a wet, miserable evening several nights later, Podric and Archie were sitting in Archie's laboratory. The doctor was preparing a G-Byte gun to implant microchips into their wrists. The chips were about half the size of a grain of rice and would be barely visible when inserted below the skin.

"Alright?"

Relaxed, Podric nodded. Archie fired the pellet into the boy's left wrist. Taking another chip and reloading the gun, the games creator began to prep himself, sterilising the area of epidermis he would shoot into.

"Want a hand?"

"Ha! Very funny. No thanks. Don't want you waving any sharp pointy objects at me!"

"This earpiece eye connection is interesting."

Podric looked at the minute hearing aid-like device Archie had been working on.

"You won't see it. It'll sit right in the ear."

Archie fired the gun into his wrist, then placed a piece of cotton wool over the tiny mark the insertion had left, holding it there for several seconds.

"The connecting pulse would sync to the optic nerve so we'll somehow 'see' the game inside ourselves."

Archie inspected his handiwork. Now micro-chipped, the tiny object was barely visible.

"You ever thought about moving matter?"

"Yeah. I talked to my dad about it just before he was killed. Some Einstein-Rosencrantz."

"Bridge. Einstein-Rosen Bridge theory."

"That'll be it. But that was never what this is about."

"No, you only need to *feel* transported."

"And be a part of it, interact. It'll create the sensation of an alternative reality – an ultimate alternative reality."

"That's good. Ultimate Alternative Reality – UAR; I like it."

The internal house phone rang. Archie picked up the receiver. Listening for several seconds, he turned to Podric.

"Your mother's here with the police. Apparently, they have some information about your accident."

Minutes later, Podric sat with his mother, Sergeant Paxman and PC Leslie Jenner in Alannah's little study.

"The analysis we've run from the paint sample on your bike plus the available CCTV footage shows a Jaguar of that same colour at the Wendbury Drinkwell intersection just five minutes after the incident."

Sergeant Paxman sipped the coffee Alannah had given him.

"We've located the vehicle. It's recently had some respray work done. The owner's a Mr. Raymond Sturridge. Mr Sturridge is currently being interviewed at our regional headquarters."

"Is the proof categorical?"

Barbara sat forward, tense.

"We believe it's the car involved."

"That's not what I asked."

The two police officers looked at each other briefly.

"It's the vehicle alright Mrs. Moon, but there's something else."

"Go on."

Sergeant Paxman cleared his throat.

"The CCTV footage suggests there was only one person present in the car and that the owner may not have been driving."

Neither Barbara nor Podric responded.

"Right now, we're getting the image further enhanced, but at current level of examination, the person behind the wheel looks younger, possibly a youth."

*   *   *

On his way to school next day, Podric had difficulty getting his head around the fact that Barney Sturridge might have deliberately 'borrowed' his father's car and driven into him – either to scare him or even worse. The car having been into a paint shop supported the police's belief that the owner was keen to have any scratches removed from enquiring eyes. Whether Mr. Sturridge had challenged his son privately or had deliberately covered up for him, was hard to contemplate.

"Podric."

Preoccupied with his thoughts, Podric turned to see Catherine Halliday.

"I...heard you got a game deal. That's amazing."

Podric muttered something about it still being in development. Catherine smiled.

"Wondered if we could meet up sometime? I mean away from school..."

"Er, yeah."

"You don't play computer games *all* the time, do you?"

"Ha! No. I'm doing other stuff right now."

"Uhuh?"

Podric didn't reply. Catherine had an amused glint in her eye.

"What – or do you mind me asking?"

It was Podric's turn to laugh.

"Well it is with computers, but it's a bit different."

"Okay. Will you take time out and meet me on Saturday?"

Podric nodded.

"Sure. Great."

Miles Willoughby appeared.

"Podric, you're wanted in Mr. Dromgoole's office. The Old Bill are back."

Moving away, Podric's expression didn't alter. Catherine glanced at Miles.

"Computer work not getting him into trouble?"

"It's Barney the bully. Reckon they're going to bang him up for what he did to Pod."

Catherine looked at Miles quizzically.

"You know, Podric's bike accident. It was Barney who hit him. Nicked his dad's Jag they reckon."

Summoned to the head teacher's office, rumours were already abounding of how Barney had tried to kill Podric using his father's Jaguar. With the arrival of a police car delivering Sergeant Paxman and a CID officer, excitement around the school was palpable. Shown into a meeting room, Podric sat down opposite the two cops.

"Hi, Podric."

Podric greeted Sergeant Paxman.

"This is Detective Inspector Richards."

"Podric. Great name by the way."

DI Richards was in his mid-thirties, clean cut and bright. Although he was the senior officer, he allowed the sergeant to lead.

"Sorry to take you away from your studies, but there have been some developments. Mr. Sturridge has admitted his car was missing and we've established Sturridge junior was driving the vehicle at the time of your accident. Although of legal age, he hasn't attempted a driving test and had taken the vehicle without permission."

Richards took over.

"I know Sergeant Paxman has interviewed you previously, but Mr. Sturridge's admission casts a different light on things. At the very least, he'll be implicated in a cover-up and his son charged with dangerous driving. We're here to find out if you wish to press charges?"

"What would be the point of that?"

The CID officer gave a slight shrug.

"If found guilty, Sturridge junior could face a custodial sentence."

"You mean go to prison?"

"If convicted. Right now, he'll likely be held in remand, and sent to a Young Offenders Institution to serve out whatever's awarded."

"If I decide not to press charges?"

"The police will continue their inquiries. In the light of the evidence, an appropriate decision will be made as to how to proceed."

"So it doesn't make much difference if I do or I don't."

"That's not quite the case."

Richards sat forward.

"Look Podric, what concerns us are the circumstances surrounding this incident. We know how you were cycling. You weren't in the middle of the road, which was otherwise clear. A vehicle travelling too fast is one thing, but though unlikely, we're not discounting the possible deliberation of the driver's actions."

This thought had been going through Podric's mind since his last meeting with the sergeant.

"You mean Barney intended to hit me?"

Richards nodded.

"As bizarre as it sounds."

The CID officer's mobile vibrated on the desk. Glancing at it, Richards picked it up.

"I better take this. Excuse me."

Standing, he left the room. Podric and Sergeant Paxman looked at each other.

"His father's full of bluster, but Sturridge seniors acknowledged his son is something of a lout. It's like the boy had a vendetta against you. What do you think?"

"He's a bully and my dad always told me bullies are really cowards."

"That maybe so but if this was deliberate, he's a dangerous one."

DI Richards re-entered the room.

"That's rum. . .Sturridge senior has just reported the disappearance of his son. Looks like the lad's done a runner."

This disturbing news had a strange effect on Podric. Whilst not exactly scared, it somehow spurred his motivation, propelling his determination to create what both he and Archie now referred to as UAR: Ultimate Alternative Reality.

Podric spent his every spare waking hour in the Lighthouse computer lab. One afternoon working at the bench after school, Cosima Light appeared with Dog.

"So, you and daddy big buddies now – reinventing those little kiddy computer games he so loves to play with..."

Cosima picked up one of her father's old virtual reality visors and put it on.

"Ooh...the world according to escapism. Can I come in?"

Dog nuzzling into his crotch, Podric tried to push the enormous animal away.

"He doesn't."

Taking off the visor, Cosima looked at him.

"What?"

"Like to play them."

"No..?"

She put the visor down on the bench.

"You do though, don't you? Surely, it's time you started playing other things..."

Provocative, Cosima's lovely face was very close to Podric's.

"Don't you want to play with me or are you still only really a kid?"

The look on Podric's face was intense. Time seemed to stand still. Somewhere in the depths of the Lighthouse, a door opened and the lift activated. Although his senses were heightened, when thinking back on the scene, Podric couldn't quite work out how Cosima had left without Alannah ever realising she'd been there. He could hardly believe she had; only Dog's continued presence served as a reminder.

"There you are, you great thing. Wondered where you'd gone?"

Alannah straightened one of the Facel Vega pictures.

"Too bound up in what you're doing to hear the phone?"

Glancing at Podric, the housekeeper mistook his look for a pre-occupation with work.

"Ah, the computers. When they get you, it seems like a drug. Come on animal."

Alannah and Dog exited the lab, and it was several seconds before Podric regained his normal equilibrium. Even when his composure did return, his concentration was fractured and a short while later, he packed up his things and went home.

Walking back to Briony Close through Drinkwell that evening, Podric initially thought no one was in the house, number 5 being in darkness. Then, searching for his key, he remembered his mother had said that she would be late that night attending an evening meeting at Tweeney's. They had adopted her 'waste disposal sucks' publicity campaign and were working up a media launch. Podric wasn't sure where his sister was but assumed she would be out with one of her friends. It was a surprise therefore, when coming into the hall, he heard Amy's voice.

"Don't turn the light on Pod."

Podric looked up. Catching a glimpse of Amy on the landing, she briefly flashed a torch.

"Come up."

Doing as he was bid, Podric climbed the stairs.

"I'm in mum's room."

Podric went into his mother's bedroom to find his sister standing on a stool peering out at their little garden.

"Someone's in your shed."

"Saw them, did you?"

"Yeah."

"What do they look like?"

"Didn't get a clear view but. There – see that?!"

Keeping her voice low, Amy was excited. Podric saw a brief flash of light.

"Who do you reckon it is? Someone on the run – a serial killer?"

His sister's particular imagination was operating in its ever-original vein.

"Better call the police."

"Can't you do something like you did to the bully the other day?"

Ideas flashed through Podric's mind. What he'd done on the sports field had been programmed but there was no time for that now. Hearing things being smashed in the shed, he quickly came to a decision.

"Dial emergency!"

Running from the room, Podric jumped downstairs and ran through into the conservatory. Charging across the garden and yanking open the shed door, he discovered Barney Sturridge busily destroying his computer equipment. Momentarily surprised at being disturbed, Barney looked round. Podric took the chance to grab a garden hoe and thwack his nemesis. The bully being much stronger than Podric wasn't disadvantaged for long, and crouched to charge.

Diving back out into the garden, Podric slammed the shed door behind him. A second later, a pair of sheers smashed through the timber. Barney began wrenching the door from its hinges. Podric spied his old football lying in the grass.

The shed door came flying off. The villain stood in its opening.

"Ha! Thought my destruction of your nerdy junk might rouse you; no techno crap to save you now Moonface."

"Oh, I don't know? Your ball skills were well off the other day. Maybe you're better at goalkeeping? Catch!"

Throwing the football at the bully, Barney instinctively ducked. Podric's view was suddenly blocked by a macaw's large wing. Eamon was on the loose again!

The beautiful bird dived and squawked, completely freaking Barney out. A car's headlights materialised in the drive, followed by another sporting a revolving blue beam. The surreal trilogy of his mother, the police, and Mrs. Bickerstaff appeared. That said, Podric was never happier at being reintroduced to the recalcitrant bird!

Led away by a policeman, Barney seemed almost relieved to be free of Eamon, who swooped and squawked around the garden, showing off.

"Came in handy, didn't he my boy?"

Officer Ravelious was less impressed.

"You got a license for that buzzard?"

Insulted, Ivy Bickerstaff's lonely lower molar wiggled excitedly in her otherwise tooth free gums.

"He isn't no buzzard you ignoramus. Don't you call my scarlet beauty that!"

Banking around and coming to rest on top of the shed, the macaw's fabulous coloured plumage feathered out. Podric managed to get hold of Eamon's cord and handed it to Ivy.

"Saved you this time, huh?"

The stout Mrs. B was proud.

"A lucky second escape. Hope neither of us needs a third."

Minutes later things were quieter. Their mother made tea, as brother and sister began clearing up the wreckage Barney had caused.

"The football trick was good."

"Bird that did it for him, though."

"Combo then."

They put the broken door against the side of the shed.

"Pity he wasn't still wearing his footy boots. You could have given him a real dance - even more fun than the bird of parallel."

In the darkness, Podric smiled at his sister's misuse of words. It had been an eventful evening.

Chapter 11

The World of UAR

It was the last Saturday before the end of the term and Podric had completely forgotten he was due to meet Catherine. A text from her reminding him of the fact, Podric had promised Archie he'd finish off some details on *Agrolution*. Explaining this to Catherine prompted the response that she'd 'like to see where you work'.

Standing in the Moon's garden, a mug of coffee in his hand, the shed was still as he and Amy had left it. Straightening out a few pieces of timber, Podric heard a scooter approach the house. Walking round to their short drive, he discovered Catherine parking a metallic green Vespa.

"Want a coffee?

"Thought you were going to work? I can give you a lift!"

Tapping a spare helmet attached to the rear seat, she took Podric's mug.

Entering his house, Podric reappeared in less than a minute with his backpack to find Catherine standing beside what was left of the shed.

"I can see why you moved to Mr. Smoothie games partner's quarters. Cyberspace get you?"

"Something like that."

Going into the shed, Catherine righted a smashed computer unit.

"This was your workshop."

Podric didn't reply. Catherine studied one of his old virtual reality headsets.

"Some attack. I hope whoever did this was caught."

Not normally keen on imparting anything private, Podric felt an intimacy between them.

"You know who."

Catherine looked at him, her expression transforming into one of incredulity. Close now, their intensity was strong, but it wasn't weird like it had been with Cosima. They kissed.

"He didn't hurt you?"

"Saved by a bird."

"Ha-ha. Were the police involved?"

Podric nodded.

"Always bad that one, but he's been worse since you arrived. You've got to him in some way."

Tempted to ask if he, Podric got to her, they kissed again.

Heading out of Briony Close, Catherine and Podric had only just turned onto the main road when a Facel Vega appeared travelling too fast. Taking immediate action, Catherine guided her scooter onto the pavement as the beautiful car swept by completely out of control. Seconds later, it collided with the village sign. Seeing steam pouring from the broken radiator, Podric clambered off the scooter and ran over to the car. Managing to get the driver's door open, he discovered Cosima behind the wheel. She appeared to have suffered no physical damage (the FV had no airbags) and got out. Standing precariously, Cosima grabbed Podric then saw he was with Catherine.

"A little girlfriend for a little boy?"

Cosima's grip on Podric weakened as she slid down his legs. Podric realised she was drunk.

Driving back from the supermarket, Alannah pulled over. Shocked at what she saw, the housekeeper was quickly centrestage.

"Is she hurt?"

Podric leaned closer to Alannah.

"Smell her breath."

Alannah did so.

"Drunk. 'Picked her moment. The doctor will kill her."

"Where is he?"

"On his way back from town. He stayed the night at his club."

"You'd better call him. I'll stay with the car if you can get her home."

Whilst leaving the scene of an accident wasn't strictly correct procedure, no one else being involved they decided to get Cosima back to the Lighthouse. Helping her into Alannah's car, she was a sorry sight.

"Made a nice mess of the sign."

Catherine was philosophical.

"And the car."

Looking at the beautiful Faciella, Podric was rueful. Out of all of Archie's Facel Vegas, the Faciella was the prettiest.

*   *   *

Several hours later, working in Light's lab, Podric completed the necessary work on *Agrolution*. He and Catherine were about to leave when Archie returned from the railway station where he'd put a sobered up Cosima on the train to her mother's. The honourable Charlotte currently living with her boyfriend, a wealthy Columbian diplomat at his house in St John's Wood, Archie had called his estranged wife informing her that their daughter totalling his car was the last straw; she would have to leave.

'You're always so dramatic!' Charlotte's retort betrayed her irritation, but Archie managed to get a commitment from her that she would meet Cosima at Paddington.

Sitting in the laboratory, the eventful day behind them (or so they thought), Catherine relaxed in one of the high-tech leather chairs, a glass of sparkling water in her hand. Sitting in the other, Archie nursed a large whisky and Podric, perched on a bench stool had a can of beer.

"It'll do well...your game, I'm sure."

Catherine sipped her drink.

"Mostly down to the skills of your hero."

Archie had a slug of his. Maybe it was because he felt he'd lost his daughter or because he'd already had a couple of glasses of scotch or because Catherine was attractive, but Archie seemed to like having her around. Podric kept it light.

"The ultra-override engine's yours."

"Ha! Glad I made some contribution."

Archie drank some more whisky.

"Has he told you about the mad crazy idea that really drives him?"

Podric didn't look pleased. Catherine's eyes narrowed catching his shift in mood.

"What's not my business, isn't my business."

Archie laughed.

"Attractive and a philosopher – impressive in one so young."

He stood up.

"I need to make some calls. You should confide in your girlfriend Podric. Maybe she's got an angle on it?"

He went out. The only luminescence coming from the beam of a microscope, the room was in shadow.

"I must go."

"Yup, I'm done."

Podric finished scrutinising a couple of components.

"I think you should stay."

She put a hand on Podric's arm.

"I need to get back. It's actually my first time out on the wheels…"

"What about later?"

"Not tonight, I'm afraid. Some domestic stuff at home. Boring but…"

Podric looked at Catherine.

"What he said…"

"You don't have to say anything Podric."

They kissed.

"Well… Maybe he's right in a way."

Picking up two minuscule electronic parts of a tiny hearing aid, Podric stood up and crossing the lab, placed them in a tray.

"You know enough about me being a computer games ninja. Maybe you know a bit about how tired I am of them…"

Podric turned back to her.

"Have you ever wanted to escape reality – and go somewhere different?"

"Often."

For some reason this surprised Podric, but he continued.

"I've been bored with games for a long time. Recently I've been working – trying to make something different – so amazing it'll change my life."

For a second or two he seemed lost in thought.

"What I want to create is an alternative reality *inside* a game where a player exists *within* the adventure. You'll think it's crazy, but I've partly proved it. I came up with this Outside-in Reality – seeing real life and a game at the same time but it's crude. I know I can get what I want though. I can feel it!"

"Mind games then."

Podric laughed.

"You could say that – but not exactly."

He had a swig of his beer.

"Since then, I've been working on trying to manipulate the creative process, create a kind of techno pathway to an alternative reality one, but it's difficult."

"I would think it is."

He looked keenly at Catherine for any sign of mockery, but her face was completely serious.

"So, you're within a game's world – like you're living in it."

"Uhuh. I'm also profiling other people in – people from school, friends and family – who can appear as characters in whatever game I'm inside."

"Would they know where they were?"

"I don't know. I haven't got in yet."

Catherine stood up.

"Well, it does sound pretty far-fetched."

"That's fair. It would be. But think of the adventures..."

"More than real life's?"

"What do you think?"

"I think I'd better make a move."

She picked up a small bag she had with her.

"It's been an interesting day. You more than lived up to expectations Podric Moon."

She kissed him lightly on the cheek and headed for the door.

"By the way, his daughter Podric – she's beautiful."

"She's also crazy."

Catherine smiled.

"Travel safe in your alternative reality. Who knows, maybe I'll see you there sometime and if you do include me, make sure it's an interesting game." With that, she was gone.

From his den window, Archie gazed out at Catherine departing down the drive on her little Vespa.

"Why can't I have a daughter like that?"

"Because you spoiled her, that's why."

Putting on several practicals, Alannah wasn't having any of her boss's indulgent self-pity. Emerging from the lab, Podric helped himself to another beer. Archie looked around. Dog leaped about beside him.

"Nice girl. You'll be alright there."

Though Catherine was the best-looking girl at Wendbury High, Podric felt it was far too early to think of a future. The way Archie was speaking about her, it was as if he already envisaged a pipe and slippers!

"There's no doubt this has been the worst day of my life."

Alannah looked at Podric and rolled her eyes.

"What are you most upset about, turfing your daughter out or the fact she pranged your car?"

Staggered at Podric's utterance, Alannah burst out laughing! Archie didn't.

"You little shit. I've a good mind to turf you out."

"Well, the contracts are signed and you've got your game. Guess we could part company."

"Thought you wanted to get your ultimatum reality rubbish sorted?"

"I do. Can I go and get on with it before you tip me over the parapet?"

"Piss off."

Podric went out.

"Little shit. 'Am I more upset my darling girl's gone or that she bust up my Faciella?'"

"He's got a point."

"Not you as well."

Archie poured himself another drink.

"Podric's been the best thing to come into your life in years. You've been more motivated since he appeared than you have since I've worked for you."

Alannah finished tidying the room and prepared to leave.

"You said what your daughter got was long overdue and damaging one of your precious cars only highlights that. Now stop feeling sorry for yourself and go and help Podric."

"He doesn't want my help."

"Rubbish. You being with him when you're sober is much more important than working on computers. In spite of how he is sometimes, the boy needs a father figure."

"Think I can make a better job of it than with my own flesh and blood?"

"I'm not even going to bother to answer that. Good night doctor. Your milk and brandy are in their usual place."

Alannah departed. Passing the lab door, she looked in on Podric who was busy working.

"Little harsh Podric."

Podric looked up.

"So, what do you think made him madder?"

Alannah smiled.

"Okay. He'll have her back in due course. If you stay over, there's a bed made up. Good night."

An hour went by, but to Podric it could have been a minute. Working intensely, two completed sets of ear components lay on the bench along with a PlayStation.

"You staying the night?"

Archie stood in the doorway. Drink in hand, he dropped into a leather chair. Dog bustled in and sniffed around Podric's legs.

"Good details they have in some of these historic games."

Looking at a monitor, Archie saw that Podric was viewing *Napoleonic Wars*. Its details were impressive – campaigns, battle plans, even options for alliances, along with weather, ordnance and supply elements.

"Took me months to write. Why's it up?"

"No particular reason. Thought it might be fun to profile people I know into something out of a different time, that's all."

Archie snorted.

"How about Brodie and Dog then? He'd be good to have along at Austerlitz, wouldn't you old pal?"

Archie ruffled the giant wolfhound's head. Working on another screen filled with data, Podric tapped in some details.

"How far are you away from making it work?"

"Done a lot..."

"Not what I asked."

Archie looked smugly sarcastic.

"Why don't we give it a try? Never know, might make for a bright end to my God awful twenty-four hours. Anyway, I could do with a laugh."

Catching the mocking tone in Archie's voice, Podric picked up one of the little earpieces. Gently guiding it into his auditory canal, it fitted deep inside rendering the tiny unit invisible. Podric handed the other ear piece to the games creator.

"Well, if you want to try going in..."

Deprecatingly, Archie began fitting the earpiece, clumsily fiddling with the delicate device. Podric was sharp.

"If you don't insert it properly, it won't work."

Archie stuffing the earpiece into his ear, Podric walked over to a cabinet.

"Want to be with us, come along for the ride?"

Dog's big face looked at Podric then adoringly at his master.

Taking a microchip from a drawer, Podric placed it under the microscope then adjusted further data. Similar to the ones they'd inserted in their wrists, Podric undid a little identity screw tag suspended from Dog's collar and placed the microchip inside.

"How's he going to sync with that? Got it programmed for hounds?"

"I've adjusted some spare chips but animals have a separate folder."

Not quite sure how serious Podric might be, Archie had another gulp of scotch.

"You might as well put the village idiot woman's macaw in while you're about it."

"They can be profiled in the next batch. I've done enough for now."

Archie burst out laughing. Podric tapped keys and adjusted calculus.

"You don't really understand the first thing about this, do you?"

"Damned right I don't. I've failed myself ever letting you even talk to me about such a cockamamie idea."

"The only reason I've chipped Dog is that we're actually trying to go into UAR with him. People – selected friends, relatives – birds and dogs for that matter I know I've profiled – if it works, they would *appear* to us in the game and *seem* to be part of the action, but not actually be in it like we are."

"Who's to say Dog won't end up at Alma and us in Borodino?"

"Unlikely if we all go in together. Anyway, we might be at sea. As you know, Maritime's part of *Napoleonic Wars*."

"Hmm... The Nile, Trafalgar –'bout the only victories we had for a while. What campaign are you challenging?"

"You started the game in 1793."

"Obviously. That's when Napoleon first came to prominence bigtime."

"Yeah?"

"Given we're conducting this farce, under Battles it should have Toulon."

Podric clicked through the game options. Selecting Battles, the Blockade of Toulon appeared which he highlighted. Archie stared at the screen.

"Want any dates, times? They're listed."

"I don't know."

"You don't know – you Mr UAR!"

Archie finished his scotch and looked stupidly at Podric.

"Ooh, exciting."

For anything to work they would have to activate the microchip in their left wrists. Not trusting Archie to touch his own properly,

Podric placed the games creator's other hand over it.

"Now press!"

Doing the same to himself, Podric remembered he saw Archie obey.

Whether either of them thought anything would happen, for a second or two nothing did. But Dog suddenly got excited and Archie starting to remonstrate, seemed to become opaque along with his wolfhound. The sensation experienced was one of falling through space, time and everything else. In fact, they were on their way to entering the brave new world of Ultimate Alternative Reality!

Part 2

Life Inside the Game
Combating Napoleon

Chapter 1

Napoleonic Wars

Raucous screams could be heard coming from the tavern next door as Podric Moon stirred. Not that he knew it was a tavern or exactly where he was, but his eyes gradually adjusting, it felt surreal. Podric peered around. A light in the neighbouring building revealed that he was wearing strange clothes and in some kind of outhouse. Hearing, rather than seeing his business partner, Podric suddenly had his face nudged by a dog. Dog! He'd come into UAR's world with them!

Getting up, Podric moved to the edge of the building and looked out. It was difficult to see much, but what he could didn't seem to resemble the twenty-first century. Podric looked down at himself. He was dressed in some kind of a uniform – gold braid and blue cloth – and wearing stockings and buckled shoes. A cocked hat was on his head. Taking it off, he stared at it in bafflement. What had he done? Where were they?

Podric anxiously moved his right index finger across his left wrist and activated UAR. Data appeared along the top of his vision. The game booted up and he heard a series of electronic sounds in his ear (that would be the aural element activating). This was followed by other retinal images. He was seeing the PlayStation Virtual Reality game of *Napoleonic Wars* with himself inside it. Incredible! So Outside-in Reality had been a precursor to Ultimate Alternative Reality!

Comforted by this knowledge and not wishing to immediately remove himself from the new world he'd just entered, Podric pressed his wrist again and deactivated the game. The data disappeared; he now had clear vision inside UAR!

The Napoleonic Wars...Podric wished he'd paid more attention to history, but recently he'd been so busy creating Alternative Reality, the subject had rather passed him by. He sort of knew who Napoleon was but... A loud crash outside was followed by the appearance of two men. Peering through slats in the outhouse door, Podric watched as they undid their belts and began to pee against the far wall.

"Trouble there'll be if that arse Sturridge dun't shut his gob."

"Reckon 'e's got it comin' the silly bastard. He's a mutinous bugger."

"What say we take off and go ter Sal's place?"

The other laughed and hitching up their trousers, the men disappeared into the night.

"Oh God, my head. Get me a paracetamol."

Podric looked around. Lying nearby, the computer games creator stirred.

"Oh, bl... Dog, get off me!"

A disgruntled and hung-over Archie Light sat up. He stared around him stupidly.

"What the..? Where the hell am I?"

"Don't know exactly but we're in your *Napoleonic Wars* game."

"Wha..?"

"I checked it. We're back several hundred years in the world of Napoleon."

Archie jumped up.

"What the hell? What have you done Podric? What am I wearing?"

"Some kind of uniform."

"Good Lord! My Chr..! You mean we're actually 'in'?"

"Uhuh."

"Well, how are we going to get out?"

"Programme ourselves, I guess."

"Well, let's do it!"

"You can, but I'm not. 'Only just got here."

"God damn stupid idea!"

Stumbling about in the straw, Archie staggered up. Dog nuzzled into to him.

"You even got the bloody hound in. Get off!"

"Yup. It all seems to have worked."

"You say you checked it."

Podric nodded.

"Let's get out then."

"I said I'm not. You go if you want to."

"Okay, I will."

Archie started trying to activate UAR but didn't seem to get very far.

"Oh God, you do it!"

"No way. We're in now and let's take a look around."

"But I don't want to. I want to get back to the Lighthouse, have a couple of Anadin and lie down!"

"You don't."

"Don't tell me what I want to do. You know I'm older than you, indeed old enough to be your father!"

Even within Archie's thick-skinned subconsciousness, he realised he'd said the wrong thing.

"Sorry. I didn't mean that."

Podric looked at Archie in the half light.

"Think Archie. Think what you left behind and when you do, you might consider the potential adventures that are going to come our way in this different world we've just entered. 'Could make a welcome temporary alternative...I mean, just being here."

"Okay, as long as it *is* temporary!"

Inspecting himself in the half light, Archie had a look at Podric.

"But are we actually playing? I mean this seems real to me."

"I think what's happened is we're in the world of the game. Now if you remember you wrote a whole lot of criteria for *Napoleonic Wars* – setting up battles and campaigns along with other stuff like weather, supply and ordnance – loads of things. But Archie, I don't know the whole nine yards of this because I can't imagine anyone's ever done what we're doing before."

Listening to Podric, Archie walked about. Preening himself in his uniform, he suddenly began to laugh hysterically, then felt his head again.

"God, I don't know what they used for headaches on board an

eighteenth-century warship?"

"What do you mean?"

"These are Royal Navy uniforms. You're a midshipman and I'm a Lieutenant or don't they teach you any history at that school of yours?"

"Hmm... Haven't been paying too much attention."

"I'll bet you haven't. Too busy playing bloody computer games!"

"Or writing them."

Archie smiled.

"Touché. So, you think we should go and experience some of this then?"

"Could be interesting."

"Guess it could at that. You don't know what you're letting yourself in for."

Archie inspected himself.

"Me, a lieutenant in the eighteenth century Royal Navy. Couldn't organise a bit of promotion next time, could you?"

"Archie, I'm still finessing the damned thing. I don't know anything about the navy, eighteenth century or otherwise."

Suddenly, all hell broke loose as some other dimension to the game kicked in. Podric and Archie watched as the brawl anticipated by the two urinators got underway. Men and women bundled out of the tavern into the courtyard in front of them. Fists flew and cutlasses flashed as the combatants grappled with each other – the women fighting with equal ferocity clawing at their foes. One lad bigger than the rest fought like a bull. His fists flew in all directions. Matters got further out of hand when a fire started, flames licking the building's timber frame. Grabbing Podric, Archie hustled him out of the byre. With Dog at their heels, they passed the mêlée but someone struck out at Archie who took a swipe back. Podric also kicked a passing body then amazingly, he was right in front of the big lad. It was Barney Sturridge! The person who Podric knew as the school bully and his potential murderer looked at him for a second too long. That split second allowed an attacker to hit Barney over the head. Unable to assist or attack – and unsure which he'd opt for anyway, Podric was swept away by the throng. Glancing over his shoulder, the last he saw of the startling apparition was Barney falling to the ground.

"Over here!"

The sound of whistles cut through cries and screams. Archie pushed Podric into the shadows of a doorway. Scarlet-clad marines carrying muskets ran by. The moment they'd past, the games creator and his young colleague dived down an alley into the night. Of Dog, there was no sign.

"You know it's an offence not to salute a superior officer."

"Sir."

Archie stammered, and came shambolically to attention.

"Who are you?"

The voice was pleasant. Even in the darkness, Archie could make out the slight figure of a captain.

"Er, Light...sir. Lieutenant Light."

"And you?"

Unsure how much eighteenth-century naval knowledge Podric possessed, Archie interjected.

"Er...Midshipman Moon, sir."

"He can speak for himself, can't he? What ship?"

Archie thought fast. What ships were stationed off Gibraltar at that time because that's where they must be. If they had entered *Napoleonic Wars* in 1793, he'd make a stab at a choice of vessel.

"Er...*Zealous* sir? The way he spoke it could have been half a question.

"Really? But she's back with the in-shore squadron."

The voice was sharper now.

"We er...we were sent ashore with the court martial party, sir."

It was a gamble, but the twenty-first-century computer man felt he had no choice. If it didn't work, they'd be hanged for desertion just minutes after entering their first (only?) Ultimate Alternative Reality adventure. Archie wasn't quite sure how such a demise would sit within UAR!

"Hmm – and you've executed the duties Captain Foley entrusted you with?"

"Sir."

"What were his instructions regarding your return?"

"They were... He wasn't very clear sir. 'Said we were to await further orders."

Archie was getting the hang of things - the right amount of deferential vagueness.

"You can berth aboard my ship. We sail for Toulon at dawn."

The young captain began to move away.

"Your dunnage is at The Star?"

"We have but little, sir."

"Very well. Be aboard at four bells."

"Begging your pardon sir - what ship?"

"Why *Agamemnon*, of course."

Then, as if he felt it necessary to explain his ship's location, he added.

"She's berthed at the mole."

Agamemnon. Agamemnon. My God, he was...he was talking to Nelson! A Nelson, who had not yet lost an arm at Calvi or an eye at the Nile, those actions not having yet been fought!

Manhandling Podric along the wharf, Archie spied another bar into which he propelled his young friend.

"I need a drink!"

Entering the rough tavern, Archie pushed his way through the crowd to the bar. He called to the barmaid.

"A brandy. Two. Large!"

"My my - don't get many officers coming in 'ere."

She began pouring two large brandies into tankards.

"That'll be three pennies gen'lmen."

The girl caught sight of Podric and gave a start. So did he; more hesitatingly, she said.

"Three pennies sirs."

Suddenly realising he had no method of payment, Archie picked up his tankard and began quaffing the liquor.

"We'll be having another."

Normally insistent on immediate payment, the girl only paused because she'd seen Podric. She stared at him. Nudging his youthful partner, Archie moved away. Finding a bench, the two sat down.

"Know her, do you? She looks as though she's seen a ghost."

Podric tried some brandy and coughed.

"She's Jane Cartwright at Wendbury High. 'Plays in the school hockey team."

For once, Archie didn't expostulate. He drank some more brandy and was thoughtful.

"Podric – I don't know exactly what's happening here, but I owe you an apology."

Podric didn't seem particularly affected by Archie's comment.

"When you used to bang on about this – about UAR, I thought you were a daft nerd."

Podric stayed silent. He looked at his tankard but didn't lift it.

"But...what's happened – what we're into now – it's not only more than a game, it's another life! Amazing. I think we may have the chance, the possibility to change what happened in the past!"

This also didn't seem to overly impress the creator of Ultimate Alternative Reality who gingerly took a sip of the fiery alcohol and screwed up his face in disgust.

"God!"

Podric cleared his throat. Archie said.

"Have to get used to that if you're going to hang out in these times..."

"Archie, it's a game – remember? We're inside a game."

Archie drank more. Perhaps he thought additional alcohol would make his headache go away.

"You reckon? Surely the point of all this is you wanted what would seem like real life adventures in another world. But this is so real, what if it was? What if we could change things, change the course of history? Don't you see what that would mean, what a profound thing UAR would be?"

Archie was getting excited.

"We can't Archie. We're currently existing in an artificial environment – the world of a computer game. That's the alternative reality we're experiencing. We've arrived here via mind pathing. UAR's enabled me, us – to alter the senses controlling our imagination but when we want to, we'll come out of the game and get back to our normal lives."

Archie banged the bench they were sitting on.

"Does this feel artificial to you?"

Fired up, he quaffed still more liquor.

"Some graphics card, huh? This bench is real Podric. These clothes, these people – they're all real. What you've done is transport us back in history, real time."

"That can't be."

"Alright – let's get out then back in now then. Activate UAR."

Putting his hand to his wrist Podric was about to do so when another brawl started up across the bar. People seemed to get into a lot of fights here whatever world they were in. The loudest voice raised was American.

"I don't give a dollar dime for the British navy. We use lemons on our ships – no cheap limes – and no British limey's gonna tell me where I can sail my boat or when!"

Rolling away from the group amidst raucous banter, Captain Saul Prendergast caught sight of the two officers.

"Well, that's a first. A British officer's ale house, now is it?"

Prendergast lurched over to Podric and Archie.

"Say, don't I know you? Your arrogant face looks familiar. And you boy, I've seen you somewhere..."

"Ha! Did I impound your vessel for smuggling or out sail you before the wind?"

"Why you stuck up-."

"'Nough of that, you."

The bartender appeared. An enormous man, he put a hand on Prendergast's shoulder.

"Get off me! Lousy bloody British."

In taking a half-hearted swipe at the barman, Prendergast's money bag somehow came loose and fell unnoticed between Archie's legs. The game's inventor wasn't slow in covering the windfall.

"Be on your way then, right enough."

"You... Don't think you've seen the last of me."

Archie laughed.

"I won't."

Prendergast turned back to Archie.

"And when I catch you..."

"That's something you'll never be able to manage Captain Prendergast."

Prendergast stopped in his tracks.

"How d'you know my name?"

"Put it down to the superior knowledge of the Royal Navy, Saul."

"You know this man?"

The bartender was surprised.

"It's been my misfortune to have some dealings with him."

"Get out you!"

The barman was more forceful toward Prendergast. His massive form towered above the American.

"I'm darned if I know what's going on here, but when I get to the bottom of it."

The bartender kicked Prendergast out the door. Unnoticed, Archie picked up the American captain's money pouch and pocketed it.

"Something else you'll never do Saul old boy."

The barman re-entered and Archie smiled.

"Our bill and one for yourself."

"Thank you, sir. Four pence in all then."

Archie took some coins from his pocket.

"American coinage do? Have some more for your trouble."

Putting several additional coins into the barman's hand, he turned to Podric.

"Now my young friend – we must join ship."

"Which'll that be sir?"

The barman was civility itself.

"Why *Agamemnon* – Admiral Nelson's."

At this, laughter broke out amongst the general gathering.

"Why he isn't no admiral that slip of a man – oh no sir. 'Can't see 'em ever being that. You'll be dreaming that one."

Archie laughed.

"Of course, you're right. You never know, perhaps..."

"He's got no connections, no one to give him a leg up. A man's got to 'ave connections for advancement in the navy. Still, I don't need to go telling you that sir. I hear Cap'n Nelson has a fine ship."

"And may Dame Fortune smile on him."

With an enigmatic look on his face, Archie led Podric from the bar. Janey the barmaid looked on intensely as the midshipman and lieutenant went out.

"Don't get ideas above yer station, girl."

"Who said I 'ad ideas. I knows 'im."

"Hear that lads – Janey here knows the young snotty!"

"Does she now? How might that be? Knowin' 'im – or *knowin'* 'im?"

Lewd merriment followed the two naval officers as they went down to the harbour.

Chapter 2

Aboard the Agamemnon

A night watchman's swinging lantern cast dancing shadows across the wharf as Archie and Podric made their way along it.

"You didn't tell me you profiled Saul Prendergast into UAR."

"You didn't ask."

"Fair enough. Why him?"

"Thought it might be interesting since you've alienated Secorni's management, and Prendergast in particular."

"You're certainly possessed of a particular sense of humour, Podric."

Archie stopped and stared at his wrist.

"Right, activate UAR. Let's get out of here now."

Some broken barrels and old fishing nets lay in disarray at the back of the quay. Squatting down, Podric took hold of Archie's left wrist and right index finger, activating the game.

"My God!"

Archie couldn't believe what he was hearing and looking at. Marshal music played in his ear and superimposed across the top of his eyes the games standby screen featured an image of Napoleon with armies, navies, and maps of Europe behind him. At the top of his field of vision icons gave Options from Battles (land and maritime) to Politics and Diplomacy, Strategy and even Religion. Awed by the experience, Archie suddenly became aware of other sounds – sounds that were outside the game and in his current surroundings.

"I know that bark!"

Looking around, Archie saw behind the game three men and Dog appear along the quay. The animal's senses locating his master, the hound bounded up to him.

"Thank heavens for that!"

A relieved young midshipman dusted his coat.

"Thought I was never going to get rid of him."

It was Billy Johnson! Having adjusted his uniform, Billy watched Dog leap all over Archie. Grabbing Archie's right hand, Podric pressed his index finger to his left wrist.

Seeing Light's rank, Billy came to attention. Archie suddenly realised that UAR had disappeared and his vision had returned to normal. He shook his head and coming to, saluted.

"Sir."

Billy Johnson stared at the lieutenant. Perceiving his error, Archie was about to bluster when he noticed Billy's gaze had turned to Podric.

"Dog is somewhat possessive of me, idiot animal. You alright Mr..?"

Years of discipline having been drummed into him, Billy snapped out of his reverie.

"'Sir. Johnson sir. William Johnson. 'Thought I recognised this snotty sir – sorry, midshipman."

"Oh, Mr. Moon... What ship are you from Mr Johnson?"

"*Agamemnon*, sir."

"Then we're to have the pleasure of your company. Captain Nelson's invited us to sail to Toulon with you. We're to re-join our ship *Zealous*."

"Delighted I'm sure, sir."

"What's he like, Captain Nelson?"

"Why sir, he's the best captain in the fleet."

"How do you quantify 'best'?"

Billy Johnson thought for a minute. Podric had seen this look a thousand times before in the twenty-first century – in the village, on the bus, at school.

"He's...he's not like other men, sir. He is sort of, but he's special. He...has a knack, a way of making you do things you'll likely not want to do – yet you do them for him, as though you were making him happy by carrying out his wishes. He's easy, but he can be tough. He's different."

The sound of a boat's oars splashing in the harbour coincided with shouts and laughter of men and women coming along the jetty. Dog sniffed around Archie in anticipation.

"You're...not bringing him, are you, sir?"

Several sailors appeared with two girls in tow. The blonde caught Archie's eye, fluttering her lashes provocatively. Further laughter engulfed the group.

"If Captain Nelson allows women aboard his ship, he's hardly going to disallow our four-legged friend."

The sailors and girls began climbing into the long boat.

Four-legged friend – I suppose that's what he is, sir."

Podric and Archie got aboard. Dog leaped in after them. There was chaos as an uncertain wolfhound tried to move about the little craft.

The coxswain leaned over and placed his shoulder against the jetty. Putting the tiller down hard, he expertly guided the boat out into the harbour.

"He's a bloody big bugger that dog."

The following morning found *Agamemnon* wallowing in a torpid Mediterranean Sea – grey sky and little wind.

"Weather could get up quick sir. 'Mark my words."

"I will Quartermaster, I will."

Captain Nelson paced the deck. In spite of the dullness of the day, his spirits were bright. Spying Archie Light amidst an array of officers, he called over to him.

"Berthed satisfactorily, Mr. Light?"

"Very well sir, thank you."

"And Mr. Moon settled in with the young gentlemen. Settled in is a misnomer. I never knew a young gentleman yet who ever 'settled in'."

Several officers standing nearby chuckled.

"I gather we have another visitor. I must say Mr. Light in all my years at sea, whilst you're not the first officer to bring his pet aboard, ribbons and bows tend to feature rather more prominently than man's best friend. Your wolfhound is certainly the largest I've ever seen. May I ask how you came by him?"

"He was one of the several dogs involved in a television commercial - advertising paint. When a particular campaign finished, the director was going to have him, but the man was killed in an accident. I knew the PA and she called up asking if I'd take Dog."

Archie was suddenly aware that several heads were turned in his direction - their eyes staring - as were Nelson's.

"Sir."

"Mr. Light - you are English, are you?"

"I am sir."

"What pray, is a television commercial? And why would anyone wish to - what did you say? - 'advertise' paint..?"

Realising he'd allowed himself to relax into the twenty-first century Archie began to sweat.

"Don't mind me, sir. My mind..."

"Were you called at the court-martial?"

"Yes, sir."

Archie lied.

"Hmm. Stressful business. Still, advertising paint, promoting paint - extraordinary. Wartime, we're always short of the stuff."

Archie grabbed at the conversational straw.

"Do you think it will be a long fight, sir?"

Nelson stared out at the lumpy sea.

"I do. We can survive because of the navy. On land, it is more difficult. We dine at three. You'll join me."

Without further ado, he turned on his heel and went below.

"...And that gentlemen, is a quadratic equation."

Crouched in the midshipmen's cramped quarters Lieutenant Hammond, *HMS Agamemnon's* third lieutenant, dropped the chalkboard carelessly on a chest. Picking up a notebook, he idly turned its pages of numerics.

"Who did this gibberish?"

"Me sir."

Billy Johnson stood his ground.

"Wasn't aware you could use a chronometer, Johnson."

"'Sir."

Hammond appeared irritated.

"What are your navigational skills like Mister Moon? Non-existent I expect, just as all the other imbeciles are, it's my misfortune to nurse."

Podric didn't comment.

"You children...how are we ever to have an effective navy?"

Hammond glared at them unsympathetically.

"Quarter of the hour. On deck with your sextants ready."

"Sir. Captain Nelson invited us to dine, sir."

"Well, we'll get fifteen minutes then, won't we."

"But it won't even be that, sir. You know what the Captain's like about punctuality."

"Are you presuming to disobey me, Johnson?"

"No, Hammond."

"*Mister* Hammond to you snotty!"

"'Sir – Mister Hammond."

The Third Lieutenant took out a fob watch.

"Twelve minutes."

Hammond turned on his heel and clambered up the companionway, leaving the two midshipman standing awkwardly.

"You don't know me in this world Billy, but I know you."

Drawn to Podric, Billy smiled shyly.

"How?"

Podric looked around.

"We don't have much time."

Reaching into his ear, he removed the tiny earpiece. Billy looked at it with uncomprehending eyes.

"What's that?"

Podric sighed.

"I don't know where to begin."

Eleven minutes and fifty seconds later, Billy and Podric appeared at the fo'c'sle. Billy carried a sextant and a worn log book under his arm.

"Where's your sextant, Moon"?

Hammond barked the question.

"I don't have one...Sir. I'm with Lietenant Light. Were aboard, sailing to re-join our ship."

"You're really going to benefit from a navigation class."

Hammond's sarcasm was belittling.

At that moment, another officer appeared on deck, his First Lieutenant's uniform immaculate. Unaware of this, Podric spoke up.

"I know where we are though, sir."

"Really?

Hammond's tone was sarcastic.

"And..?"

"43°7'0"N / 5°55'59"E."

"A likely story. You young midders-."

Catching sight of the First Lieutenant, he stopped abruptly. Hinton came over to the group.

"Actually Hammond, the boy's right. I've just checked."

Hinton turned to Podric.

"What's your name"?

"Moon sir. Podric Moon."

"Oh yes. You came aboard with that other cove – er... Lieutenant Light and his dog, didn't you?"

"'Sir."

"You'd better come with me. Carry on Hammond."

About to depart, Hinton looked round again.

"Come to think of it, Johnson you'd better look lively. Captain Nelson invited you to his table today, did he not?"

"'Sir."

"Have a good watch, Hammond."

That afternoon as Midshipman William Johnson looked around the table, he couldn't quite believe the conversation he'd had with Podric Moon an hour or so before. Looking across at his friend, there didn't seem to be anything odd about him. His hair was a little shorter than the others, but he looked well, normal. That is except for what Billy knew Podric had in his ear. What a strange object. And it was the other thing in Podric's wrist they'd used to calculate their position from Billy's battered logarithm book. It was all very weird. Someone was talking to him. What was the chaplain saying?

"Mister Johnson, are you quite well sir? That's the third time I've had to remind you that the port is with you."

Snapping out of his reverie, Billy quickly poured himself a glass and passed the decanter. Catching Lieutenant Light's eye, Podric had told him the lieutenant and his dog were also with him.

"Was there something..?"

The lieutenant's manner was neutral.

"Oh er, no sir."

Luncheon breaking up, Nelson led his officers on deck. Looking out to starboard, land was faintly visible.

"We'll shortly be off Toulon and under the services of my Lord Hood."

"You're pleased to be at sea again, sir?"

Archie was deferential.

"Of course. Seven years on the beach is more than enough for any sailor."

"Do you..? Do you consider yourself destined, sir?"

Nelson looked round at Light sharply.

"That might be regarded as impertinent, Mr. Light."

"I didn't mean it in that way at all my lor...sir."

"You're a strange fellow Light."

Nelson stared across the deck, his gaze suddenly far away.

It reminded Archie of a look Podric sometimes had.

"It's a strange thing the future. Something we cannot foretell – what it may hold. D'you think you know the future Mr. Light?"

Archie considered Nelson.

"What if I said you would become a very great admiral – your country's hero?"

"Excuse me sir. Signal from *Theseus*."

Lieutenant Hinton stood by respectfully. Nelson turned to Archie.

"I should say that you were quite possibly the biggest charlatan I ever laid eyes on – or would you have me believe you're a character of some prescience..?"

Hinton was growing impatient as Nelson and Archie stood looking at each other.

"Sir..."

"Yes, yes Hinton, the workings of the ship. What does *Theseus* want?"

"Lord Hood wishes an audience with you on board the flagship at your earliest convenience."

"Signal 'Acknowledge'."

"Lord Hood's aboard *Victory* sir?"

"Indeed Mr. Light. You know his lordship?"

"No sir."

"The ship then?"

"Sir. A little."

"Fine ship. You're going to tell me I'll command her and a fleet one day?"

Nelson turned away.

"I think we'd better leave our dreams for now and attend to more immediate concerns."

Archie continued eyeing the slight figure whose face seemed strangely lit up.

"I believe the captain means 'duties' Mister Light."

Hinton was smiling, but there could be no mistaking his meaning. With a brief acknowledgement, Archie went below.

Stepping down the companionway with Dog at his side, Archie entered the darkness that was *Agamemnon's* below decks underworld. To him, the activity was fascinating - all life living cheek by jowl. Livestock and fowl snorting and crowing; men and some women - maimed and palsied, drunken and dissipated - all shared the cramped and stinking deck.

Reaching another stairwell, Light tripped and fell headlong into the ever-deepening darkness of the orlop. When he regained consciousness, Archie discovered he was slung between his young business partner and Billy Johnson. Laying him on a rough bed, Billy was attentive.

"You all right, sir?"

Touching his head, Archie grunted.

"I would say that I am not all right Mr Johnson - not all right at all."

"I'll leave you then, Doctor."

Edging his way out of the gloom, Billy's footsteps died away.

Archie sat up.

"Where are we?"

"What they call the hold, I think."

Dog nudged into his master.

"Bloody animal. Bloody leaking bloody wooden ship. Why is it since I've entered this alternative reality, I've had a constant bloody headache and seem to always wake up in stinking smelly straw!"

"Thought you liked the historic navy."

For a second or two neither said anything. Both listened to the sounds of the sea running along *Agamemnon's* side.

"Wait a minute? Did that boy call me doctor?"

Podric grunted.

"You told him then."

In the half-light Archie could just see Podric nod.

"Wha-? He couldn't have believed you."

"I showed him the earpiece. Then using the chip, 'worked out the most accurate position this ship will ever have."

Archie sat up.

"So are we real, or unreal?"

"We're real existing in the game's world."

"You can say that again, but it's not like a game. 'More like real life. I believe I've *met* Nelson, I'm *on* his ship. In which case as I said in the bar, feeling that we're living in this existence, we might actually have a chance to change history."

Archie was animated. Podric said.

"Oh I've told you. However real you feel here, you're inside the game you wrote!"

"I don't care. I know I've met Nelson. I know he's going to die in twelve years' time as Admiral of the Mediterranean fleet aboard *Victory* at a battle he doesn't even know he's going to fight. I also know that Lord Hood is bombarding Toulon and that a young major in the French artillery is going to save the day for the enemy. That man's name is Napoleon Bonaparte and he is going to change Europe."

"So what? *You're still in a game.*"

Archie scrambled up.

"Okay, we're in a game – as you say a masterpiece I created. Let's have some more adventures then."

This did have appeal to Podric.

"What have you got in mind?"

"If we stick around here things are likely to get tricky - meeting Foley and so on... We'll go to London."

"Why?"

"Because I want to meet William Pitt, the Prime Minister."

"What do you want to see him for?"

"He can call off the siege."

"What will that achieve?"

"If he called off the siege, Napoleon would never get started."

"*But it's a game!* It's only relevant if it's some game manoeuvre."

Archie burst out laughing.

"Maybe that's how to play it in UAR? Live it to our advantage."

Archie dusted straw off his jacket.

"Come on Podric, indulge me. What have you got to lose? You invented UAR for adventure. We're having some."

The sound of distant cannon fire jolted their thoughts and prompted Dog to howl.

Not trusting Archie to manage syncing UAR, Podric took hold of his wrist and right index finger activating it, then did the same to himself.

"Spool through Options."

Moving his finger across his left wrist, Podric highlighted Options. Various data appeared.

"Now 'Politics'."

Podric clicked on the subject. Dates and political events were featured.

"1793."

He highlighted the year and up came 'Hostilities with Britain'.

"Check 'Siege of Toulon'."

Podric went back to Options and Battles. A lot of information was presented including the protagonists, their leaders, and dates of engagement.

"Highlight the last."

'18th September - 19th December' came up.

"Incredible detail. I'm better than I thought. Okay, middle of September...now go back to Politics then Capital Cities."

Paris, Vienna, London, Moscow, Lisbon, Madrid – the cities flashed into their layered vision.

"London."

Podric selected it.

"Okay so 1793, Siege of Toulon, London programmed."

"Let's go then."

"What about Dog?"

"What about him?"

"Better not leave him here Archie, just in case."

"Maybe I should. One way to get rid of the damned animal."

Aware he was being talked about, Dog licked his master.

"That won't wash, you old bugger."

Ensuring Archie depressed his left wrist, Podric did the same.

Whilst he couldn't speak for his business partner, the sensation Podric experienced this time in UAR felt very much within the game world. Images of eighteenth-century frigates, field guns, faces of men clad in regimental and naval uniforms, women in bustles and gowns, horses, carriages, banquets, balls and cannon fodder – all comprised the visions of *Napoleonic Wars*!

Chapter 3

London Rendezvous

"What a bootiful dog? Ain't seen one like 'im before. My, my, you're a handsome one an' all darlin'. Few pence for yer girl now."

Pushing a grimy hand at Archie, the beggar woman smiled her gummed smile, cackling with delight.

Shaking his head in an attempt to clear it, Archie took some coins from the pocket of his naval uniform and discovering he still had some American currency, handed several pieces to the woman.

"Wos this? Wot you givin' me? That ain't farmer George."

"It's all I've got and all you're having. Good day madam."

"Oh, good day, good day to you – stuck up sailor."

Finding themselves in a wynd, Podric, Archie and Dog slowly walked out into Whitehall. Approaching Downing Street amidst the busy thoroughfare, there seemed little or no security, but as Archie reflected, Number 10 was still a relatively new Prime Minister's residence.

Banging the knocker, the two naval officers and their dog stood waiting on the step. A liveried footman opened the door; his large tummy stretched his waistcoat. Claude Linklater, who Podric knew as the Wendbury School bus driver, stood on the step.

"Yeees?"

"Mr. Linklater. You're well I hope."

Linklater looked nonplussed, then flustered.

"Er..."

"This is my friend Lieutenant Light and this is Dog. He's quite friendly. We've called to see Mr. Pitt. Is he in?"

"Er..."

Linklater tried to recover himself.

"Mister...mister..."

"Moon. Podric Moon."

Podric, Archie and Dog stepped across the threshold.

"Moon...you, you can't come in here. You don't have an appointment – er...do you?"

"The Prime Minister will want to see us, Mr Linklater. It's important."

Podric set off across the lobby.

"Mister Moon. You can't... You can't just enter like this!"

Two soldiers suddenly appeared blocking Podric's way. Archie came up.

"You should let us through. We have news that could change things about the war."

The guardsman looked impassively at Archie.

"What's going on here? Linklater, who are these people and what's this dog doing here?"

An elderly gentleman came out of an office, his wig slightly askew.

"Sorry, Mr Fitzgibbon. They're leaving. A misunderstanding about an appointment."

"With whom?"

Archie turned on Fitzgibbon condescendingly.

"With the Prime Minister, sir, Mr Pitt."

"I'm aware who the prime minister is Lieutenant..?"

"Light sir. Late of His Majesty's ship *Zealous.*"

"*Zealous? Zealous? Zealous* is in the Mediterranean."

"Indeed she is sir, but having had the privilege to fall in with Captain Nelson, we've travelled post haste with dispatches."

"Nelson? What's the little upstart meddling in now?"

Archie silently made a mental note of Fitzgibbon's attitude towards the man who would one day be his country's hero.

"I can see sir, that we've wasted our time."

Archie turned on his heel.

"One minute. I haven't dismissed you yet."

Fitzgibbon approached Archie.

"If you have naval dispatches, why didn't you present them at the admiralty?"

"Because they are not naval dispatches. As I said sir, I can only communicate with Mister Pitt. No one else."

"For a lieutenant, you are an extremely conceited popinjay."

"And you sir, are a tired and withered secretary. Good day to you."

Fitzgibbon made a rapid sign as several more soldiers suddenly appeared, blocking Archie and Podric's way.

"Seize these men."

A scrimmage started – Archie shouting protestations and a barking Dog bounding about. It was into this chaos that the Prime Minister entered. Pitt said nothing as he stood watching the fracas before him. Finally, two soldiers fell back and Archie picked himself up from the floor. Pitt turned to his secretary. In low tones Fitzgibbon began whispering into the Prime Minister's ear. Making a curt comment, the PM crossed the lobby and walked off down a corridor.

"Against my advice, the Prime Minister has granted you an audience. In my opinion, you deserve nothing less than a night in the cells."

"Then sir, it is fortunate there are those who can appreciate wisdom and intelligence, as you clearly cannot."

Fitzgibbon's face went a strange colour and it was only with the greatest difficulty that he managed to restrain himself.

"You will present yourself here at four o'clock. Whilst you will be punctual, be prepared to wait."

He turned icily to Linklater.

"Show these gentlemen out."

Fitzgibbon's enunciation was so loaded no one could be in any doubt as to the secretary's real appraisal of Archie and Podric's standing.

Outside on the street, Archie burst out laughing. Podric was more subdued.

"I'm not sure inventing UAR is such a good thing for you."

"Oh? Why's that?"

"Because you could become even more of a pain, knowing you'll always be able to escape."

"Ha! Don't worry yourself. No change there; I've always known I'd escape from anything."

Reaching the end of Downing Street, Archie turned to Podric. He was more serious.

"Sometimes Podric it takes an arrogant bastard like me to recognise another arrogant bastard like him. We've got a meeting –that's all that matters. Don't look so glum."

Archie stared across a heaving eighteenth century Whitehall.

"Architecturally not so different, but so much more bustle. You don't know London – even twenty-first century London, do you Podric?"

"It was on the west side where I saw Fred S. Chiswick, wasn't it?"

"Chiswick. Ha! There won't be anything like Pasaro, let alone the building that houses the computer giant in 1793 Chiswick! There's half a dozen miles of fields and meadows between here and that little hamlet. But this London *is* different, and it's time you, Mister Moon had some experience of it. Come, we'll walk up to the Garden."

"I hate gardens."

Archie laughed.

"Come along Dog. I need to find a place that sells port of a superior kind."

He must be in a good mood thought Podric, as they strolled across The Strand into St. James's. Arriving at a shop, Archie uttered a satisfying 'Ah' and turned to his young business partner.

"I'm going in here."

He took some coins from Saul Prendergast's money pouch, and put several into his young friend's hands.

"Amuse yourself. What with one thing and another, I may be sometime. There's an ale house, a pub – the *Rose Tavern* off Drury Lane. They'll look after you."

Archie turned and entered the premises of Berry Bros & Rudd.

Podric studied the American money. Left with Dog, the giant animal's big eyes looked up at him.

"You look lost young sir."

Norris Widget aka 'The Widge', Podric's class mate at Wendbury High stood beside him.

"It's a dream. It's all just a dream."

The Widge looked at Podric.

"If you say so mate."

He began to move away. Podric spun him around.

"I do say so, Norris Widget!

The Widge was stunned.

"Get off!"

"I'm Podric Moon. *Podric Moon!*"

"You could be the man in the moon for all I care. You ain't no mate of mine, least I..."

Like Billy Johnson before him, Norris Widget looked a little disconcerted.

"Oh Widge, I don't know what I've invented. It's doing my head in."

"You don't 'alf 'ave some strange words, mister midshipman."

The Widge kicked pebbles across the dirt street with his wooden clog-like shoes.

"Come along 'a me. Young gentleman like you needs cheering up. I know just the thing."

Following the Widge's skinny back, Podric stumbled down Piccadilly.

Arriving at Covent Garden, the opera house and church were recognisable to modern eyes, but the piazza was much livelier; farm animals – goats, sheep and cattle roamed, and were slaughtered on the spot. The Widge led Podric through the crowd towards the theatre.

"I'll be leavin' yer now mate. Enjoy; it'll do yer good."

Podric looked around but the friend he knew from school had disappeared.

Podric and Dog entered a vast auditorium. In semi-darkness, several people were rehearsing on a large stage lit by candlelight. As his eyes became accustomed to the shadowy dimness, Podric edged forward into the pit. Hearing voices, he made out some rooms along its periphery; sounds of a conversation came from one of them.

"You know he's keeping her in the country. They have children. I don't know how she can possibly show herself in London."

"She's not showing herself in London. She's working. She's doing what she was born to do."

"No woman's born for anything, except propagation."

"What a reactionary beast you are Brinsley!"

"And no man's born to be compromised."

"Reactionary's too mild. Philistine's more appropriate. When the new play is ready, you're going to want her in it, you mark my words."

"There are others."

"There is no one, Mrs. Siddons included, who can touch her right now. Besides the scandal you spoke of…"

The speaker paused.

"What of it?"

"Such…things never harm the box office. Might even add to the play's success."

The two men laughed. Podric stole silently by.

On stage two actresses were at work. One was in her thirties, and a beautiful woman. The other was a teenage girl who Podric couldn't take his eyes off. The girl was speaking.

"'No? When nature hath made a fair creature, may she not by Fortune fall into the fire? Though Nature hath given us wit to flout Fortune, hath not Fortune sent in this fool to cut off the argument?'"

The older woman replied, her voice lilting.

"'Indeed, there is Fortune too hard for Nature, when Fortune makes Nature's natural the cutter-off of Nature's wit'."

The girl responded, "'Peradventure this is not fortune's work neither, but Nature's who perceiveth our natural wits too dull to reason of such goddesses and hath sent this natural for our whetstone'."

"No, Miss Halliday, no – not like that at all. Celia is more melodramatic. She is the opposite of Rosalind's cool disposition."

A man whose voice Podric recognised as being one of those he'd heard talking in the anteroom, bound onto the stage.

"'Peradventure this is not fortune's work neither but Nature's, who perceiveth our natural wits too dull to reason of such goddesses and hath sent this natural for our whetstone' and so forth – but with a lighter touch my dear. Not so strained, hmm? We break, returning to rehearse the Duke's closing scene."

Miss Halliday burst into tears. The older actress put an arm around the girl's shoulders.

"You mustn't take it to heart, Catherine. Mr. Kemble is only looking to improve us all."

"He never criticises you like that."

Catherine sobbed into the woman's breast.

"You have talent. You just need to let it come to you a little – not try so hard."

"Oh yes, you have talent ma'am – wonderful talent!"

Podric had spoken before he realised it.

"Who's there?"

The woman brought out some spectacles. Podric emerged from the shadows.

"A sailor no less. You think Miss Halliday has talent, do you young man?"

"I do, indeed ma'am. I think she is the most beautiful sight I have ever seen."

"Pretty she maybe, but talent is something quite different."

Podric said nothing.

"What's that beside you?"

Podric turned. Dog wagged his giant tail. Catherine laughed.

"Do you always take your dog with you to the theatre?"

"I...wasn't going to the theatre when I started. I just sort of came here."

The actress smiled into a fan she was using.

"On leave no doubt. Father a parson I'll wager. No money and up from the country."

"Where do you come from Mr..?"

"Moon. My name is Podric Moon."

"An unusual name. You're not from London then. A star per-haps."

Podric smiled.

"No, I'm not extra-terrestrial."

"What?" she asked.

"Extra-terrestrial – you know from another planet."

"My my...a scientist no less."

"Dora, Dora, can I interrupt you? We need to discuss Scene Two – Orlando's 'then there is no true lover in the forest'."

John Kemble was at his most earnest. Dora Jordan smiled down at him. No wonder she could melt hearts; her smile was one of sweet directness.

"Mr Kemble, I shall give you my full attention."

Mrs. Jordan leaned across to Catherine and spoke quietly. "Have him attend us later. I'm sure you can keep him amused."

With that, she departed.

Catherine stepped out from the edge of the stage and approached Podric.

"He is a beautiful dog. What's his name?"

"Er...Dog."

"That's not a proper name for him Po...What did you say your name was?"

"Podric."

"That's funny too. Mrs. Jordan's got a friend – Padraig – which is a bit like it. He's from Ireland, I think. Come, let us take tea. You drink tea, don't you?"

Staring at Catherine who was moving back stage, Podric appeared mute.

"Come."

Like someone in a dream, he followed the beautiful apparition.

Chapter 4

10 Downing Street

Archie Light had been busy since he and Podric parted. True, much of his afternoon involved purchasing alcohol - the finest port Berry Bros & Rudd could supply. This was made especially challenging as the only form of payment Archie possessed was Saul Prendergast's American coinage - but then this was the sort of challenge he thrived on.

Whilst unable to negotiate a case of twelve he'd been hoping for, Archie managed to procure half a dozen bottles of their superior vintage using a mixture of new world currency and the promise of the balance signed to the account of 'Lieutenant Archibald Aloysius Light, His Majesty's Navy'. The address he gave was White's Club of St James's where he requested the wine be delivered. 'Well, I will be a member there one day' he muttered as he walked back towards Downing Street, for once on time: 'It can be a long-term investment for them provided Billy Pitt doesn't drink them all!'

Archie was still chuckling when a few minutes before the appointed hour, he rapped on the door of Number 10. Podric's acquaintance, Claude Linklater, appeared, apparently no happier to see Archie now than he had been earlier.

"Got me into a lot of trouble I can tell you" the doorman moaned as he led Lieutenant Light across the lobby and along a hall.

"Sorry about that Linklater."

"And that's another thing. How'd your young midshipman know my name? Hey? You tell me that."

"Not now Claude. Wouldn't want to spoil your siesta."

"Siesta? Bah! Extra duties more like."

"Bogs and drains?"

Archie entered the Prime Minister's antechamber. It was a beautiful room and as there was no one else waiting, he took the opportunity to look around. Pictures included two Reynolds and a Gainsborough. The fireplace was Adams; on the marble mantelpiece stood a magnificent ornamental advancing refractor clock by Bernini.

Time ticked by. Tired, Archie sat down on a chaise longue and closed his eyes. Within seconds he was dreaming – seeing himself dancing with Kaliska Monroe at a ball presided over by Napoleon. Kaliska was beautiful but Boney, he'd got to stop him. Wasn't that what he was doing here – trying to prevent Bonaparte from ever becoming the tyrannical conqueror of Europe? Archie was shaken awake. It was dark, and bending over him was the Prime Minister!

"Lieutenant. Lieutenant Light."

Archie sat up.

"Oh... Oh!!!"

"I'm sorry I kept you waiting so long. Urgent business. Would you be able to have dinner with me, sir?"

"Er...yes..."

"My club is White's. I trust that's satisfactory."

"Perfectly."

*   *   *

'If Archie could see me now'. Podric lay back in the box bed wondering quite what world he was in. Holding Catherine tenderly in his arms stroking her long blonde hair, he decided whatever or wherever it was, it was paradise.

When she'd led him backstage he couldn't have known anything of the world he was about to enter; it defied all expectations. Almost as fanciful as the one he had created, the exotic combination of grease paint and the acting world was intoxicating. Podric had never encountered such an environment before and it fascinated him.

Not as much as Catherine did though.

Taking him to a private apartment and later into the funny little curtained bed they now lay in, the casualness with which she undressed amazed him.

"Wha...are you tired?"

His innocence made her laugh – a lovely rippling sound. He fancied her in class, but in school life she seemed unobtainable.

"Have you..? Is it your first time?"

Podric knew what she meant but didn't want to admit that it was. Catherine looked at him, her grey eyes studying him reflectively.

"You needn't be shy, Podric Moon."

She smiled.

"I shall call you 'Man in the Moon' – my 'Man in the Moon'."

"I love you, Catherine Halliday."

*   *   *

William Pitt studied the bottle the waiter proffered him.

"Douro '82. I know the grower. You have good taste Light. And a half case. You obviously have private means sir; that's a considerable sum for a lieutenant in His Majesty's Navy."

Pitt nodded to the waiter who began opening the bottle at a small serving table.

"I presume your arriving at my office was not some coincidence, nor was it to simply provide me with fine port."

Archie looked at Pitt; a brilliant man, the young prime minister worked too hard and if the historians were correct, Archie was about to find out how much he drank.

"I hardly know how I may speak."

The waiter returned with the opened bottle. Archie addressed the man.

"Do you have a large – er...glass receptacle?"

The waiter was momentarily hesitant.

"I think we may have something, sir..."

"Be kind enough to bring it to the table if you please."

Archie was quickly catching on to eighteenth-century manners.

"Shall I pour for you, sir?"

"No. If you'd just leave it here and bring what I ask."

The waiter departed. Archie faced Pitt who had been idly watching proceedings.

"Have you ever heard of a man called Napoleon Bonaparte?"

"I don't think I recollect the name."

"A major in the French artillery, he's about to save Toulon for the republic defeating our blockading efforts and in half a dozen years, will proclaim himself Emperor of France."

Pitt allowed himself a small smile.

"If said to the wrong ear, your first comment could be interpreted as treasonous."

"In leading the French, this man will attempt to attack Egypt, be defeated by Nelson at the Nile and Nelson will ultimately die in a battle fought some twelve years from now off Cape Trafalgar."

"Captain Nelson?"

"The same. He'll be made Admiral in '97."

Pitt laughed.

"What you say is of course, fantastic. This Napoleon...what will become of him?"

"After having been master of Europe for several years, he will ultimately be defeated by the Duke of Wellington – Arthur Welles-ley – at a place called Waterloo. He will then be incarcerated on the island of Saint Helena and die there in 1821."

At this point the waiter returned, carrying a large glass bottle. Not a proper decanter shape, it was about the size of a jeroboam.

"You say Mornington's younger brother will defeat this man Napoleon?"

"I do sir. All that I say will occur unless we can do something about it."

Archie picked up the bottle of port and with a look of careful concentration, began gently pouring it into the larger carafe.

"One day all that I've said will come true unless you and I can change it. And one day, what I'm doing now will be done each time one drinks fine port wine."

Archie gently relaxed the angle of the bottle and when complet-ing his task, put down the decanted liquor. Holding up what was left of the port, an inch of sediment remained. Pitt was appreciative and quietly clapped. Several other guests who had watched the perfor-mance, did likewise.

"Very well done, sir. The process is called decanting I believe."

"Indeed."

"You find it improves its drinking?"

"Certainly."

Pitt sipped a glass and nodded appreciatively.

"So, what do we do with these assertions of yours, Lieutenant Light?"

"I'm afraid they're not assertions Prime Minister. Unless we do some 'decanting', they will become facts."

"And how do you propose to avoid that?"

"Ensure that you never hear of Napoleon."

Pitt looked quizzical. Archie continued.

"Because if you never hear of him, it will mean that he has lost at Toulon and that the subsequent European war will have been concluded before it ever really gets started."

"That would be desirable," Pitt spoke flatly.

"The prevention of such death and carnage, this country's near bankruptcy and your premature death due to overwork - yes, it is desirable."

"You have the date of my death?"

"Yes. Eighteen hu-."

Pitt held up his hand.

"This is knowledge that I do not seek nor want."

The Prime Minister sipped his port.

"Returning to your 'information'. Acting on it, we strengthen Lord Hood's squadron."

"Exactly."

Archie was amazed how casual Pitt was in his apparent acceptance of Archie's claims.

"How is it you have come before me now?"

Pitt eyed Archie evenly.

"That Prime Minister, is a fantastic story."

"Why do I believe you, Lieutenant Light?"

Was Pitt lightly mocking him?

"I don't know sir, but if at the end of it, you consider me no more than a scoundrel, then all you will have lost is a little time and gained five bottles of vintage port."

"Perhaps only four before we're done?"

Pitt laughed and enjoyed some more of his drink.

"Pray continue."

"Well..."

Archie began the tale of his life – whatever world it related to.

Chapter 5

Love And Longing

Emerging from the depths of slumber, Podric awoke to Dog licking his face.

"Oh. Off! Off Dog!!"

The room in semi-darkness, a single candle provided the only light. Women's voices were speaking in low tones - soft but urgent. Podric peered through the bed's curtains to see Catherine clad only in a chemise, talking to the actress he had seen earlier on stage. Mrs. Jordan was dressed in an evening gown which showed off her décolletage to great effect.

"You must hurry. We have to leave shortly."

"What about..?"

Catherine sounded far away and almost childlike.

"Oh - you wish to bring him?"

She nodded towards the box bed from which Dog's tail protruded.

"You suggested he attend us."

Dora Jordan smiled.

"I did."

She took Catherine's face in her hands.

"It's all right my sweet, don't look so disturbed. His uniform is passable. Besides, he's probably never attended a levee. The experience will do him good. But hurry now. Come along. Vite, Vite children!"

With that, Dora Jordan left the room. Catherine turned to face Podric, who had drawn back the curtains.

"I want to stay like this forever."

"Yes, but not now."

Podric stood up and put his arms round Catherine.

"Podric – we must dress!"

"What's the hurry?"

"A levee with the Duke of Clarence is the hurry. He's one of the king's sons and we *must* be on time."

Pushing him away, she opened a cupboard. Inside were various clothes – lace bodices, ball gowns in silks, velvets and heavy muslin. Taking out several dresses, Catherine selected one – dark red and ruched in style. Even held to her, she looked fabulous.

"Come on Podric – get your clothes!"

"You're so beautiful."

"And we'll be so late if you don't get a move on!"

*   *   *

At White's Club, The Prime Minister sat listening to his unusual guest.

"A most interesting story. Perambulating cars, people travelling into the constellations – by Jove, I shall never look at the stars in quite the same way again! Did you tell Captain Nelson all this?"

Pitt nearly said drivel but managed to restrain himself.

"No, sir. No, it was never necessary."

"Good. One doesn't want to disturb people's balance if possible. Nelson's highly strung and I wouldn't wish the navy feeling any more troubled than it is already."

Pitt drank some more port. Archie was beginning to look the worse for wear.

"Your young colleague, is he from the future as well?"

"Podric? Yeesh."

Archie's words were a little slurred.

"Podric invented it really, the little..."

"You don't like him?"

"I told you sir, I invent these, these games."

"Jealous then? He's a young rival. You're jealous of the boy?"

Archie didn't reply. Pitt looked at him steadily.

"Where is he now, this Midshipman Podric?"

"They don't teach history very well in the future, least not at his school. Not knowing London in the twenty-first century, I advised him to study it in the eighteenth and suggested he went to the theatre."

"Ha! I trust the experience will enlighten him."

Pitt leaned forward.

"Do you have any proof of all this? Anything you could show me that would help reinforce my belief in your...fantastic statements."

Archie pulled his earlobe. He was severely tempted to produce the little aural device, but something in the back of his mind told him not to. He decided on another tactic.

"No. No Mister Pitts Sir. You can believe meesh or you can disbelieve meesh. It's up to yoush." With that Archie's head dropped onto the table and he started to snore.

William Pitt finished his glass of port and stood up. One of the colleagues who had admired Archie's decanting operation – Thomas Townsend, Lord Sydney, approached. A member of Pitt's cabinet, the prime minister turned to him briefly.

"Whether he's from this time or any other Thomas, the fellow can't drink."

"Nice job of decanting though."

"Yes. Let's see to it the club continues the practice and...make a note to have Hood reinforced at Toulon."

"We're already stretched in the Mediterranean, Billy."

"Hmm. We can divert a couple of frigates assigned to Jervis's West Indian squadron. Probably a waste of time but... Ha! What an evening. I must get back to work."

"Do you want me to do anything with him?"

"You have a suggestion? No, let him sleep it off. If nothing else, he provided some diversionary entertainment."

"And several bottles of excellent port."

"Bonaparte. Napoleon Bonaparte. I wonder if we'll ever hear more of the fellow."

*   *   *

As with all levees, there was a hierarchy waiting to be presented to the evening's guest of honour – that night, His Grace, the Duke of Clarence. What was surprising was that as a midshipman, Podric Moon was placed so near the front of the gathering. This was due to the Duke's mistress, Mrs. Jordan being pre-eminent. As a protégé of hers, Catherine was also at the fore. The young actress whispered in Podric's ear.

"Remember to make your leg."

"My what?"

"Your leg. Watch the other men."

Podric saw a man nearby put one leg in front of the other as he bowed to the Duke.

"Miss Catherine Halliday and Mister Midshipman Moon."

The sonorous voice of the Master of Ceremonies echoed across the ballroom as Catherine and Podric were announced.

Later, Podric couldn't quite remember how he managed his social performance, but whatever he did seemed to pass muster. The Duke of Clarence nodded to Catherine but turned to Podric.

"Ah...a young midder. How do you find the service my boy?"

"Very good. Thank you, sir."

"Excellent. Good. Where have you been serving?"

"Toulon. *Zealous* sir. Captain Foley..."

"Ha! Foley. Didn't meet Captain Nelson, I suppose?"

"Er, yes, as a matter of fact, I did sir. Indeed, it was Captain Nelson who took me from Gibraltar to join my ship in *Agamemnon*."

The Duke of Clarence looked delighted.

"*Agamemnon. Agamemnon* and dear Nelson has her. Come, come and sit with me. I wish to know all about your adventures. You may know the service is very dear to my heart, very dear to me indeed."

Disregarding the several hundred other guests, the Duke put his arm round Podric and guided him across the floor to a throne chair situated on a dais. Seeing the Duke's approach, a flunky rapidly placed another smaller seat alongside it. The Duke sat down and indicated to Podric he do the same. Brinsley Sheridan sidled over to Dora Jordan.

"Your young protégé's naval buck's made quite an impression. Not entirely to her liking methinks."

They looked across at Catherine who was clearly put out.

"Don't you think I'm not aware that where the sea is concerned, I'm His Grace's second mistress?"

Dora smiled at Sheridan before strolling away towards Catherine. The actor/manager watched her cross the room.

"And men think they rule... Ha!"

*   *   *

If Lord Sydney or Pitt had been outside White's Club, half an hour later they would have seen a surprisingly sober Lieutenant Light emerge from its doorway.

Standing by a railing, Archie took a surreptitious look up and down the still busy street. What was he to make of the evening? It didn't really amount to much: Pitt dispatching two additional frigates to Hood, it was unlikely that the small reinforcements would affect the outcome of Napoleon entering his place in history. That meant returning to Toulon which meant finding Podric. Fast.

Having suggested he meet his young friend at the Rose Tavern in Drury Lane, Archie set off towards Covent Garden. Arriving at Pall Mall, he approached the Carlton Club. The building's interior lights were brilliant, attracting the gaze of passers-by as carriages waited on the good and great. Archie stopped at the entrance where two impassive doormen stood sentry.

"Quite a party."

Neither man acknowledged the naval lieutenant's existence. Archie peered into the lobby as two fops were leaving.

"Frightful evening. Sailor Billy's preoccupation with our illustrious matelots - quite the end. Fawning all over that young midshipman - makes you deride the seas. I shall most definitely remain terra firma."

"Do I hear the senior service's name being taken in vain sir, that you're critical of his majesty's nautical servants?"

"Oh, George - send me to the deep!"

Archie's fist hit the effete dandy squarely on the nose. Blood immediately poured from the man's face. Light didn't wait for any reaction but turned to one of the doormen.

"Can't tolerate offence to the service; unacceptable."

Amidst cries of 'Do something! Arrest him!' Archie suddenly saw Podric standing beside an overweight man, the sash and Garter star emblazoned across the man's chest.

"Podric! Podric!!"

For a second his young friend didn't respond and it was as hands descended upon him that Archie yelled "P O D R I C !" at the top of his voice. Both Podric and the Duke of Clarence turned to see Lieutenant Light being forcibly restrained by the now active doormen.

"Oh sir, your grace – the lieutenant is the friend I came to England with. I believe he's had an important meeting with the Prime Minister."

"Not necessarily the greatest of entrées Podric, but perhaps I shouldn't hold that against him?"

Clarence waved a hand at the doormen.

"Release him there. I say release him!"

With some reluctance, the two men dropped their hold on Archie. Looking dishevelled, he straightened up and adjusting his uniform, entered the building.

"Archie, er... Lieutenant Light sir, lately HM ship *Zealous*."

Archie made his bow with an elegance that surprised Podric.

"Lieutenant Light, welcome. Mister Moon has been telling me something of your exploits. I gather you've recently come from a meeting with our Three Bottle man."

Archie looked quizzical. The duke continued.

"Ah, I see you're not acquainted with colloquialism."

The Duke of Clarence wiped his brow.

"...On account of Billy's taste for Duoro's finest reserve..."

Replacing his handkerchief, he said,

"And how did you find our Prime Minister?"

"Well enough sir. I tried to suggest the inshore squadron off Toulon be reinforced, it being vital if we are to be victorious."

"Did you by Jove? And what was his reaction?"

"He volunteered extra frigates sir, but I fear they won't be enough."

"Hmm. You think not?"

"No, your grace. Defeat at Toulon will shift the balance in France's favour and put the whole Mediterranean at risk."

"My own feelings Light, my own feelings entirely. Reinforce the Mediterranean squadron. I'm always telling their Lordships at the Admiralty the very same. Before we know it, these Frenchies will take over the Eastern Mediterranean and it'll be the devil's own job to drive them out if they do."

"That's very prescient your grace. Would you excuse me if I had word with my young colleague?"

"Yes, yes – certainly. Dora, where's Dora?"

The Duke of Clarence turned away and was instantly surrounded by the levee's throng.

"Dora...that's right Clarence...Clarence becomes William IVth and his mistress who he has umpteen kids with, was the actress Dora Jordan. Ha-ha... Strange looking at everything like this."

Archie noticed that Podric was staring at someone across the ballroom.

"You alright?"

"Mrs. Jordan is beautiful but not as beautiful as my Catherine."

"Wha..?"

Following Podric's gaze, Archie realised who he was looking at. Recognising her as Podric's twenty-first-century girlfriend, it wasn't apparent from Catherine's attitude that she was reciprocating Podric's adoration.

"Which of your friends haven't you profiled?"

Podric didn't respond.

"We've got to go back."

Podric still gazed at Catherine.

"Do you hear me? Toulon. We've got to go back to Toulon."

Podric still didn't react. Archie shook him.

"Podric – stop being so childish and pay attention!"

His partner's attitude remained indifferent. Archie abruptly walked away. Crossing the room, he approached Catherine, surrounded as she was by a group of admirers. Podric watched as Archie introduced himself and saw Catherine's initial disinterest gradually give way to merriment and laughter. Several times they turned to look at Podric; it slowly dawned on the games champion that he was the butt of their amusement. Colouring up, Podric dived into a group of guests, disappearing amongst the glitterati.

An hour later with just the last few revellers remaining, a butler found Podric sitting disconsolately under a tree in the gardens of Carlton House.

"Mister Moon?"

Podric looked up but said nothing.

"For you sir."

The butler presented a note that he proffered on a silver salver. Taking the sealed envelope, Podric ripped it open and read. 'She awaits you, Drury Lane. Meet at The Rose tomorrow breakfast: LLNL'. The last letters meant nothing to him, but Podric recognised Archie's handwriting.

*   *   *

The first glimmer of dawn was breaking as Midshipman Moon stood outside the deserted theatre. A cat fight started; its screech-ing row caused the night watchman to stir from his slumber. Somewhere deep inside the theatre, Dog howled. The watchman looked at Podric.

"Can't get in there young sir."

"I've got to! I'm... I'm meeting someone."

"I'm sure you are but you ain't getting in – not unless you give the password."

Disconsolately, Podric took out the crumpled note from his pocket. LLNL – what was that?

"Wos 'at?"

The watchman's pukesome breath made Podric wince.

"LLN..L.."

With surprising alacrity, the itinerant turned away, threw back several bolts and swung open a side door.

"You think someone like me has no intelligence."

'Tis a consummation

Devoutly to be wished. To die, to sleep––

To sleep—perchance to dream.'"

Podric stared at the man open-mouthed as he recited Hamlet.

"Go on, go on - or dreamin's all she will be doin'."

Podric entered. The watchman locked the door behind him. It was pitch black inside and letting his eyes adjust, UAR's creator slowly picked his way forward towards the back-stage area. After several wrong turns and a fall, he found the stairs. His heart beating excitedly, Podric began to climb. At the top, he tapped on the door and was surprised when Catherine's voice immediately responded.

"Say the code."

"Er, LLNL?"

The lock clicked. Dog began to bark but quietened by Catherine, only wagged his tail and licked his young friend. Catherine was still in her ball gown. Turning to her dressing table, she picked up two glasses of wine. Handing one to Podric, Catherine crossed the room.

"Come with me."

On the far side of the attic apartment, Catherine opened another door. Stairs led to the roof and soon the two stood outside leaning on a balustrade. The slumbering city of London lay beneath them. Catherine sipped her wine.

"I must have sat up here a week of my life."

Silent, Podric looked at the city.

"You can talk now."

"I can't."

Putting down her glass, Catherine laughed and placed an arm around Podric.

"You're going to tell me that I've to go back to Toulon."

"I'm not going to tell you anything."

"Did my partner - colleague, flatter you?"

"Of course."

Catherine smiled more intimately.

"Podric. Such a funny name... I know lots of Lieutenant Lights. I meet them all the time. This city is full of them. You must go back because you must go back."

"But I..."

Catherine put a finger to his lips.

"Come to me when you know you can – when you can stay."

"Forever?"

She smiled slightly and removing a pin from her hair, pressed the ornamental clip into Podric's hand. Podric ripped a nickel button from his tunic and gave it to Catherine who kissed it.

"Now we shall sleep – just for a little. Go along. This is my special place; I'll be down in a minute."

Podric walked slowly towards the roof top door.

"LLNL..?"

"Shakespeare of course. Loves Labours *Not* Lost! Your friend thought it up."

"He would."

"He cares about you Podric."

Podric went down the stairs.

"So do I."

A tear trickled down Catherine's cheek. Perhaps in the 18th century people grew up even faster than they do in the 21st?

*   *   *

The twenty-first-century Podric didn't go to pubs much and when he walked into the Rose Tavern, Dog panting by his side at ten thirty the following morning, he was amazed at the level of drinking being conducted. The place was raucous with people already drunk!

Moving through the crowded bar, Podric found his friend cavorting with one of the numerous barmaids.

"Your boyfriend dearie? Didn't know you were like that lieutenant? And what a big dog the boy's got."

The woman's mountainous breasts shook with laughter at her lewd wit. Archie didn't seem to mind and only smiled.

"Another for me and wine for my friend."

The barmaid climbed off his lap.

"Yes m'lord, no m'lord. What about me?"

"Of course. And porter for you Bess of Bermondsey."

The woman turned into the crowd surrounding the bar.

"Move!"

Archie's hissed whisper seared into Podric's ear.

"Wha..?"

Archie was already manoeuvring through the throng and Podric tentatively followed. Slipping into the street, cries of annoyance were heard from within.

"They'll get beadles. Run!"

The two naval figures sprinted away from Drury Lane towards the river; law officer's whistles were shrill behind them.

Standing under a wooden bridge on a Thames mud bank, Archie looked at the river. How busy it was. The place was alive with life – boatmen ferrying people, lighters carrying loads of anything and everything that was needed by a voracious city; cattle carcasses, timber, wine and clothing – all were transported along London's aquatic artery. In spite of the stench and filth, it was wonderful – far more exciting than the modern day sanitised waterway he was used to. Archie felt invigorated and energised – his attitude very different to his partner's, who now appeared resigned.

"It's okay. She told me I've to go back – but what are we going to achieve?"

Archie took out a small earthenware flask, uncorked it and had a swig. He turned to Podric who was pulling up his cuff.

"Want some?"

Podric shook his head.

"Wrist."

Archie proffered it.

"It's my fault. I thought I could persuade Billy Pitt to do something that would prevent Napoleon from succeeding – that what will happen, never would. So...the only way now to stop him is being there."

"What do you mean?"

"The battle. There's a point when the French get their artillery to the heights overlooking Toulon. It's the moment things turn in the siege campaign."

"But I keep telling you Archie this is only a game. We can enter UAR and play it – not go back there."

"Fair enough, but I'm going anyway."

"You mean you want to?"

Archie kicked a large stone into the river.

"Yeah. I admit it Podric. Making a lash of reality, its ultimate alternative is becoming life for me. I prefer it."

Looking around the corner of the timber arch, the games creator became aware of the need for urgent action. Led by Dog, a gang of men and women, including several beadles and the large, threatening figure of Bermondsey Bess were bearing down on them. The gargantuan woman was wielding an enormous spiked club.

"Podric. I've got to go!"

Podric sighed.

"Press your right finger over the chip in your left wrist."

Seconds later UAR's interface optically appeared across Archie's upper vision.

"Is that it?"

His eyes were looking at the top of his field of sight.

"It is...you've got games options and all that."

"Incredible. You'll have to tell me sometime how you did this."

"I did tell you."

"Oh?"

"You were drunk."

"Well then, another time"

"Move your finger."

Archie did, but he was slow. Realising his friend wouldn't make it, Podric quickly took control and reverted to previous settings. Dog leaped at them.

"You handling this Podric? We need to activate Play quite soon. I mean very soon! I really don't fancy being on the receiving end of that woman's club."

Whether or not Archie and Podric were real, Bess's massive cudgel only struck thin air. The ferocity of her action caused her to topple into the mud. Those accompanying her found this highly amusing. That is, until extricating herself, she struck one of them, a cockler named Hugh Nosey. Something of a gargoyle himself, what teeth Nosey had possessed disintegrated after Bess's blow, he being rendered unconscious for the rest of the day.

Chapter 6

The Siege of Toulon

"The French seem to be bringing up more artillery sir."
Straining in his saddle, the aide-de-camp snapped his telescope shut. Turning to his commanding officer, General Charles O'Hara, these were the last words he ever spoke. A cannonball decapitated him and the young ensign beside him. The general's horse reared, and much of his aide's blood spattered across O'Hara's chest.

"Warm work."

Speaking to no one in particular, the general regained control of his mount and wheeling it, trotted off down the lane. Seeing two riders emerge from a defile, the general let out a holler.

"You two. I say dragoons, are you?"

The older of the two reined in. The younger fellow, little more than a boy, looked decidedly unstable astride his cob which shied nervously as several more cannon balls plummeted about them.

"What regiment?"

The older man seemed to briefly try and look into his collar then studied his sleeve.

"Know what battalion you're from, don't you?"

The fellow suddenly pushed the general out of his saddle and O'Hara was lucky that he did. A shell exploding beside him, completely vaporised his horse. Archie dismounted and walked over to the general who lay on the ground.

"Life Guards, sir. Captain Light and Ensign Moon at your service."

He was a cool one, this hussar – O'Hara had to give him that.

"I believe I'm in your debt, sir. Not the normal way a junior officer greets a general, but I'm grateful."

Archie gave a slight bow. The general began wiping his tunic in an effort to clean himself.

"Look here, my aide and ensign have gone down. I'd be obliged if I could temporarily assign you to my staff. Who's your commanding officer?"

"Attached to Sir Robert Boyd, Gibraltar sir."

"Must have just missed you then. I was Lieutenant Governor. Recently arrived here?"

"Indeed."

"Bloody mess – what with the navy interfering all the time. We'd better get down and see Mulgrave. No doubt he won't have a plan. It's what makes it so damned annoying trying to deal with that titan Hood."

O'Hara mounted Archie's horse.

"We'll er...follow on then sir."

"Where d'you get these horses? Don't recognise the numnah colours."

"We just...fell upon them, sir."

"Ha! Damned funny business. Ride double. The mute doesn't seem too comfortable anyway."

With that O'Hara galloped away down the hill.

"Where do we go then?"

"His HQ I suppose. The way he's heading, it'll be in the city. I'd better get in the saddle and you hang on."

Dog appeared.

"Oh, here you are. Might have known you'd show up."

Podric clumsily dismounted and Archie got in his saddle.

"'Must say Podric you don't seem too comfortable riding a horse."

Hanging on to Archie, Podric clambered back up behind him.

"That's because I never have."

"A reasonable reason. Hold tight."

Digging in his spurs, Archie got the animal moving. In seconds they were chasing after their new commanding officer. Podric yelled in Archie's ear.

"Are all army officers so weird?"

"Usually more so!" came the reply.

*   *   *

"For God's sake Grainger – how many times do I have to tell you, I require my eggs runny on the inside – not raw, damn you!"

The Commander in Chief, HM Land Forces Toulon, Lord Mulgrave, was unhappy with his breakfast. The victim of his wrath, fusilier Grainger stared at the general for a moment then averted his eyes to avoid rebuke for insubordination.

"Sorry sir. It won't happen again."

"It certainly won't. I'm replacing you."

"Sir. Very good sir."

Grainger had been threatened by Mulgrave more times than he cared to remember and now played his trump card.

"I've made up your gout lotion sir. It's warming in your bed chamber."

"Damn and blast your eyes!"

An officer knocked on the door.

"Sir?"

Grainger began clearing away his lordship's breakfast dishes.

"Leave that and get out you oaf!"

Grainger put down the tray and left the room. Without looking up, Mulgrave took a spoon and began to eat one of the eggs he'd rejected, devouring it with such voracity, yolk spilled down his chin.

"What do you want Drummond?"

"General O'Hara's here sir – arrived from the fort."

Mulgrave continued his grotesque mastication. Drummond waited quietly; his commanding officer finally replied through a mouthful of raw egg white.

"Show 'im in."

Drummond bowed and withdrew.

*   *   *

General O'Hara was sitting in his breeches reading a report when

Drummond returned to the adjutants' room.

"Lord Mulgrave will see you now, sir."

"Damned right, he will!"

Grainger appeared with O'Hara's semi-cleaned jacket.

"Best I could do in the time, sir."

Standing, O'Hara grunted. Slipping into the garment and beginning to button-up, he turned to Drummond.

"I'm expecting a new aide and ensign shortly. A fellow named Light. Guards captain. He's with a youngster. Rum cove – appeared mute. Devil I know where they come from."

"Pomphrey and Lulworth sir?"

"At peace, I hope. Grainger's removed most of what was left of them."

He looked down at his tunic, flicked a piece of something from the fabric, and left the room.

*   *   *

"Phipps."

"I dislike your familiarity, O'Hara."

Mulgrave sat slumped on a button-backed velvet three-quarter chair. Sipping wine, his feet rested on a stool. O'Hara moved around the room restlessly.

"Henry, you may be in token command here, but that's all it is."

Mulgrave coughed and moved his body uneasily.

"Now that Baron d'Imbert has proclaimed the young dauphin Louis XVII, it's my belief this action has spurred our republican friends to some determined activity. They're bringing up more artillery and obviously plan to cut off our supply line."

Mulgrave made no comment and slurped his vin rouge.

"We should consult Lord Hood immediately as to how best to manage the naval campaign. As for our own position, we must attack the French without delay."

"Really?"

Mulgrave put down his glass and pushing the stool over, got to his feet.

"A very interesting analysis Charles O'Hara; gambling bastard,

Charlie O'Hara, the illegitimate son of a Portuguese whore who had to clear out of England for not paying up at the tables. Don't you lecture me about being 'token'. I'm in command here and it's only under sufferance I allow you to stay."

"I think not. In Whitehall circles, Lord Mulgrave is regarded as having bought his way to command."

"How dare you, sir! You will withdraw that remark or..."

"Or what? Is it really fitting for the two senior commanders here to fight a duel – that is if you're up to it Henry!"

Having stared Mulgrave in the face, O'Hara turned away. When he spoke his voice was quiet, almost matter of fact.

"We should attack. I'll take responsibility if it fails, so you'll not be affected if we suffer any reverse. I cannot stand by and watch the enemy's activity. I will require a conference with Lord Hood – we have to cooperate with the navy. Perhaps as senior commander, you'll be so good as to sign the signal when it's drafted."

O'Hara couldn't escape a touch of bitterness entering his voice. Mulgrave smiled gloatingly.

"With pleasure."

He turned towards the window. A strange scene was playing out on the lawn.

"Good lord!"

Dog was jumping around Archie and Podric, who were doing their best to restrain the animal.

"Upon my word that's a hound. Never seen an Irish like it."

"My new aide. What *is* he doing?"

"He's got a fine taste in wolfhounds, whoever he is!"

Emerging from Lord Mulgrave's private quarters, General O'Hara walked briskly down the corridor. Reaching the adjutant's office, the room was empty except for Captain Drummond who studied a map.

"I want you to prepare a plan of attack. Not a large force, two companies will suffice – a night sortie."

O'Hara peered at the chart.

"Here's what needs to be taken; I've heard they call the battery 'Convention'."

"General Mulgrave's decided to strike then?"

Drummond's voice was neutral.

"The decision's been made and he will sign the necessary orders."

O'Hara rifled through some notes.

"Have an initial draft ready tonight. Oh, and the moment my new aide has finished his canine activities, send him along, will you?"

Pulling out a more detailed topographical chart, Drummond's concentration was abruptly disturbed when a minute or two later, the largest Irish wolfhound he'd ever clapped eyes on burst into the room. The animal moved about boisterously, threatening to upset desks and tables. Temporarily thrown, Drummond was further decomposed when Captain Archibald Light of the 4th Life Guards entered followed by Ensign Moon of the same regiment.

"Get down Dog. Bloody animal! It's the same wherever we go. He really is the limit."

Drummond noted Archie's captain's pips.

"Drummond, 2nd Dragoons."

He paused.

"Gazetted April '91."

Having brought Dog in hand, Archie looked across at his fellow captain.

"Light. January, same year."

A look of distraction flitted crossed Drummond's face.

"Welcome. I'm to take you along to General O'Hara. I believe you're replacing Pomphrey and young Lulworth."

"Ensign Moon."

Archie announcing Podric, Drummond gave a brief nod.

"Is there anywhere we can leave the animal?"

"Your ensign can keep an eye on him while you get briefed. Wait here Mister Moon."

Drummond and Archie went out. Podric walked over to the table. Maps and documents were spread all over it.

"What are you doing?"

Drummond had made a prompt return.

"Er, nothing sir."

Obviously suspicious, Drummond's eyes roamed about.

"How long have you served with Captain Light?"

Deciding on a twenty-first-century truth, Podric replied.

"About six months" then belatedly added, "sir."

"Seen much action?"

"Bit. We were with Captain Nelson then in London. Archie – er, Captain Light had a meeting with Mister Pitt."

"The Prime Minister?"

Drummond was incredulous.

"Yes sir."

"I have a feeling I'm not going to like you, Moon."

"'Sir."

"Not like you at all."

Drummond was almost sneering. Dog suddenly began to bark at him. Although a docile creature, the animal looked threatening. Drummond drew back, tripping over a table leg.

"Call the bloody thing off. Now, damn it!"

Dog barked more and louder.

"G-e-t h-i-m o-f-f!"

"Wha...?"

The gout-ridden figure of Lord Mulgrave stood in the doorway. He had a glass of wine in his hand and a night cap was perched on his head.

"What's going on Drummond?"

Podric brought Dog to his side and the two stood docilely before their C-in-C.

"The animal was out of control sir."

"Looks remarkably under control now. It's you who look désordre Drummond."

Mulgrave turned to Podric.

"What's your name boy?"

"Moon sir, Podric Moon."

"Rum name. This your dog?"

"No, sir. He belongs to Captain Light."

"Does he, by Jove? And a damn fine animal he is too. Trained, is he?"

"Well er, sort of sir."

Mulgrave laughed.

"Never known a hound yet I couldn't train. Come with me. And you Drummond, straighten yourself up. Uniform's a disgrace."

In General O'Hara's office, things were going better. The general had a papier-mâché model of the heights surrounding Toulon and he and Archie were engrossed in the detail of O'Hara's proposed sortie.

"I can't emphasise enough sir – it's vital we take the 'Convention' battery, hold it at all costs and I know – er...I'm sure they'll try an attack on Little Gibraltar."

"My thoughts entirely. 'Admire your forcefulness Light. Speak as though you're a visionary."

"What I say could happen, sir. What I mean is, I feel that's what they'll do."

"Important then, this attack."

"The most important attack of the war. Could even end it, sir."

"Ha! You think the republicans will give up if we drive 'em back? Toulon is only one of several fronts."

"But it's pivotal. Right now, they're poorly led but that will – er... could change. And if it does, then so will the world."

"My my...this is strong stuff. Odd we didn't meet on the Rock. Man of your vitality I'd have remembered."

Archie became more subdued.

"Now don't go off the boil, Light. Lord Hood's coming here to-night to give us support. He's with some kind of volunteer who he's making a Commodore or whatever they call 'em in the navy."

"Sir Sidney Smith."

"That's the man. My God you are well informed. Fortunate I came upon you – fortunate indeed."

O'Hara picked up a welded strip of little metal blue soldiers.

"I've got Drummond working on the details, but I'd like you to take a look at what he comes up with. I've requested the attack be only two companies."

Deep in thought, Archie said.

"With another in reserve..."

"Of course. Of course. You'll go far young man."

O'Hara re-positioned the soldiers and inspected the miniature battlefield more closely.

"Last time we attacked, they weren't much more than a rabble. They'll need much better organised defences if they're to stop us this time.."

Archie looked at the model, his expression bleak.

Chapter 7

Lose or Leave

Toulon in 1793 was an historic port and a sailors' town. This meant that it was always lively, often rowdy and not infrequently depraved! Walking along the bustling streets leading to the harbour, Podric Moon wasn't aware of any of this.

In the past few days since he'd begun to experience eighteenth-century life, Podric was surprised at how quickly he'd adapted to it – the poverty, filth and overt public lewdness of men and women. Although it was a cold night, French female voices called out to him from doorways. Podric smiled to himself. Thanks to Ultimate Alternative Reality, he knew he'd already experienced something precious. Love. Nothing was more important than that. He did wonder how he would be able to look Catherine Halliday in the eye when he returned to twenty-first-century reality, knowing he'd held her so intimately in his arms. Somehow, he didn't fancy his chances in quite the same way when back at Wendbury High in real life! But what was real life? By discovering a way to live inside a computer game, everything seemed pretty real – eating, walking, sleeping...loving. Surely nothing could be more real than that?

"What could be more real than that, a real English penny you ignorant bunch of Spanish pieces of eight!"

His reverie broken, Podric turned to see Barney Sturridge land on his backside in the street. Several burly Spanish marineros emerged from a tavern and stood around him.

"Spanish Main – British Main more like!"

One of the Spaniards knocked him on the head and Barney fell forward into the dirt. Laughing, the Spanish sailors re-entered the bar.

* * *

Clearing him up, half an hour later in another tavern along the quay, Podric sat at a rough table opposite a bleary-eyed Barney. There were times in the future when the games neoteric would wonder if he'd done the right thing. Serving as a young British soldier in his self-created alternative reality inside the *Napoleonic Wars* computer game, Ensign Moon was beginning to understand how much time and circumstance could drastically alter things.

"Good health."

Podric raised his tankard; the longer he was in this world, the better the 18ᵗʰ century alcohol was tasting.

"This is the second time I've seen you in a fight."

"Yeah?"

"When I first came here, you were fighting outside a bar on Gibraltar."

"So?"

"You always seem to be fighting."

"Nothing odd about that. We all fight. We're here to fight."

"Not each other."

"Da! Half the ship's company are dagos. Wouldn't trust 'em further than knife 'em."

Barney drank some ale.

"Why d'you get me in here anyways? You didn't set me right for charity."

"I have my reasons."

"Yeah? And what might they be?"

Podric looked at him.

"The officer I'm with has got the crazy idea of trying to kill someone, someone who if he wins now will make a lot of trouble in the future. Irrespective of how much I tell him he's daft, it makes no difference. I could do with some help."

"How d'you know if you don't kill 'im he's gonna make trouble?"

Barney was never thick, possessing an innate intelligence.

"You wouldn't believe me if I told you."

"Na. Prob'bly not."

He quaffed some more beer.

"When are you gonna try and get him?"

"There's an attack soon. Then."

"Huh. 'Knew there's something brewin'. I'm in Sir Smith's squadron. We've been told there'll be some action ashore.

"Is that why you're here?"

Barney suddenly grabbed Podric across the table.

"Askin' a lot of questions, aren't yer ensign? Maybe you've got other reasons to get me in 'ere?"

Podric was surprised how steadily he was able to look the school thug in the eye.

"I just wanted to see what you're really like."

For several seconds they studied each other. Letting go of Podric, Barney stood up and finished his drink.

"You're weird."

Watching him disappear out of the door Podric felt he could only agree.

"I'll give you that one Sturridge. But things are going to get a whole lot weirder yet."

Returning to headquarters, Podric discovered the place was a hive of activity. Walking past the guard house, he watched as carriages filled with senior officials drove away. Other officers including the man Podric recognised as General O'Hara, rode out on chargers. Amidst this throng, he suddenly saw Dog running around accompanied by Lord Mulgrave. The general was apparently more preoccupied with the animal than in the professional activity surrounding him. Becoming aware of Podric's presence, Dog ran towards him. Podric did his best to calm the giant hound as General Mulgrave came wheezing up.

"He's quite a challenge. Do you think Captain Light will sell him to me?"

Podric didn't tell Mulgrave he thought Archie would probably give Dog away, but because it was their first UAR foray, an odd bond had fostered between them; he'd become attached to the big pet.

"I couldn't possibly say what Captain Light's intentions might be regarding the matter. We came here with Dog and have been through some adventures together."

"Oh indeed, indeed."

Mulgrave looked at the wolfhound who stood panting beside him. Podric bent down and taking Dog's collar, made some adjustment to it.

"On the other hand, I would pay handsomely."

A stressed Fusilier Grainger appeared.

"Er, General. Excuse me General."

"What is it, Grainger?"

Mulgrave was irritable.

"Come quickly, sir. You've got to come quickly. There's some trouble in the 'ouse."

"What sort of trouble?"

"Captain Drummond sir; he's taken a sword to the new fellow, Captain Light."

"He's done what?"

"Threatened him, sir. They're about to fight a duel."

"Damn and blast Drummond. Fellow's a surly devil at the best of times."

Mulgrave, Grainger and Podric set off. Rounding a corner, they were just in time to see Archie attacking Drummond.

"Cease gentlemen! Put up your sabres. Now!"

Mulgrave's words echoed across the courtyard. Drummond's face was furious, but Archie's demeanour left one in no doubt that he was about to deliver a coup de grace. Mulgrave approached the two men.

"Were it not for this attack I'd have you both in irons. Captain Light, you are new to my staff and I'll make some allowance. But be aware sir, I will not have my officers involved in duels. Is that understood?"

Duly admonished, Archie gave a nod of acknowledgement. Mulgrave turned to Drummond.

"You Drummond, I intend to remove from my staff at the earliest opportunity. You will not take part in the forthcoming activities and are to be confined to quarters awaiting further orders. Your sword, sir."

Drummond's face looked like death.

"General I really must pro-."

Mulgrave was apoplectic.

"You dare argue with me, sir? Guard – take this man's sword."

Two soldiers appeared but before they could accost him, Drummond handed Mulgrave his weapon hilt first. Taking it, the general cocked his head to the soldiers who escorted Drummond away.

"I meant what I said Light – I allow no duelling on my staff."

Archie stood quietly, his face impassive. The general's attitude suddenly changed, becoming almost over familiar.

"I wanted to ask you about your magnificent wolfhound. 'Wondered if you'd care to sell him to me? Would the sum of six guineas be acceptable?"

Rarely at a loss for words, it was a second or two before Archie could speak.

"I'm not sure if it would be right to sell him sir. You see he's something of a mascot to Ensign Moon and myself on our travels."

"I'll go ten. That would buy several talismans."

Their conversation was interrupted by the sound of shells exploding near the compound. Soldiers poured out of the garrison and under orders from their NCOs, began forming up.

"If you'll excuse me, sir, perhaps we can discuss this on another occasion. I must attend to my duties."

Saluting, Archie turned to Podric and the two hurried off accompanied by Dog. Mulgrave was left gazing after them.

"Confound this damned siege!"

Entering the stables, Archie and Podric found numerous grooms hard at work saddling horses.

"Captain Light and Ensign Moon."

"Oh yes, sir. General O'Hara's taken your horse. I've another for you and er...the general said something about a quiet mount for the ensign."

"Did he now? How thoughtful of the general."

The grooms continued their work a pace. Archie turned to Podric. "Podric."

Archie kept his voice low. Podric watched one of the stablemen saddle a particularly frisky horse.

"Whether this is real or not, it seems pretty real to me. Given

we're back here at my insistence, I'll understand if you don't participate tonight."

"What do you mean?"

"Not go up there – the heights, Napoleon, you know. It was my
idea to come back. I wanted to do this."

"Yeah – taking me away from Catherine!"

Archie looked at his young friend.

"Youth... Fanciful in their imaginings, aberrant in their crea-
tions..." Podric looked at him blankly. Archie continued.

"Right now, let's leave aside our reality debate. In history –
O'Hara goes to Paris but gets traded – swapped with the enemy. He
says he'd try and get as many royalist allies out as he could but under
the Suppression, the Republicans murder several thousand of their
monarchist countrymen in Toulon."

Podric took hold of Archie's wrist.

"Okay Archie, I've had enough of the history lesson and you
listen to me. I may only be an inexperienced boy in your eyes but
coming from London, making it with the girl of my dreams – you're
right – it didn't feel like a dream! But I'm back here now and there's
no ways I'm not going to see some action."

Podric lifted Archie's wrist.

"If we get separated and have to get out of this world fast..."

Podric moved his own finger over Archie's left radiocarpal joint.

"Use your index finger to activate UAR. Your finger's the cursor.
Move it across the chip and hit 'Exit Game'. Got it?"

"Is that it – no other programming?"

Podric smiled.

"Made it easy for you."

Podric released his business partner's wrist.

"Still don't see how it works. What about our four-legged friend?"

"I've already set his exit. You just concentrate on getting yourself
out."

"Thanks for the vote of confidence."

Podric nodded outside the stables where General Mulgrave was
stroking Dog.

"Anyway, if he did stay behind you know he'd have a good home."

"Your mounts sirs."

A groom led two horses into the yard – a stallion for Archie and a smaller gelding for Podric. Whether it was because he was pumped up in anticipation of imminent action but unlike the previous afternoon, Podric felt calm – stroking his horse's neck and mounting without any trouble.

"Thought you said you hadn't ridden. You don't get into the saddle like that without having been on a horse before."

"School said I'm a quick learner!"

With that, Podric pushed his heels into the animal's flanks, and rode out of the yard with a confidence that wouldn't have shamed a more experienced rider.

*   *   *

Galloping into the hills, the scene that greeted Podric and Archie the night of 9th December 1793 was chaotic. The muddied lanes were full of soldiers trying to deploy themselves along the heights and it wasn't until the first light of dawn that the two Life Guards were able to present themselves to General O'Hara at his forward command post.

"At last."

"We..."

Archie thought better of remonstrating. O'Hara seemed animated.

"We're attacking the 'Convention' battery within the hour. I intend to lead the attack myself. Sergeant Tweeney!"

Two cries of 'Sir!' rang out. Exasperated, O'Hara turned to Don Tweeney.

"Sergeant Don. You'll be under the command of Captain Light. Have C Company at the ready."

"'Sir."

"Sergeant Ralph you're with me. Was there anything else Captain Light?"

Archie looked hard at O'Hara.

"No sir."

O'Hara turned away and busied himself studying a map. Dismissed, Archie and Podric left the tent and walked out across the hill-top where a clearer picture of the battlefield was visible. The French had constructed a series of fortifications that would enable them to fire more accurately on British positions. Remounting and heading off along the ridge to their allocated place in the line, Podric realised that he and Archie were being followed by a hundred or more men. At their head was Sergeant Don Tweeney!

"So, you and your brother are both sergeants then."

"Sir."

"Are you in the Engineers and Sergeant Ralph more in the organising line?"

Sergeant Don eyed Podric.

"You'll be right, sir. I'm with the Artillery and my brother is a quartermaster in Supply."

Podric smiled.

"Do you er, know of us then sir?"

Don Tweeney looked perplexed. Shells and cannon fire began exploding about them.

"Kind of."

Tweeney stared at Podric. Reining in his horse and dismounting, Archie shouted to take cover. Podric slid neatly off his mount.

Over on the right side of the allied lines troops began to advance. General O'Hara could be seen leading, but their pace was slow. Giving his horse to Ensign Moon, Archie issued orders.

"Sergeant. Have the men stand at the ready."

Archie turned to Podric.

"Tether them over the ridge."

Leading the two horses away, Podric set off along the escarpment. Climbing the crest of a hill, musket fire singing about his ears, Podric saw a crude corral below containing stores and boxes of ammunition. Guarded, several men were preparing a gun carriage. Tethering his two mounts to a hitching post, Podric turned and scrambled back up the ridge.

Opening the leather pouch on his bandolier, Podric took out a pair of binoculars. Adjusting focus, he began scanning the horizon. Spotting Archie's section advancing on the French position, his part-

ner's men were moving forward in a crouched position rather than
standing bolt upright.

The French artillery barrage suddenly intensified causing the boy
to dive for cover. Hearing horse's hooves Podric looked round. A pair
of mounts pulling a caisson reared up, the field gun behind them
perilously close to overturning. Bodies of the dead driver and his
assistant lay across the limber's small seat. Podric leaped aboard and
seizing the flying reins, brought the two horses under control.

Other shells dropped nearby as they raced down the hill – wheels
barely touching the rough ground. Getting the excited horses under
some sort of control, Podric managed to swing the field gun round
into position. Sergeant Tweeney and another soldier grabbed the
hauling pin, and released it from the caisson. Feeling their load light-
en, the horses shot forward. Podric let go the reins and jumped from
the driver's seat.

"Thanks Don."

"Experienced ensign aren't yer? If you'd pick up some ammo sir."

Don Tweeney already had the loading pin ready and was lining
up the 9 pounder. Podric took a shell and helped another soldier
insert it into the breach.

"Now, let's see what we can do."

Sighting the barrel at the 'Convention' battery, Tweeney made a
crude elevation adjustment and placed a burning firing stick to the
vent tube. Exuding an enormous roar, the gun recoiled as a brigade
of French cavalry charged out of their fortified position.

Grabbing a musket from a fallen comrade, Podric thrust the
weapon's bayonet this way and that. Barely twenty yards away Archie
felt, rather than saw, a difference in the action across the ridge where
O'Hara was attacking the battery from the other flank. During a
brief lull, he clambered up on a piece of artillery in time to watch
men in blue uniforms swarming around the distant allied position.

A few seconds later the colours fell. A huge cheer went up from
the French as Neapolitan and Piedmontese troops fled the field. Realising the British position was now exposed, Archie spun around.

"Fall back. Fall back Second Company!"

A young soldier carrying the regimental flag was hit by a musket ball and collapsed. Catching the lad in one arm, Sergeant Tweeney thrust the colours into Podric's hands.

"More than your life!"

Podric waved the standard.

"Fall back. Fall back steady and in order!"

Archie's voice was urgent but controlled. The men gradually closed up and began their retreat from the battery.

At Podric's part of the line, the last charge by French chasseurs nearly killed him. Leaping aside from a cavalryman's swinging sabre, Podric stabbed the colours between the legs of the Frenchman's horse throwing the man. Up in a flash, the lancer immediately attacked Podric, who parried the enemy's sword thrusts with his broken staff.

It was the flag that saved him.

Seeing the battalion's colours wavering amidst the swarming French cavalry, Tweeney led a platoon back into the fray. The fighting was fierce and bloody but the French were driven off.

"Where have you been fighting Mr. Moon, sir?"

Sergeant Don was angry.

"You *never* ever use the colours as a weapon – even unto death. They're to be defended."

Podric was so surprised by this outburst, for a moment he stood dumbfounded. Climbing wearily up the slope towards the British lines later that afternoon, he met Archie coming out of the field HQ.

"Our allies are quitting the field. O'Hara's section's surrendered. Your attack on that cavalry troop made enough diversion to slow the enemy down and help keep our men retreating steady. Without that, they would have routed us."

"If the General has surrendered what do we do?"

Archie looked at Podric keenly.

"We *know* what could happen and what we're trying to stop. I thought of attacking tonight. It's not in the history books, but..."

Leaving Archie to his plans, Podric went to assist the wounded. He helped orderlies carry soldiers with ripped arms and shattered limbs into a crude field hospital. It was there he bumped into the indestructible Sergeant Don, pulling a cart with yet more injured sappers from the battlefield.

"Captain's told me about the night attack. I'd try and get a bit of shut-eye if I were you, sir."

Wrapping himself in a blanket and huddling under a gun carriage, Podric drifted into a fitful sleep. When he awoke, several inches of snow lay on the ground and he was grateful for the mug of sweet tea thrust into his hands by a field cook.

Entering the makeshift tent, Podric noticed bags under his partner's eyes. Having sent off a runner with a message to General Mulgrave reporting their position, Archie sat down on a stool.

"He's where we attacked today. I know it. The artillery is much better organised there and that'll be his work. You know what he looks like, don't you?"

"Er, sort of small I think. He was a bit fat in pictures."

"That's how he was later. He wasn't fat when he was young. Right now, he's only twenty-four."

Archie got up and pulled back the tent flap. They stared out through the dimming light at the battery across the valley.

"When we go in, stick with me. I'm going to find him, even if it's the last thing I do..."

"Well it won't be, will it? The last thing you do..."

Archie's eyes had a faraway look.

"I'm going to get him. I'm going to change history."

Podric considered his partner. Although so much younger, he was much more realistic than the older man.

"Archie, I shouldn't be bothering to tell you any more about our life here. We've come here because of a game. We can leave all this when we want. We don't have to be here!"

With great effort, Archie seemed to pull himself together.

"Oh yuh – 'course."

"If we get separated or we need to get out, I've shown you what you've got to do – several times!"

"Sure."

Podric didn't look satisfied but Archie snapped back.

"I know, I know, hit Exit. Okay, you created the damn thing but I do have some computer knowledge!"

"Not much UAR."

Sinking back, Archie sighed.

"Yuh, yuh. Well thanks to your help, I'm sure I'll manage."

"With all you seem to be feeling, I don't think we should look on this as a joke, Archie!"

"You're right Podric, it's deadly serious."

Then as if coming out of some intense reverie Archie turned away and began studying deployment details.

"'Couple of hours before we go, I've got things to do."

Leaving the tent, Podric wondered whether the preoccupation with stopping Napoleon from ever becoming who he was in history hadn't in some way unhinged his partner. Was Archie really serious about killing Napoleon and what would it mean if he did so inside a game? Perhaps he'd just win? But this was more than playing anything, this was living it.

UAR had started out as an adventure – a means of escaping life's humdrum – but it wasn't evolving like Podric had imagined.

Staring at the bleak landscape he suddenly didn't want any more of where he was.

"Looking lost."

Don Tweeney glanced at him.

"If you've got a minute, come with me, sir."

Podric followed Sergeant Don across a track to a stone redoubt. It gave a little shelter from the falling snow.

"Got a feeling about this attack – a strange feeling."

Taking a swig of brandy, Don passed the flagon to Podric who tipped it up and happily swallowed some of the fiery liquid.

"Unreal?"

Sergeant Don shrugged.

"Strange for sure. You're a rum lad."

Podric didn't comment.

"You fought with the Captain before?"

"Ever since I've met him."

"'Coves, the pair of you."

He wiped his mouth.

"Can't work out what's drivin' him."

Checking the muzzle of his firearm, Don Tweeney removed the percussion cap and began cleaning the hammer.

"He thinks he can change history."

Taking another swig, Podric lowered the flask.

"Change what happens in history."

"What rubbish you talk. How's he going to do that?"

"By altering events."

"But what happens tonight hasn't happened yet."

"You said it was strange."

Refitting the components of his weapon, Don held the musket up to what light there was, and studied his handiwork.

"Crazy. Still, at least he's fighting. More than some of them other Rodneys."

*   *   *

Almost from the start, the attack was a disaster. Mounted, Archie led his troops headlong at the 'Convention' battery like a man possessed. Podric rode one of the caisson horses with Don Tweeney astride the other, pulling the limber behind them.

Getting the field gun into position just eighty yards from the enemy, Podric began preparing shot. Readying his gun, Tweeney sighted it and ignited the fuse. The barrel recoiled. Their shot made a breach in the timber wall. The next thing Podric saw was Archie charging through the gap followed by redcoats. The fighting became dense. Attempting to cut his way through smoke and men, Ensign Moon fell among the mass of convulsed soldiers – hacked and hewn legs and torsos flayed at his side.

"That's him! That's him!!!"

Hearing Archie's shout, Podric somehow managed to get up. Moving forward, he pushed bodies away and propelled himself to the forefront of the fighting.

Archie stood in front of an enemy artillery battery that was being directed by a slightly built figure wearing an overlarge cocked hat. Long hair hung loosely around his gaunt face. Although the British were now close to the guns, the figure moved steadily between his cannon, quickly sighting each one and managing things with a cool efficiency. Raising a pistol, Archie lined up on his target. A barrage of firing simultaneously wiped out Podric's view and when the smoke cleared his partner was nowhere to be seen. However, the little French artillery officer was still at his position tending his guns.

Swinging a sabre, Podric ran forwards getting below the enemy's redoubt. He could see Napoleon quite clearly but whilst trying to clamber up between two field pieces, French infantry attacked the boy. Fighting desperately to survive, out of the corner of his eye Podric saw Sergeant Don challenge Napoleon thrusting his bayonet at him. He thought he saw the artilleryman buckle, but Tweeney was overwhelmed and went down. An enemy sharpshooter raised his rifle. Podric lashed out with his sword slashing the man's arm. The attacker screamed away in pain but blue coats were swarming all around him...

From where he lay Podric Moon heard an order being issued. The battery ceased firing and looking up, the young games champion saw the artillery major gaze down at the carnage he'd rent. Turning his body into the earth Podric took his left wrist in his right hand. He couldn't do anything else now. He hoped Archie would get out okay but with his hearing deafened, UAR images began swimming across his half blind eyes. Escaping this bloody ordeal seemed like the only possible thing to do.

Chapter 8

Back Home

It was night time in the lab. Dog lay asleep on the floor and Podric and Archie were sitting at the bench where they had been when entering UAR. Returning to reality consciousness, Podric glanced about, initially unable to absorb his surroundings. Dog stirred; the giant wolfhound also seemed dazed (Podric didn't want to think how UAR would affect an animal's mind). The huge hound got up, walked around in circles before barking loudly to be let out. Going downstairs, Podric opened the side door into the back garden and Dog trotted off.

Taking the lift back up to the den, Podric re-entered Archie's laboratory. Approaching the games creator, it was interesting to see the insensate state. Archie's eyes were closed and he was sitting perfectly still. Wondering if he hadn't managed to activate UAR and leave the battle, Podric studied his partner intently. Archie muttered several times and his eyes fluttered; once, he even cried out. Concerned about his ability to remove himself from Ultimate Alternative Reality, Podric decided to leave Archie for a while. If he didn't return to normal reality reasonably soon, Podric would go back and retrieve his friend. That's what Archie was Podric decided – his friend. People could say what they liked about the man being a surrogate father figure but the moody, irresponsible Archie made that a mockery. Why, there were times in their recent adventures when it was Podric who felt like the parent!

His phone vibrated on the counter. Podric picked it up. He had several messages – a text and voice message from his mum and two texts followed by three voice messages from Catherine. His mother's asked what time he was likely to be home; Catherine's were requests that he call her.

Going through to the den, Podric sat down on the sofa. His mind was in a whirl. He and Archie had gone into UAR and what adventures they had had! Ultimate Alternative Reality already exceeded his wildest dreams.

"Oah...!"

Archie staggered into the room clutching his head.

"Where am I? Nurofen, oh Nurofen!"

"Funny, that was the first thing you said on Gibraltar."

"Wha..?"

Looking around, Archie spied Podric sitting on the sofa.

"Where? Wha-?"

"You're home Archie - in your den and it's 11.30 on Saturday night!"

Archie looked at Podric stupidly, then slumped down in an easy chair opposite him.

"And you've still got a hangover."

"My God... But..."

The sound of the Lighthouse door opening and the lift descending seemed artificially loud to the two UAR adventurers. Moments later it returned and Alannah Brodie stepped out along with Dog. The wolfhound seemed to have recovered his boisterous spirit - charging over to his master who hugged him! This display of affection surprised the housekeeper who was more accustomed to her employer irritatingly dismiss his pet.

"My word - you alright doctor?"

"No, I've got a damned headache!"

Alannah looked at her boss archly but made no comment.

"You must have both been busy. I've been calling on the house phone this last half hour. Your mum said she tried you several times Podric. She just wants to know if you're staying over."

"I'll text her now."

Recovering more quickly than Archie, Podric sent his mother a message.

"You'll be staying then?"

"He will."

It was Archie who replied.

"Sorry to have disturbed you I'm sure."

Sensing she'd interrupted them, Alannah was tart and turned to go.

"Oh, Mr Zaentz is in London and wants you to call him. He says you have his number. Something about a meeting…"

In spite of his head, Archie chuckled.

"Cy Zaentz, huh? Ha-ha…"

"Want me to take your new found canine compadre?"

"He can stay."

Alannah widened her eyes and shrugged.

"Make sure you get some sleep. I tell you, when you two are working, it's like you're lost to the world."

For a little while after the housekeeper had departed neither Archie nor Podric spoke. When their reverie did break, the intrusion was caused by Podric's phone vibrating. It was Barbara replying to her son's text. Arche sighed.

"I've got to go back."

His voice sounded tired but fatalistic.

"No, you don't."

Podric got up, went to the fridge and took a beer.

"Want one?"

"Yeah."

Taking out another, Podric handed it to his partner.

"What happened when you got out?"

"I nearly got him Podric, I nearly got him!"

"You didn't Archie."

"Who says?"

"I do."

"I damned well did – I know I did!"

Archie stood up and began pacing around the room.

"We were storming that Convention redoubt – fighting hand to hand. I was in front of him. I thought I'd shot him but some clod got in the way. I fell and got trampled. When I came to at the bottom of the defile, the French were bayonetting bodies. I didn't fancy getting stabbed so I activated UAR...but I've got to go back."

Pulling the tab on his beer can, Podric had a swig.

"Archie, I'm running out of ways to tell you about UAR. When you're in it, what it is..."

He took another gulp of his beer.

"Although it feels real when we're inside - for the umpteenth time, it's only a computer game."

"I don't care. I want more of it - it's where I want to be."

Archie was passionate.

"But it isn't reality."

"That's rich coming from you. You created the damn thing! Anyway, it is to me. It's as real as I'm standing in front of you now."

Archie allowed himself a chuckle.

"You've done too good a job Podric. You've created an alternative reality and it really is the ultimate."

Standing by the window, Podric enjoyed his drink.

"Archie, I invented UAR as an alternative reality to escape into for adventure, but I didn't want it at a cost of my real life."

"Really? I don't think you're right Podric. I think you wanted to create a dimension which in some way, might connect you with your dad."

Speaking more intimately, Archie leaned forward.

"You told me he was keen on computer games and apart from father son, your being the player you are - it was something that bound you both."

Opening his own beer can, Archie took a swig.

"I've also wondered about our meeting... If it was random, it was an amazing coincidence. I think it was meant."

"Why should it have been? We just met, that's all."

"Ha. You can say what you like and fine, it doesn't matter what your intention was - even subconsciously. But I'm going back because I want to escape where I am right now.."

Gulping down his beer, Archie tossed his empty can in a trash bin. He was heading for the door when Podric spoke.

"Two things. Don't try and go in right now and if you do I'll disable it!"

Podric was strident.

"Nothing will change until you return inside Archie because UAR only activates when you enter it."

"Why should I wait?"

"Because having been in, there are some things I want to finesse – or at least understand more before either of us go again."

"Like?"

"Greater knowledge of how it works. We were actually in *Napoleonic Wars* for two hours, yet our adventures seemed weeks. Obviously, there's game time and real time which I suppose stands to reason."

"So what?"

Podric gave Archie an irritated look.

"It reinforces my point about UAR only being a game. What you think and feel you're experiencing, is only because you're in that state."

He finished his beer.

"You can't re-write history Archie. That's not what UAR is all about – but you can go have adventures. What you say about my dad maybe true. Another dimension to life is why I wanted alternate reality, and that's an okay reason to have it."

"What about anything that's done to us physically? If we get stabbed, wounded or even killed – what would happen?"

"I think one would be stabbed, wounded or killed in a game context just like one kills or destroys an opponent in any game."

"Hmm... I see. But if we were wiped out in that sense, it would presumably give us a problem activating UAR."

"That's one of the things I need take a look at – try and figure out."

Removing the tiny audile membrane from his ear Podric studied it.

"I also want to work on the aural device, syncing it better with the visual chip."

"How long will that take?"

"I don't know. I'll work on it the next few days."

Podric and Archie were close to each other.

"Make sure you do."

"And you make sure you don't go back in without checking with me. Promise?"

Archie was sweating and the look on his face was intense. Podric stuck out his hand. After hesitating, his partner finally accepted it.

"Promise."

*   *   *

The preoccupation Archie had about re-entering UAR bothered Podric. Contacting his mother, he decided he would stay over at the Lighthouse and work on the alternative reality programme after a night's sleep. He also sent a text to Catherine replying to her tentatively romantic messages. Communicating with her energised him and his mind began to race with alternative reality questions and possible solutions.

Finding sleep impossible and unencumbered by Archie's presence, the small hours of Sunday morning found Podric working feverishly writing new codex – data becoming metadata at a rapid rate. A lot of the work questioned his own formulas. This drove Podric to attempt new solutions which were necessary where inaccuracies had thrown out his figures.

By seven o'clock on Sunday night Podric's configuration appeared to be confirmed and he sat back from the bench exhausted. His phone vibrated; it was Amy.

"May we see you traveller?"

Podric smiled to himself. His sister and her particular ways.

"Five."

"Minutes, hours, years or game time?"

"You work it out."

It was actually seven minutes later when he arrived home.

"Darling – you're here. Would you like some supper?"

His mother appeared around the conservatory door removing her gardening gloves.

"Love some mum."

"Spag Bog – your favourite."

Entering the house, she kicked off her flowery-patterned wellies.

"How's the suction business?"

"Right now, going down the proverbial plug hole. Don had a dust up with Ralph a couple of days ago. Very odd."

Podric took a sip from a glass of red wine standing by the hob.

"I like Don."

Barbara smiled.

"Big pal of yours, is he?"

"Sort of. He's a good guy."

"I'm sure he'll be pleased to know you think so."

"He already does."

After supper, Podric went up to his room and wedged his bedroom door shut. Dropping on to his bed, he spooled through Catherine's increasingly suggestive texts. He was about to write a reply but stopped. Instead he put down his mobile, took his left wrist in his right hand and activated UAR.

Becoming more comfortable with the strange optics – *Napoleonic Wars* on Standby appeared at the top of his vision. It was just like a computer games menu. Using his right fingers over the chip, Podric spooled through Options selecting the same detail he had when going to London from *Agamemnon*. Highlighting the year – 1793, instead of Politics, he chose Social Background. There was only one person he was interested in seeing again. The good and great could wait.

Chapter 9

Love Across Time

For several days carts had been transporting equipment to the beautiful park on the far side of London's Mayfair. Unpacking crates, an enormous gantry was constructed. A vast silk sack suspended from it, was vertically held in place by leather straps that hung to the ground. Underneath the giant envelope, a bonfire was built. A wicker basket yet to be connected, had been placed nearby.

This activity aroused considerable interest. By the third day, construction had ceased and the bonfire was lit. Although the weather was bright and cold and the winter air crisp, carriages bringing society from all walks of life converged on the scene. Nobility, politicians, judges and bishops jostled with grocers, hawkers and no doubt villains, for a seat to view the spectacle.

The acting profession was well represented. Brinsley Sheridan and Sarah Siddons with her Kemble brothers arrived meeting Dora Jordan, who was accompanied by her young protégé, Catherine Halliday. As hot air from the bonfire continued to inflate the enormous balloon, viewers gazed in anticipated wonder.

Sitting in her carriage, Dora Jordan greeted Stephen Kemble who walked over to welcome her.

"Stephen!"

The actor/director kissed Dora's outstretched hand.

"Your sister appears in good health."

Seeing her brother in conversation with her rival, Mrs. Siddons gave a slight bow from her carriage.

"The London stage is fortunate indeed to have two of the finest actresses treading its boards."

"You flatter sir."

Kemble eyed Catherine, whose expression was subdued.

"Miss Halliday."

"Sir."

"You are excited by the day's activities."

Catherine sighed. "A bag filling with hot air to take flight, who knows where men might travel next?"

Grasping her meaning, Kemble burst out laughing.

"Well said, Miss Halliday, well said. Bags of hot air – perhaps there's more surrounding the envelope than filling it!"

Dora and Kemble laughed. Catherine managed a smile. Kemble raised his hat and walked away, still chuckling.

"Your wit covers your mood, Catherine. I know how désarroi you've been since the departure of your young matelot, but men coming and going are a woman's fate."

The Duke of Clarence and his royal entourage arrived in several carriages. Although bows and smiles greeted Mrs. Jordan, no intimate acknowledgement was made. A man emerged from a group surrounding the balloon and came over to them. Bareheaded, he made his bow.

"Noting your presence ma'am and recently admiring you on stage, I beg to present myself."

Dora Jordan smiled.

"Shawcross, a colleague of Signor Lunardi."

"The balloon man. A pleasure I'm sure."

"I wonder if you'd do me the honour of allowing me to show you the dirigible and its gondola?"

"Honoured sir, but I'm well satisfied with my position thank you. However, perhaps my young friend would like to avail herself of your kindness?"

Shawcross bowed again and looked at Catherine who did not seem best pleased. Nevertheless, alighting from Mrs. Jordan's carriage, she allowed herself to be led towards the balloon.

Surrounded as it was by an assortment of people, its owner, Vincenzo Lunardi was rhapsodising on the wonders of flight. Shawcross guided Catherine through the throng and stopping a few paces from the basket, began explaining the rudiments of aviation – 'science' 'hot air', 'lift'.

"...the whole rising upwards do you see?"

Gazing at the ridiculously small pannier now attached beneath the giant balloon, Catherine was dubious.

"It looks very dangerous."

"It's the future."

Lying at the bottom of the basket, Podric pushed off some canvas covering him and looked down at himself. He was back wearing his midshipmen's uniform, complete with buckled shoes and stockings. That was good; programming himself precisely would be the only way any recognition was currently possible to anyone profiled in the game.

Sitting up, Podric heard a man talking nearby. Peering through the gondola's wicker slats, he identified his beloved listening to Ian Shawcross! The pilot called away, Catherine looked at the crowd.

"Catherine."

The girl turned and gasped as she saw Podric standing in the basket.

"Podric?"

Dusting tarp residue from his coat, Podric looked up at the vast balloon. Catherine walked over to him.

"What are you doing here?"

"Er...testing something."

"A balloon?!"

Love flooding back, they gazed at each other.

Suddenly, a gust of wind rocked the gigantic capsule, uprooting its pegs and the rope guys it was attached to. The lifting basket snagged Catherine's chemise, and a piece of her garment was caught in the woven willow.

"Hold me."

Disturbed at the gondola pulling her gown, Catherine dropped her parasol and grabbed Podric. Another sudden swirl of air pulled the balloon clear of its anchorage. Clutching his lover, Podric fell backward. Both he and Catherine collapsed on the wicker floor inside. Their first instinct to embrace was interrupted by cries of amazement and concern. Standing, the two looked down at the scene. Floating thirty feet from the ground, desperate attempts were being made to catch the dangling ropes that hung tantalisingly close to flailing fingers. As one, the crowd bellowed and gawped as the balloon took flight.

Inside the basket things weren't quite so romantic. Although all appeared serene from the ground, the gondola bucked around violently. The young people were compelled to grip its sides to avoid falling out. Still, the sight below them was amazing; eighteenth-century London in all its magnificent squalor spread into the distance. Whilst bright, the winter's day was cold and Podric took off his jacket, draping it around Catherine's shivering shoulders.

"I love you Podric. I think you're crazy, but I love you."

The simple way she spoke made Catherine's sentiment all the more powerful. Podric would have told her that he loved her too, but just then the basket gave a particularly violent lurch. Using one of the guys, Podric whipped it around their bodies, tying them to the gondola. Air in the balloon seemed to be sustaining their height – if anything they were climbing – England's capital fast receding beneath them. Scanning the horizon, squally weather could be seen approaching.

"Podric, I'm scared."

Despite giving Catherine his coat, the girl's teeth were chattering; her knuckles were white as she clung to his side. Podric could have admitted he was too, but just said, "It'll be alright. We'll get down okay."

"Okay? What's that?"

Whatever Podric's answer was got lost in the wind.

Clouds gathered and the light faded. The hour that followed was a terrifying experience. They climbed into thick weather then plummeted earthwards with uncontrolled velocity.

The balloon looked as though it would crash into the ground, but for some inexplicable reason levelled off fifty feet above rain-swept fields. Even though the weather was foul, people were working on the land and watched in awe at the crazy sight unfurling above them.

Though there was little to identify their position, Podric believed they'd travelled west from London. He thought he recognised Wendbury church spire with its crooked steeple, well known in the twenty-first century. So near yet so far. The balloon whipped away in a different direction and dropping even lower, only increased their sense of speed.

In and out of consciousness, Catherine was hypothermic. Podric knew that for her to have any chance of survival, they would have to land quickly. He looked down at the ground with increased desperation. The gondola hurtling over a ploughed field, Podric caught sight of a haystack.

"Catherine! Catherine!"

In her distressed state, the girl was barely sensible. Podric slapped her.

"Catherine. You must do as I tell you."

Catherine looked at him with a blank expression.

"I'm going to climb out and I need you to get on my back. You're roped to me so nothing bad can happen. Understand?"

Podric wasn't sure if she absorbed anything he'd said but they had reached a point of no return. Roped to the basket, he somehow managed to get them both over the side. Then, with a firm grip on Catherine, he undid the rope binding them. Nearing the stack, Podric calculated the angles and at the critical moment, let her go.

"I love you!"

The girl tumbled into the haystack. Podric watched as a ploughman ran to her aid. He could only hope Catherine was alright but seconds later another gust caught the balloon rocketing it skywards into clouds and lost from sight forever.

No trace of the balloon was ever found.

*   *   *

Returning to reality in his bedroom at Briony Close, Podric savoured a feeling of extreme well-being. Although he knew he would continue to fine tune his invention, this latest experiment

paved the way to enabling a participant, providing they were programmed, to automatically leave UAR. He could also now con-
firm to Archie that any accident or misadventure experienced
inside the game would only be just that – a *game* accident, a *game*
wound, a *game* death. The physical aspect of their games experiences had bothered Podric but for a different reason – his relationship with Catherine. After all, didn't he *feel* his love for her?
Surely it was as much a sensation (though of a happier kind) as a
rapier wound or even death by misadventure!

Getting up, Podric went over to the laptop on his desk and logging in, made some minor adjustments to the revised exit methodology. Going into UAR this second time, he'd made a big step forward.

*   *   *

Sally Frost had recently decided to get fit. Clad in tracksuit and
trainers, she was out jogging on the tow path running beside the
River Wendle early on Monday morning, and was thinking about
her friendship with Catherine Halliday.

Catherine was Sally's closest friend and their propinquity was
particular. Although overshadowed by Catherine's good looks, Sally
brought a lot to their relationship which had recently been affected by
the arrival of Podric Moon. Initially, Sally felt her position threatened
by his presence and her friend's interest in him, but she was gradually
changing her mind, finding Podric's shy diffidence appealing.

Approaching an intersection, Sally noticed movement in some
bushes ahead. Pausing briefly to check her Apple wrist sports band,
she was about to take the other path when a motorbike came out of
nowhere and roared up behind her. Jumping out of the way, Sally
tripped, winding herself. Skidding, the motorcycle narrowly avoided
the river, but Sally couldn't and tumbled headlong into the water.

The bike roared off.

Panting as she came up for air, a shocked Sally sank beneath the
surface. She wasn't conscious of strong hands grabbing her, hauling
her out of the water and dragging her to the bank. Her lungs partly
filled with water, the same powerful fingers pressed Sally's back and

then pushed her over, rocking her forward and causing her to spew. Lying back, when Sally came to there was no sign of her rescuer.

Arriving at school that morning, Podric was accosted by Miles Willoughby.

"Hear Big Barn's out?"

Miles couldn't hide the worry in his voice. Listening to this news, Podric felt less concerned than might have been expected. Given all his recent UAR adventures, he felt flat and disconnected. Somehow bumping into Norris Widget made him even more so. The Widge picking a giant bogey out of his left nostril reminded Podric that he'd been doing exactly the same thing in eighteenth century UAR!

"When did you last see me Widge?"

Norris rolled the enormous bogey between his fingers.

"Hmm... Friday was it Pod?"

"You don't remember meeting up again anywhere different?"

"What do you mean?"

Podric looked at him.

"Oh, nothing."

Podric began to wander off.

"I did have some weird dream. All over the place, I was - like in another time..."

Satisfied with his nasal excretion, Norris flicked it away. Podric turned back.

"Anything else?"

"It was a bit crazy - things kept flashing by. I was in an old town with smells and stuff. Stank a lot."

The school bell sounded.

"Liked it."

The Widge smiled.

"Got to go Pod - Miss Mullins has me on roster duties and you know what she's like for time. See yer."

Chapter 10

Impossible is not French

Archie, restless at waiting for Podric's report, decided that he must do something. Sleeping badly since they'd got back from their recent adventures, he rose early, showered and dressed. He then did two unusual things – he packed himself a valise and going downstairs, collected Dog. The animal and its master strolled out to his Facel Vega HK 500, then hit the road heading for London.

Checking into his club, he left Dog with the janitor who always spoiled him and going to a room, unpacked his overnight bag. He intended to go by Secorni's offices during the morning and see Cy Zaentz, who he'd heard was in the UK before touching base with Monty Limmerson and perhaps meet Kaliska Monroe.

Thinking about his solicitor's new head of corporate affairs, the games creator reflected how he must ask Podric about profiling her into UAR. Indeed, as he thought about their discussion, Archie conceded that he must consult with his young partner more deeply about Ultimate Alternative Reality and its workings, period. With this in mind, he went down to breakfast.

Returning from his repast, Archie picked up a message from Podric requesting that he go online. The teenage games genie's email outlined the codex strategy Podric had been working on predetermining an individual's exit from the game. Archie replied, enquiring if he was sure it worked and was advised that it had been tested.

So...his young friend had already been in again! When they'd parted Podric had demanded Archie didn't resume any UAR activity unless accompanied. This irritated the games creator. Normally a fiercely independent man, he hated the idea of being reliant on his young partner where UAR was concerned. For his own self esteem, Archie needed to prove to himself that he could manage his alternative reality adventures unassisted.

Deciding it would be preferable to be somewhere quiet – away from people and a place where he wouldn't be bothered, meant for Archie one thing. A call to Mrs. Evans.

Checking out of his club that same morning accompanied by an excited Dog, Archie guided his Facel Vega west, speeding down the M4 towards Bristol, the Severn Bridge and Wales. When married, one of the few genuine pleasures he and Charlotte had enjoyed was their time at Bwthyn Anghysbell. A few miles from Aber Village, the remote cottage was situated in the hills above the Talybont Reservoir in the Brecon Beacons. Completely isolated, its great advantage was its relative proximity to London. A call to the owner, Mrs. Evans had established the place was free for a month. Archie immediately booked it.

Arriving later that day, he took Dog for a walk up Pen y Fan, and returned to discover Mrs. E stocking the fridge with basic provisions. Adding his own fermentedly vintage liquid supplies, Archie closed the door. Making himself comfortable, he considered his upcoming adventures with eager anticipation. He was ready!

*   *   *

Looking down the mountainside at the desolate scene below – the smoke-filled city in the distance, frigates and ships faintly visible on the grey sea behind – a column of dejected allied prisoners made their exhausted way over the scraggy terrain.

A bruised Life Guards captain, his tunic ripped and breeches torn, carried another man on his shoulders. Prodded by a bayonet, Archie Light fell forward and dropped his burden. The French soldier kicked and rolled the other over. Don Tweeney's dead face stared sightlessly back at them.

"Wasting your efforts prisoner. He'll see no more action. Vive la République!"

Spitting at Tweeney, the Frenchman clubbed another struggling survivor and moved on. Archie looked around in despair. All his intentions failed, the intensity of the conflict and his attempt to remove Napoleon before he ever established himself as a major force, had left him empty and exhausted.

"Déplacer ton cul!"

Mounted on a charger, the chasseur interrupted Archie's thoughts.

Getting up, he began to think about the course of events after the siege. Certainly, Bonaparte was promoted and his influence on the army and France rapidly grew, but where had he gone after the evacuation of the city?

Having toiled their way down to its gates, the prisoners entered Toulon through the Porte d'Italie. Stopping in the Boulevard Strasbourg, Archie was vaguely aware of being segregated. He and several other British officers were removed from the column and escorted up the drive to the property that had been the Allied headquarters, but was now taken over by the French.

Led to the rear of the house, Archie and others were pushed down some steps into a fortified dungeon. The door clanged shut behind them and for several seconds Archie could see nothing. His eyes gradually adjusted; the grate under the courtyard allowed a little light into the cell. Finally, a figure emerged from the gloom.

"Heard you'd played the hero Light. Didn't get you very far, did it?" These words of welcome were uttered by Captain Drummond.

"Being confined to quarters is no path to glory. You missed a good battle, Drummond."

"Why you-!"

Despite his situation, Archie smiled.

"I seem to recall I'm your senior by several months and accordingly you can address me as 'sir.'"

Whatever reality he was living in, Archie hadn't lost his provocative touch.

"You-!"

Drummond's remonstration was abruptly cut short by the sound of the door being reopened. Several fusiliers stood guard as French General Jacques François Dugommier entered accompanied by a

British general who Archie recognised as Charles O'Hara.

"Here are your captured officers General. You may select one of them to assist you."

O'Hara moved around the cell looking at each man in turn. On seeing Archie, a glimmer of recognition crossed his face but he continued to walk amongst the men a little longer before turning to Dugommier.

"Captain Light will suit my needs. Thank you, General."

"Sir, I really should..."

Drummond interjected.

"Captain Drummond..?"

Although sounding tired, O'Hara's voice was mild.

"I've been serving on your staff for over six months now."

"Correction. You were serving on General Mulgrave's staff and he confined you to quarters. Anyway, its Captain Light's services that I require."

"But sir, I really must protest!"

O'Hara turned back and cut across his subordinate.

"Captain Drummond. I trust it won't be necessary to remind you that where orders are concerned, the British army takes a very dim view of insubordination. Right now the report that will be written on you is likely to be distinctly unfavourable but don't make it worse for yourself. I advise you therefore to hold your tongue. General."

O'Hara indicated to Dugommier that he was ready to leave. Archie stepped forward to accompany the departing party.

Arriving upstairs O'Hara headed towards his old office and signaled Archie to follow him. Two French soldiers stood guard at the door.

"A gallant attack."

O'Hara kept his voice low.

"A failed one."

"Yes, but at least it was attempted."

"Irrelevant in the scheme of things."

"My dear Light, you mustn't be so hard on yourself."

"Why not? Failure has no friend."

O'Hara didn't have a reply to this and Archie continued.

"What's the situation? Where's General Mulgrave?"

O'Hara gave a snort.

"Departed with Smith's inshore squadron. They're rounding up all our senior allies - especially d'Imbert and the French royalists. There's been talk of taking a few of them to Paris under Dugommier."

"To be tried."

"Surely. But the journey - whether it offers escape or not, these blooded revolutionaries will kill every man, woman and child they can find in the city. I fear the worst. They want a purge - a suppression they call it."

A great howl began outside, temporarily rendering further conversation impossible.

"Ah, he's appeared."

"Your damned dog. Apparently everyone loves the animal. Even Dugommier wants him now. 'Always seems uncontrollable to me."

Dog barked some more.

"Maybe we could use him as a secret weapon?"

Archie was light. O'Hara stared out at the courtyard below. It was several seconds before Archie realised that the general was laughing.

"Given me an idea...do you think you could actually get him under control?"

It was Archie's turn to chuckle.

"Rarely been known but I suppose I could try. What do you have in mind - some kind of canine attack?"

"If your dog can be obedient - show that you're his master, it might give us some leverage."

"You're not serious. My dog?!"

"The world's turned on stranger things Captain Light."

"Hmm - if you say so..."

A knock on the open door and a French subaltern appeared.

"General Dugommier awaits your presence."

Acknowledging, O'Hara nodded curtly.

"Sir, if you intend me for other duties may I suggest you re-instate Captain Drummond?"

"Rum suggestion."

"He's not incapable as a secretary and might be useful."

"Huh."

Collecting a document case, O'Hara crossed the room and picked up a bridle lead hanging from a wall peg.

"Come, Captain, your destiny awaits."

Archie smiled. Still uncertain what the general had in mind, it appeared that Dog was pivotal. Hilarious!

In the Grand State Room, long tables were positioned - a top table with shorter ones running directly off it at either end. Leaders of the Republic including Robespierre the Younger, Antoine Louis Albitte, Paul Barras and Stanislas Fréron along with several generals including Dugommier, presided. Escorted to one of the side tables, O'Hara and Archie sat down beside Baron d'Imbert, General De Lángara and their staffs.

"Very well General O'Hara. You have prepared your surrender documents?"

O'Hara removed several sheets of paper from his case.

"Before discussing the relevant terms, I wonder if I might have a private word with General Dugommier. A personal matter."

O'Hara flicked the leather lead between his fingers and eyed the French general expectantly.

"It is most unorthodox. The matters before this session must be deliberated immediately."

As judge presiding, Robespierre the Younger was petulant. Dog let out an enormous growl outside the chamber.

"That animal!"

Dugommier shifted his weight.

"I think we could adjourn for five minutes."

"No!"

Robespierre was vehement but Dugommier rounded on him.

"I remind civilian members of this sitting, you are only here because of the military's victory."

Other members of the Council of the République never knew exactly what passed between the French and British generals but it was with renewed spirit that both returned to the table. O'Hara having instructed his aide about other duties, Archie was leaving the room when he met Captain Drummond.

"Consigned to the kennels, Captain Light?"

Drummond's smile was false, as was Archie's.

"I've learned a lot about handling dogs since joining this cam-paign Drummond. You've been of great assistance."

It was probably just as well that Drummond didn't know about Archie's role springing him from the dungeon.

Walking through the residency, Archie was amazed how quickly it had become shabby. In just a day or two, the place had a run-down feel, furniture broken and windows smashed.

Approaching a door to the courtyard Archie became aware of voices in an anteroom. Looking around, he saw a French officer lying on a low ottoman, his face drawn with fatigue. A medico was bent over the man's wounded thigh. Removing the field dressing, a nasty gash lay beneath. The man seemed oddly indifferent as the doctor worked to stem the flow of blood. It was with a faintly quizzical look that the patient turned a soldierly eye towards the British captain.

"What are you staring at? Never seen blood before?"

It was Napoleon! Napoleon Bonaparte. Britain's nemesis, the man who was to become France's greatest leader and the man Archie wanted to destroy before he became famous.

Looking at Bonaparte's wound, Archie wondered if he'd been the one who'd inflicted it. He thought about finishing him off now but he had no weapon.

"Staring at a man for more than a few seconds causes paralysis of action. Are you going to help him or kill me?" Speaking in his rough Corsican dialogue, Bonaparte's French made it difficult for Archie to understand.

"Why should I help him? You're the enemy and might bleed to death."

Napoleon laughed and then winced.

"Do that again Hernandez, the job will be over whatever he does."

The doctor turned to Archie.

"Can you Monsieur? If you could hold this strap it would greatly assist."

'What the hell am I doing?' thought Archie. I've come back into this weird game-life to try and kill this man and change history. Now his doctor wants my help! From underneath his pillow, Bonaparte produced a pistol.

"Perhaps this might centre your mind?"

Archie kept tension on the tourniquet as Jean-François Hernandez swiftly worked on Napoleon's leg. His deft hands cleaned the open laceration before applying a lint dressing. The doctor was binding up the wound when Dog began again, his bark more of a snarl.

"I have to go. I've been instructed to take control of the animal."

Bonaparte looked surprised.

"Shoot if you like but those are my instructions. It's why I'm unguarded. I was going to the stables."

"Are you a dog master of some kind?"

Archie laughed. Could he really be talking to Napoleon about Dog?

"He's mine. They're having trouble controlling him."

"Why not kill him?"

"I wouldn't let them."

Archie was surprised at his own utterance. In the past, he'd often felt he'd do anything to be shot of Dog.

"You English – you love animals more than people."

"True – and gardens more than houses."

Hernandez lowered Napoleon's leg on to the divan. Standing by the door, Archie fiddled with the bridle General O'Hara had given him.

"You won't win, you know."

"What are you talking about?"

"The conquest of Europe; we'll defeat you."

"As well as dog loving gardeners, the English are mad."

"Also true. It's our secret weapon."

Without waiting for a response, Archie turned and left. Coming out into the courtyard, he couldn't quite believe the previous few minutes. Dabbling with attempts at changing history obviously wasn't for him. His philosophical thoughts were disrupted by the fearsome sight of Dog leaping through the air only to be throttled by

a choker chain around his neck. The animal was a sorry sight – dirty
and unkempt. That this had happened in such a short space of time
disturbed Archie. French guards backed away from the snarling wolfhound as he tenderly approached his pet.

"Hey hey."

Dog's initial response was to try and get his jaws around his master's throat – an action that brought the old Archie back to life.

"Dog, you damned animal! How dare you?!"

The transformation in Dog couldn't have been more dramatic if
he'd been Saul on the Damascus road. He whimpered and nuzzled
into Archie's crouched legs.

"You poor old bugger. Let's get you cleaned up."

Archie became aware that people nearby – French soldiers no
less – were clapping and shouting with admiration. Looking at them,
he continued to stroke Dog, whispering in his ear as he unclipped
the leash.

"They don't know anything about us do they, huh? They don't
know how we came here and if it's going to be like this, we'd better
get you home."

"You are a dog trainer."

Archie turned to see Napoleon on crutches, hobbling towards
him.

"He's my animal. If I can't control him..."

"You wouldn't be the first owner who couldn't manage his dog.
He's a big specimen. What type?"

"Irish wolfhound."

"Looks as though he could be dangerous; are the Irish dangerous?"

Bonaparte sat down on a bench.

"They're a passionate people – sometimes hot-headed."

"And ill-treated by the English."

Archie stroked Dog.

"What did you mean about conquering Europe?"

Archie took his time before replying.

"A French attempt to dominate the continent."

"We're in the middle of a revolution."

"A country cannot stay in a constant state of upheaval. But France will emerge from it and what better opportunity than this to create a proud nation, a triumphant France."

For all his frailty, Napoleon laughed.

"A philosopher and a dog trainer!"

Feeling strangely calm, Archie saw Captain Drummond emerge from the residence.

"Captain Light. You're requested in the State Room – sir."

Drummond's last word was virtually spat out. Archie stood up. With Dog now quiet, he dusted his uniform and made his way towards the building.

"But captain – how could you be so sure the English will win?

Archie stopped. From where he stood, Toulon's harbour was just visible.

"Soldiers always think land battles will give them ultimate triumph, but we British inhabit an island which has already built itself up as a successful trading nation. That means one thing."

"Yes...?"

"It's there before your eyes."

Not waiting for a response, Archie followed Drummond into the residence. Dog padded along beside him. They entered the State Room; the session was obviously in another recess. A murmur of amazement went around the French contingent at Dog's docility. Detaching himself from the group, O'Hara came over to Archie.

"Well done. Magnificent! Matters are delicately poised – whether any royalists are allowed to leave the city and face trial in the capital."

"Otherwise?"

"They meet a certain fate here."

O'Hara rubbed his eyes.

"If they go to Paris, I'm to travel with them."

"You're to be tried?"

O'Hara smiled.

"They just say that. I'm worth more to them alive than under a guillotine blade. No, I'll be traded. But those of Bourbon persuasion won't be so fortunate. However, the prison guard will be under the command of General Dugommier, who as I explained, is enthralled by your dog – even more so now that he can be controlled."

"It would seem my animal has a unique ability to excite military staff – be they friend or foe."

"Indeed! I can probably organise your immediate release from here but I would count it a great service if you'd accompany the prison party to Paris."

Archie was unable to answer as at that moment Dugommier himself approached.

"It is fantastic – this beautiful animal and your control of him, Captain. I look forward to learning your technique. It's a long road to the capital."

Archie smiled. Dugommier turned to O'Hara.

"We must resume the session."

The British general nodded. Archie bowed to both men, who re-entered the assembly.

Unexpectedly alone, Archie and Dog walked along a broad corridor past several state apartments before arriving at a smaller one. The door was ajar and peering into the room, Archie saw thirty or so people, most of whom were in a languid state. Bewigged and dressed in what had been court attire, the group was now bedraggled. Whilst a few gave off an air of arrogant condescension, the overriding sentience was one of fear.

For several seconds Archie and the group stared at each other. Then a young girl of about fourteen skipped across the room and approached him.

"What a beautiful dog. Is he dangerous?"

Her French was refined and Archie replied in a similar manner.

"He's so dangerous you can stroke him."

Light smiled. The girl put out her hand which Dog began to lick.

"What's your name?"

"I'm the Vicomtesse Louisa d'Angoulac."

"Louisa huh? A pretty name."

Archie bent down.

"That's it, he likes a big pat. Why are you all here?"

"We were brought with the Duchesse. She's a member of the royal family. My mama says we're to go to Paris."

"Louisa!"

A young woman's voice caused Archie to look up – straight into the eyes of his daughter.

Chapter 11

Troubled Realities

At school that day, Podric's mind drifted between listlessness and excitement – indifferent to being at school but elated by his recent adventures. Glancing at Catherine, she seemed preoccupied and receiving a text, Podric noticed she became agitated. Not wishing to intrude, he left her alone and it wasn't till lunchtime they met. For a little while neither of them spoke.

"Sally had an accident this morning running by the river. A motorbike spooked her and she ended up in the water."

"Is she okay?"

Podric was concerned.

"Shaken up. Reckoned she was drowning but someone pulled her out then disappeared. It's freaked her."

"Anything I can do?"

Catherine shrugged.

"Don't think there's anything to do. She's okay – just in shock."

They walked away from the school building, a feeling of restrained tension between them.

"Difficult to get hold of you later on Saturday night."

Podric didn't immediately reply.

"Busy were you..?" She suddenly turned to Podric.

"Did you go into your computer world? You did, didn't you? You've been in – Catherine was intense. Podric looked at her.

"Well say something!"

"Yes. I went in."

"You really did?"

"Yes, I really did!"

"What was it like?"

Catherine was smiling, obviously interested.

"Amazing."

"What did you do?"

"It was in *Napoleonic Wars*. Met Nelson, William Pitt..."

"Wow! Anything else?"

"Some theatre – an actress called Dora Jordan and the Prince of Wales...met you too."

Podric smiled.

"Podric..!"

"You were this young actress working with Dora..."

"An actress? Me?! I can't act to save my life!"

Podric hesitated before replying.

"Do you feel any different?"

"How do you mean?"

"Sense anything? Anything changed..?"

"Between us? Since last Saturday?"

Catherine considered Podric more thoughtfully.

"In your game's world, in *Napoleonic Wars*, did we get to know each other?"

"A bit."

Podric's attempt at being casual sounded hollow to himself.

"How much of a bit?"

Podric shrugged, and assumed nonchalance.

"Some."

"You're lying."

Podric looked embarrassed.

"We had a number, didn't we?"

Podric didn't reply.

"Did we have a number?"

Partly playful, Catherine laughed – but it was brittle.

"A computer games number..."

"But if this world you're creating is so alternatively real..."

She was close to him.

"Podric that's not fair. I thought you were going to tell me if you were going in and I was there."

"I was – would have. It was a bit sudden, the second time."

"You've been in twice?"

"Had to – to check out a problem."

"And I was involved?"

"Uhuh, deliberately."

"What happened?"

"We were in a balloon."

"I hate flying."

"I know."

Podric couldn't help smiling.

"But it was alright. Things worked out okay."

Partly mollified, Catherine became reflective.

"Glad they did. I wonder, do you think your..?"

"UAR. Ultimate Alternative Reality."

"UAR – could help Sally?"

"What do you mean?"

"She doesn't know what happened to her? I thought – maybe with your computer knowledge, you could somehow find stuff out."

"Maybe I can but not with UAR; UAR's an alternative reality inside a game's world."

Catherine looked thoughtful.

"Hmm... Be more useful if you could figure things out in this one."

"Think so?"

"Yeah... Well, maybe not. Just don't do that again – putting me inside without telling me. It's unfair. Promise?"

Only a few days previously Podric had extracted one from Archie but now the boot was on the other foot. He nodded.

"Wouldn't you like to come in if I'm with you?"

"I...don't know Podric. Sometimes I find this life quite challenging enough."

"Which is why I invented UAR."

"To escape."

"Exactly!"

Pulling his sweatshirt, she became coy.

"Maybe I do feel a bit different..."

*   *   *

Archie was staring. The haughty young woman standing beside the Comtesse Louisa could not be his daughter – she simply could not. But she was – the look, bearing, her beauty – Archie was transfixed.

"Are you alright?"

In his trance-like state Archie hadn't realised General O'Hara had walked in.

"I say, Captain Light."

With great difficulty, Archie pulled himself together. Unable to take his eyes off the young woman he was convinced was Cosima, Archie was still in a daze as he and the general left the room.

"You're as white as a sheet man – quite ghostly. We'd better let the doctor have a look at you. Perhaps that last raid on the battery caused some internal injury?"

"No. No – I'm fine."

O'Hara led the way to a small ante-chamber. The general sat down on a window seat, Archie slumped on a nearby bench. When he spoke, his voice had a faraway remoteness.

"What time do we leave?"

"Dawn, but the Council have agreed your parole; you don't have to come."

"I'll be with you."

Archie stared out of the window. O'Hara looked troubled.

"We journey together and will be interned till an exchange is agreed. Although there will be a show trial, I fear the dye is already cast as to the fate awaiting the prisoners."

Outside the residence, wagons, coaches and carriages were loosely formed up. Military impedimenta required for a baggage train would be protected by a company of cavalry.

As Archie stood watching, a group of British sailors marched into the quadrangle under guard. Brought to a halt, the men appeared to have complete disregard for their captors, casually talking to one another, trading tobacco and bits of food. This ill-disciplined behaviour provoked a vigorous response from the French who began firing their carbines in the air. This having little effect, one of the prisoners nonchalantly strolled over to Archie.

"Nice dog."

Archie looked at the young man – no more than a big boy really. The games creator was sure he'd seen him somewhere – some friend of Podric's perhaps. Friend... Friend..? Or was he..?

"He bites."

"Reckon not."

Several French soldiers ran up and were about to manhandle the lad. Dog growled and the caporal dragoons hesitated. Ignoring the French guards, Barney stretched.

"I was thinking – yer know, going to Paris."

The soldiers continued to hover as Dog continued to growl.

"You're gonna need someone to give you a hand, look after the animal."

"Really? I'm not quite sure what services you could provide."

Barney looked down at Dog. Whilst not a 'horse whisperer,' Dog became strangely calm beside him. The guards saw this and drew back.

"I'm good with animals – got a way with 'em. Not birds though; I really don't like birds."

"I'm sure someone will find this information of interest. Where are you lot going?"

Archie nodded at the motley collection of sailors.

"Likely into French ships. That's usually what happens."

"Ah..."

Barney stroked Dog.

"Were I to bother requesting to our captors I require your services attending the convoy in some capacity, what reason do you suggest is offered."

"How about that I dragged you out from under the battery at 'Convention'? But if you don't think that's appropriate, I'm sure you'll come up with something, sir."

Giving Dog a final pat, Barney turned and walked back to his colleagues who were still carrying on in their insubordinate way. For once, Archie was speechless. The youth couldn't have been lying. He owed him his life.

The royalist nobility General O'Hara had negotiated the passage to Paris for were escorted to carriages. Watching the scene, Archie couldn't fail to notice how quickly these people looked pathetic – as though it was only their fancy finery that had given them any grandeur. Able Seaman Sturridge appeared but had the sense to remain silent. He gently stroked his new charge. Speaking quietly Archie said, "I've got a first job for you. I wish to ride in the carriage of that young lady."

He nodded towards Cosima, who stood waiting with the Comtesse Louisa.

"The elder girl – and if you make the smallest inference regarding my intent, I'll ensure that you're pressed into a French ship so fast you'll make the tide!"

"Begging pardon sir, there is none in the Mediterranean – tide that is."

Moving away to carry out the order he'd been given Barney left Archie staring after him.

"Ah Captain of dogs. Your duties take you to the capital." Napoleon appeared. Limping and walking with a cane, he was unable to suppress his excitement.

"And you to take up your new command in Nice."

The recently appointed Brigadier General's eyes narrowed; his face changed from glee to displeasure in a second. Archie laughed.

"The posting isn't a success. Your relationship with Robespierre will cause you to be briefly imprisoned but your star will rise to great heights before it's finally extinguished."

Given his massive ego, even Bonaparte couldn't completely hide a faint look of unease. His chaise and escort arrived.

"Beware hussar. These are dangerous times and your tongue does you no favours."

Napoleon departed. Archie turned to see O'Hara on the steps with Drummond and General Dugommier.

"There you are Light. The General was just asking for you. He's anxious to have a chat. Something to do with your animal no doubt."

Barney appeared.

"Begging pardon sir, I've er...organised your coach."

O'Hara smiled.

"Got yourself a footman, Light. Commendable."

The general moved away. With Dog in tow, Archie followed Barney along a line of carriages.

"I'll ride atop sir along with the Frenchie guard. The hound can come up as well. He'd take up a deal of room otherwise inside."

"You're welcome to him. Dog – up you go!"

They arrived at their carriage. With some handy assistance from Barney, the great animal leaped on the roof causing cries of delight from the Comtesse Louisa.

"Your dog is travelling with us, sir. This makes me very happy!"

The girl was delightful.

"The popularity that animal has. If I ever come back as something else, it'll be him!"

"Safer perhaps."

The speaker was a tired looking man who sat in the corner seat. His careworn face and cadaverously bent torso aged him more than his years.

"I am just happy to have such a beautiful dog with us! He will bring us good luck I think."

Louisa attempted to lean out of the window but at that moment the coach gave a lurch and she fell back.

"I should introduce myself. I am Captain Light of His Britannic Majesty's 4th Life Guards. Currently a prisoner of the Republic, I'm accompanying General O'Hara to Paris."

"To be traded when we arrive."

"To whom do I have the pleasure of addressing?"

The old-before-his-time man turned his tired eyes in Archie's direction.

"My name is for my friends."

He sighed.

"Valois."

Archie knew the ancient title of Valois was used by members of the Bourbon household when travelling incognito.

"Aren't you going to ask who *my* friend is?"

The now oppressive atmosphere couldn't reduce the Comtesse

Louisa's exuberant spirits.

Archie turned to the other young woman who immediately lowered her eyes and looked away. Yet in those few seconds he felt some strange intimacy pass between them.

"Well, as it appears she's suddenly become mute, the lady is the Marquise Badeni of the famous Austrian family currently attached to our royal household as a Lady in Waiting."

'Wow, that was a turn up'. Archie couldn't imagine 'his' Cosima waiting on, or for, anything – be it a lady or anyone else! Archie racked his brains. He knew there was some European family history on his wife's side – French/Italian connections he thought; he might have heard the name Badeni but couldn't be certain of its origin.

The convoy of coaches began trundling through the city, the mood of the growing crowds becoming uglier at each turn of the road. The feeling of violence increased, and orders were given to lower the blinds. Valois hurriedly closed his. Taking the cue, Archie did likewise.

Darkness enveloped them. There were cries and shouts outside. The coach picked up speed, lurching dangerously as it charged along the crowded boulevards. Archie pulled his blind slightly and saw a maddened scene. The blooded mob were lynching their victims mercilessly. Truncated limbs and dismembered bodies hung from pillars lining the route, jeered at by the horde.

Turning back in the half-light, Archie caught the deadened expressions of Valois and the Marquise. A look of serenity on the face of the Comtesse, it was as if all the terror outside was not of the world she inhabited. Shots rang out from the coach roof as the driver whipped up the horses to a pell-mell pace.

The carriage rocked about at a terrifying speed. A loud bang beside Archie caused him to open his blind. Barney was hanging upside down in front of him!

"Beggin' pardon sir – suggest the ladies lie down and er, these could be handy. Cutting up a bit rough up here."

Barney shoved a pair of pistols into Archie's hands and disappeared from view. Quite how they'd been procured the computer man could never find out, but they felt comforting to hold. As if to

reinforce their usefulness, part of the door was shot away by a sharp
shooting marauder. Splinters flew all over the carriage. Lowering his
window, Archie leaned out and fired one of his newly acquired weapons at the revolutionary. Despite the coach's terrifying pace, the man
was trying to grab a rail and swing himself on board. Shot at point
blank range, the frondeur fell back screaming.

They were now at the outskirts of Toulon and thankfully the
mob began to thin. By the time the coach reached the countryside,
all was peaceful. The frightened internees abruptly found themselves
in pastoral tranquillity. The release of tension was palpable, and the
driver brought the horses to a trot. From the sound of laughter above,
entente cordial prevailed.

During the course of their flight the convoy had become separated. A number of carriages hadn't made it out of the city. For those
that had got through, coming over a gentle rise revealed a peaceful
scene. Groomsmen were watering the exhausted horses and Dog instantly leaped from the roof to bound about. Experience of the recent terror actied as a bond. Guards and prisoners alike mixed freely,
relieved at their survival. Able Seaman Sturridge was communicating animatedly with their French coachmen and someone threw a
rope swing over a bower.

Watching the young Comtesse Louisa being gently pushed by
courtiers, her rippling laughter completed the translucent image of
a rural idyll. Captain Light made his way down to the river bank.
Coming upon Valois in intense discussion with the Marquise Badeni, their voices dropped as he passed by. Exhausted by the horrors
of the morning, Archie stared at the water.

"The Duc wants to know why you're accompanying us."

Lost in thought, Archie turned to the marquise.

"I believe he still has a tongue in his head."

Cosima laughed – but it was a dark laugh, a laugh that had seen
too much evil and been touched by fear's hand.

"At the moment but why-."

"Your name is Cosima, isn't it?"

Archie cut in. For the first time the young woman looked surprised.

"How do you know?"

"Do you know me? Do you think we've ever met before?"

"Well...I saw you at the Residence."

"I didn't mean that."

"I... I'm not sure..."

Archie was thoughtful.

"You know you have to escape."

"What do you mean?"

"Just that. Escape."

"You're not serious Captain?"

"Scared?"

"Of escaping? Ha!"

"What then?"

"You are strange. You don't understand."

Archie waited for her to continue.

"I was with the king and queen."

Archie still made no comment.

"They wanted to guillotine me but the Austrian ambassador intervened. I was under house arrest in Versailles."

"Some prison."

"M'sieur, why do you think these people are indifferent as to where they lay their heads? Whether they sleep in a stable or palace is of no consequence to them."

"Historically, I suspect that wasn't the case."

"Of course not!"

Cosima Badeni was hard.

"But when you have lived in fear and terror for weeks – months on end, endured brutality and bloodshed, life changes its perspective. It is not difficult to become detached from one's surroundings."

She stopped speaking and following Archie's gaze, looked across the river at the French countryside.

"The ambassador came to me asking if I would help get some of the court out of Paris. The d'Angoulac family is ennobled to the Kingdom of Two Sicilies. The royal family assisted them escaping under diplomatic protection. All was in secret and the guards let us pass. We got as far as Toulon. Now we are captured."

"And Valois?"

"Several of the royal family took flight. Toulon was seen as a hope."

"But you...you are not obligated to these people."

"There you are mistaken sir. Everything binds me to them. You think I would betray the Comtesse? I would rather die."

Whether she really was his daughter, whether he was experiencing some strange life within a game or actually living in January 1794, this girl and he were related alright. The stubbornness he knew so well reinforced that!

Their conversation at an end, the Marquise took Captain Light's arm and they climbed the slight gradient re-joining the rest of the company. Dog was barking madly at the arrival of generals O'Hara and Dugommier.

"Thank god you made it through. We lost a third of the convoy."

Although tense, O'Hara looked much calmer than his pale aide-de-camp, Captain Drummond. Cosima left Light's side for the Comtesse.

"As you said general, it's a long road to Paris."

Chapter 12

Dual Identity

Friday night was proving a long road to Drinkwell. The school bus had broken down and unencumbered by the responsibility of Amy, who was off school with a cold, Podric decided to get off and walk. Billy was dubious.

"We're supposed to stay on the bus."

"Might be hours yet and the village is only a mile..."

Linklater, buried in his mobile phone ranting at the delay with whoever was coming to their assistance - the boys began trudging down the road.

Podric had been surprised that both Norris Widget and Catherine had even a vague sense of experiencing anything of his recent UAR adventures. They only being profiled, he wondered if somehow, the mind pathway created was affecting their subconscious? Deciding he wouldn't bother questioning Billy about their encounter, his friend surprised him.

"Strange dream the other night - at least I think it was a dream. It was like super intensive - seemed almost real."

"Yeah?"

"We met on an old wooden ship, and were wearing funny clothes - historic stuff."

"Go on."

Podric tried to keep any excitement out of his voice.

"All a bit weird."

"What happened?"

"I was some rookie officer and you appeared with that computer man up the road. It's crazy - you had that great dog of his - charging about all over the ship like a thing possessed it was."

Podric's head was in a spin. He knew it wasn't a dream Billy had had. Although only UAR profiled, the normally latent part of his imagination had been stimulated.

The Johnson's living in a different part of Drinkwell to Podric, Billy turned off the main road.

"When you get home, can you write down everything you remember about what happened – anything, however weird you might think it is?"

"Yeah, reckon I could. You researching dreams then, Pod?"

"In a way."

With the light fading and deep in thought, Podric continued along the road. Approaching Archie's darkened house, he began walking down the drive when he was set upon. His attacker pinned him against the garage wall.

"Moon."

Podric couldn't miss Barney's sinister cadence.

"Not very bright tonight."

"Ha-ha. Very funny. You know if you move, my fingers could paralyse you."

Podric made no sign of concern or fear.

"Out on my Community Service – thought I'd do some, if you get me."

Barney laughed.

"Have a little catch-up – your kindly putting the finger on me."

Looking at his own positioned in Podric's neck, Barney laughed some more before removing his metacarpal weapon.

"What's the matter – cat got your tongue or has all that mucking about in your geeky computer world meant you can't speak?"

Podric looked at him.

"Do you feel anything different, strange?"

"About what? My lovely spell in the Young Offenders Institution – or YOI to us inmates."

"You're right about my being in my computer world – but not mucking about. I've met you there – twice."

"Unimpressed. What did we talk about, ratting?"

"Even in the eighteenth century, you were an aggressive bastard."

"Ha! Pirate, was I?"

"Deckhand, but with subversive tendencies."

"Yeah, right on."

"The kind of guy who drives into a cyclist but pulls a girl out of the river."

Barney whipped around on Podric.

"What do you mean?!"

"Driving into me and fishing Sally out of the water."

"How d'you know I did that?"

"What hit me or save her?"

Barney grabbed Podric, who continued.

"So, I'm right. I didn't know but you being out, I checked you hadn't gone home. There aren't that many people living rough in Wendbury."

"Look, Moon, I don't like you, I've never liked you and I'm never gonna like you – you and your smart-arse technology shit."

Prizing himself from Barney's grip, Podric looked the bully in the eye.

"What I want to get is fusion – now and then."

"And the fact you always speak gobbledygook. Riddles ain't in it."

"Connecting you with your past. Might just do you some good."

"How could you do that?"

In spite of himself, Barney was interested.

"If you want to know, you'd better come with me."

Without looking back, Podric continued down the drive. Bypassing Archie's front door, he headed for the Lighthouse.

*   *   *

The number of monarchist and enemy prisoners had been considerably depleted as a result of the Terrors of Toulon. Whilst there were rumours of other carriages escaping, only seven of the original group now made their way towards the French capital.

The road was unpaved and no more than a lane meandering through pastoral France. The coaching inns varied and, like now, their comfort depended on the quality of the hotelier. Some were pleasant – linen sheets for those who could afford them, and decent food; others were squalid in both their accommodation and fodder.

For several days after their dramatic flight from the city, Archie felt physically and emotionally drained. Sitting in a corner of the carriage, his mind was numbed and his body exhausted. An irritation on his wrist caused him to scratch. Looking down, he studied the tiny scar made by the microchip insertion.

For the first time in what seemed like an age he thought about his partner. What had happened to his young friend? Where was he? Was he still in the twenty-first century? He hadn't shown up here but the games creator decided that Podric's non-appearance wouldn't deter him. This business of whether these people were real wasn't easy to solve. He was convinced Cosima was his daughter or her manifestation, and though she was ambivalent in her recognition of him, Archie knew she felt a connection. He needed to explore that.

"Sir, beggin' yer pardon – can I 'ave a word?"

They were at a wayside inn changing horses. Archie looked around. Barney was bent over Dog.

"Ought to check his coat sir, fleas."

Under the guise of grooming the wolfhound, the officer and his subordinate began their conversation.

"There's somethin' up sir. 'Cos I don't speak the lingo proper, I dunno what it is exactly but there's somethin' afoot or my name ain't Barney Sturridge."

"What especially is arousing your suspicions?"

"Well for a start, our coachmen. We're close like. One speaks a bit of English and I can sort of parlez the vous a little. They all get together of an evening and though I'm not much involved, I've a feeling some of the royal folks are plannin' to make a run for it."

"How would you know that from the drivers?"

"'Cos the toffs can't do it without bribing 'em. Horses – and maybe creatin' a distraction or somethin' when they scarper."

"How many to run?"

"In our carriage, the Duc; in fact, I think he's the leader."

Barney abruptly changed his attitude.

"That's a jigger an' a half sir. The size of that."

He picked a large flea out of Dog's coat.

"Sacre bleu! Vous êtes un grand puce!"

Dugommier was attentive to the two Englishmen's efforts at cleaning Dog's coat. Their work was now interrupted by the announcement that fresh horses were ready and the convoy could continue. Knowing how Dog loved to play, Archie broke into a wolf-hound howl. The animal rose up on his hind legs in a crazy balletic movement. Awed, Dugommier clapped his hands with delight at the trick. Briefly turning his back on the French general, Archie whispered to Barney.

"Find out as much as you can."

*   *   *

Lit by a single anglepoise lamp, Podric and Barney sat in shadows in Archie's lab high up in the Lighthouse. Each had a beer.

"So, what's with this other reality then?"

"Life within a computer game."

"That sounds underwhelming. 'Sort of geeky thing you would do."

Reaching into his pocket, Barney pulled out some tablets.

"So real it feels like it is."

"Yeah? And that's a big deal, is it?"

"Ha. You could say that."

Podric had a swig of beer.

"You go around bullying people for what you think is fun - why? Part of the reason's inadequacy, but part of the reason's you're bored. Why not have adventures that take you out of yourself - another time, another place? More exciting than running people down or fishing them out of rivers."

Taking a couple of tablets, Barney gulped his beer.

"Got a headache?"

"You're enough to give me one, prat."

Podric smiled.

"Why don't we see if I am or not? Scared - or don't you want to try it?"

Barney scoffed and snorted.

"What have you got to lose? What else are you doing tonight?"

"Having another beer."

"Help yourself. You know where they are."

Getting off his stool, Barney headed for the door.

"This better be good Moon or you're meat."

Hearing the television switched on, Podric sat back thinking fast. Having recently solved more elements of UAR, he still wanted further experimentation. Profiling people as he had been, their appearance was random, but his intention to programme Barney would be a major step. It would mean the school bully would be the first person, other than Archie or himself, to enter UAR as a participant (though at this stage Podric wouldn't tell Barney that).

Deciding not to enter with the bully, he tapped a keyboard activating one of the computer screens full of calculus. To programme Barney would require a designated microchip and taking one from the cabinet drawer, Podric began logging its details.

Whilst putting Barney into alternative reality was an impulsive decision, Podric reckoned the school bully would be more useful in a tight corner than many of his friends – Miles, Norris or even Billy. A light went on in the house. Brodie must be home. A second or two later the internal phone rang. Podric picked up the receiver.

"Hello."

"Podric?"

"Hi, Alannah."

"I noticed the tower alarm had been deactivated. You're doing some computer work, I expect."

Podric smiled to himself.

"That's it."

"Don't know whether you knew, but the doctor's going to be away for a while. He's up in Wales and taken Dog with him. Very strange."

Podric's brain was in overdrive. Archie gone to Wales. There could only be one reason. He'd gone into UAR again! Alannah was still talking.

"I'm having a few days off – making a trip home. The house will be locked, but if you're working here you'll only need the Tower. Just make sure it's all secure when you come and go. Give my love to your mum."

Hanging up the house phone, Podric turned back to the bench. The little transponder was already linked to *Napoleonic Wars* and rather than search around trying to find Archie, he'd simply link Barney's entry to that of his partner. Ultimate Alternative Reality should do the rest – or so he hoped. If Barney got 'lost' that was a bridge Podric would have to cross subsequently. That is, if he could be bothered to try and find the thug. Leaving him roaming around in UAR might be an option. It would certainly solve a lot of problems!

Taking a tiny earpiece and the microchip insertion gun, he loaded the little programmed pellet into its chamber.

Walking into the den he looked down at Barney, who lay sprawled on the sofa. A packet of *Eszopclone* sleeping tablets was half out of his pocket – the bully was out to the world.

Not wasting any time, Podric inserted the aural device into Barney's ear and took hold of his left wrist, firing the microchip into it.

Shocked in spasm, the bully half woke from his drugged stupor but Podric's grip on his left wrist was vice-like. Never completely coming to, Barney's body relaxed and he was soon oscitant again.

Relaxing his grip, Podric studied Barney. His state was different to his previous slumber – not trance-like, but insentient. Because he'd been cybernetically encoded into UAR, logic dictated that he would remain in that condition until appropriately released. Given Archie's limited knowledge of the system and the fact that Barney wouldn't know how to deactivate himself, it was inevitable Podric would have to re-enter ultimate alternative reality soon in order to complete his experiment.

*   *   *

Dinner at the inn was a strange, artificial affair with Duc Valois being in especially high spirits. Aware the escape attempt was imminent, the joviality of some of the prisoners was too obvious for

Archie's liking.

The Bourbon prisoners disappeared after supper and with other military men including O'Hara and Dugommier also drifting off, Archie sat alone at the table. Lighting a cigar, he wandered back to his quarters under the watchful eye of the guards.

Opening the door of his room, Archie was astounded to see Barney Sturridge lying on his bed! An agitated Dog sat beside him. The boy was insensate.

Spying a package on top of his portmanteau, Archie opened it. Wrapped inside were several phosphate matches. Certain they weren't there when he went down to supper, the highly combustible fire sticks had to have been planted. Dog slobbering over Barney, the lackey stirred.

"Oh sorry, sir..."

"Unlike you Sturridge, asleep on the job."

Barney sat up shaking his head from side to side.

"Oh, my sight's funny. I'm seeing two different pictures."

Having only been mildly interested in Barney's AWOL nap, Archie was suddenly attentive. Taking Barney's head, he turned it and peered into his ear. Deep inside was a tiny aural implant, its size no more than a miniscule membrane. Checking Sturridge's left wrist, the small mark of the microchip insertion set the games creator thinking. What had Podric said about programming? Archie thought he remembered that coming across profiled characters inside the game was random but this was different. Podric must have deliberately decided Barney should enter *Napoleonic Wars* as a participant which meant that he would be conscious of being in the games world in the same way they were.

Why had Podric done that? What was the point? Perhaps he hadn't told Barney and it was some kind of test? Podric was forever adjusting and finessing his pet creation and maybe putting the bully in like this was part of the process?

"How are your eyes?"

Barney looked at him.

"Alright now. I was just seeing other things as well."

"What sort of other things?"

"I...was half asleep. Can't say really. Figures I think."

Recalling that double vision occurred by keeping the right finger over the left wrist proved beyond doubt that he'd been programmed. Archie found the knowledge of Podric's actions oddly comforting.

"So, this possible escape...have you discovered anything else or does your siesta mean you missed developments?"

"I'm afraid I don't know, sir."

Archie smiled.

"Then you'd better get along and see what's happening. I'll come and find you shortly."

After Barney and Dog had gone, Archie paced around the little room. Whoever had planted the combustibles meant him to use them but it was likely to be a trap. What should he do? Ignore the lure or take the risk? Despite the promise he'd made to himself about helping Cosima, Archie knew whichever reality he was alive in, doing nothing wasn't an option.

Picking up the sailcloth packet, he extinguished the guttering candle and lifted the door latch. Peering into the empty corridor, Archie slipped out of his room and began moving quietly along the passage. He was keyed up for adventure.

Arriving at the rear of the main building, Archie came out into a large deserted courtyard. Gingerly, he began working his way around its perimeter. Pausing at an intersecting track, the silence was unbearable. Peering into the darkness, he could just make out the shape of an old wagon nearby.

Shots rang out. Horses panicked and Archie instinctively dived for the cart. Amidst shouts, hollering and further shooting, he flipped open the pouch and struck one of the matches against a metal wheel rim. The fusée burst brightly into flame.

Throwing it into a hay load, the straw immediately began to burn. Putting his weight to an axle, Archie got the wagon moving. The cart rolled into a shed and smashed into the hostelry wall. There was pandemonium as flames shot up the building – horses, guards and elusive figures galloping away into the night. Ducking into shadows, Archie threw the rest of the phosphate sticks into a barn. It also rapidly caught fire before exploding. The yellow and orange blast dancing before his eyes made for a fine image, perfectly coinciding with a club that descended on his cranium. Archie saw stars.

Chapter 13

A Gaming Bird

Turning into Briony Close, Podric found Catherine's scooter parked in the little drive. Walking into the house, he took a biscuit from a tin on the kitchen counter and went through to the living room. Amy was sitting on the sofa nursing her cold and Catherine was shuffling some playing cards, entertaining her.

"Mon bro. Back in the land of the living."

A wailing started followed by a House of Horrors laugh. Amy checked her mobile and the crazy ringtone ceased.

"Basanti. Hold."

Stirring herself, Amy got up and speaking into her phone, wandered out of the room.

Struggling with his sister's eccentric behaviour, Podric sat down. Finishing a slick card shuffle, Catherine placed the pack on a side table.

"I've decided I do want to go into your UA – whatever it is."

Her grey eyes studied Podric evenly.

"Why the change of heart?"

"Thought I'd like to see what all the fuss was about and what some of these experiences you've been extolling are really like."

Walking over to him, she broke off a bit of the biscuit he was eating and put it in her mouth.

"Isn't that what you wanted – me to be a participant in your alternate world? Or do you doubt my spirit of adventure Podric Moon?"

"I've put Barney in."

"Sturridge the thug? I thought he was already inside – in both senses."

"He's been sleeping rough in Wendbury and I've just programmed him. You know he fished out Sally."

Catherine looked at Podric.

"No, I did not know that. Are you sure?"

Podric nodded.

"Given he deliberately hit you on your bike, that's very strange
behaviour."

"He's a very strange guy which is why I've done it."

"You mean you've inserted him in the game like you are so that
he's a participant – really aware. You're as weird as he is."

"Maybe. I haven't activated him yet but I've got to go back in soon
and some of the things I'll likely come up against – Barney's got the
skills I'll need. What do they say about keeping friends close and
enemy's closer..?"

Podric finished what was left of his biscuit.

"All very melodramatic but what do you mean you've *got* to go
back? I know you've invented your alternative world Podric but it's
not the real one."

"That's not the point. Archie's in there and because he didn't
pay much attention when we created UAR, I'm not happy about him
roaming around in it."

"Where is he now?"

"In the middle of the French Revolution."

Catherine walked to the end of the room and studied a photograph of the Moon family. Sean centre stage, had an arm around
Barbara. His other was around Podric and Amy sat on his lap.

"How does time fit into UAR? I mean it's Monday night for us
but when you were talking about balloon flights and...me that must
have seemed to take a while."

"Days, weeks, months...UAR time doesn't relate to real."

"Kind of time warp then, is it? An out of body experience."

Amy appeared.

"Out of body out of mind – mum left supper. Toad in the black
hole of elastic. She's cool with the cards Poderici. Impress."

Amy walked out again. Podric got up and Catherine came over
to him.

"I'm not coming with you, then."

Podric didn't reply.

"Daft really. I mean you can't actually die or get hurt inside your alternate world and it's not as though you're actually going to take part in a battle, but somehow it feels like it."

"I'm still finding out how UAR works."

"And you want to check on your partner."

"And Dog."

Catherine looked quizzical. Podric smiled.

"His pet Irish wolfhound."

"Is he in UAR as well?"

"Yuh. When we first went into *Napoleonic Wars*, we arrived in a cowshed on Gibraltar. Funny start to it all really. Dog was licking us."

"Sounds like a warm welcome. This is all very weird Podric. Have you seen what someone looks like in the real world when they're in the UAR state?"

"Uhuh. It's different to sleep, more sort of semi-conscious."

"Who did you see?"

"Archie, and now Barney."

"Where is the thug – I mean physically?"

"On the sofa in Archie's den."

"Comfortable then. 'Sure you won't let me come with you?"

The two were close now. A loud call from Amy advising them that the toad was rapidly disappearing down her own hole, broke the mood. Food over desire. Even with young love it could be a difficult choice.

*   *   *

Scorching sunlight pierced Archie's eyes. He painfully became aware that he was strapped to a chair in the inn's front parlour.

Looking down at his body, Archie saw that his clothes were ragged and that he sported a scorched boot on one of his feet. If he felt wretched, he looked worse!

Other people were in the room. The only person Archie recognised was a disconsolate General Dugommier. Archie laughed.

"Where's my dog?"

His face was whipped.

"You don't speak unless I allow! You English - you love dogs more than people."

"And gardens. Yes, yes..."

"You are a dog!"

A coarse-looking man appeared in Archie's vision.

"I recognise you from history. You're one of the two Jacques – either Roux or Hébert."

The man was momentarily taken aback. Archie continued.

"I'm a British soldier. As such, you have no right to treat me this way."

"You are an enemy of France, who has assisted in the escape of royalist scum. You have no rights."

"You should be careful what you say. General Bonaparte may have beaten us at Toulon, but he won't like you mistreating officers – even enemy ones."

The whip lashed out again.

"This Bonaparte is nothing. Just a jumped-up artilleryman. We of the revolution control France now!"

"Think so? You don't control anything. Paris is in turmoil. You shouldn't be guillotining me just yet. Your little Corsican corporal had some information he wants passed to Robespierre."

At this Jacques Roux hesitated.

"What lies are these?"

Through his scarred face, Archie forced a broken smile. Roux approached as if to strike him again. Other people in the room stirred and he held back.

"Take him out – but have him chained in the wagon."

Unshackled from the chair, Archie was dragged outside by two soldiers. He couldn't but notice the havoc his explosion had caused. Barely half the buildings were left and most of those were burned or in ruins.

General O'Hara stood talking quietly to Drummond as Archie was hauled across the yard. Thrown into a crude wain - vertical slats allowed the occupants a restricted view of the world outside. Already full of bedraggled aristocracy, Archie joined their manacled number.

Fainting as the cart moved out, sometime later he was vaguely aware of his brow being wiped.

Opening a swollen eye, Archie looked into those of the Comtesse Louisa.

"You are very brave M'sieur."

"And very stupid."

Turning his head painfully, he saw that the cart was rumbling slowly along a track. Cosima was bent over some other poor wretch helping him drink from a small tin mug.

"The marquise managed to slip her chains; I learned from her."

Louisa smiled weakly but her vivaciousness had gone. Archie tried to move his aching body.

"Make sure you've got them on when the wagon stops."

Hours later when the cart slowed, the girls were struggling to get back into their chains. The rudimentary rear door opened and Archie screamed. Taken aback by the prisoner's delirium tremens, the chasseur knocked him senseless. The few seconds diversion allowed both the Comtesse and Marquise to regain their shackles.

*   *   *

It wasn't until they approached Paris several days later that Archie began to recover. Watching through the slats of the cart, he witnessed the baying Parisian hordes and the unreality of those in captivity. Reflecting on the chasm separating their lives, two people in the existence he was currently experiencing, he cared about. One, he loved. And they were going to die. Soon.

The Temple was all that history supposed it to be - a terrifyingly intimidating citadel, grey and massive. Clattering into the keep, the portcullis gate clanked shut behind them. Moans of desolation cried out from the cart. Most of the older nobles were already too weak to walk properly. Punched and kicked by their guards, the dishevelled aristocrats were herded into the dungeon deep underground.

Pressed into an already overcrowded cell, the welcome that greeted the newcomers was no more than irritated indifference. Stumbling about in the ever-deepening gloom, they tried to find space for themselves.

"Oaf!"

"Who's that?"

"Évreux."

"Son of a whore."

"I know that voice Montbazon. Still shooting your servants?"

Amidst such mutterings, Archie managed to guide the two girls to the side of the vile chamber.

Although she hadn't outwardly reacted to their entrance into prison, the Comtesse Louisa was clearly very tired. Now, despite the disgusting smell, she sank to the floor. Lines of fatigue were visible under Cosima's eyes. The marquise bent over her young charge and made her as comfortable as she could before standing and facing Archie.

"Do you know what fate awaits us?"

"I've a good idea."

"But they must allow a trial."

"You think so? Look around. How many of these people do you believe will walk free? I can you tell you. Of the eighty or so here, less than a dozen."

"Unfortunately, you seem to have confidence in what you say."

Archie didn't immediately reply.

"But you'll be one of the freed."

"How do you know?"

"Because I'm going to see that you escape."

"You know that I won't leave without the Comtesse d'Angoulac and her family."

"I'm not sure that I can achieve that."

"Then the only place I'll be going is with them."

Deciding not to debate the issue further, Archie looked at her.

"For some crazy reason, I'd better track down my dog."

"Goodness sir – at such a time. It's true then, what they say of the English-."

"Yes, yes – obviously we're a cliché the way you continentals carry on. Animals and flowers, that's us!"

PODRIC MOON and the Corsican Tyrant   237

Archie began picking his way towards the iron-grilled gate on the far side of the dungeon. Two guards sat on sentry duty, bored and desultory.

*   *   *

The fact that Podric was supposed to be doing revision work for his exams which allowed him swatting time at home didn't particularly influence his decision to go back into UAR.

The morning after he'd programmed Barney into *Napoleonic Wars*, Podric decided he would go and check on him. He also decided going in from Archie's lab would be best as it would enable him to keep an eye on the bully both in this world or another! Making his final preparations, Podric told Catherine where he would be which she seemed to appreciate. Whilst he didn't know how long he'd be gone, trusting her, Podric gave her the alarm code to the Lighthouse in case of an emergency.

Walking through the village that morning staring up at the vapour trail of a jet high in the sky prompted Podric to think about his dad. Suddenly, a squawking mass of colour appeared above him.

"Come here my beauty. That's Podric. Leave him be!"

Finally brought under control, the macaw drew in its magnificent wings, landing on the village sign. Although not frightened of birds, Podric was guarded.

"Eamon don't mean no harm."

Ivy Bickerstaff sat on a bench seat scratching her chin reflectively.

"How are your computer things coming along?"

Despite being something of an oddity, Ivy was sufficiently clued up about who was doing what in Drinkwell.

"Coming along."

Podric sat down beside her.

"He likes you."

"Yuh?"

"He doesn't like most people."

Podric was about to say that she could have fooled him when Eamon gently lifted off his perch and settled on the bench between them. Podric studied the macaw. Scarlet, his plumage was fantastic and Podric recognised what a beautiful specimen Eamon was.

"He's rare...you know they were hunted down. Always been prized. People 'ud pay a king's ransom for 'em. They were popular in courts of Europe. That French queen – the one who had her head chopped off, she was painted with 'em."

Preoccupied with Eamon's head movement and how the bird appeared to be inviting him to stroke its neck, Podric hadn't been paying much attention to Ivy's chatter. Now he looked round at her.

"You mean hundreds of years ago – in the French Revolution?"

"That's it."

Podric sat up and made an immediate decision. There was no particular logic to it but there and then he decided to profile Ivy and Eamon into UAR. Pulling out his iPhone, he activated it and hitting the camera app, pointed the lens at Ivy.

"Smile."

"Crazy boy. What d'you want my picture for? He's better looking than me."

Responding to her comment, Podric also took one of Eamon, who cocked his head.

"Wants you to capture his best side."

"You better get him an agent."

Turning into Archie's drive, Podric let himself into the Lighthouse. Resetting the alarm before taking the lift to the upper floor, he entered the den. Checking on Barney, Podric went through to the lab. Activating several PCs, he began profiling Ivy Bickerstaff and Eamon's details.

The process Podric used to place his friends inside UAR as games characters was disarmingly simple. Imaging them, he logged their details then entered the information as encodes in the games bitmap using its codex sequence. It had been one of the many things he'd had problems with Archie about. The games creator just couldn't understand the relevance of such a dimension within the project.

Whilst Podric admitted it was an emotive thing – wanting friends in his current life as characters within a computer game – the opportunity to place people you knew in the contemporary world inside a different existence was something that gave UAR another dimension. It was interesting to see how those people reacted in their alternate surroundings.

Walking back to the den, Podric looked out at the countryside surrounding Drinkwell. He wondered what adventures his partner had been in since he'd left him on the Heights of Toulon. Taking a seat in one of Archie's comfortable leather chairs, Podric settled himself. His index finger poised over his wrist, in a few moments time, he'd be able to find out.

*   *   *

Sitting in a large, sparsely furnished room, its view high up in one of the Temple's towers overlooking Paris, Captain Light gazed out over the city. He had been permitted to rejoin General O'Hara at the express wish of the reinstated General Dugommier. Posted to fight in Spain, the general had stipulated the British captain must be allowed to look after his magnificent dog in anticipation of Dugommier's victorious return when he would claim the animal! However, much to the concern of O'Hara, Light had insisted as part of the agreement, that he return to the dungeon at night.

Reluctant to provide any reason for this, Archie only said that he wished to offer comfort to the terrified prisoners – a sentiment O'Hara admired wholeheartedly.

With Dog sitting at his master's heels, the two men watched Madame Guillotine busy at work. Large numbers of the Parisian populace surrounding the evil contraption, a constant stream of victims were led to her razor-sharp blade.

"This Terror – it must be one of the worst crimes in history."

O'Hara was grave.

"What's the situation with the d'Angoulac family?"

"Their trial is set for the day after tomorrow."

"Is the Marquise to be tried with them?"

"It's all of a one I believe sir – if trial it is..?"

A banging outside was followed by the door crashing open. Looking very much the worse for wear, Captain Drummond was pushed into the room by two Citizens of the Republic. Wearing their red Phrygian caps, the revolutionary's attitude was full of arrogant swagger. The first Citizen, who appeared the senior, approached O'Hara.

"So, you are making plans to escape."

O'Hara stared at the Frenchman coldly. The revolutionary laughed.

"If all your soldiers are so cowardly as this piece of shit..." He looked disparagingly at Drummond. "...we'll take the entire continent when we please."

Spitting at Drummond, the man turned to Archie.

"And you being allowed here is to stop immediately. We're to take you to Prosecutor Robespierre who will hear your dispatches from General Bonaparte, after which you're to be sent below where you belong. The crimes you've committed are of such filth you're to be tried with the monarchist scum."

"I protest. You cannot try this man. He's a British officer."

O'Hara was as forceful as he could be.

"He's a spy and an activist. The Council has decided he's forfeited his soldiers' rights. Citizen Roux has decreed it. Come!"

Archie was surprised he hadn't been called before and felt quite calm. General O'Hara obviously believed this was the end.

"I'll see you're freed somehow."

Nodding to O'Hara as he was escorted from the room, Archie couldn't resist a parting comment to Drummond.

"Chin up Bulldog. If not Paris, we'll always have Toulon."

Chapter 14

The Big Escape

L ed ever deeper into the depths of The Temple, Archie realised they were leaving the building. Their route was to take them across Paris via a series of underground catacombs.

The men who had showed such conceit in the tower were now reduced to quiet grumblings as they made their damp way along the subterranean sewer. At times, it narrowed so much that they had to crawl on their hands and knees; at others, the tunnels expanded to hall-like dimensions. Finally, a turn brought them to some spiral steps at the top of which was a door. Opening it, they entered a backstairs corridor that fed into a large chamber.

It was a chaotic scene. Members of the Committee of Public Safety and other Revolutionary Citizens scurried about in all directions flitting between impromptu meetings. Crossing the forum, the two guards stopped in front of a small lobby. One of them knocked on a door which was opened by another guard. The tree men led Archie along a passage to a far entrance and pushed him through it.

"You're to wait here."

The door slammed shut.

Archie's eyes gradually adjusted to the murky darkness. The only light came from a single taper. The room he found himself in appeared to be an empty courthouse.

"I told you I don't give a damn about your bloody alternative reality!"

Archie nearly jumped out of his skin. It was the sound of his own voice!

"Wha..?"

"Archie!"

His name hissed, the voice appeared to come from behind some
brocaded drapes.

"Er...Who's that?"

Archie kept his voice low.

"Don't you know your partner's voice?"

"Where are you?"

"Behind the curtain you idiot!"

"Come out then."

"It's better I don't."

"Why?"

"Come nearer."

Archie moved closer to the heavy curtain.

"Why the secrecy?"

His question met with a derisive snort.

"You're the one who's supposed to have been experiencing the
revolution."

"Okay... How did you do that – my voice?"

"Ever heard of mimicry?"

"Ha! Not bad. And finding me?"

"There have been a few developments."

"Thought so."

Archie peered around the chamber.

"What's with the thug coming in as a participant?"

"Dormant at the moment I trust?"

"Uhuh."

"Figured we might need some help – active assistance at some
point. He's got the sort of talents that could be handy to have around."

"Hmm... So why not appear, oh wise one?

"Ever heard of The Terror?"

"Of course I have."

"Work it out then. I haven't come back as a somebody...I'm the
Supreme Being."

"You've flipped."

"Think so? It has its advantages. Everyone's terrified of everyone
around here. No one sees me...no one is allowed to see me; I'm the
voice of the revolution. Today I speak for Robespierre, tomorrow it

could be Talleyrand. Nobody knows. I can go wherever I want, do as I please."

"Right little Hydra."

"Wha-?"

"Greek stuff. Don't worry – maybe another adventure one day."

"God, keep on the case Archie. Now listen. You and your lot's trial's been brought forward to tomorrow morning."

"How d'you know-?"

"Skip interrupting! They'll be a diversion. Do you remember Ivy Bickerstaff in Drinkwell?"

"Er…"

"The old dear with the macaw."

"The nutter?"

"Well – maybe she's not quite so crazy. Anyway, she's here in Paris now."

"How?"

"I profiled her. Whatever happens, you're to do what she tells you. You'll have some protection but you *must* follow her instructions."

"What about the others I'm with? You know I've found…"

"Cosima. Yes, I know. She'll go with you and the little French countess and her mum and dad."

"Mum and dad? The Duke and Duchess… How?"

"Enough! The guards are coming back."

"What about Robespierre – my report from Bonaparte?"

"The Incorruptible has other concerns."

There was a commotion in the passage.

"One last thing…"

The curtains ruffled slightly.

"Make sure you have Dog with you."

"That animal."

The guards appeared at the court entrance.

"Talking to you yourself prisoner? Guilty as accused!"

The men laughed heartily as they led him away.

A trial always resulted in big crowds at the Convention and this one was no exception. The public jammed the Palais De Justice to witness the junta's quick removal of the aristocracy. Tried and sentenced in minutes, groups of twenty or thirty were condemned at a time. There seemed to be no counsel for prisoners' defence. The accused themselves pathetically attempted to fight their cases. A tyrannical looking man – Antoine Quentin Fouquier-Tinville – sinister in demeanour and possessing the customary revolutionary arrogance – was attorney for the prosecution.

"Because of these crimes against the state, I request...no, demand the accused be pronounced guilty!"

"Condemned. Next!"

Judge Presiding Saint-Just was peremptory in his sentencing and the mournful people were taken roughly from the court. The notary called the next witnesses to take the stand.

"Bring in the Duc and Duchesse d'Angoulac, the Comtesse d'Angoulac, the Marquise Badeni and the man presenting himself as a British soldier but who in fact is an agent spying against the Republic. Vive la République!"

The crowd roared its appreciation. The arrival of these prisoners was somehow different. The French duke and duchess, their daughter and the marquise all entered with dignity. Captain Light of his Britannic Majesty's 4th Life Guards strode in with a positive swagger. Accompanied by his enormous Irish wolfhound, the dog barged court officials who backed off. This allowed the captain a brief moment centrestage.

"The prisoner will stand with the others."

"Citizens, I protest this trial is invalid on the grounds that I am not really here."

Archie's French was not perfect but the crowd got his meaning and looked nonplussed. The judge advocate was unimpressed.

"Get this idiot out of here. He's holding up proceedings."

"But his trial?"

"He'll go with the rest. Just remove him from the court."

The official turned to several attendants.

"Seize the prisoner!"

Officers of the court began to converge on Archie. Sensing his master could be in trouble, Dog let out a mighty roar causing the men to hang back. The Judge Advocate had had enough. "Call the guard!"

The guard attempted to enter but the courtroom already in confusion, now experienced a further interruption in the form of English housekeeper, Ivy Bickerstaff. Her single tooth blackened and her hair awry, a giant macaw sat perched on her shoulder. Ivy's appearance was fantastic and excited the masses. The magnificent bird began to flap its multi-coloured wings. The jostling crowd gave way to the woman as she swept up to Archie.

"You must be the British cap'n. Your dog ready to have some fun?"

"Indeed he is, Mrs. Bickerstaff."

"Right then. Get 'im going and you and 'em follow me."

Ivy nodded towards the dock where the d'Angoulacs and Cosima stood watching the spectacle as enthralled as everyone else.

"Your hound'll be alright. Eamon'll keep an eye on 'im."

Smiling, Archie calmly took a military baton from an open-mouthed sergeant-at-arms. Waving it in front of Dog, he threw it into the crowd. The giant animal barked ferociously and leaped into the throng. With Eamon flying above, chaos erupted. The ensuing pandemonium allowed Archie to attend his fellow accused. The Marquise Badeni was already guiding the Duc, Duchesse and their daughter away from the stand, and the party was able to slip out of the frenzied courthouse.

"English entertainment."

Cosima laughed. Ivy Bickerstaff was nearing the door as other cries and shouts went up.

"The prisoners are escaping; seize them!"

Several smoke bombs exploded causing further bedlam. Outside, a stunned Archie couldn't quite believe what he'd just experienced. Little encouragement was necessary to press the escapees, who scurried after Ivy as fast as their legs could carry them.

The eccentric woman moved through Paris's back streets with surprising speed. The residence Mrs. Bickerstaff took them to was set in its own substantial grounds. Approaching a set of rusted gates, she let out a low whistle. A small side entrance unlatched and they quickly slipped into the overgrown garden. Walking up the drive, much of it was covered with weeds. The property had a run-down look about it.

"T'is how we like it, see. Dilapidated. But when Frenchie's come a snoopin' they get trouble, that's for sure."

Mrs. B's cackling laughter announced her arrival. The front door opened and a man in his forties, nondescript save for a slight stoop, stood aside.

"Mickle, we 'ave visitors."

Ivy turned to Archie.

"'E's 'ead of defence. 'E'd been his lordships' valet but stayin' on, e's good with his hands; fixed up that gate so we could open it from the 'ouse."

Eamon flew out landing on Ivy's shoulder and seconds later, Dog came bounding up to Archie. Ivy laughed.

"I'd 'ave 'ad a florin they'd be 'ere afore us."

Inside, several reception rooms led off what had been a grand hallway. Ivy took the group into one of them. A large drawing room, its furniture was shrouded with white sheets. Standing by a marble fireplace, Podric Moon stood talking to a middle-aged man. As the newcomers entered, the latter bowed and left.

"Ah, Citizen. 'Ere are your guests."

"Thanks, Ivy. Any problems?"

"None we 'adn't thought of. Smoke was good. I'll er...show these..."

She nodded to everyone except Archie.

"Some rooms. 'Spect the wimin 'ud like a rest."

Ivy spoke a patois to the aristocrats who readily agreed to follow her. Podric and Archie were alone.

"You found me then."

"No problem. When out of the game, I did some work to re-enter in synch with another character. Profiled characters like Ivy who don't know us as UAR characters, can be locked down and involved in particular events. Witness recent activities. That man who went out, Braxby – he's Wendover School's caretaker. Few issues there, though his tastes are probably less of a problem for him right now than they will be in the future. Mr. Micklediver who's sorted the defences here, he teaches metalwork."

"So, Cosima is my daughter?"

"As a games character, she's the Marquise Badeni."

Rather than fly off the handle, Archie was thoughtful.

"And the chips now track a programmed participant enabling them to be located at any point precisely... That's good. Why did you programme the thug and not profile him?"

"Another test and...fun. Where is he, by the way?"

"Last time I saw him he was all over the place. You'd just programmed him."

"Thought that might give his loutish brain a few issues. The sooner he starts learning that not everything can be sorted by bully-boy tactics, the better.

"Didn't you want him here for his bully boy tactics?"

"It's a long-term thing."

Archie looked at his young friend.

"Hmm... So, these are the clothes of 'The Supreme Being'? Seems like yarn cloth and twill to me. Boots are alright though."

Podric was wearing a rough shirt and dark breeches with leather calf length boots.

"What's the plan?"

"An immediate challenge will be to thwart the revolutionaries and get the hostages to safety."

"Obviously – and Podric, don't keep telling me it's just a game; It's too damn real. Somehow Cosima's profile has created her as a distant relative. My wife has foreign blood and Badeni is part of the bloodline. How do you account for that – Mr. Ultimate Alternative Reality?!"

Engaging *Napoleonic Wars*, the two creators immersed themselves in its world. Selecting French Revolution and Political Infrastructure, the game requested further criteria – Location, Details of Participants and Political or Military advantages. His eyes flicking out of UAR, Archie sat back.

"'Afraid we're slightly off piste."

"We can reposition via 'Bourbon Royalty'."

Archie sighed.

"You know Podric, I don't really want to play *Wars* like this."

Ever the games player, Podric continued to move his right fingers across his left wrist probing the challenge.

"What do you mean?"

Archie inspected himself. His dragoons uniform looked shabby now.

"I want to go with whatever hand is dealt me inside this reality world."

"What, not activate it like we did with Captain Nelson then moving to London? That was exciting - being inside *NW* and going through different Options."

Archie lay back in his chair.

"That was before I'd really begun to live inside UAR. You know how I feel about the situation we're in. Anyway, you said our next challenge was to get the prisoners out."

Disengaging *Napoleonic Wars* and UAR, Podric blinked, clearing his eyes.

"We will, but like you say, we've got side tracked into this adventure since the Fall of Toulon. *Napoleonic Wars* revolves around Napoleon - *his* battles, *his* strategy, *his* career - making himself emperor, *his* enemies, opposing alliances..."

Podric relaxed.

"I kind of understood how you wanted to stop him when we were still learning about life inside the game, but the whole point of UAR is to give us another mechanism whilst playing. We still want to win - beat Napoleon, but in a form of reality which is unique to us."

Archie stretched. He looked tired.

"I'm just staying with it Podric. I know I was sceptical but for me, UAR has turned into much more than an alternate games world. I feel I'm communicating with my daughter now and reconnecting with my life."

Not quite believing what he'd just heard, Podric looked at his partner who drifted off to sleep. Getting up, UAR's inventor left the room and went into the library where he sat down to think. Archie's desire to use Ultimate Alternative Reality as a replacement life worried him. Podric had invented UAR for adventure but Archie apparently wanted to make it his life which suggested it had taken over his reason for being. That was awry.

The afternoon gloom wore on. Ivy appeared in the doorway.

"Beggin' pardon Podric but your people 'ave been bathed – terrible 'abit – and I was thinkin' of supper. I expect you've been making plans. It er, wouldn't be clever for you to be 'ere too long. There'll be a terrible uproar about the escape."

Archie walked in.

"Have the revolutionaries been here before?"

"Oh lord, yes sir. But they usually stay away 'less they're very suspicious – and I expect them to be *very* suspicious. It's the bird. Someone'll remember 'im from 'ere for sure."

"What about your escaping?"

"Oh, don't worry about us. We're more sorted than you think."

"All your weapons of mass destruction eh, Mrs. Bickerstaff?"

Ivy Bickerstaff looked at Archie blankly.

"He means the defences Mr. Micklediver's devised Ivy."

"Oh them. You ain't seen nothin'. You want to see when Eamon's dive bombin' 'em. That really gets 'em jumpin.'"

Chapter 15

Vaulted Walls

In spite of the day's traumatic escape, dinner that night was surprisingly fun. Though simple, the food was plentiful and the atmosphere convivial. Whilst initially nonplussed about their hosts and how they came to be in the empty British ambassadorial residence, the Duc and Duchesse were glad to be alive and entered into the banter that suffused the table.

The d'Angoulac family had been in almost continuous attendance at the Court of Versailles for a number of years and had run into debt – so much so that the Duc had been forced to sell off most of his property. The king assured him that he would one day reinstate their possessions but his and the queen's subsequent demise rendered the family both homeless and financially impoverished.

"Have you thought of escaping to England?"

Archie looked up, catching his partner's eye. The Duc was thoughtful.

"Would we be welcome in England m'sieur?"

Podric nodded.

"Yes."

"Is it a good country?"

The Comtesse Louisa was beguiling.

"It's better than your being in France right now."

"I hear many who can afford it are escaping there, but we have no money."

The Duc was sombre.

"I think I may have the answer to your difficulties."

Taking a pouch from his leather bag, Podric poured out its contents. Gold Louis coins covered the table. A huge sigh went up from the diners.

"Perhaps this will resolve your difficulties? A little something from the revolution."

Podric separated out some coins.

"Some must assist the settlement of our account here but there will be enough for your needs. It would help you reach England – your family and the marquise."

Looking down at the table, Cosima suddenly got up and left. A minute or two later, Archie followed. He found Cosima in the darkened drawing room staring out at the overgrown garden.

"You feel in a dilemma..?"

Apparently ignoring him, the young woman continued to stare at the unkempt wildness.

"Your home in Austria-."

"What is England like Captain?"

Cosima abruptly cut in. Archie was thoughtful.

"It's not perfect, but then where is?"

He walked over to the window.

"'O England! Little body with a mighty heart. Were all thy children kind and natural!' So says Mister Shakespeare. The English are not always kind or natural, but it's unlikely what's going on here would ever happen there."

Archie took a last look at the bedraggled grounds.

"I don't know when anyone can ever say what a place is like... Is France simply the murderous bloody country it appears to be right now? And your country – mountains, lakes..."

"Home."

Archie closed a shutter.

"Yes. And home is home – good or bad."

Sounds came from the hall and there was a light tap on the door. Ivy Bickerstaff appeared, candle in hand.

"Sir! Mickle says they're a comin'. You've to follow me – quickly now!"

Taking Cosima's arm, Archie led her into the hall where Braxby was already guiding the d'Angoulacs into the cellar. Ivy went over to Podric.

"I'll say goodbye here, Podric. Braxby'll show you a way out of the city alright."

"Thanks, Ivy – and thank you for all your help. 'Couldn't have done it without you, Eamon and friends."

Taking a smaller pouch from his bag, Podric pressed it into her hand.

"Oh, I don't want no money."

"What, not from the revolution?!"

Podric and Mrs. B laughed. The sound of musket fire drew things to a rapid conclusion. Ivy tucked the money into her bodice.

"Just let them try getting hold of that!"

With a cackle of mirth, she turned on her heel and imitating Eamon's squawk, summoned her magnificent bird. Appearing from the depths of the residence, the macaw circled once around his mistress before descending on her shoulder.

"Now my beauty, time to put you to work. A little extra diversion. A few of Mickle's flying firecrackers should do the trick."

Seconds later a trap door banged shut over the escapists heads. A taper flickered into light followed by another. Giving the second one to Podric, the caretaker shuffled to the head of the little group.

"We'll go along underground. Come out on the edge of the city. 'Bout an hour."

With the sounds of shouts and bangs above ringing in their ears, they headed off along subterranean passages.

The hypogealic journey deep below the streets of Paris that night would be an experience that would haunt the party's memories for a long time to come.

In spite of being unfit, the Duc was uncomplaining as was his wife; extraordinarily Dog sensed her collapse and the woman now rode on his back! Whilst quieter than usual, the Comtesse Louisa was stalwart and what little Podric could see of the Marquise Badeni, she also appeared to bear the ordeal with grit. At one point they came to a blockage of fallen mortar. Braxby began clearing it with a steady relentlessness.

"'Aven't been down 'ere a while."

Assisted by Archie and Podric, a few minutes work saw the rubble shifted and the fugitives on their way again.

After what seemed an age - most of the group was sleepwalking by now - the caretaker brought them to an abrupt halt. Podric worked his way past the others to the front.

"Thanks very much Mister Braxby."

"That's alright Podric. You go forward and do as I told you. Come back by the count of sixty or I'll send the others on."

Podric moved forward and rounding a bend in the passage, saw that a grate ahead allowed a little light. Making his way to the end of the tunnel, he counted back several stones and pressed a slab. Nothing happened. He did the same thing again, only this time pushing a stone next to the original one he'd tried. Very slowly the grill slid open. Stepping past it, he entered what appeared to be a crypt - tombs in recesses lining the walls.

The others joining him, explored the macabre chamber. Podric reached up to a lintel, and took down a large rusty key. Fitting it into the lock, the noise seemed terrifyingly loud. Pushing the corroded hinged timbers, the ancient door swung back revealing a vestry. Standing in the empty room, Podric could hear mass being sung in the church. He turned to Archie.

"The only thing to do is lock you in."

"Can't think of anywhere I'd rather be. I love a heavenly choir."

"The way you're all dressed, we wouldn't get to the end of the street."

"What are you going to do?"

"Organise the sort of transport you've become accustomed to."

"Right now my Facel Vegas are just a dream."

"Ha. Had a change of heart? Thought you wanted to settle down in our alternate world."

Looking tense, Archie forced a smile. Podric said.

"If I'm not back in two hours, return to the residence. I'll knock three taps of two. To reopen the grate, push the fourth stone on the left, three up from the floor."

Podric turned to leave. Dog, now free of his aristocratic burden, pushed into him. Archie chuckled.

"Why don't you take him? He'll only get in the way here and

might just be useful. The Frenchies love him."

Podric and Dog left the crypt. Turning the medieval key, Archie locked himself and the remainder of the party inside.

"Well folks – I'm afraid we're in for a slight delay whilst our travel arrangements are finessed. I'm sorry, but this is all I can offer you by way of sustenance." And with that, he took out a flask of brandy.

"You have an odd way of speaking, Captain Light. Some of your phrases are quite bizarre."

Leaving him to sleep on a sarcophagus, the Comtesse Louisa began deciphering Latin 'in memoriam' inscriptions to pass the time. Quickly in slumber, to Archie it seemed only seconds before he was being shaken awake by the vision of his daughter.

"The tapping noise. Come!"

Stumbling towards the ancient door, Archie listened for several seconds."

"That's not the code. We'd better get back to the residence."

An enormous crash threw him to one side. The doorway's timbers splintered in all directions. Through dust and debris, a platoon of Citizens rushed the chamber waving staves and ancient flintlocks.

"Rats in a trap. Let's do 'em 'ere."

A more senior Revolutionary appeared. The man commanded a measure of discipline.

"Cease! Bring them as instructed."

Archie was about to remonstrate but for some reason, refrained. The entrapped group left their morbid hiding place and under guard, trudged into the church.

Outside, two carriages were drawn up in a dimly lit lane. The Duc, Duchesse and the Comtesse Louisa climbed into the rear carriage while Archie and the Marquise Badeni were led to a smaller one in front.

"Why am I to travel in this coach?"

"Orders!"

The Citizen was brutal. Bundled inside, the marquise had no time to protest further as Archie was pushed in after her. Dog began to lick them both ecstatically. Sitting in the shadows on the far seat was the 'Supreme Being' otherwise known as Podric Moon. The coach moved off.

"What happened to knocking?"

"It didn't work out like that."

"I'll say. Couldn't you get the car? I've had enough of seeing France at five miles an hour."

"That's a turnaround from staying here and reconnecting with life."

"Yeah, well – some things... Nice bit of theatre, though a tad 'am dram' for my taste."

"What rubbish do you speak? I must return to the Duc and Duchesse."

"You can later, Cosima."

Although he was the youngest person in the coach Podric was very much in control.

"It's just a precaution in case there are problems."

"That's of no consequence. If there are it is all the more reason I should be with them."

Podric didn't reply. Archie tried to peer round a drawn blind.

"Where are we heading?"

"Officially, Arras."

The partners looked at each other.

"Robespierre came from there, didn't he?

Podric shrugged.

"When I told him I had you all, he said to take you for private interrogation."

"As I recall, he's in trouble – pressure's mounting and other members of the Committee are closing in on him."

Giving up his attempt to look outside, Archie relaxed.

"You know in history he never makes it out of Paris... Not trying to change his outcome, surely?"

Archie was tongue in cheek.

"Only where it affects the game."

"You're both insane."

Cosima was angry.

"Okay, okay... And our unofficial destination?

"Calais' a port now, isn't it?"

"Well it doesn't have RoRo ferries yet, but the mail packet's continued running during the revolution."

He pushed Dog's panting head to one side.

"Passengers though...sometimes they had to be slipped aboard undercover."

Before Podric could reply the carriage swayed dangerously. Shots rang out nearby.

Releasing the window blind, Archie took in the violent view. Flames licked buildings and streets which had been quiet, were now filling with people – panicking, screaming and crying. In spite of the driver cracking his whip, their way gradually slowed.

"If I'm not mistaken, we're shortly going to see whether 'The Incorruptible' has become 'The Tyrant' in which case your position isn't only vulnerable, it's terminal."

With a final lurch, the coach came to a stop.

"Get on the floor – quick!"

Pushing Archie and Cosima down, Podric threw a cloak over them and sat back. He didn't have long to wait. Wrenching open the door, a rough looking gamin – pimple nosed and uncouth, appeared.

"Who goes there?"

Revealing as little of himself as possible, Podric spoke coolly.

"Know nothing, see nothing, hear nothing"

The ruffian paused.

"You hesitate, Citizen."

Podric was pushing his luck. The man brandished a pistol.

"On whose authority do you travel?"

"By order of Citizen Tallien."

"Papers!"

Podric took some documents from inside his shirt.

"Wait here."

Leaving a couple of bedraggled near-do-wells to stand guard, Pimple Nose disappeared towards a barricade. He was intercepted by another Citizen who loomed into view. A felt hat was pulled over his eyes which largely covered his face.

"These aren't completed."

"They give the bearer...I'm instructed to take prisoners out of the city."

"Your destination?"

"Seine-et-Oise."

Felt Hat laughed darkly.

"Wrong road citizen."

An explosion erupted nearby. Several houses collapsed and debris flew in all directions. Some of it landed around the coach and two men were hit. Felt Hat seemed undeterred. Podric dusted himself.

"Tried moving around the city tonight?"

"No, and neither should you be. Guards – seize this man and the coach behind!"

As henchmen advanced towards the carriages, Archie leaped up and pulled out a pair of pistols. Shooting Felt Hat, he turned his other piece on the carriage's driver. The man fell forward and the horses careered into the terrified revolutionaries. Taking advantage of the Citizen's disarray, Archie took control of the lighter chaise they were in, and Podric ran round to the carriage behind.

Grabbing reins and whip, Podric's experience on the battlefield at Toulon now stood him in good stead. Astride the foot rest, he brought the animals under control, driving them forward through the broken barricade.

With all-around an inferno, it was hard to see where the road led. Catching sight of the smaller coach Archie was driving, Podric drove his team after it. Managing to keep his partner in sight for a bit – all of a sudden, he was gone. Peering out in desperation Podric rounded a corner pell-mell, realising too late that the way before him was engulfed in flame. With no time to stop, the carriage plunged through the fire and into oblivion.

Chapter 16

A New Player

Struggling in the depths of the swirling river, Podric experienced a strange twenty-first century sensation of learning to swim. He was a child and in a swimming pool on one of his dad's air bases. An image of his father flashed before him as he looked up at the dark waves above.

Becoming aware of something brushing against his side, Podric finally broke surface pulling a woman's inert body with him. A few seconds later, his feet touched the ground and he crawled onto the muddy banks of the Seine.

Coming to, coughing, and spluttering, Podric looked around to see the Comtesse Louisa bent over the body. Her father stood nearby in a stupor. Getting up, Podric stared along the shore. A filthy piece of clothing hung from a log. Taking a closer look, he recognised it as a frayed red jacket of the 4th Life Guards. Tied with it were ripped remnants of the marquise' shawl. A dogs' collar hung on a post nearby.

The new Duchesse Louisa slowly looked up from her dead mother.

"The other coach…"

"Did you see it go down – where it went?"

Louisa shook her head. She and Podric stared at the river as the last wheel of their conveyance sank into its depths.

"Now she's dead."

Podric murmured "Only in the game perhaps."

Louisa looked at him sharply.

"Life is not a game m'sieur. The vile revolutionaries want to exterminate our very existence."

The young duchess was passionate.

"I have been so many miles with the marquise – the bravest woman I ever knew."

"The captain's gone too – and his dog."

Louisa began to sob. Podric continued quietly.

"We're on the edge of the city. We must find shelter away from it."

As they prepared to depart, Podric went in search of a place to leave the dead duchesse. Finding a coffin-like box in a timber yard on the waterside, the three of them laid her body inside it. The Duc recited a few words in memory of his departed wife, then they joined the thousands of other bedraggled people trying to make their way out of Paris. Struggling through the interminable night, dawn found the exhausted little group collapsed in a derelict barn. Fatigued though they were, they had at least escaped the horrors of the revolution, if only temporarily.

*   *   *

Lying on an old sofa, Archie was inevitably welcomed back into contemporary Wales by Dog slobbering all over him. The computer man aggressively remonstrating with his animal only sent the hound into paroxysms of adoration. This resulted in him being put outside.

Padding about the cottage, Archie took a shower then lit the log burner. He readmitted Dog and fed him his dinner, before sitting down to make some notes on his adventures. Pausing over his journal, Archie reached for his mobile phone. Activating it, he viewed several messages. One was from Alannah advising him of her vacation and a couple were from Kaliska requesting he call her.

Checking his watch, Archie saw that it was Tuesday. Something he hadn't got used to was the time differential, adventures in UAR having no bearing on real hours and days. Gazing at the Welsh mountains, Archie decided that before contacting his solicitor's office, the person he most wanted to connect with was his daughter.

*   *   *

Inside UAR, Podric awoke to discover himself looking up the barrel of an ancient flintlock pistol! Brandished by Barney Sturridge, the school bully was clad in a striped shirt, sawn off British sailor trousers, and sported the cockade hat of the revolution.

"Oh God. Where have you come from?"

"What's it to you?"

Feeling tired in spite of his slumber, Podric pushed the barrel away.

"Frankly, nothing."

Podric got up and stretched.

"I was with the Cap'n and that great dog of his along with the French toffs after we got kicked out of Toulon."

Barney seemed sulky rather than threatening.

"You didn't make the trial though."

"Been a bit dazed, strange."

"No change there, then."

Looking round the barn, Podric scratched himself and ran his fingers through his tousled hair.

"Where are the Duc and his daughter?"

"Why do you want to know?"

"Oh, for God's sake! Is your auto reflex always so negative?"

Podric was angry.

"Up the road in a tavern. Right state they are about the other girl disappearin'. More upset than losing his old woman. Daft bugger."

"Why? He's old and scared, she's young and vulnerable."

"Got a note from her, haven't I."

"What do you mean, you've got a note? From whom?"

Barney pulled out a screwed-up envelope and handed it to Podric who quickly read it.

"She's in England."

"So?"

Podric began pacing about. Archie's knowledge of UAR must have been sufficient to move Cosima around inside the game before leaving it himself with Dog. This showed that his partner had learned a bit more about UAR's methodology.

"Last time I saw you, you were face down in the dirt."

Barney looked at Podric quizzically.

"Toulon. The evacuation. You'd been set on by some Spanish sailors."

Barney scowled.

"Bloody scum."

"You said much the same then."

Podric abruptly took hold of Barney's arm.

"Hoy! What yer doin'?"

"Has this irritated you?"

Several scratch marks around the pellet's insertion suggested that it had. Podric grabbed Barney's other hand, and pressed the bully's fingers onto his wrist. Holding them there for several seconds activated the chip.

"Wha-?"

Barney rocked back, his eyes blinking rapidly. Putting up his hands, he shook his head as if trying to clear his vision.

"Sit down."

Podric was authoritative. Barney did as instructed, and sat down on a bale of straw.

"Don't try and look around your eyes. The detail in your peripheral vision is alternative reality information and having been programmed, you'll now be aware of who you are in this games world and the adventures you experience. It's a privilege but there's no need to thank me."

It took several seconds for Barney to engage in the milieu Podric had put him in - but he didn't understand it.

"You'll get used to it - maybe."

Barney's eyes still caused him problems. He looked down at his eccentric attire and the rustic surroundings.

"What? What have you done to me? Where am I?"

"You're in a computer game called *Napoleonic Wars* because of something I've developed which I told you about at Drinkwell. In the game, we're escaping from revolutionaries who are busy murdering anyone they can find who they think disagrees with them, in Paris. The year is 1794 and the revolution's in full swing. You have heard of the French Revolution, have you, Sturridge?"

Barney scowled.

"All bollocks."

"In what sense – the French Revolution or your being in it?"

"Dah. I'm going to smash you!"

Podric laughed.

"That's more like it. But it's not me you're going to bully. I want to see how you perform against some of the eighteenth-century thugs we're up against. Our challenge now is to get the Duc and his daughter out of France."

Barney shook his head and flicked his eyes as if still trying to clear them.

"I'll get rid of that for you – unless you'd like to know more about UAR."

Barney stared belligerently at Podric.

"Guess not then."

Taking Sturridge's wrist, he used the index finger of Barney's other hand to depress the area over the microchip. UAR's optical imagery disengaged.

"If you ever want to know where you are, do that twice and the information will reappear. I'll have to teach you how to operate it more and move around in the game sometime."

Barney seemed stultified by the recent experience. What Podric didn't tell him was that three longer depressions followed by two short ones would remove him from his game existence completely. For some reason the young co-inventor of Ultimate Alternative Reality thought this knowledge would be best kept to himself.

Walking up the muddy track towards the tavern Barney said. "I hate you Moon. The next time I take you out, I'll make sure I do a better job of it."

"You definitely suffer from repetition, Barney."

Podric stopped.

"But I should advise you – try it now and you're stuck here. A real person locked inside a computer game. Rather than experiencing the adventures of a lifetime, you'd be stranded in a nightmare of eternity. Think about that before you pull the trigger, bully Barney."

*   *   *

The tavern was a lowly affair – poor and filthy. Its interior dirty, the floor was strewn with dung and straw. The proprietors – a slothful man and his severe, narrow-eyed wife – presided mistrustfully over their penurious customers. A contradictory character, Barney touched Podric's arm and strode over to the plank that served as a counter.

"The old man and the girl I sent up here. Where are they?"

Barney's lingua franca was crude but from the way the innkeeper's eyes darted about, Podric knew he understood sufficiently well.

"What are they to you?"

It was the woman who spoke – her voice thin and weaselly.

Barney's answer was a deft move pulling out two flintlocks. The landlord twitched, but the woman didn't flinch.

"You're a fool. You're covered from every quarter."

Eyeing the habitué's, Podric saw sullen eyes furtively watching proceedings. Barney was breezy.

"Won't stop you two from going, will it?"

"You're our enemy – an enemy of the revolution!"

The woman was venomous, and spat out her words.

A gun went off and it wasn't Barney's. Turning, Podric saw a Citizen crumple to the floor. Knife in hand, he was poised to throw it at Sturridge's back. The Duchesse Louisa appeared from the shadows. White-faced, she clutched a small pistol. Smoke drifted from its barrel.

Speaking his strange argot, Barney moved back slightly.

"Alright, you lot. Allez vites!"

A dozen of the proles got the message and began shuffling towards the door. The proprietor made a move for something underneath the bar.

"Whoa. Leave it sunshine!"

Barney's pistol waved at the inn keeper.

"You can serve us some drinks – wine and a brandy for the gir... young lady."

The man looked at his wife, who gave a barely perceptible nod.

Her husband sullenly went about his permitted task, placing the alcohol on the bar. Barney took the brandy and gave it to Louisa who
still clutched her little handgun.

"I've carried it for two years."

Pouring himself some wine, Barney took a big gulp.

"Amazed it worked love. Still, good shooting."

Looking pale, Louisa sipped her liquor. Podric came over to her.

"May I take wine to papa?"

"Where is your father?"

"Outside in the stable. It wasn't safe in here."

Picking up a jug and mug, Podric began leading her from the inn.
Looking at the proprietress, Barney reached over the counter and
removed the blunderbuss from underneath it.

"We'll shortly be on our way. Try anything and I'll torch the
joint."

The woman's hard gaze met Barney's unblinkingly.

"Guess you're not really getting it."

He fired the big bored gun at the wall behind the bar. Bottles
shattered and lath and plaster covered the man and woman. The
Wendover school bully grinned.

"Have a nice day."

Outside, the Duc was propped against a crude shed tended by
his daughter and Podric. Looking about, Barney was alert.

"We'd better move. The bloke's a load of piss but the dame's
likely to cut up trouble."

An old cart stood to one side of the stables and inside, an equally
old nag. Podric spied one of the down-at-heel drinkers being berated
by a harridan.

"Horse man, are you?"

The dishevelled peasant looked up. Podric slipped a silver Louis
into his hand. The man gawped at it for several seconds.

"Hitch the nag to the wagon and there's another."

The woman continued to harass the imbiber who took a swipe at
her and entered the stable. The termagant's decibels reached screech-
ing levels. Barney swung a pistol in her direction and fired just above
her head. Yokes and tackle went flying. Dishevelled-man not turning

a hair, continued his task of harnessing the horse. Lifting the Duc gently on to the back of the wagon, Louisa sat beside her father. Podric tossed the man a second coin and clambered onto the driver's seat. With Barney alongside, the cart rolled out into the yard and set off down the lane.

A new remonstrance began as the Madame Defarge proprietress tried to galvanise her lethargic men. This was thwarted by the unkempt hostler who picked up a besom, lit it and quietly set fire to the place, burning it to the ground.

Chapter 17

Making it Right

If there was anything the honourable Charlotte McCorquodale missed from her marriage to Archie Light, it was their time in Wales. During a rare moment of simpatico early in their relationship, they had discovered the cottage set at the eastern end of the Brecon Beacons with its view of the Talybont Reservoir.

Charlotte quickly realised that she'd made a mistake marrying her self-made engineering scientist beau, who evolved into a creator of what she considered the lightweight business of computer games – highly lucrative though they were. But Bwthyn Anghsbell was somewhere they both loved and kept returning to even when things got tough between them. Such was the impression the place made, they had spent their last long weekend together at the cottage before parting.

Charlotte being largely to blame for their marital failure and her determination to separate from her husband, Archie had asked they stay a couple that final trip and for that he had her grudging respect. Now, as her Land Cruiser turned off the motorway and headed up the valley into Powys, these memories came flooding back. Her daughter yawned, stretched her long legs, and gazed out of the window.

"Bloody Wales."

"You wanted it."

"Bleak as shit."

Cosima's stay with her mother had been a disaster. Apart from having a negative effect on Charlotte's relationship with her Columbian diplomat boyfriend, her daughter's surly behaviour made for an unbearable atmosphere. Consistently rowing with her mother, Archie's surprise call had resulted in Cosima declaring she'd be 'better off with dad'. Taking her at her word, Charlotte responded.

"Okay then, to Aber we will go."

Advising Archie on the course of action, her husband also astonished Charlotte by accepting, even encouraging the decision. The girl thumped the door panel.

"What am I going to do here?"

"Don't ask me. You were up for coming."

"That was just to get away from you."

Charlotte laughed at her daughter's conceit.

"Well, you'll have achieved that if nothing else."

Charlotte concentrated on the winding road.

"Get out and take some exercise. The country's wild and you can take Dog for a walk."

"Oh God no – Dog! He's not there, is he?"

"I'd be surprised if he wasn't. For all your father's denial, he's got something going with that animal. In fact, as I recall the more he berates him, the more slobbering Dog gets."

*   *   *

The wagon lurched along the bumpy lanes of northern France. Preferring to drive, Barney had the reins. There was little he could do with the withered cob other than gently encourage its stumbling pace. Podric sat on the back with the Duc and his daughter. Having made the old man as comfortable as they could, Podric and Louisa watched the countryside slowly pass by.

"Where are we going?"

"Calais."

The young duchess looked at Podric.

"The port?"

Podric nodded.

"It's not safe for you to stay in France. Besides, there's someone in England you'll want to see."

Pulling out Cosima's crumpled note, he handed it to Louisa. Opening the stained envelope, the girl began to read and seconds later, let out a squeal of delight.

"She escaped. This is wonderful! But how did she do this?"

Podric shrugged.

"Does it matter? We must get you and your father to safety there as quickly as possible."

With their present pace of travel, the irony of his words wasn't lost on Podric.

"You are very kind to us m'sieur."

Louisa folded Cosima's letter.

"Do you have a plan?"

"Yes. No. Maybe."

Podric smiled.

"I'll be happier the more distance we put between us and Paris."

The Duchesse Louisa looked thoughtful.

"Perhaps..?"

Podric looked at her.

"This part of France is famous for its ancient monasteries. The friars and novices are known to be very independent."

For all her graces, the young duchess could be beguiling.

"And we have money."

Louisa's manner was coquettish.

"A donation to an abbaye is always welcome."

*   *   *

Supper at Bwthyn Anghsbell was a strange affair. Although Char-lotte had initially stated that she would head off after a coffee, one thing led to another and having had a glass of wine, it seemed better to stay. José was abroad with some trade delegation and there was nothing in town to hurry back for.

After what appeared to be a perfunctory greeting with her father, Cosima elected to take a shower. Sitting in the living room, a peat fire blazing and Dog snoring beside it, Archie and Charlotte got a bottle of red wine on the go. They looked like the ideal couple.

"So, what have you been up to my fine bucko?"

Archie studied his wife. She could be flirtatious with anyone –

even him.

"You wouldn't believe me if I told you."

"Probably not. Try me."

Looking over the rim of her wine glass, she eyed Archie who kicked Dog in an attempt to stop his noisy ululations.

"'Few months ago, a young lad arrived at Drinkwell. He'd piled off his bike and was brought to the house."

"The Irish leprechaun must have loved that. Blood all over her kitchen."

"Brodie discovered Podric was a computer games player of some ability. It was she who pushed me to meet him."

"Must have been a Paddy thing then if he's called Podric."

Charlotte had some more wine.

"Why did you agree?"

Archie put another peat block on the fire.

"Things haven't been so bright lately."

"What, your creative genius in that deeply intellectual field of light entertainment's not on the wane, surely?"

"I'd forgotten how catty you can be."

"Meow."

She laughed. Archie smiled.

"The kid and I created a game and it's taken off."

"Wünderbar. I'll worry no more and Cosima's sorted."

Archie's face darkened.

"No, Charlotte. That's not the way it will be."

"Really? Life can be a bitch, but it's a bigger bitch without the dollar."

"That's hard earned – and something which long overdue, I intend our daughter discovers."

"Good luck with that one m'lord. Her silver spoon's been in a while. To pull it out now and have her face reality will be some task."

"You know Lady M you never said a truer word. Reality's the thing, but in creating alternative reality I might just have found the answer."

A little lost at this, Charlotte shrugged.

"You always were a quirky bastard Archie, which when I was in the naivety of youth, had some appeal."

"Glad you thought so."

Archie uncorked another bottle of wine. There was something in his manner – an unfeigned confidence, that surprised Charlotte. This was an Archie she didn't know.

"That's an assertive little vintage. I trust you've cooked up some culinary delights to match?"

"Boeuf bourguignon – as I recall, a favourite of yours."

*   *   *

Giving a determined company of Citizen soldiers the slip, Podric, Barney and father and daughter d'Angoulac heeded the young duchess's advice, finding shelter at the Abbaye of St. Pierre.

Podric proffering his revolutionary funds on their arrival pro-duced a particular luminescence. Tossing the money casually on to the table, the glitter in the prior's eyes matched the cascade of golden Louis coins.

Awarding the abbey the largest private endowment it had ever re-ceived – whether it was because of the prior's Christian consideration towards the fugitives or the result of such charitable generosity by them – plans rapidly got underway for the party's continued journey towards the coast. This time it would be with the Order's protection. "The Convention doesn't like the church. It feels threatened by it. A little divine assistance can but surely help you on your way." The abbot positively gushed his support for them.

A pilgrimage was organised to the neighbouring monastery at St. Omer. A procession of monks, complete with a covered supply wag-on, made ready for the morning. Inspecting the conveyance, Barney and Podric were particularly interested in a little secret compartment in the wagon. At a squeeze, it was capable of hiding two people. The ways of the church were undoubtedly deep and inscrutable.

*   *   *

The Welsh weather was for once clear and bright.

Stepping out of the cottage, Archie and Charlotte walked towards her Land Cruiser. Dog ran about in front of them.

"Quite like old times."

"Quite."

Charlotte laughed.

"You know I rather envy you."

Archie feigned surprise.

"I always loved this place.

"I know."

"Do you ever wonder about us?"

"No."

Charlotte laughed some more.

"Liar."

"How long are you staying?"

"Don't know right now. A while maybe."

Charlotte looked at her husband.

"There's a change in you Archie Light, something I can't quite fathom."

"Bugs you, does it?"

"No. It's rather attractive."

"I am 'rather attractive'."

"You're an unmitigated, difficult bastard and well you know it."

"And rather attractive."

Charlotte laughed.

"Mistake One for this morning. Don't tell your estranged husband you fancy him."

"You'll get over it."

Cosima appeared wrapped up for a walk. Mother and daughter seemed awkward, their hug perfunctory.

"Bye ma."

For a second Charlotte choked up.

"Love you."

They hugged again, this time for longer. Lightening her mood, Charlotte turned to Archie.

"As for you..." She didn't approach him but swung into her jeep. Father, daughter and Dog watched the Land Cruiser move down the winding track towards the road. After a while, Archie spoke.

"How are you feeling?"

If he'd asked his daughter the same question a few weeks ago he would have received a surly response. Now, turning to look at him as they got ready to set off, she was thoughtful. Cosima was a lovely girl and Archie loved her dearly.

"I don't know...different somehow."

Smiling, Archie adjusted his Barbour.

"What are you laughing at?"

"If I told you what I believe has happened, you wouldn't trust me."

"Try me."

"Come on then."

Walking up the hillside path, Archie began to relate the fantastic tale of UAR – the alternative reality state that he now believed had a subconscious effect on a person in reality even if they were only profiled into a game, and how he had deliberately freed himself from *Napoleonic Wars*.

"I didn't have to with you because of that, but then I re-set you or Marquise Badeni to be in England in 1794. Right now, Podric will be bringing these French aristos out of France to safety unless he decides to get out of the game himself, but I rather doubt he will. I think he wants to experience the adventure for what it is. He's in there with his Wendover school bully, who for reasons best known to himself, he's programmed into it."

Surprisingly, Cosima didn't scoff her father's words out of existence.

"So a person profiled is only subconsciously aware of the experiences they have in that state, but a programmed person is fully."

"Bingo."

"In that case pa, I want to go back in – programmed."

Climbing over a fence, Archie took in the view.

"For that my dear, you'll have to wait. Although I managed to get myself out having paid just enough attention to my junior parner's instructions, I need a further briefing from him to be able to programme you."

"You mean you have to rely on master Podric? That's not like you Dr. Light, mister control freak."

Archie straightened a piece of dry stone wall.

"I didn't believe Podric at first. I thought all his UAR stuff was mumbo jumbo, schoolboy nonsense."

Archie continued his wall building, and gathered up several slates lying in the field.

"He couldn't have created anything inside a computer game without me and he knows it. He didn't have the algorithmic abilities, but he's got incredible games skills and an astounding imagination. I *wouldn't* have created UAR without him – the feeling of living in other worlds and the fantastic adventures."

"But you don't actually move matter – you stay where you are."

"Why I came here; there's no one around and I knew I'd be alone."

"It's all in the mind then."

"Isn't so much of life?"

Chapter 18

Lies & Secrets

The following morning the d'Angoulacs, Podric and Barney joined the monks on their pilgrimage. About twenty men made up the party. The two boys clad in habits, had their hoods up against the weather. The Duc and his daughter sat inside the wagon with two friars, one of whom drove the oxen. Prior Boniface rode a donkey, his presence amidst his brothers, pious and dignified.

Leaving the monastery by a small lane, their route climbed away on a track that bypassed Arras, and cut cross country towards St. Omer. However, although their journey was remote, a troop of a dozen Citizen cavalry caught up with the clerics.

"You would challenge pilgrims of the church?"

"We're looking for escaped enemies of the state."

"Then go and find them."

Prior Boniface was derisive.

"What's the name of your abbey?"

The prior ignored the question. The Citizen captain rode up alongside him menacingly.

"I demand you identify yourself."

"You can demand all you like. Whether I deign to oblige you is another matter."

"What do you carry in the wagon?"

Boniface looked at the officer as if he was a retarded minnow. The captain called out to his men.

"Search it."

"On whose authority?"

The prior had a powerful voice when he chose to use it. The

soldiers approaching the wagon, dithered.

"When men of God visit others of their kind in piety and faith it is customary gifts are taken to their hosts. Other necessary items include vestments for celebrating the holy mass and also books from our library, used when entering discourse with our colleagues at St. Bertin."

Watching two troopers peer inside the canvas, the prior spoke up.

"I am Prior Boniface. We are the Abbaye of St. Pierre under the diocese of his holiness the archbishop who was recently consulted by the Convention."

"Why?"

"Are you not informed, Citizen? The ignorant man is a stupid man."

If the prior was pushing his luck, his attitude was one of disdained contempt. A soldier called back from the wagon.

"Nothing here we're looking for."

Prior Boniface looked at the angry captain.

"The Convention has been anxious about the church because the church holds the key to the people. Your influence is only temporal and at best, flimsy."

The procession filed past the soldiers. The Citizen captain watched it with extreme suspicion.

"If I hate royalists, I loathe the church."

Leading off his troop, he didn't notice several of his men surreptitiously made signs of the benediction as they rode away.

*   *   *

"Good heavens, Dr. Light! I thought you'd disappeared."

Archie had forgotten the appeal Kaliska Monroe's husky voice held for him. Sitting in the Welsh cottage talking to her on his mobile, he wondered how he could explain that in a manner of speaking disappearing was exactly what he had been doing. She continued.

"I'm sure you've been busy."

Archie agreed.

"I've got some details on your new company and a draft contract. I could mail them though several of the clauses are quite lengthy. If you want to discuss them, I wondered if you were in town at all..?"

The computer games man explained that he was currently in Wales with his daughter but would arrange to come to London the following week.

*   *   *

Entering St. Bertin's abbey that night, two cramped figures emerged from behind the wagon's tiny false partition. The Duc and Duchesse Louisa receiving care and sustenance, Podric decided that first light must see them on the road for the final dash up to Calais. A covered trap was found and pulled by a pair of strong horses, the conveyance rattled off in the early morning under Barney's control.

The thirty-mile journey from St. Omer to the coast was made through driving rain. The horses driven at a cracking pace – whilst the windows were up and the occupants hidden, the vehicle didn't go unnoticed as it sped its way northwards towards the channel. 1794 France was a nation of spies, betrayers and betrayed.

Calais was dismal and grey, its dwellings huddled along the shore. With blustering sea air whipping through its streets, Podric found a coaching inn near the port. Having set aside funds for the d'Angoulac's future, he spent the remainder of the revolution's money securing rooms for the travellers.

Seeing the aristos ensconced and the day fading to early evening, Podric and Barney went to the bar. The bully, dressed in his potpourri attire of Jolly Jack Tar and Phrygian-hatted French revolutionary, and the computer genie in the clothes of the Supreme Being (not that anyone could say what they might be), Barney nursed his hidden weaponry. In skittish mood, Podric ordered a jug of ale.

"Jumpy, aren't you?"

"Nah. Just don't trust the Froggie's."

Yet another furtive landlord brought their beer. Paying him, Podric and his bullying compadre quaffed their pints.

"I thought you had a thirst for adventure. Anyway, I need you to get down to the dock and check when the next packet's sailing for Dover."

Barney looked at Podric blankly.

"Packet – you know, mail boat."

Barney scowled.

"When are we splitting from here permanently – I mean outta here?"

"Oah. UAR huh? Old time escapades too much for you, are they?"

Barney drank his ale.

"Didn't believe me did you – a life in a computer game?"

Podric poured more beer into their tankards.

"Feels real doesn't it? I mean you're living it!"

He looked around the room and lowered his voice.

"Clever lad like you would have worked out we're nearing the end of this particular adventure, but we've still got to get them aboard."

Podric stood up.

"Let me know about the boat and stay sharp. They're not out of here yet."

Walking through the inn, Podric could feel people's eyes on him. Crossing to the stairs, he didn't let his concern show.

Admitted to the d'Angoulac's suite by Louisa, Podric glimpsed the Duc lying on a bed in the adjacent room.

"Your father sleeps?"

"He is very tired."

Putting his hand inside his jerkin, UAR's Scarlet Pimpernel took out two pouches.

"These contain gold."

"The last of your money."

"It wasn't ever mine. I just looked after it for a while."

Podric put them into Louisa's hands. Turning away from him, she hitched up her skirts and tied the pouch strings of each to the girdle of her undergarments.

"It will enable you to survive. The revolution doesn't last forever and one day when all this is over you'll have your lands restored to you."

"You speak with authority."

Podric shrugged and Louisa readjusted herself.

"Why are you not coming to England with us?"

"Because hanging out with you finishes with your escape."

"Hanging out? You use some strange phrases m'sieur."

She suddenly reached out to him.

"I want you to come with us, with me!"

Surprised at her passion, Podric was embarrassed. The young duchesse was intense.

"You must know that I have feelings for you."

Hearing a noise outside the door, Podric put his index finger to his lips indicating silence. Doors banged, shouts were heard and a shot rang out. Hurried footsteps up the stairs,   Barney called through the door.

"We gotta get out – now!"

Admitting him, Podric shut and bolted the door.

"There's a ship, but the bastard Revo soldier's about. I've given him a sore foot but it ain't enough to stop him."

"Backstairs from the Duc's room."

Louisa had already gone into her father's bedroom and had begun to raise him. The old man put a brave face on things and was hustled downstairs.

The exit emerged at the side of the building and ships were berthed across the quay. The jetty was busy – traders, sailors and soldiers crowding the wharf. Barney programmed into UAR now paid dividends. He required no further prodding to put his brutish talents into action.

Grabbing a torch from a passing cart, Barney thrust it into another carrying bales for shipment. Although a light rain was falling, the cargo quickly caught fire. Spying several cages of wild animals, Barney promptly unhitched them and slipping their bars, let loose two bears and a leopard. In seconds, the whole place was mayhem.

With his twenty-first century nemesis active, Podric led the d'Angoulacs across the quay to the ship moored at the end of the harbour. The tide on the turn, the English vessel was making ready to set sail.

As they neared the gangplank, the limping Citizen captain appeared from the shadows with his soldiers. The Duc shook off his daughter, who had been supporting him and stood alone before the revolutionaries.

"I thought it was you, Carl. I wasn't certain spying you secretly on the road, but seeing you now, there is no doubt."

Far from dismissing the old aristocrat, the Citizen captain was impassive.

"I know your mother well and I'm sure she will be proud of you. She put great store in your education."

Although he maintained a cold bearing, to the shrewd eye, the Citizen captain was wrestling with conflicting emotions.

"Captain. We must seize these people!"

The Troop Sergeant moved forward.

"Prepare to cast off for'ard."

Standing by the gangplank, Podric saw Arthur Johnson, Billy's dad on the little quarterdeck!

"Wait! Mr. Johnson!"

Arthur looked around.

"Wha..? Cap'n to you young man."

"Two passengers to come aboard."

"Belay there."

Captain Johnson addressed a seaman. The Tar stood at the bow holding a warped rope in readiness. The Duc eyed the Citizen captain.

"Do my daughter and I proceed?"

"Captain, we must arrest them!"

The sergeant was apoplectic.

"Not on my ship, you don't."

Captain Johnson wore a piratical look. The sergeant reached for his sword to strike the Duc but was attacked by the leopard.

So incredible a sight – sailors, guards and guarded all gawped at the spectacle. The animal ripped into the sergeant's jugular. None of his colleagues going to his aid, it was left to Barney hurling a length of metal chain at the predator, that drove it from its quarry.

The sergeant writhed on the ground, blood spurting from his

throat. Two members of the troop belatedly began to help him but their efforts were feeble and too late. Guiding his daughter up the gangplank, the Duc turned back to his bastard son.

"Your mother never told you?"

The expression on the revolutionary captain's face was intense.

"Give her my regards when you see her and tell her any assistance I gave was made with great affection."

Without waiting for an acknowledgement, the Duc and the Duchesse Louisa stepped aboard *Drinkwell Girl*. It would be later that night the Duc's daughter would ask her father to explain the denouement of their escape – a tale involving intrigue, romance, and infidelity.

Podric walked up the gangplank and approached Captain Johnson.

"They have money for their passage captain."

Captain Johnson laughed.

"Of course they do. If they didn't, they wouldn't be sailing!"

The Duchesse Louisa hitched up her skirts and removing one of the pouches, undid its cord.

"Two silver Louis for our passage sir."

Captain Johnson inspected the coinage.

"Three. Each."

Louisa eyed Johnson.

"You drive a hard bargain."

"I drive you to safety from this accursed country."

"It is my country, captain."

"Then if you're sailing with me, you'd better say goodbye to it. Cast off for'ard."

Barney appeared with the d'Angoulac's small trunk and swung it on deck. The ship began to move. Podric gave a slight bow to the Duc, who took his hand. The boy started to do the same to Louisa but the girl kissed him.

"We're not sailing then?"

Barney was expectant. Podric shook his head. Captain Johnson gave orders to his crew, and the two youths made for the creaking gangplank.

Drinkwell Girl caught the breeze, and Podric and Barney turned back to the quay. Soldiers carried the lifeless form of the troop sergeant away. The Citizen captain stood watching the bears being recaptured and prepared for baiting.

"An aristocratic bloodline's certainly an unlikely credential for a revolutionary captain, particularly as you hate them so much."

"Go to hell."

"Don't know whether the twenty-first century's quite that mate, but we'll be making a move right enough."

The Citizen captain looked at Barney as if he was from another planet.

"Don't worry cock. You can always get the frills out when the revolution's over." Barney slapped his hand down on the Revolutionary captain's.

"High five – and look after that foot!"

Chapter 19

Back to Reality

It was early morning when Barney returned to normal reality in Archie's study.

"Oh God, where am I?"

Looking around, he saw Podric sitting opposite in one of Archie's expensive leather chairs.

"Find that dull, did you?"

"Ha. Dunno what you mean?"

"You know exactly what I mean. You were programmed so you're fully aware of the adventures you've just had."

Barney got up. Stretching himself, he was a bit wobbly.

"Right dick that Revo captain... What was he saying about letting them go?"

"The duke was obviously his father. What was he going to do?"

"I'd have taken 'im out. The old fella was on his last legs anyway. Got any coffee?"

"Yuh. 'Reckon you would have."

Podric went through to the small kitchen and turned on the expresso machine.

"So it didn't do anything for you, alternative reality?"

"S'alright. Better than school I suppose."

"Not saying much; only activity you seem to enjoy is beating people up."

"Paid off for you though didn't it in your altercating realism."

Podric smiled and prepared coffee.

"Altercating's good where you're concerned. What are you going to do now?"

"None of your business."

"True. But you've skipped YOI – that'll give you grief."

"You put me there."

"No, you put you there."

Barney scowled. Podric poured out two americanos.

"What's it to you anyway?"

"Nothing."

Podric sipped his coffee.

"Do you know why I wanted to programme you into UAR?"

"'Cos you're a geeky burk."

"Because you're a con. You're not thick Barney and you need a positive challenge to stop behaving like you do."

Taking a gulp of coffee, Barney banged down his mug.

"Yeah, rock on. Finished with the psycho shit?"

"Where's your phone?"

Barney fished in his pocket.

"What do you want it for?"

Taking it, within seconds Podric was into it tapping out details.

"Wha-? How'd you get into that?"

Podric handed it back.

"'Cos I'm a geek. I've inserted my number so you can skip jumping me."

"Yeah, likely I'll call you Moon."

Podric had some more coffee.

"Yuh, likely you will."

Shaking his head at the idiocy of this comment and without any farewell, Barney legged it downstairs.

Watching him go, Podric's mien was older than his years. It was as if his latest adventures had somehow given him a maturity. Going through to the lab he took his own phone from his bag. There were several messages – most of them from Catherine. He speeddialled Archie's number.

"So, you're back."

"You too."

"How mutually observant we are. Where are you?"

"The lab."

"You went in from there?"

"With Barney."

"The thug you programmed? How was it?"

"Interesting."

"Back out now, is he?"

"I brought him. Where are you?"

"Wales."

"Only been through it."

"On your way to the bogs no doubt. Talking of which, any sign of the leprechaun?"

"Her car's not here and the house is locked."

There was a pause in their dialogue.

"You went to Wales to go in?"

"Clever boy. I'm with Cosima."

"And Dog?"

"Yes, and bloody Dog!"

"Coming to town?"

"Next week. What are you up to?"

"Working."

Archie laughed.

"I'll surmise, not academic."

Podric didn't reply.

"Planning something else?"

"Tell you when you get back."

Putting down his iPhone, Podric felt deflated. He'd begun to realise that experiencing life inside UAR gave him such a high that returning to normal reality left him feeling not only physically drained, but mentally wrung out.

Making himself another coffee, Podric sat for a long time staring out of the window. He loved the view. From the top of the Lighthouse, one could see for miles – the gentle English landscape with its meandering river, a tiny tributary trickling through the garden below. Archie's lab had become his world – the place he felt most at home. Having invented Ultimate Alternative Reality in it – in a sense he felt it was his home. Sort of.

Opening his wallet, Podric took out the dog-eared photograph of his father. Sean's face smiled back at his son.

"Is it so wrong how I feel dad?"

Staring at the snapshot, he could almost swear Sean winked at him! Podric's phone vibrated. Checking it, he saw that it was Catherine.

"Hullo."

"You're back."

"Missed me?"

"No. Where have you been? With buddy Boney?"

"Sort of."

"Presume you're in your lab den."

"It's not mine and anyway, I might be at home."

"You're not. Is the thug with you?"

"No one's with me."

"Want to meet up?"

"Sure."

"Don't sound so keen."

"I am."

Catherine clicked off.

Feeling better, Podric put down his coffee and sighed. His mind wandered this way and that. As he thought about the wonders of Ultimate Alternative Reality, he began to consider one last challenge – one that would complete whatever he could create for UAR. It was something he'd never envisaged when formulating his idea and something so audacious that even as he thought about it, Podric could barely reconcile how it might be achieved.

Bringing a character from a computer game into normal reality.

Although it appeared that people profiled into UAR were only subconsciously aware of their adventures in the alternative reality state, Podric was confident they would be able 'see' a person out of a game. He was equally aware that no one else would. But even with this limited audience, how fantastic it would be to have someone from inside a game outside it – to hang out with them, here and now. Then he would have the best of both worlds.

Enthralled with the concept, there was only one person he wanted to attempt this with – the man who gave his name to the game – Napoleon. Napoleon Bonaparte, Emperor of the French, conqueror of Europe. The man who created so much of France's infrastructure – legal, economic, and political. But these dimensions of the great man Podric only had limited knowledge of and wasn't why he desired bringing him out of his game existence. Podric wanted to challenge Bonaparte while playing *Napoleonic Wars*!

Walking through to the lab, Podric booted up the PC system. To extract Napoleon from the game he'd have to profile him, but programming could wait till he was in normal reality. This would be essential otherwise Napoleon couldn't be aware of the experiences he was having. To make a start, Podric had Napoleon's DOB and the date of his death but he wasn't sure in creating the codex, if such data would reverse a character out of a game as he and Archie had been able to go into it.

Still contemplating this when he heard Catherine's scooter coming down the drive, Podric let her in using the top floor's visual intercom system. Returning to his lab work, he heard the lift descend and half a minute later Catherine appeared.

"Working. What is it about you Podric that makes me want to be with you? Perhaps it's because I never quite believe you're the mad boffin type, but who knows..?"

Podric was still immersed in his thoughts. Catherine didn't attempt any intimacy and walked back to the kitchen, making herself a cup of coffee. Returning a little while later with a steaming mug, she came over to him. She put down her drink and forcibly turned his head towards her, kissing him.

"How are you doing with school stuff?"

"Trying to spoil a nice day? How do you think I'm doing?"

"Hmm. Average I guess. What are you cooking up now?"

Podric sat back and in his particular way, tried to explain the challenge he'd set himself.

"And you're going in to bring him out."

Taking the news in her stride, Catherine was matter of fact. Podric nodded.

"That's great. When are we off?"

"I'm...er?"

"Don't even start Podric. You promised you would take me the next time and bad things happen if you go back on a promise."

The two of them looked at each other.

"Some of these adventures are dangerous."

"How can they be? UAR's just something you've created to get inside a computer game."

Podric laughed.

"Maybe so, but it feels like the real deal."

"Want me to sign something?"

They both laughed.

"What day is it?

"Saturday morning. Why?"

"I sometimes lose track of time. Life in UAR doesn't relate to normal reality."

"Can't you plan a time out?"

"Haven't done so far."

"Something else to work on then."

She turned away, picked up her mug and sipped her coffee.

"Let's get started. The sooner in..."

Podric looked at her again.

"Hmm... Guess we won't be long. This is a strictly in-out operation to see if it works for you."

"Well then."

Podric reached over to the store box and opened one of the metal cabinet's sliding drawers. Taking out a packet of microchips he removed one, logged its number into a PC and began to programme it with Catherine's details.

"You know I have to shoot this into your wrist."

"Does it hurt a lot?"

"No more than a prick."

"Podric!"

Catherine suddenly looked nervous.

"When you..."

Catherine appeared increasingly hesitant. Podric laid aside the microchip implant device.

"When you said we had a number in UAR – how much of a number?"

Podric shrugged but it was artificial.

"Well..."

"Podric, I'm really upset."

"Huh? Why?"

"Well... I haven't done it before. And, well, I think I... Oaah."

"What?"

"I've got feelings, you know."

"What sort of feelings?"

Catherine became exasperated.

"Podric you can be the most frustratingly obtuse person. For you, you idiot!"

Podric was briefly reminded of the Duchesse Louisa's similar declaration, but that was experienced in his alternate state. Ultimate Alternative Reality and reality. . . He looked at Catherine for several seconds.

"What if I told you that I loved you when you were acting with Mrs. Jordan."

"Did you?"

Podric nodded.

"I'm glad you said it – even in UAR."

She held him tightly, her head on his shoulder.

"Are you okay if we keep it like that for now?"

"What do you think?"

"I think I love you in this real world."

"Better get going then."

Chapter 20

An Important Guest

The snow falling on Paris during the night of 24th December, 1800 was thick and deep. To the casual eye, the French capital looked picturesque under its white blanket but the city was far from being festively serene. A feeling of deep unease lurked below its surface. The revolution had calmed a bit, but the country remained unstable. Napoleon, now First Consul, maintained control through constant military conflict. He had recently defeated the Austrians at Marengo, driving them out of Italy and consolidating French dominance there; his plans of aggressive expansionism for la belle France were limitless.

Dressed in a jerkin and breeches the recently converted monarchists, Podric Moon and Catherine d'Alliday sat on the running board of a cart surrounded by wine casks. Peering over them, Podric glimpsed the two men driving the contraption. Having selected a particular moment in *Napoleonic Wars*, he knew them to be Joseph Carbon and his friend Pierre Limoëlan.

Turning into Rue Saint-Nicaise, the wagon came to a halt. A figure appeared from the shadows. Podric recognised the man as Pierre Robinault de Saint-Régeant. The two drivers departed leaving the other to take charge. Saint-Régeant offered a girl a dozen sous and requested that she look after the horses for half an hour. The scene that history records, was set.

Nudging Catherine, Podric and she slipped off the cart and walked around to where the girl, Pensol was standing. Seeing several people huddled beside a rough brazier nearby, Podric gently took the reins from Pensol's freezing fingers.

"Go and warm yourself."

"M'sieur, I have been paid to watch the cart."

Taking a pistol from a leather sleeve on the side of the driving seat, Podric handed it to Catherine.

"I'll take care of it. My friend will go with you."

Pensol reluctantly allowed herself to be led by Catherine over to the fire. No sooner had they departed than Podric clambered aboard the wagon and got it moving.

Aroused by the activity, Saint-Régeant ran back to the vehicle and was easily able to catch it up. However, rather than challenge Podric, he walked beside the rear of the cart and started lighting fuses protruding from several of the wine casks. When this was accomplished, Saint-Régeant threw a firecracker in amongst them.

Panicking, the horses found an energy they didn't otherwise possess. The wagon careened into the Rue du Faubourg Saint-Honoré, Podric hanging on for all he was worth.

The First Consul's coach and one following it containing his wife Josephine, her daughter and other family members, approached L'Opéra. The cart Podric was attempting to steer, shot through Bonaparte's Garde Consulaire cavalry escort. The boy had a final yank of the reins before jumping off. The wagon veered and narrowly missed the carriages, detonating nearby.

The street being full of people attending the evening's performance, panic ensued and Napoleon with his family, entered the building, shaken.

Getting to his feet, Podric sprinted towards the carnage surrounding Napoleon's coach. Pushing aside his drunken driver César, he took control of the carriage, and drove it away from devastation.

The evening calming, Napoleon enjoyed Haydn's *Creation* and seemed unruffled. Other members of his family were distressed and it was decided that they would leave. Their respective carriages ordered, standing on the driver's platform of Napoleon's covered phaeton, César's hat thrust low over his forehead, Podric pulled up at the doors. The First Consul climbed in alone. The phaeton moved off smartly. Leaning back in his seat, Napoleon didn't seem particularly surprised to find Catherine sitting opposite him.

"To what do I owe the pleasure, mademoiselle?"

Whilst her costume was boyish it didn't fool Bonaparte.

Catherine would forever regard the ride back to the Tuileries as surreal. Dubious of Podric's UAR claims, the experience was so life like that it was inconceivable she wasn't in Napoleon's coach and that this wasn't 1800! With some difficulty, Catherine managed to reply.

"How could any woman resist such an opportunity?"

Napoleon laughed.

"Let alone a girl."

Bonaparte sat back.

"Your French is good but like me, you're not native."

"No."

Catherine said nothing more. Napoleon raised an eyebrow.

"Am I being abducted?"

"Sort of, but not perhaps quite the way you think."

"There is only one way to think as far as abduction is concerned."

"Perhaps it's better if I leave any explanations to my partner."

"Who drives us."

"That obvious?"

"Indeed. It's better handled than that oaf César."

The journey being a short one, they were soon rattling into the palace courtyard. Napoleon noticed the pistol Podric had given Catherine rested on her lap. He smiled and showed mock horror.

"Be careful with that. We don't want any accidents."

Disembarking, Napoleon called out to his guard.

"Organise the carriage stabled. I wish to talk with the driver. My companion and I will be in my apartments."

Catherine emerged and she and Napoleon entered the building.

Candlelit, Napoleon's private apartments were tasteful. The winter snow outside gave the ante-chamber a heightened sense of intimacy. However, the First Consul's mood was far from such. Picking up a decanter, he poured two measures of brandy and taking one, handed it to Catherine. She was about to sip it when there was a knock at the door. A guard entered, followed by Podric.

"Sire, this lad is an imposter."

"That is so but he drives better than César. Dismissed."

Spluttering in protest, the guard made his exit closing the doors behind him. Napoleon handed the other glass of brandy to Podric. His manner was now far from amused.

"You have one minute."

Having recently sampled brandy in UAR, Podric put the snifter down untouched.

"If that's all I have there is little time for explanation. We're here to take you on an adventure – or try to."

"Your escapades couldn't match my own. I am Napoleon!"

Sipping her brandy, Catherine choked and coughed.

"The girl cannot even drink. Children!"

"We'll see."

Ignoring Bonaparte, Podric used his wrist operation to activate *Napoleonic Wars*. Immediately data appeared at the top of his vision. Selecting a games configuration of his own making marked 'Present' Podric turned to his convulsed girlfriend.

"I told you ultimate alternative reality was the real deal."

Moving his right index finger over his left wrist, he watched the cursor reach 'Play' and pressed.

*   *   *

Podric and Catherine were on the couch. Dazed, Catherine began to cough. Slumped on one of Archie's easy chairs, Napoleon sat sprawled opposite them. His vision now clear, Podric got up and went through to the kitchen fetching Catherine a bottle of Badoit.

"So, you believe me now?"

Catherine sipped her water.

"Some trip."

Going through to the lab, Podric picked up a pre-selected microchip he'd left in a glass sterilization tray and took out the implant gun. Returning to the den, he approached Napoleon.

"You're right. It is a kind of drug."

"If programmed people aren't very careful, life inside UAR could become more desirable than normal reality. I'll give you half a day and you'll want to go again."

Recovering, Catherine was thoughtful. Podric inserted the pellet into the G-Byte's chamber.

"Why did you want to bring him out then?"

"For the same reason I wanted to create UAR – excitement, adventure and to see if I could – plus in his case, the challenge; playing the man at his own game."

"How's he going to know how to play a computer game?"

"As he keeps telling us, he's Napoleon. You really think it's going to take him that long?"

Bending over the First Consul, Podric slipped the little aural fitting deep into Napoleon's ear. He then pressed the gun to his left wrist and squeezed the trigger. This caused an involuntary spasm. Putting down the insertion device, Podric took Bonaparte's pudgy right hand and holding his index finger, activated him. A few seconds later Napoleon came to.

Regarded by history as the possessor of genius, even Bonaparte couldn't help being surprised by his new surroundings. He got up and looked around before turning his gaze on Podric and Catherine.

"Ah, Orphée et Eurydice."

"Let's hope not. We might appear to be in and out of this world but lost forever we are not."

Catherine turned to Podric.

"At least that's not the plan, is it Podric?"

She smiled.

"Anyway, Napoleon and Josephine..?"

The phone rang. Napoleon jumped. Podric picked it up.

"So, you're still there."

Podric decided that he'd wouldn't tell Archie he'd just been back inside UAR and out again let alone what he'd been doing and who he had with him.

"Still working on whatever little idea you had?"

"Something like that."

"I've decided to come back early."

"Had enough of Wales?"

"Things to do. Besides, got to check out what you're up to."

"When are you returning?"

"Tomorrow night. My erratic housekeeper's also on her way home."

"Family gathering then."

"Make sure you leave things tidy."

"Jawohl mein herr."

At this use of German, Napoleon pricked up his ears.

"Vous parlez allemand? Un peu que je comprends. Mieux que l'anglais."

"Who the hell is that?"

"It's a bit of a story."

"I'll bet it is. 'Sooner I get back the better!"

The phone call concluding, Napoleon began jabbering away in his Corsican French. Because he was UAR programmed Podric when activated, could speak and understand French though Napoleon's thick accent was demanding.

Clearly agitated, Bonaparte's imperious dynamism vanished. Pacing up and down, he obviously didn't understand where he was or what he was experiencing. A situation being out of his control wasn't something Napoleon had ever known!

Catherine decided to leave them. Napoleon watched her depart on her little scooter. Podric went through to the kitchen and began making coffee. Napoleon followed him and was instantly fascinated by the technology of the machine.

"This - how? What?"

Electricity, the internal combustion engine - let alone computers and space technology - it was some hours before Podric had finished explaining to Napoleon who he was, what time in history they were in and what they had done. He also had to explain how, in spite of Napoleon appearing to be in the twenty-first century, no one could see him unless they'd been UAR profiled as characters in his game *Napoleonic Wars.*

"So, we are a secret life within life."

Podric was right when he said Bonaparte would have little difficulty mastering a computer game. His rapid understanding of what had happened bore testament to his terrific intelligence and Podric was keen to introduce his new...well what was Napoleon to him? Not really a friend, more an historic acquaintance perhaps.

"It's time we were going home. You need to meet my mum and sister."

"Ah, votre mère et votre sœur? Qu'en est-il De votre père?"

Podric explained that he had no father, his dad having been killed in a flying accident. This led them into the lab. Podric showed Napoleon Royal Air Force fast jets and the type his father was killed in on the laboratory's virtual reality system. Other questions arose about war usage – missile systems and their destructive powers. Napoleon was wondrous.

It was late afternoon before he and Podric left the Lighthouse, Bonaparte's incessant questions peppering their departure.

Chapter 21

Living the Future

Twilight as they walked through Drinkwell, Napoleon's excitement turned to reflection.

"So, in this alternate world, you know what's going to happen to me?"

"Yes, and you will when you play the game."

"When do we start?"

"Soon. Are you in a hurry?"

"Napoleon is always in a hurry."

"I thought maybe just a little time in this world for you to see some things."

Turning into Briony Close, Podric found his key and opened the front door of Number 5. Amy stood in the hall wearing a space helmet.

"Moon landing."

Her voice came through the headset speaker. Napoleon was entranced.

"Where's mum?"

"Attending her inner self. Who's that?"

Barbara Moon appeared in the kitchen doorway.

"Unless I'm much mistaken 'that' is an actor dressed up as Napoleon."

"For your information, he is actually Napoleon."

Though he hadn't come across them yet, Podric had profiled his mother and sister into UAR from its inception so Barbara and Amy were able to identify Napoleon's image.

"Oh? Does he know where he is?"

"Yup. All been a bit of a shock to him but he's clever."

Never a man who enjoyed being at a disadvantage, Bonaparte looked irritated.

"Bonjour empereur. Je crois que vous êtes bien."

"He's not emperor yet mum. I've been into *Napoleonic Wars* and brought him here in 1800."

"So, he's First Consul."

"Wow." Podric was impressed.

"To whom do I have the honour of addressing?"

Speaking French in his Corsican accent, Napoleon was all courtesy.

"I'm Podric's mum. We're just sitting down to supper. Won't you join us?"

"Enchante Madame. Les rosbifs?"

"No, that's a traditional English Sunday lunch, but I presume you're staying a little while."

*   *   *

Alannah was already home when Archie, Cosima and Dog arrived back from Wales the following day. The house was spotless and Archie could find little fault with the state of his computer laboratory.

Not knowing what had brought about the change in Cosima, Alannah was interested to see how much her boss's daughter had altered. All Archie would say was that they had had a heart to heart. Whatever had happened, the moodiness and ill manners were gone, replaced by a strikingly independent young woman.

Archie hadn't been back an hour when the H-V HK500 was down the drive and crossing Drinkwell. Pulling up outside the Moon's house, Archie pressed the bell. The door was answered by Barbara waving an artist's paintbrush.

"Dr. Light. Welcome."

"Is Podric home?"

"He is – in the garden with our guest."

Barbara didn't wait for Archie to enter but went back through the house out into the garden and her studio – the shed reclaimed from Podric.

Vaguely following in her footsteps, Archie found his partner sitting in a hand painted deckchair.

"Back from Wales then."

"No Podric, I'm an illusion!"

"Tell me about it."

Podric twisted a chair around but Archie walked a few paces away.

"So, what have you got?"

Podric returned to his recline position.

"This and that."

"You can be..."

"Has Podric offered you a cup of tea?"

Barbara, brush in hand, leaned out of her studio.

"No, but I won't. Thank you."

Given he'd decided to visit Podric rather than call him, Archie felt more infuriated by the second. Laughter was heard coming from upstairs in the house.

"I want you to programme Cosima into UAR. She wants it and I want it."

"You know where the microchips are."

"Don't be smart Podric. It's my daughter we're talking about."

"You mean because it's your daughter, you don't want to risk an attempt because you don't know how to do it."

"You little..."

Just then Amy ran into the garden followed by Napoleon. Podric's sister wore a Mexican poncho complete with sombrero. The First Consul had taken off his coat revealing his waistcoat and breeches.

"Kids party, is it? More amateur dramatics?"

Napoleon burst into some jolly French/Corsican invective as he slumped into the chair Podric had offered Archie.

"He's quite good."

"He should be."

The sun dipping, Podric pulled off his shades.

"The image you can see *is* Napoleon – or at least Napoleon in *Napoleonic Wars*."

"Crap!"

"I brought his games self out."

"You're joking."

"Really? You can see him, can't you?"

Archie didn't reply but he obviously could.

"Why?"

"Because I want to play the game with him - here in our time - challenging *him*."

"And that's a big deal?"

"I reckon - plus it's all part of understanding what UAR can do."

Archie walked up to Napoleon.

"Do you remember me? We met in Toulon in 1794. You'd been wounded and I assisted the doctor attending you."

Archie's French was quite good.

"Unlikely he'll know you. He wasn't programmed then."

Napoleon shrugged.

"I do not recollect."

"I had my dog with me. Big wolfhound."

Archie turned to Podric.

"So, seeing him, how are we now?"

"We're in an outside-the-game UAR state. Anyone profiled can identify Napoleon, otherwise, he doesn't exist."

"A big dog you say? You're its master?"

"I have that honour."

"Ha! The English and animals."

"Are you as arrogant as history records?"

"I am a genius."

"So am I."

"Really? What have you achieved to suggest such?"

"A twenty-first century scientific brain creating a reality other people only dream of."

"You didn't do that."

"Who says? 'Think he could have done it by himself? Anyway, I wrote your game. You're just about the most conceited ogre to ever sit astride Europe."

Archie was back in a sneering mode now.

"Napoleon. Tortillas, are you coming to make them?"

Having run into the house, Amy called from the conservatory, her mobile on Google translate.

"Of course, cherie."

Napoleon got up. Although only thirty-one, he looked older. His hair was thinning and the rotundness he was later noted for, was already beginning.

"*Napoleonic Wars* simply reflects my achievements."

"Allowing a player to challenge you."

"Maybe I will get to play you?"

Napoleon studied Archie.

"But I believe I am right about your Achilles heel. Arrogance usually hides inadequacy."

"Is that what drives you then?"

"The dream of France drives me."

"A cover for your own ambition."

"Hmm. Yes, likely but I changed my world."

Archie watched him go.

"I hope you're pleased with your little experiment. Have you played him yet?"

"I was going to this evening."

"Make sure you destroy him."

Archie turned, intent on leaving.

"And Podric, given you're the genius, you'll ensure to programme Cosima. Partner! Talking of which I've got a meeting in town tomorrow about our agreement."

"Looking to terminate?"

"Like that, would you?"

"Your call. You're having the meeting."

Arriving at a little hedge that divided the garden from the drive, Archie turned back. For several seconds, he said nothing.

"Enjoy yourself tonight and remember, nothing less than annihilation."

Some hours later, Podric's intentions to play *Napoleonic Wars* were thwarted when told that the First Consul was left handed!

"You wish to play me at my game, but I cannot be so disadvantaged."

Deciding he couldn't face going to Archie's laboratory to get another microchip and the gun, rather than play conventionally (Podric could barely remember virtual reality games where he used Xbox or PlayStation controls), he activated alternative reality. Not playing *Napoleonic Wars*, Napoleon and Podric sat in Podric's bedroom looking through the game.

Navigating the First Consul through the challenges – Options, Tasks, and Criteria – was initially amusing. The period 1794 to 1800 largely triumphant, Napoleon was all too aware of what he had achieved. Whilst thwarted by Nelson when waging his Egyptian campaign, he laughed with glee at the Battle of Marengo – 'the ordnance was more difficult and if I'd had the supply I demanded, my victory would have been even greater!'

However, the first years of the new century were mixed and unknown to him. He watched the aborted conquest of England, his coronation, Trafalgar and then his triumph at Austerlitz. This was a high but Napoleon's distress mounted with the advent of the Russian campaign.

"Stop!"

Agitated and opening his eyes, Napoleon got up and began pacing about the room.

"Release me from this state."

Podric did so.

"Never mind playing your partner's little game, I do not wish to see more."

Napoleon looked out over the Moon's garden.

"Viewing the future – it is more than a man can bear..."

Podric studied a virtual reality visor. To his eyes, it seemed archaic.

"It was my mistake to bring you out. I'm sorry. Forget Archie, I just wanted to play you at your own game."

Napoleon turned and put his hand on Podric's shoulder.

"You did not do wrong. With your réalité ultime, you have created something amazing my young friend. Amazing and compelling. But you will have to be careful that this alternative life of yours does not take over your existence."

"I sometimes wonder if living in it wouldn't be so bad."

Napoleon laughed.

"How can you say that with your crazy mother and sister? Don't forget Podric, they need you. But what you've invented for yourself is another dimension. Adventures whenever you want them."

Napoleon turned away, reflective.

"You know – seeing a little of my fate, life was simpler in 1800. Live. Die. Eat. Starve. The things we have spoken of – electricity, space, this!"

Napoleon held up his left wrist.

"What you have inserted into me has more technology than the whole world had two hundred years ago!"

Picking up his green coat, Napoleon flicked some dust off the fabric.

"There is one thing I wish to know. When I return into my game's existence, will I be aware of these experiences?"

"You should be unless I remove the microchip."

"Ah, the wrist again! If this remains inside me, it will add an interesting dimension to my life in the future."

Podric reflected that this was an important moment. Although his was only a computer game entity created by Podric's warping, Napoleon in UAR obviously felt himself to be alive. Such was the craziness Ultimate Alternative Reality had thrown up.

Chapter 22

To Play or Not to Play?

Next morning, Napoleon announced that he would attend Wendbury High. This put the Moon household into chaos as everyone was trying to leave within a few minutes of each other.

Bonaparte taking time with his toilette caused a log jam for the bathroom. Being intrigued by the lavatory cistern, Napoleon began taking it to pieces exploring its construction! Barbara banged on the bathroom door.

"Napoleon, Podric and Amy have gone. The school bus - they had to go."

Opening the door, Napoleon was crestfallen.

"They went without me?"

"We were all calling you, but they couldn't miss the bus."

"I am Napoleon."

Barbara looked at him.

"Yes you are, and while I know you're a great man, driver Linklater is unlikely to be so appreciative."

Bonaparte's shoulders sagged. He could be like a child on occasion.

"Come on. Come and have a cup of coffee."

The two went downstairs where Barbara found her phone vibrating. A message from Podric suggested that she drop Napoleon at the Lighthouse on her way to work.

*   *   *

Passing the school bus in his repaired Faciella, Archie headed up the London road. A couple of hours later he negotiated his way into the city, and parked his car in Mayfair. Walking around to his solicitor's offices, Archie requested Kaliska Monroe, and was shown into a meeting room.

For all Archie's recent adventures, nothing had diminished the stylish Kaliska's appeal. He made a note to ensure that she was profiled into UAR at the soonest opportunity.

"Dr. Light. Thank you for coming in."

Archie made a brief reply. When attracted to someone, he often appeared abrupt. Sitting opposite him, Kaliska opened a file and took out some documents.

"This is the draft agreement for MoonLight. It isn't complicated."

Kaliska paused. She looked at Archie with her clear blue eyes.

"But it's not the contract I wanted to see you about."

Scanning the papers, Archie looked up.

"Oh?"

"Pasaro want to sign Podric exclusively."

Archie's face went hard.

"Exclusively?"

"Personally. For a lot of money."

"How do you know this?"

"Because while contacting them about *Agrolution*, Mr Schepesi told me that they want the game but they also want Podric."

Archie stood up, furious.

"The-!"

"You know Podric has been under a non-exclusive contract with Pasaro as a consultant for a while."

"They can't. I won't!"

"And it seems Secorni have also been after his services."

Not only was Kaliska extremely attractive, she was tough.

"He's hot."

"You've got me here to tell me this?!"

"No. Podric has informed me he doesn't intend to sign with either of them unless it's through MoonLight."

"How do you know?"

Kaliska was slightly exasperated.

"I just said, he told me."

"Wha-?"

"The only deal he'll do is via MoonLight and wishes Secorni and Pasaro to know that if they still want his services, all business transactions are to go through the new company."

Archie's expression displayed conflicting emotions.

"Podric has further advised that apart from *Agrolution*, he has an agreement with you about some other project you're working on which commits him to MoonLight."

Kaliska sat back.

"He was quite adamant about it."

"You seem to be having plenty of communication with the boy wonder."

"No more than you would expect."

Archie took a turn around the small room.

"You think I'm lucky to be associated with Podric, don't you?"

"I do. I also think he's fortunate to be in business with you."

"In spite of..."

"In spite of nothing. Podric may only be sixteen but he's a smart lad. I think it's highly unlikely he'd sign up to anything he hadn't thought about at some length."

Archie sighed.

"He-. That family."

"Interesting, aren't they?"

"You've had contact with them as well?"

"Mrs. Moon called me about this and we've had a bit of visual messaging."

Kaliska tapped the draft agreement.

"As Podric is under 18, she had to approve."

"And what did Mrs. Moon say about me?"

"You have no right to ask me that. Now, are you going to buy me lunch?"

Snapping shut her file, Kaliska stood up.

"I thought you corporate types didn't do lunch anymore?"

"Whatever gave you that idea?"

She smiled and at the door, turned back.

"I didn't tell you this but Barbara's attitude was similar to my own. She actually thinks you're good for Podric. I'll be in reception in five minutes."

*   *   *

Going into school Podric found it difficult to concentrate. Meeting Catherine at their usual lunchtime rendezvous underneath an oak tree on the farthest edge of the playing fields, he was distracted.

"History on your mind?"

Podric looked at her.

"How is France's greatest leader?"

"Still entranced by your intellect."

"Yeah."

Podric smiled.

"He was going to come to school but decided to take the loo cistern to pieces and missed the bus."

Catherine laughed.

"Played him yet?"

"Uhuh. He's had a look inside the game though."

"And?"

"It freaked him out. Us going in at 1800, everything was alright up to then because he'd lived it, but things after that upset him. Trafalgar, Russia..."

"I am not surprised. Aren't you glad you can't see into the future?"

Podric didn't reply. Catherine continued.

"Did he get to Waterloo?"

Podric shook his head.

"We stopped before that."

"Do you think you'll play him?"

"That was the idea."

Sitting with their backs against the tree, Catherine kissed Podric.

"I think he should go back."

For a little while they shared an intimate silence before Podric replied.

"So do I."

*   *   *

Dropping Napoleon off at the Lighthouse half an hour after Podric and Amy had gone to school, Barbara introduced the First Consul to Alannah. Already UAR profiled by Podric, it was remarkable how casually the housekeeper accepted Bonaparte in her matter of fact Irish way.

"My, I'm a lazy bones. Just making breakfast now. Would you like some?"

Alannah didn't speak French and Napoleon looked at her quizzically. Translating, Barbara derided her own earlier efforts of toast and instant coffee. She suggested that this would be far superior cuisine. Casting an eye around the high-tech kitchen, croissants warming and an aroma of the real thing flowing from the fanciest of percolators, Napoleon tapped his tummy.

"Very sensible."

Barbara turned to go.

"I'd better get to work. Podric will be along for you after school."

Advising Alannah to pull Google translate up on her phone, Barbara hugged Napoleon. He seemed lost.

"Mon dieu Barbara. You are my friend."

Barbara smiled.

"You'll be alright. Podric will see that you are."

Watching her go down the drive heading for Tweeney's Waste Disposal in her battered old VW, Napoleon sighed. An emotional man, he was ruthless yet could be sentimental. In an environment he couldn't control, his character was diminished. Sensing his inadequacy, Alannah led Napoleon back into the kitchen.

"Let's wake Cosima. Her French ought to be good. Those posh academies and finishing schools must have taught her something."

Cosima was in fact not only up but had been out for a run. Minutes later, she returned to the house. Not intending to come into the kitchen, she was collared by Brodie as she entered the hall.

"We have a visitor."

Napoleon was standing in the kitchen winding his pocket repeater Breguet.

"My not speaking French, I need your help."

"Is he...?"

"So Barbara says."

"This must be via dad and Podric's reality thing."

"If you say so."

Hot from her jog, Cosima walked over to Napoleon wiping her face with a sports towel. In spite of sweating, now that her indolence had evaporated, she had an easy grace and charm.

"Swim do you sir?"

The verb was in the wrong place but Cosima spoke French with confidence.

"No mademoiselle, I do not. Water is for fish."

"Then I'll teach you. Bring your coffee."

Left with the choice of a non-French speaking Alannah and the young woman before him, Napoleon opted for the latter. He picked up his cup.

Rarely has a friendship developed so rapidly. Although he refused her offer of a swimming lesson, Napoleon was relaxed watching Cosima's svelte form cruise effortlessly up and down the pool. After her swim, they sat in the garden and talked – about everything. Napoleon told her about Josephine and his other loves, his ambitions for France and his place in history. Cosima, about her father and mother, their relationship and her rapport with them.

"Your father is troubled, I think."

"He's always been like that. He's a clever man, a proud man but socially he has issues. My mother is titled and made him feel that he's not good enough for her."

"Titled?"

"She's a lady – in society's terms."

"Ha! The English and class – they are obsessed."

"If you're speaking from an eighteenth-century perspective – as far as that's concerned, not much has changed!"

They laughed.

"Tell me about Podric."

"I don't really know Podric. I was in a bad place when he came on the scene. He and pa seem to have a particular relationship. Brodie says he's good for dad."

"Brodie?"

"Alannah, the housekeeper."

"Ah, nom de famille."

Cosima laughed.

"Okay..."

Napoleon was thoughtful.

"He wants to play me in my game."

"So that's why you're here. He wants to challenge you."

"You don't play these...computer games?"

"Afraid not."

"Not even the one your father created?"

"He's written many."

"It is his work, no?"

"Hmm... My mother laughed at him, children's science she said, but it's big business. He's very successful - or was."

Napoleon looked quizzically at his young hostess.

"In the last year or so his games haven't been doing so well. It's very competitive and the marketing companies said he was losing his touch."

"*Napoleonic Wars*...as if I am constantly at war."

"That's what we're taught."

Napoleon bowed his head.

"To be remembered this way..."

"It's a successful game."

Napoleon looked up.

"Of course! So, you don't play?"

Cosima shook her head.

"You are alone then, I think. I am told everyone does."

"People are crazy about them."

"Is Podric?"

"He must have been but I think they started to bore him. That's why he wanted to add a dimension to virtual reality and create an alternate one where he could exist inside the game's world and have whatever adventures he wanted, for real."

"For someone who doesn't play, you seem to have a lot of knowledge."

"How could I not? My father doing what he does, I had to pick up something."

She sat back.

"I don't think Podric likes me."

"Why do you say that?"

"I wasn't very nice to him."

"He is a clever boy, Podric. He has vision."

"You think?"

"This alternative reality...the idea of having another life in a different world; it is interesting and the technologie - ha!" Napoleon looked at his wrist.

"I rest now. When Podric returns, I will leave."

"You depart so soon?"

"I do not wish to play the stupid game. If I challenge Podric and your papa, the contest will be réalité!"

"But your existence is inside the game."

"If that is so, it is at least an actual existence for me there."

Napoleon got up.

"I leave Paris in the Year 9. I have some more life ahead. A man's destiny is not proven until he has lived it."

He looked at Cosima.

"The tower - it is quiet there?"

"The Lighthouse? 'Should be."

"Lighthouse?"

"My father calls it that. His name is Light."

"You bear the same name, do you not?"

"I've been using my mother's."

"Ah."

"But I might revert."

"He shines more brightly for you?"

Cosima laughed.

"Sometimes."

"You are a lovely young woman. Will you come and visit me in-."

Napoleon paused. His next words were obviously distasteful to him.

"*Guerres Napoléoniennes?*"

"You can count on it, sir. I will."

Podric and Catherine arrived at Drinkwell after school and went directly to Archie's lab where they found Napoleon fast asleep on the sofa.

"You're very familiar with this place."

Unnoticed by either of them, Cosima sat in one of Archie's leather chairs.

"I...come here a lot."

"Obviously."

"Your dad and me, we build games-."

"And Ultimate Alternative Reality."

"You know about that."

"My father's told me. You're going to programme me."

"I am?"

"Yes."

Cosima stood up.

"Now."

Her tone stopped short of rudeness - just. Turning to Catherine she said.

"Cosima - Dr. Light's daughter."

"Catherine - a friend of Podric's."

There was the faintest twinkle in both their eyes. Cosima noticed Catherine's wrist.

"A particular friend, I think. Shall we get on with it?"

Grunts and mutters from the sofa suggested Napoleon was waking up.

"Meird - my head! Where am I?"

Seeing Cosima, Podric and Catherine, his mind gradually cleared.

"Poderique. You will return the vision you see to his game. Ha! Perhaps I am unfair about your alternative reality. After all, in a sense, life itself is little more than one."

"A moment."

Cosima was as imperious as Napoleon.

"Before you go, Podric has another task to perform."

"What could have greater priority than Napoleon?"

To answer him, Cosima raised her left wrist.

Chapter 23

Stresses and Strains

Podric having returned Napoleon into the game bearing his name, Catherine prepared to leave. Outside the Lighthouse, she unlocked her Vespa.

"There's something about Napoleon I don't quite trust."

Podric looked at her.

"His wanting to know all about getting in and out of the game – if you read your history, Napoleon was a master strategist. Now he's learnt about UAR, he won't rest till he's planned something using it to his advantage."

Archie's Faciella swung into the drive.

"I'll leave you to your high-powered games business but you want to think about it. Napoleon's not the sort of man to let anything go."

She swiftly kissed Podric's cheek and put on her helmet. "Thanks for taking me. You're right about one thing. It is life changing – literally."

Archie parked his car by the front door. His expression bore a look of dissatisfaction.

"Off she wobbles into the night."

Archie walked into his lab.

"Buddy boy Nap gone?"

"She actually rides pretty well."

Archie grunted.

"Yes, Napoleon's back inside."

"Where he belongs. Bloody fiasco if you ask me. 'Gather he wouldn't even play."

Podric realised Cosima must have told her father about the First Consul's refusal to play him but thinking about his experiment, he wasn't sure it was such a failure. He'd learned things about Bonaparte he knew he otherwise wouldn't have.

"Trust you programmed my daughter."

Podric nodded.

"There's one more person I want to go in."

Archie handed Podric an envelope.

"Only profiled. I'll say goodnight."

With that, Archie got into the lift and ascended. Opening the envelope, Podric saw that the details were Kaliska Monroe's.

Sensing that he wasn't welcome, Podric hitched his bag on his shoulder and set off down the drive. He was nearly at the road when Barney leaped out.

"Not the bushes again!"

"When are we going back in?"

"How do I know? You're the one doing time."

"Not Young Offenders dummy – your reality thing."

"Oh, the adventures you thought boring and couldn't wait to get out of."

Podric laughed. Barney was sullen. He looked rough.

"Yeah well, when are we going back?"

"Dunno yet. Where can I find you?"

Barney held up his mobile and Podric glimpsed the small mark on his wrist. Enough people were programmed now. Podric would comply with Archie's request to profile Kaliska Monroe, but he wouldn't programme her or anyone else. Otherwise if they weren't careful the unique world they had created would be lost.

"I'll let you know. I'm sure it won't be long."

*   *   *

Whatever it was that caused Archie to behave as he had, after their parting outside the Lighthouse, Podric decided to leave his business partner alone for a while. His recent adventures – their inventing UAR and Napoleon's visit to the twenty-first century – had left him drained.

For several days Podric's life seemed to return to normality, but it didn't last long. While Pasaro had secured the rights to *Agrolution*

and the launch was imminent, Secorni still circled. Both companies
had been advised that Podric's work was going through MoonLight,
but that didn't stop them from trying to pursue him independently.
Cy Zaentz was particularly aggressive in demanding a meeting. With
these pressures, it was an irritation to Podric as to why his partner
should behave in such an erratic way.

Walking home from the school bus with Amy one afternoon,
Podric was surprised to see Cosima in Briony Close.

"Brodie told me your number but I forgot it."

Cosima was obviously distracted.

"Numéro cinq."

Skipping off, Amy was her usual particular self. Podric shrugged.

"Napoleon. Right now, everything's French in Amy's life."

Cosima smiled.

"You're wondering why I'm here?"

Podric didn't comment.

"It's pa. He's drinking again."

They began walking towards the Moon's house.

"I need to talk to someone, someone who knows him."

"But I'm-."

"The nearest thing he's got to a friend."

"You're kidding?"

They stopped outside number 5.

"You'll have worked out my dad's a troubled soul and-."

Cosima was uncomfortable.

"Is there somewhere we could go?"

Entering the house, Cosima was immediately accosted by Amy
who dragged her upstairs. It was several minutes before she was able
to re-join Podric. Sitting in the conservatory, he was flicking through
one of his mother's art magazines when she came in.

"I can see why pa's lucky to have you as his partner."

Podric looked up from his journal.

"You need a trophy room."

Cosima sat down at the kitchen table.

"I was shown. I didn't mean to pry."

She sipped some tea that Podric had made.

"This game you've created with dad is going to be a success but he feels inadequate as it's really your work. Because of that, he drinks."

Podric took a sip of his own builder's brew.

"If Archie's so screwed up, why doesn't he go back inside UAR to escape? He has before."

"I think it's because of me."

Podric looked at her.

"Although you programmed me, another of dad's hang-ups is he doesn't know how to put me in. Not properly. He wants to be with me when it happens, but he's not confident."

"Archie not confident?!"

"If you know my pa, you'll get what I'm saying..."

Cosima spoke quietly.

"I'm not his life coach!"

"No one's asking you to be."

"But it's like I've got some solution." Podric stood up.

"What do you want me to do?"

"Come and see him."

Podric was thoughtful.

"If I do, I'm not putting you in."

"Why not?"

"Because until he understands programming, really understands it, it wouldn't be safe."

"What do you mean?"

"UAR for Archie has become an escape prop to his life. Having him blunder about *Napoleonic Wars* is one thing but having him blunder about in it with you is quite another."

"He's pretty good with games..."

"Was."

"You're saying he's out of touch."

"Yes, and UAR takes gaming to a height no one ever thought possible. It's a different league. Its challenges are out of this world."

Collecting their mugs, Podric went to the sink and rinsed them.

"He wanted me to profile someone. I'll come over and do that sometime."

*   *   *

Sitting at the lab bench, Podric profiled Kaliska Monroe into Ultimate Alternative Reality. Unsure when he might be returning to the Lighthouse, Podric took the opportunity of updating several UAR files. It was while he was doing this that he heard the lift. Half a minute later, Archie stood in the lab doorway. He looked dreadful – tired and haggard.

"Don't tell me what I look like."

Finishing his work, Podric turned to him and pushed the envelope Archie had given him containing Kaliska's details along the bench.

"The profile you wanted."

"Thank you."

Archie sat down on the other stool.

"Aren't you going to ask why I'm not boringly aggressive?"

"Why are you not boringly aggressive?"

Archie laughed.

"Shit. Because I've come to learn about UAR, Podric."

"You know a lot about UAR. You helped create it."

"Ha! I was pissed half the time – either because of alcohol or you; still am, but I've got to master it."

"Why?"

"Because if I don't, I'll die."

Chapter 24

Deceptions and Disguises

Napoleon was in a rage. Stomping about the empty ballroom that served as his Boulogne invasion office, he railed at the incompetence of the rehearsal. Standing silently in front of him, Admiral Magon of Bonaparte's Navy bore the brunt of his onslaught. Other senior army officers present included Marshall Soult and General Bertrand. The emperor's Chief of Police, Joseph Fouché was also in attendance.

Bonaparte was exhausted having spent the previous thirty-six hours desperately trying to salvage anything he could from the recent debacle. Worn out from his efforts and rantings, he slumped into a chair. Dismissing the military men, Napoleon indicated Fouché to stay behind.

"These damned shallops. The sea is so unpredictable - winds, tides... Such difficulties don't exist for generals. Yet Perfidious Albion, each day I wonder. Do I need to conquer her or will I rue a missed opportunity..?"

"I wouldn't presume to understand your strategy, emperor."

Fouché was circumspect. Napoleon sipped some wine.

"I am surrounded by incompetence. My forces are complete, yet they fail me. They blame everything but themselves and I am compelled to oversee everything."

"As your chief of police, emperor, I cannot comment on the efficacy of your military commanders but forces other than these are at work and they are intent on disruption."

"Spies, Fouché. You always talk to me of spies, saboteurs and espionage!"

Fouché gave a slight bow.

"That is because your plans are threatened by such people. I have explained how the town is alive with agents and informers. They have been determined in their efforts to discover details of the invasion."

Napoleon fiddled with some documents but made no comment. Fouché continued, "You will also be aware that gathering information takes time – what is accurate and what is misinformation. However, my people have been busy and I am pleased to tell you that we have unearthed the senior British agent in Boulogne."

"What information has been compromised?"

"Naval operations and the six-month plan."

Napoleon scratched his wrist.

"How was this possible?"

"The emperor will know of Admiral Bruix's collapse..."

"The idiot who put my fleet to sea."

Inspecting his silver-topped cane, Fouché sat back.

"The admiral is seriously ill, probably dying and his wife was sent for. Arriving from Paris two nights ago, the woman went straight to the admiral's side. Unfortunately, Bruix was in the habit of taking confidential papers home with him and whilst she was in his chamber, they were stolen."

"By his wife? Fouché your imagination surpasses itself."

"By a beautiful British agent who supplanted his wife."

"Where is this agent now?"

"Here."

"You have questioned her?"

"An initial interrogation has been conducted."

"And compromising documents have been found?"

"Unfortunately, she had already passed them on."

"How so and to whom?"

"I will know that shortly."

"Ha. So as of this moment Fouché, you have no proof the woman is an agent at all."

"The real Madame Bruix arrived in Boulogne this morning."

Napoleon rubbed his wrist again.

"That in itself doesn't prove the imposter is a spy."

Bonaparte began studying a file.

"I will see this highly placed agent. Have her brought in."

"You wish me to remain for the interview?"

Napoleon didn't look up from his papers.

"I do not."

His face impassive, Fouché left the room.

The irritation on Napoleon's left wrist caused him to inspect it. The carpal joint bore a small red spot where the microchip had been shot under the epidermis. Viewing the tiny grey pellet just visible when the skin was stretched, accelerated Bonaparte's thoughts. He began to pace the room.

There was a knock at the door and Kaliska Monroe was ushered in. Two guards were in attendance. Napoleon couldn't help but admire her beauty.

"Madame, be seated."

Napoleon indicated a chair in front of his large desk and then turned to the guards.

"You may leave us."

The two men eyed each other. One of them thought to remonstrate but decided against it and they left. The doors closed behind them. Napoleon eyed Kaliska.

"Were you his wife, Admiral Bruix would indeed be a fortunate man."

"So fortunate he will be dead in a few hours."

"With the real Madame Bruix now arrived from Paris, at his bedside."

Napoleon walked over to French windows.

"You are accused of being a spy. Do you have anything to say?"

"You will understand my predicament."

Napoleon turned, bemused.

"How so?"

"Because since you have taken power, you have been in constant motion. Ever at war expanding France's horizons, you cannot stop for fear that if you do, others will destroy you. Not only do the allies range against your armies, but those within your own country."

"A pretty speech, though I fail to see what comparison you might make."

Kaliska Monroe sat forward.

"Emperor, although you are brilliant, you are a man. Whether I am a spy or I am not, a woman – particularly an intelligent woman, has to learn to live by her wits. It is a constant. She can never rest."

This philosophy appealed to Napoleon, but he wasn't deflected.

"You will be tried."

"So sir, will you."

A noise outside in the corridor disturbed their riposte. Seconds later, Quartermaster Lumière aka Archie Light burst through the doors followed by several soldiers. Before he could be restrained, the games creator walked over to Bonaparte and took hold of his left wrist.

"Ah, the games man. I've been waiting for one of you to arrive."

Removing his arm from Archie's grip, Napoleon ran his right index finger over the microchip.

"I wish Podric had transferred the composant to my right."

Archie looked quizzical.

"I am left handed!"

The soldiers parted as Joseph Fouché appeared.

"You're familiar with this quartermaster, emperor?"

"Oh yes, quite familiar. You may leave us."

This time it was Fouché who considered protesting, but he too accepted Napoleon's order.

Left to themselves, the three people in the room made a picture – Kaliska enigmatic, the two men, foes. Napoleon was the first to speak.

"This woman passed my plans to you. Where are they?"

"On their way to England."

Napoleon closed on Archie.

"You are supposed to be a French naval quartier-maître."

Kaliska stood up.

"As I advised – 'those within your own country'. You will excuse me. It has been...interesting."

Making a brief curtsy, she left the room.

"I presume she is a part of my game."

"As I advised, I wrote it."

"But on my existence."

Archie actually laughed.

"She is profiled."

"Why did you do that?"

"Because I wanted to see how she was in this world."

"Ah, a fantasist. But she does not play."

"Correct. Being profiled is different to being programmed as you are."

Archie watched Napoleon work his forefinger over his microchipped wrist.

"You wish to play?"

"Where is Podric?"

"At school, I hope."

"You play your réalité alternative with him?"

"So far, we haven't much. We've preferred the adventures inside UAR to unfold. That itself has given us the ultimate game."

Napoleon considered.

"Alluring but escapist. One must be victorious!"

Napoleon was concentrating. His finger moved with increasing urgency around the area where the tiny processor was buried under his skin.

"Look, you depress to activate."

Napoleon abruptly started viewing the top of his eyes.

"Then moving the cursor..."

Archie's fingers manoeuvred Napoleon's.

"You click Control, then Options – but Podric would have explained this."

Napoleon appeared deeply preoccupied. UAR could be challenging – even for a genius.

Chapter 25

Whose Game is it Anyway?

Bored and forbidden to smoke, Cosima stepped out of the house into the night. Taking a packet of cigarettes from an inside pocket of her designer tracksuit, she lit the king-sized filter tip and inhaled.

Inspecting the skin where the microchip had been inserted from the glow of her cigarette, the gunned impregnation still throbbed. But she was excited. Ever since she was told about UAR, Cosima's imagination had been fired. In a very different place emotionally these recent weeks, her attitude had developed into a cool confidence. A greater belief in herself had stimulated a desire for adventure.

Finishing her smoke, Cosima looked up at the Lighthouse. Was there a tiny light at its top? Keen to see her father if he was around, she ambled towards the tower. The door was unlocked and entering the building she pressed for the lift. Stepping out into the darkened den, a glimmer of light was just visible at its far end. Hearing voices, Cosima hadn't tried to be quiet, but now she crossed the room silently.

Looking down the stairwell into the lab, she could just see her father and Podric deep in conversation.

"You were right about Engage and Release. It couldn't be simpler."

Archie sat back tapping his wrist.

"But he says he's at a disadvantage. Something to do with being left handed. Apparently, he told you."

Working at a PC, Podric finessed some data.

"For all his genius, he's likely not to be good at the game. After all, he's got no one to play against except us and we're outside off-line right now."

"So, can he be outside?"

"He doesn't know how, unless you told him."

"Not me, but he's Napoleon."

Archie laughed. Finishing his adjustments, Podric stretched.

"On the other hand, what's driving him is to beat us at our own game. That's his motivation. You left him at Boulogne?"

"Trying to get into UAR. Showing him stuff you had, he could be anywhere now."

Archie stood up.

"Doesn't matter. We can always lock up on him. That was something else that's sorted. Now we can find anyone programmed instantly."

Archie was thoughtful.

"I'm getting more of a grasp on this now Podric – programming and what have you."

"Good."

"And practice makes perfect."

He smiled and left the room. Seconds later, Podric heard his name called and putting the computer system on Standby, went through to the darkened den. Handing Podric a beer, Archie looked out of the window. A fleeting shadow left the building heading for the house. Archie was in no doubt who it was.

"Do you think she heard us?

"Why is that important?"

"Your programming her."

"Against my better judgement!"

"Alright, yes. But now she is, she'll be impatient."

"How impatient?"

Archie looked at Podric.

"Ha. Be seeing you then."

Leaving the Lighthouse to go home, Podric considered his partner. Pleased that he was getting the hang of alternative reality, if what Archie said about his daughter was true and that he would go into UAR to keep an eye on her, he'd need every micron of his new found skills.

*   *   *

"Where am I now?"
Having stopped his coach, Napoleon looked out across Russia's frozen wastes.
"Cursed reality."
In spite of the cold, Napoleon took off his glove and rubbed his left wrist.
"You will return inside my game, Podric Moon. You will come and you will challenge me and when you do, I will destroy you."

*   *   *

Snow was blizzarding as the carriage lurched along the bleak track in the rapidly fading twilight. It had no escort and the driver worked the horses hard to keep the vehicle moving. Inside, three men sat huddled against the cold. On the seat facing forward, the eldest, Polish Prince Józef Poniatowski, lay covered in rugs, seriously wounded. The two men opposite shivered in their cloaks.
Struggling over an incline, the coach finally rolled downhill towards an inn. Minutes later it rattled into a yard.
"Not a moment too soon. We'd better find a doctor."
The horses came to an exhausted stop, but no one came to help.
"You'll be joking of course. There'll be no doctor here. 'Only medicine they'll have in this god-forsaken hole is vodka. If we're lucky."
Alighting, the aide stamped his feet in an attempt to warm them. "Whatever possessed the Emperor to conquer such a barren land?"
"The same reason that compels the Emperor to conquer anything."
"Well, he can have this frozen dump."
"Hmph. Let's get the Prince inside before we all freeze. Come, give me a hand."
The two men carried their wounded commanding officer into the rudimentary building.
A desultory fire was doing little to heat the place except fill it with

acrid smoke. The two officers gagged as they set Poniatowski down in front of its pathetic flames.

In contrast to the surroundings, the atmosphere was lively - the clamjamphrie of serfs, vagabonds and brigands were having their spirits lifted by the antics of a giant wolfhound.

Making the prince as comfortable as they could, the first of his two bearers turned back to close the door when he was leaped on by the enormous animal. Letting out an oath, the man pushed Dog aside only to be beset by a further onslaught of rumbustious affection.

"Animal lover too huh, Swiatto? Almost like he knows you."

Colonel Swiatto muttered an expletive as pushing him, Dog nearly knocked him off his feet.

A door at the rear of the bar opened and a young woman entered. Dressed in travelling clothes - doublet and riding habit, Cosima crossed the room to her father.

"What the bloody hell did you have to bring him in for?"

"I didn't plan it. He was with me when I-."

"You're a dark horse Swiatto. In the absence of an introduction, Count Anatole Byrenski of the Polish Light Infantry at your service ma'am."

Byrenski clicked his heels. Cosima smiled.

"The pleasure is mine, sir."

"You will excuse us Byrenski. My daughter's arrival is something of a surprise."

Dog bounded up, keen to be in the familial mix.

"Compounded by her bringing our pet wolfhound along."

"Your daughter Swiatto? A brave girl indeed to come campaigning. I should say she was wise having some protection."

"Dog's about as much use as a pirate in a fair."

Byrenski didn't query how successful Bluebeard might have been hooking a toy duck from a goldfish bowl. Archie and Cosima retreated to a simple parlour adjacent to the inn.

"Swiatto?"

"Polish for Light I believe. It was Lumieré in France."

Archie closed the door.

"So 'Settings' are relevant. Podric's a genius."

"What gives you that idea?"

"Being here."

"If this is genius, you're welcome to it."

"Why are you so obsessed with alternative reality then?"

"Fair enough. You didn't waste any time I see..."

Cosima approached her father.

"UAR's been good for you pa. It's given you a new sense of purpose, another dimension."

"Some purpose, some dimension – being able to live life in a computer game."

"I don't know anyone who wouldn't give anything to experience what we're able to – an alternative reality."

At that moment the sound of wagons and troops was heard approaching. Archie pushed open a grimy shutter to reveal hundreds of men marching into the yard. Their horses pulled gun limbers and some light artillery behind them. He and Cosima watched as an escort surrounding a coach came to a stop. An adjutant opened the door of the dormeuse and the unmistakable figure of Napoleon emerged. The crumpled form bowed against the blustering elements, it was a different Bonaparte to the man Cosima had sat in their garden with at Drinkwell. Even catching a brief glimpse, the emperor's face looked haggard and drawn.

"As escapism, yes, but it's going to take on a whole new games aspect shortly."

"What do you mean?"

"You'll see."

Napoleon entered the building. Aides and attachés scurried hither and thither. Soldiers evicted the local populace, who howled and cursed as they were forcibly turfed out into the bitter night. The emperor approached a revitalised fire and began to warm himself. He nodded to Count Byresnki, still at Prince Poniatowski's side.

Senior officers and army commanders including Oudinot, Davout and Prince Eugène arrived. Napoleon was about to sit down with them when Dog came bounding up. An attaché immediately tried to intervene, but Bonaparte brushed him aside.

"Where you are, your master will likely not be far away."

Cosima appeared. In spite of his fatigue, Napoleon's spirits lifted.

"Chère fille."

He kissed her hand. Archie/Swiatto approached.

"And here is your father – as a Colonel in the Polish cavalry, I see."

Napoleon looked round at Byresnki.

"A colleague of yours, is he count? I'll wager only a recent one..."

Bonaparte chuckled.

"In what guise do you enter this campaign, my dear?"

"The contents of my valise suggest I'm some kind of government spy."

Napoleon burst out laughing and turned to Archie.

"Like the one in Boulogne? Surely you games writers can be more imaginative."

Cosima was nonplussed. The door opened and a blast of snow announced the arrival of another marshal. This time it was Ney. Mud and blood splattered, the lines of his face were etched with fatigue. Grasping Ney's arm, the emperor's attitude abruptly changed.

"Ney! Come! Warm yourself."

Briefly acknowledging his colleagues, the marshal kicked a log and warmed his hands by the fire. It was Napoleon who spoke.

"The Rear Guard?"

"Here emperor. We were near-routed, but we bloodied them and they're in check."

"How long?"

"A few hours at most."

"You have done well, Ney."

"I have done no more than any general in your service."

Ney felt his neck. A dried blood stained bandage was visible beneath the high collar of his uniform.

"How is your wound?"

The marshal made a dismissive grunt and hunched nearer the fire. Noticing Poniatowski, he raised an eyebrow.

"He lives and makes for Warsaw."

"We all strive for Warsaw emperor. The Berezina crossing?"

Napoleon nodded.

"We have a few hours to regroup. We dine, we plan, we move again at dawn."

*   *   *

Whilst not comfortable, the rear parlour was less cavernous than the main saloon and although it was the small hours of the morning, Napoleon worked at a portable desk. General Rapp attended the emperor, and the only other person present was Archie who sat with Dog. Most of the men arriving looked harassed and exhausted, but nearly all of them stopped to make a fuss of the wolfhound.

Sitting back, Napoleon threw down his quill and rubbed his eyes. "How many people have you been since entering my game?"

Ignoring whose game it was, Archie smiled.

"Let's see... First of all I was a naval lieutenant when we were with Nelson."

"Ah, the British hero."

"Then a captain in the Life Guards when you and I met." Napoleon studied Archie.

"You don't remember because you weren't programmed then. It was at the Siege of Toulon. I was a prisoner and you had been wounded. Indeed, as I told you when we met at Podric's, I helped the doctor with your tourniquet. Then I was a quartermaster at Boulogne – but you know about that."

"A spy!"

An aide appeared requesting a decision. Making it perfunctorily, Napoleon turned back to Archie.

"And Podric?"

"He was a midshipman first. Later, he played the Supreme Being during the revolution which seemed a bit esoteric to me, but you know Podric. Since then I believe he inserted himself into the monarchist gang who wished to assassinate you, thwarting their attempt. It was at the time he'd decided to programme you."

"Ha. His arrival mélodramatique – and with the girl."

"Surely, you would appreciate both."

Ignoring Archie's sarcasm, Napoleon studied his wrist. Less irritating now, the experience of what had happened to him held increased fascination.

"Your daughter claims she is following her father's footsteps."

"And as the possessor of information, you may find it interesting."

Archie produced a piece of parchment.

"A coup has been attempted against you."

Rapp was visibly startled. However, Napoleon showed little sign of surprise. He snapped his fingers impatiently. Archie passed Napoleon the folded sheet.

"The plot was organised by De Malet – a man you certainly mistrust. Other traitors include general's Guidal and Lahorie – both of whom were imprisoned in La Force."

"This paper – its validation?"

"If you study the watermark, three-quarters of the way down there's a smudge. Moisten and it reveals the tiny seal of the double-headed eagle. The emperor will be aware of the royal house using such a crest."

"How did she get this?"

"You can ask her yourself."

Archie stood up.

"Don't forget Bonaparte, we know this coup happened. Activate the game and you can check it out."

Napoleon considered the game's creator, a slight smile playing across his lips.

"You wanted something more from your réalité alternative I think..."

It was Archie's turn to study Napoleon. For the first time since he'd met him, Archie sensed the genius that possessed the little general. He paced around.

"When we started out in UAR, I felt one might actually change things, alter history. It took Podric's explanation and me some time to realise that whilst we have that opportunity *inside the game*, it's just that – a game."

"So is life, my friend. But perhaps you missed the point, the point of your creating a game around *my* life."

The two men looked at each other.

"I play to win."

Archie smiled.

"So do Podric and I, but at the time I wrote *Napoleonic Wars*, I didn't know I would be a part of it. That makes things more personal."

Dog stretched. Taking a turn around the room, he stood panting beside Napoleon's little desk. The emperor stroked him.

"When will Podric come?"

"Why is that important to you?"

Napoleon stood up - all 5 foot 5 inches of him.

"Because my friend, whatever this world we're inhabiting is, I intend to beat you both."

"You mean, destroy us."

Napoleon shrugged.

"To be a great general, one must know many things about men –have an agile mind - be decisive yet flexible. But above all, one must have a vision, stratégie."

Ney's aide-de-camp, De Fezensac, burst through the doorway followed by Rapp.

"Emperor, we must hurry. The Russians approach."

Two corporals began packing Napoleon's field desk, chair and unslept-in cot.

"So, what happened with this campaign?"

"Ha. Russia is the curse of all... Your daughter - where is she?"

"Sleeping." Archie was a second too late in his understanding.

"Seize him!"

Several soldiers appeared, and restrained Archie.

"As I said, you must be prompt with advantage, know who to dispense with, and when."

"What about empathy, frailty and error?"

"With these, you will not triumph."

"Podric will be here shortly."

Clutching a leather-bound document folio, Napoleon was propelled from the parlour by Rapp but called back over his shoulder.

"Then we will play to the finish!"

The scene downstairs was chaotic as men hastened in their efforts to leave. Grabbing anything they could, all food was taken as was every last drop of alcohol.

Emerging from the inn, Napoleon stepped into his chaise. Accompanied by Dog, Cosima was brought round under guard. The driver whipped up the horses and seconds later they were gone.

Bending over Prince Poniatowski, Archie joined Count Byresnki.

"Ah, Swiatto or whoever you are. It seems the great god Napoleon has departed with your daughter leaving you with us, the dispensable."

Archie busied himself making the prince as comfortable as he could.

"I'm sorry there was no physician."

Byresnki grunted.

"I approached our French comrades but they were busy with their own. However, I managed to persuade a medic to conduct a cursory inspection. He advised an operation was necessary."

"How urgent?"

"With a week to home, if we keep travelling he should make it."

"Better be on our way then."

Picking up Prince Poniatowski lying on his rough stretcher, they headed for the door.

*   *   *

"My old man got me bail but his solicitor reckons I'm going to be tagged."

Barney and Podric were in the groundsmen's inner office. It had become Carol Jensen and Jane Cartwright's new school hideaway.

After the methane blowback accident destroyed the school boiler system, Jane and Carol lost their exclusive changing room. Missing their privacy, Carol went in search of a replacement. One day she stumbled across the woodwork teacher, Mr. Czvnik in a compromising situation with the new German grounds woman Ms. Purzelbaum. The grounds men's inner office providing a perfect location, a deal had been struck. As a particular friend of Jane and Carol's,

Podric was allowed its use.

"Better than doing time though."

A girl's voice came from a behind partition and a second or two later, Jane and Carol appeared. Although surprised by the girls, neither Podric nor Barney seemed particularly bothered.

"What are you doing here thuggy? Thought you were expelled."

"Maybe I like getting your sporty knickers in a twist."

Barney fiddled with his mobile phone.

The door opened and Catherine Halliday appeared. Already changed into sports kit Jane and Carol were unimpressed by her arrival.

"Got a little meeting going here, Podric? Intruding on our space?"

Caustic, Carol went out. Jane who had always been mildly flirtatious with the computer games wünderkind, shrugged as she went by. The door banged shut. Podric turned to Barney.

"Where are you living?"

"What's it to you?"

"Your going into UAR is what's it to me."

Barney's face lit up as Podric continued.

"You know you need to be somewhere you're not disturbed."

"How about a cell?"

"Ha-ha."

Barney thought for a moment.

"I can go to the parents. No one's usually there and if they are, I never see 'em."

There was something unintentionally pathetic about this knowledge. Podric checked Barney's wrist.

"I'll text you the time but it'll be tomorrow night, latest."

The school bully turned to go but caught Catherine's eye.

"You going in and all?"

"Try stopping me."

"Have a party then. Where are we heading?"

Catherine looked at Podric.

"Yuh – where are we going?"

"Where do you think?"

Barney didn't know but Catherine looked as though she might.

"Guess there's only one place – a crossroads in Belgium."
Barney still looked blank.
"Waterloo."

Chapter 26

Gathering Up

"So...the emperor and your daughter. What lies there Swiatto?" The coach trundled along. Byresnki bit into a cigar. Archie didn't immediately reply. Although initially panicked by Napoleon's behaviour, he considered the situation.

Concerned about his daughter and her desire to experience ultimate alternative reality, he'd immediately gone into UAR after her and now in the world of *Napoleonic Wars*, assumed the emperor had taken Cosima as a ruse to unnerve him. He also understood Napoleon's intense desire to challenge Podric, though where that would manifest itself, Archie was uncertain. He supposed he should contact his partner, but was sure it wouldn't be long before Podric put in an appearance.

With all this and more on his mind, Archie turned to his Polish cavalry colleague and calmly relieving him of his cigar, used it to light his own.

"I wish I knew Byresnki but one thing's for sure, the emperor's losing this campaign and will be beaten."

Byresnki was initially struck mumchance at Archie's removal of his cheroot. Finally, he replied.

"You seem confident."

Enjoying a little of the tobacco, Archie handed Byresnki's smoke back to him.

"Oh, I am, dear count. In this bleak world, I'm very confident indeed, though how I fair in my personal hors de combat with the great man, remains to be seen. If nothing else it will be interesting and most likely, unorthodox."

*   *   *

In Napoleon's chaise several miles ahead, the emperor pored over papers. Despite fresh horses, the animals struggled along the track, covered as it was by yet another fall of snow. Sitting opposite Napoleon, Dog beside her, Cosima stared at the bleak landscape.

"Was coming here worth it? What did it achieve? Death and destruction..."

Cosima wasn't aware she'd spoken aloud. She was surprised when a little while later, Napoleon replied.

"In war, one cannot stand still. It has a dynamic of its own."

Cosima looked at the emperor.

"So, there was there no alternative to fighting?"

Napoleon looked out of the window but his eyes didn't focus on the landscape; his gaze was farther away.

"When I came to power, France was a mess. A dissipated and corrupt monarchy was overthrown by the revolution which was itself chaotic. I have made France the greatest power on earth."

"But not sea and at what price?"

Napoleon looked at her.

"You speak with the benefit of history."

"Which in *Napoleonic Wars* you have the opportunity to change."

"Supposedly it's just a game as Podric and your father never fail to remind me."

"Didn't you say life was?"

Speaking with intensity, Cosima leaned forward.

"Why not try and re-write it now? You've got nothing to lose."

Napoleon's eyes narrowed.

"Why should this be important to you? Your father and Podric will be challenging me."

Cosima sat back, reflective.

"The Light family has been pretty screwed up. Dad linking up with Podric creating UAR has given us a dimension to life we lacked. It has actually made us *come* alive. After getting Podric to programme me, I couldn't wait to be here."

"Presumably that is why your father followed you in."

"Wanting to keep an eye on me, you mean? Worried about his little girl getting into trouble." She laughed.

"He has his reasons."

"Why didn't your father programme you?"

"He's not entirely up to speed with alternative reality. Podric knows it and dad needs him."

So, the girl's father was the weak link. Bonaparte had thought as much. In contemplating his strategy, he reflected that this knowledge could be useful when battle commenced.

"When will they challenge me?"

Cosima was thoughtful.

"I don't think you've studied the whole game."

"Which includes my mortality."

"Each adventure has progressed through your life."

"Only a bad general would allow an enemy to select the battle."

Fiddling with his wrist, Napoleon was glad he'd taken the girl. Talking to her had sharpened his focus. He would study *Napoleonic Wars*. There was some battle ahead that he had lost. That was the challenge and it would be his to rectify. This time victory would be assured.

*   *   *

Barney having left the groundsmen's shed, Catherine sat down.

"When are we going in?"

Podric looked at her, resigned she would be coming with him.

"Tomorrow end of the day. It's the beginning of the weekend."

"I want to be with you, wherever we are."

"I don't want to go in from Archie's. He's there with Cosima. 'Wouldn't have to be chasing after him if it wasn't for her."

"What do you mean?"

"He went in directly she did. I still don't trust his knowledge – or lack of."

"You like her."

Podric banged the bench.

"You like her because she's difficult."

Catherine smiled. "My parents are away."

She was shy. Podric hadn't been to Catherine's house and it suddenly occurred to him that in some ways he knew so little about her.

"Do you have any brothers or sisters?"

Catherine shook her head. "I'm the spoilt brat, an only child."

"And your parents leave you in the house on your own?"

"My real mother died and dad remarried."

Podric was going to commiserate but something in Catherine's manner stopped him.

The two looked at each other.

"How are you going to fight him strategically in the game? You're too young to be the Iron Duke and Blücher was nearly late."

Becoming animated, Catherine picked up a gardening cane.

"Technically, playing the game, we can be anyone in any challenge."

"But you'll be inside won't you - fighting Napoleon in combat on the battlefield so to speak."

Catherine stood up. Podric was cool.

"Napoleon wants to rewrite history. That's what this is all about for him. Creating UAR has given him that opportunity. You're right though. For it to mean anything, we have to fight him but using the advantages of UAR."

"How will that work?"

Podric tapped his left wrist.

"Repositioning of troops, changing tactics, creating the unexpected."

"All things Napoleon's famous for."

Catherine's brain was in overdrive.

"How's the game configured?"

"Shut your eyes."

For a second, Catherine was hesitant.

"It's okay. 'Just easier to see."

Removing the cane she was holding, Podric took Catherine's wrist placing the fingers of her right hand over the microchip.

"You're not going into UAR but I'm activating the game."

The vision revealed the Waterloo battlefield. Guiding her over it, Podric highlighted Napoleon and Wellington's opening positions, the Hougoumont château, La Haye Sainte farm and Prussian movements – ordnance, the terrain, weather conditions – the details were amazing.

"You having been inside UAR properly, the experience is totally different because you're actually living in that world but the detail and accuracy you're looking at in the game are how it was written."

"By your partner."

"He did great work."

Podric moved her fingers across the chip.

"Now watch."

Blocks of red-idented troops suddenly switched positions.

"You can move anything anywhere as long as it's supported. It has to be feasibly practical. Get the picture?"

Podric shut down the game.

Catherine shook her head, clearing it.

"It's amazing; incredible."

Podric checked his own wrist control.

"I'm going to fight inside UAR but have it constantly engaged."

"You mean it'll be real, but you'll manipulate events."

"That's the plan."

"Think it'll work?"

"Find out soon enough. Got one advantage though."

Podric actually smiled.

"As he said, he's not so good with his right hand."

*　　*　　*

The partly frozen Berezina River cut like a blackened scar through the vast snowbound wastes of the Russian countryside. The freezing scene was only broken by the glow of forges. Active on the banks of the river, men carried iron fittings to a pontoon bridge that was being constructed.

Although the instigator of this industry, Napoleon stood with his back to it all. His energies were concentrated on surveying the battlefield before him. Russian infantry had formed up and were preparing to attack. Raising a telescope, Bonaparte eyed a lone rider making his way at a gallop through his tired troops. A minute later the horseman pulled up and dismounted. Ney's attaché, De Fezensac bowed.

"Emperor, the Marshal says Kutuzov is moving to outflank us."

"How far?"

"Five, six miles."

Napoleon turned to an aide.

"The bridgehead?"

The man looked over his shoulder at the pontoon workings which had begun to span the river.

"Eblé says four hours emperor."

"Tell Marshal Oudinot I desire his presence."

The marshal summoned, Napoleon resumed his classic stance. His brooding gaze studied the activity. Oudinot arrived.

"Emperor."

Napoleon turned to the marshal and indicated a portable campaign table. Several maps were clipped to it.

"I have a difficult task for you marshal." Oudinot made no reply.

"The admiral prepares for battle but I do not wish to fight him here. Kutuzov approaches and I desire you engage Chichagov – draw him off, allowing The Grande Armée to make good its retreat."

"Sire."

"Kutuzov's forces number fifty thousand which is why we must strike now."

Oudinot gave the map a last glance and looked across at the enemy.

"Then I must not delay."

"You have your orders, Comte. The glory of France awaits!"

Twilight on the river found engineers struggling in the swirling current. The weather freezing, conditions could not have been worse but the pontoon bridge was nearing completion. Sporadic artillery fire could be heard in the distance and what was left of Napoleon's army had bivouacked nearby.

Drawn and fatigued, the emperor finally entered the encampment late in the evening. Heading directly for his quarters, he dined
in conference with his staff. The meeting concluded in the small
hours when General Rapp brought more papers for Napoleon's sig-
nature.

"The young lady sire. You wished to see her?"

A cannon shell exploding nearby ended their conversation. The
earth shook and a lump of scorching metal flew through the tent.
The emperor avoided being hit but a shard nicked Rapp's arm which
started to bleed. Getting to his feet, Napoleon whipped the necker-
chief from his stock and quickly began wrapping it around the general's wound.

"Emperor, you must attend the army!"

Rapp ministered to by an aide, Napoleon went outside. The
encampment was in chaos as further shells exploded amongst the
massed troops. Soldiers needed little spurring as men and materiel
– infantry, cannon, horse and gun cart – began to pour across the
pontoon bascule. At times the unstable structure wavered alarming-
ly, the river's strong tide threatening to sweep all away. But discipline
finally reasserted itself and the French continued to evacuate their
position in some order.

Pressed against the bank in the icy river downstream, Cosima
and Dog watched the activity. Having already decided to make her escape, the Russian bombardment provided perfect cover but knowing
she couldn't stay in the water for long, Cosima climbed out. Hiding
in some snow-covered bushes near the water's edge, she hugged Dog
for warmth.

The French army preoccupied with its egress, the last broken gun
limber rolled off into the darkness. The bombardment fell silent and
the stillness was intense.

From her hidden position, Cosima caught her first glimpse
of pointed enemy hats as Cossack soldiers rode stealthily forward
mounted on their shaggy ponies. Wild looking, they seemed ominous and barbaric.

Spying a rowing boat tied to a ramshackle jetty, Cosima decided
to make for it. She and Dog wormed their way towards the craft.

Spotted, shots rang out and as she leaped for the tiny vessel, the girl concussed herself hitting her head on its combing.

Coming round moments later, Cosima stared at a large pair of fur boots. The Cossack - moustachioed and grizzled - gazed down at her. The man was taken by surprise when Dog barged him aside, knocking him off balance.

With shaking hands, Cosima managed to untie the rocking dinghy and Dog scrambling in, she cast off. More pistol shots were fired, but the little boat was gripped by the current and quickly began drifting downstream into the murky night.

Chapter 27

All Aboard!

Podric felt strangely void of emotion as he accompanied Catherine up the drive to her house on the outskirts of Wendbury that Friday night. A sizeable property, to Podric's eyes it lacked character, a sentiment shared by his girlfriend.

"We had an old place near the river. 'Bit ramshackle, I loved it, but when ma died, Dad lost the plot. Stella came along, discovered he had a bit of money and the rest is history."

She unlocked the front door and deactivated the alarm.

"I was sent off to stay with an aunt in Yorkshire for a few days. When I came back, he was married and we'd moved here. All my things were in my room, unpacked. It was surreal."

They went into the kitchen. Podric leaned against a counter checking messages on his iPhone as Catherine sorted drinks. A beer for Podric and a glass of wine for herself. The kitchen was spacious and looked out on a rear garden bordered by woods. They swigged and sipped their drinks.

"How do you feel now?"

"Okay."

Catherine put down her drink and came over to Podric putting her arms around his waist.

"I've been thinking a lot about UAR, particularly the chosen few you've programmed. By all accounts, Archie's pretty screwed up. I haven't figured out his daughter yet, but from what you say, she also seems a little twisted. Then there's Barney and we know what a delinquent he is."

Letting Podric go, she had another sip of her wine.

"And me. It's an interesting selection you've made."

Podric didn't reply but had another swig of his beer. Catherine continued.

"Of all of us, the choice that interests me most is Barney."

"There's more to him than meets the eye. Besides, I wanted him for a UAR experiment."

"Are you always so calculating?"

"Yes."

They both laughed.

"But you've forgotten the most important participant. He's the greatest question of all."

"Think you'll get to know him?"

"After I beat him you mean?"

"Good luck with that. He's one of history's all-time great commanders."

"Better get going then. No time like the present."

With reluctance, Catherine led him through to her bedroom.

*   *   *

Pressed on all sides by marauding Cossacks, the coach carrying the wounded Prince Poniatowski lurched along the track. Protected by a column of Polish hussars, the prince still lay on a seat inside, but Count Byresnki was now positioned beside the driver with a rifle to his shoulder. Mounted on a cavalry charger, Colonel Swiatto covered a flank. If the Poles had any advantage, it was the atrocious weather and moonless night.

Battling on, some of their number were picked off but the bulk of the force approached the river. Arriving a little way downstream from the crossing the French had constructed, glimmers of light could be seen at the far end of the pontoon. The remnants of Napoleon's army continued to struggle across the bridgehead.

Taking temporary command, Count Byresnki held a brief conference. It was decided a battalion would engage the Russian's and harry them while the main force bivouacked, ate and rested in preparation to cross the Berezina at dawn. Electing to be a part of the combat unit, Archie led off a troop and moved up to the empty French encampment. Engagement with the Russians became intense. Small arms were fired at close quarters and men were in hand to hand combat.

*   *   *

Podric lay on Catherine's bed. His having entered UAR several minutes previously, Catherine sat beside him gently stroking his hair. She was curious to see how he looked in his state of Ultimate Alternative Reality. Although his eyes were closed, it wasn't like sleep. It was more meditative, as if transcendental – his being removed from his body. It was strange, looking at somebody in another world. It added an incomparable dimension.

She got up. What had he said? In a few hours' time she could go in herself. Even with the UAR encounters Catherine had already experienced, she knew that alternative reality time had no bearing on its normal counterpart. By now Podric could be anywhere in *Napoleonic Wars*, meeting up with Dr. Light and having the adventures they both loved.

She hadn't really understood what a clever guy Podric was – not just bright, but original. She knew Dr. Light had been integral in providing the mathematical calculus necessary to create their alternative reality, but it had been Podric's creativity that had inspired it.

Catherine thought how attractive he was in his slightly gangling way. There was a diffidence about Podric which had immediately attracted her when they first met. Although Catherine had been dated plenty of times she was still a virgin. Without being prudish, committing herself physically to someone would in her eyes, be the ultimate sense of giving. She was certain she would make love to Podric – she wanted it to happen but it would be when the time was right. Meanwhile, their Ultimate Alternative Reality experiences would give them both climaxes of a very different kind.

Twilight gathering, the clock beside Catherine's bed indicated that it was 7.48pm. Lying down beside Podric, she'd go in at 8.30 pm; it would be one hell of a weekend.

*   *   *

On the far bank of the Berezina, the last of the Grande Armée got ashore as sappers working with night lamps, busily prepared to blow what had been their means of escape.

The road west to Poland running parallel to the river for several miles, Napoleon's field HQ had camped in a village near Borisov. An aide galloped in, asking for Oudinot. Directed to the marshal who was at conference with his staff, young Lieutenant De Willoughby hurriedly reported.

"The last of our men crossing advise that the Poles are preparing to get on the bascule Marshal."

"What of it?"

"You instructed it should be blown."

"Well?"

"Our allies, sir. Shouldn't we assist them?"

Oudinot glanced at the lancer dismissively.

"Your task ensign, is to obey my order."

For several seconds, De Willoughby didn't move.

"Return to your post immediately and see that they are."

Coming to attention, the lieutenant departed leaving behind him a wake of arrogant disdain.

Thwarted by overturned transport and dire conditions, De Willoughby's return journey proved difficult. He finally arrived at the pontoon just before dawn to discover the engineers he'd left laying charges, had disappeared.

The temporary bridgehead was supported by timber struts. Peering underneath, De Willoughby saw that all the explosives were in position but looking around, the only people he could see were the approaching Poles, who had begun to set off across the rickety structure.

"Wonker."

De Willoughby looked around.

"Wonker Will, a Frenchie officer. Ha!"

Emerging from snow covered bushes, Barney Sturridge looked a rare sight. His tunic was now a foot soldier's uniform of the Vistula legion but he still wore his red cockade hat from the revolution! De Willoughby eyed him stupidly.

"Who are you?"

"Don't be dumb Wonker. You know who I am."

But only UAR profiled, De Willoughby, didn't. To him, the scruffy figure was some sort of deranged ragtag militaire.

Removing a pouch of slow burning fuses from inside his tunic, De Willoughby selected one.

"No Miles, you're not going to do that. Podric said the pontoon isn't to be blown yet."

De Willoughby was thrown – Barney was using his forename.

"Look here – who are you, a mercenary?"

Barney laughed.

"You could say that."

Sturridge began to move towards Miles Willoughby.

"Put the fuse away Miles, get on your horse and ride off just like the good little swot you are in class."

"You're mad!"

Ignoring Barney, De Willoughby inspected the fuse and taking out a knife, began to cut it. Barney knocked him on the head with a wooden strut.

Dragging Miles over to the bushes, Barney ran back along the pontoon towards the oncoming Polish.

"Hurry guys – keep it moving."

The strange looking youth gesticulating, indicated the bank behind him.

"Chop chop now."

The Polish soldiers couldn't understand what Barney was doing there any more than De Willoughby had, but needing little encouragement, they hurried on.

At the Polish held end, fighting was fierce and Archie was under severe pressure as the Russians pressed home their attack.

It was into this bagarre that Barney arrived. It was lucky that he did. Taking a bad blow, Archie had fallen. Barney managed to pull him away, and let the immediate battle pass over them.

Lying prostrate, Archie regained consciousness to discover that he was in Barney's tender loving care.

"Oh, God. You again."

Archie felt his head.

"What have I done to deserve this?"

"Taken a bang on the head sir. Common casualty."

Helping Archie to his feet, Barney was concerned.

"You need to take it easy, sir."

The relationship Barney had with Archie was particular. The school bully had an odd respect for the computer games creator and similarly, Archie had a perverse fondness for the boy. It was as if both recognised the artificial front each presented to the outside world. However grudging, a kind of mutual understanding existed between them.

Looking around, Archie surveyed the scene. Mercifully, the Russians had withdrawn briefly to regroup but the Polish forces had got across leaving Barney and himself isolated to fend for themselves.

"Since you've been bozo, everyone's crossed over."

"Bozo?"

"Out of it; zonked."

"Your English... Can't be a lot of teaching going on at that school."

"Never paid much attention at Wendbury and grammar don't rate at YOI."

Archie looked at Barney quizzically.

"Young Offenders."

"I forgot you were a con."

Archie scratched his tired body.

"Is that Podric's common denominator for programming us – we're all losers?"

"Speak for yerself."

Small arms fire starting up nearby, musket shots zipped around their ears.

"We've got to get across! Where's my daughter?"

Archie tried to walk but stumbled.

"Taken care of sir."

"What do you mean?"

"Just that."

The penny dropped.

"So, where is my business partner?"

"He's around."

"But my daughter. I've got to find her."

"Reckon Pod will have that in hand."

"What gives you that idea?"

"Said he'd do a recce – snout her out."

"Snout her out?"

Archie's energy sagged again.

"Education. That's what you need young man."

"If you say so sir, but just now, a good fight'll do."

On the far side of the river, Podric sat in Cosima's dinghy resting on an oar. The young woman lay asleep on the burden boards and Dog's panting head rested against the gunwale.

Watching the last Polish soldiers stream ashore, Podric secured the craft nearby. Landing, he discovered a dazed Miles De Willoughby lying in some bushes where Barney had left him.

Turning his attention to the pontoon, Podric watched Barney half carry Archie across the rickety structure. The Russian army behind was beginning to make its way on to it. Podric ducked below and checked the detonating primers.

At his camp a mile or two away, Napoleon's light chaise was being prepared. Bonaparte was in a remote mood, his mercurial mind preoccupied with affairs of state now much affected by the failure of his Russian campaign.

His bodyguard already mounted and the necessary portmanteau loaded aboard, the emperor made ready to leave. All of a sudden there was an almighty explosion. Clouds of smoke and debris wafted into the sky.

Paying little heed, Napoleon climbed into his coach. Jolting along the track that ran beside the Berezina, the driver noticed a dinghy swirling around. One of its occupants waved a salute. In spite of his orders, the coachman reined in and stopped. About to remonstrate, Napoleon looked out of the window and saw the now united UAR group aboard the skiff. Standing, Podric's left arm was above his head, and as Napoleon watched, the boy raised his right hand up to his left wrist.

*   *   *

On the evening of 15th June 1815, the ballroom of the Duke and Duchess of Richmond's residence in Brussels was magnificent. Candelabra shone with brilliance and tapestries were an abundance of exotic voile. The glitterati of European society being present – the Coalition's officer corps were dashing in their resplendent uniforms. They were equally matched by the women, who dazzled amidst toile, brocade and diamonds.

Watching proceedings from the shadows, two young women stood apart. The taller of the two, the Hon Cosima McCorquodale wore a dress of midnight blue moiré which shimmied against her statuesque figure. The other, Miss Catherine Halliday, looked equally stunning in a claret velvet gown, its slashed plunging V accentuating her décolletage. Several officers showed interest in the two women but made no headway.

A tall man dressed in black and wearing a single order entered and began talking to the Duke of Richmond. Leaving his host and circulating the room, the Duke of Wellington spied the two young ladies and strolled over.

"Mesdames."

The duke bowed; the ladies curtsied.

"You find the ball uninteresting?"

"Our presence here isn't celebratory."

Cosima's response was cool.

"We know you're to fight a battle."

The duke laughed.

"My dear young lady, everyone knows I'm here to fight a battle."

"But not everyone knows exactly where and at what time – even you."

Unaccustomed to such attitude, least from a young woman, Wellington was taken aback, though his manners didn't entirely desert him.

"What possible military knowledge would you possess, ma'am?"

"The knowledge that in a minute or two, an aide to the Prince of

Orange will arrive informing you Prussian forces are in retreat and later, a second message is delivered explaining how Napoleon has stolen a march on you – if you'll pardon the expression, my lord."

Wellington had no time to respond as at that moment the mud splattered figure of Henry Weber entered. After bowing to the Duke of Richmond, he was directed to Wellington.

"I have dispatches, sir."

The Iron Duke put out his hand. Pulling open his tunic, Weber removed a leather wrapped note and handed it to Wellington.

"My lords, ladies and gentlemen, dinner is served."

The major domo's sonorous tones died away. The Duchess of Devonshire and Lady Frances Webster appeared beside Wellington.

"And remember the second message, sir. You may recall our advising you of it in the hours to come." Catherine made a small bow and to the surprise of the three nobles, she and Cosima withdrew.

"Who pray, are they?"

Lady Webster was put out. Wellington caught Weber's eyes following the young beauties admiringly.

"Young women can have lively imaginations."

"But not the experience."

Lady Webster's weighted retort was followed by a smile of intimacy.

"What did she mean by a second message?"

Georgiana Richmond was more astute than her friend.

"I cannot imagine ma'am but no doubt all will be revealed if, and when, it appears."

The drollness of this wasn't lost on the women, particularly Lady Frances, whose flirtatiousness towards Wellington was evident as she accompanied him into dinner.

Chapter 28

Waterloo

A mile or two from the village of Waterloo, a farmhouse known as Le Caillou had been taken over by French high command on the eve of battle, requisitioned for the emperor's headquarters. Having breakfasted in the small hours, Napoleon dressed in waistcoat and breeches and looking much stouter, sat with his generals who included Count Drouot, Duc De Bassano and commander of the Imperial Guard, Marshal Soult. Masticating his food thoughtfully, Bonaparte pushed aside his plate and studied the maps strewn about beside him.

"The army of the enemy is superior to ours by more than one-fourth. Nevertheless, we have ninety chances in our favour, and ten against us."

At that moment Marshal Ney entered. Not having had breakfast, he was handed coffee. Napoleon requested his opinion regarding their position.

"Without doubt Sire, you have Wellington cornered. But I must inform you that his retreat is decided and that if you do not hasten to attack, the enemy is about to escape you."

Napoleon looked up from his maps.

"You are wrong, and it is too late now. Wellington would expose himself to a certain loss. He has thrown the dice and they are in our favour."

There being much activity in the breakfast room - aides coming and going with dispatches - Ney excused himself leaving a hesitant Marshal Soult to liaise with the emperor.

"Would it not be beneficial to bring up the right wing emperor, by way of reinforcements?"

Interpreting Soult's suggestion as criticism of his tactics, Napoleon was dismissive. He jumped up and strode about the room.

"Because you have been beaten by Wellington, you consider him a great general. And now I will tell you that he is a bad general and that this affair is nothing more serious than eating one's breakfast."

Thus admonished, Soult also withdrew. Bonaparte instructed that his horse Marengo should be saddled and his staff prepare themselves in readiness. The room emptied.

Suddenly quiet, Napoleon stood alone. Scratching his left wrist, he stared out of the window.

"So few of your generals ever carry out orders to your satisfaction. 'Reckon it's easier to fight a campaign solo."

Napoleon smiled and continued to look at the gloomy view. Low clouds scudded across the horizon.

"You are right Podric, but troop movements, ordnance and supply are different in reality than in your battle electronique."

"Principle's the same though. All those things have to be taken into account in order to win."

Napoleon finally turned to face Podric who stood on the far side of the breakfast table. Dressed in the uniform of a hussar sous-lieutenant, his gangly form was contrastingly still after the bustling bodies of Gallic officers.

"I've been waiting for you."

Napoleon's face was much brighter than it had been with his staff.

"Because of the chance to re-write history – at least in the game?"

Napoleon sighed.

"I never thought Wellington much of a general."

"He beat you though."

"Pchwa. I'm unwell."

"That sounds like an excuse. Anyway, I'm not the Iron Duke or whatever he called himself. I'm a computer games champion."

"...who has an advantage over me."

Signing a document on the table with his left hand, Bonaparte raised it waving the quill in his fingers.

"Shouldn't affect any strategy of the great Napoleon. Having been inside *Napoleonic Wars* recently you'll have already reminded yourself of the reasons for your loss. Grouchy not finishing off the Prussians yesterday at Wavre, the delays and foul-ups of your orders."

Podric finally moved, and leaning forward studied a map of the Waterloo battlefield.

"But if you throw more weight on your right flank and attack Wellington faster, victory can be yours."

"How do you know I've been inside the game?"

It was Podric's turn to tap his wrist. Napoleon nodded.

"You a mere boy, giving me advice!"

Podric eyed the emperor coolly.

"Do you actually want to play?"

Napoleon resumed a sulky attitude.

"Do you think even challenging inside it, you'll really win – or would you rather re-live the battle fought without modern technology..?"

The way Podric spoke suggested he was considering a line of thought.

"To win Podric. My whole life I have lived to win!"

Still looking at Napoleon, Podric's gaze suddenly flicked up. Activating the game, *Napoleonic Wars* flashed into his top vision. With a further depression of his finger, he linked the emperor. The two of them were now participants.

"Wha-? I have not activated myself."

"My being able to do that to you remotely is another element I've been working on. Play when you want."

Podric moved his right index finger quickly over the microchip in his left wrist racing through Options to Campaigns, then Battles. Selecting Waterloo, within the support menu he opted for Troop Deployment. Caught up watching Podric's actions, Napoleon hadn't moved.

A battalion of Grenadiers moved into position taking cover along a tree-lined field on the far side of the road from La Caillou. A musketry fusillade poured into the building. Glass shattered, plaster fell from the ceiling and brick and timber fragments rent the air.

Podric pressed his left wrist again, deactivating *Napoleonic Wars*. Transfixed, Bonaparte never got started as a player, stunned as he had been by Podric's sheer speed.

The air clearing, a shattered Bonaparte looked out of the window. There was no sign of Picton's division or any other British soldiers for that matter.

"That's what you're playing with old man – in my century, using my technology. That's the game now; that's *my* game."

Napoleon sat down crumpled. Having experienced seconds of heightened intensity, Podric cleaned out a dust-filled cup and helped himself to some cold coffee from a silver pot.

"Let's leave the game challenge otherwise I'll destroy you. But we can experience the battle as it was when you fought it."

Podric had some cold coffee and grimaced.

"You still have the advantage in the field because you know what went wrong. With that knowledge, you can change the course of events within the battle but do it without using technology."

Recovering his wits, Napoleon looked at Podric.

"What will you do?"

"That's my business. But now you're not playing me, if I fight you, I'll fight you as one would have in 1815."

"Why will you do this?"

Podric had another gulp of cold coffee.

"When I invented Ultimate Alternative Reality-."

"With your partner."

Napoleon cut in. Podric laughed.

"Yes, with my partner...I, we created it to enjoy adventures we otherwise could never experience. UAR has already delivered more than we ever imagined."

Napoleon stood up and reached for his old bottle green field coat. Podric helped him into it.

"But that wasn't the real reason you wanted your alternative reality, was it Podric? You needed to find another life to help you connect with your father."

It was Podric's turn to reflect.

"But you won't find him."

"That's where you're wrong. He's with me all the time."

"You can't bring him back to life though."

"Why not? I did you."

"But I'm in a computer game. Are you going to do that to your father?!"

Podric turned to the French emperor.

"You're partly right about UAR and its origins but it was my dad who first got me into computer games. When I'm existing in this world, I feel his presence intensely."

"More than in your real life?"

"Yes. He was so wired computer wise – sometimes when I'm doing things in alternative reality I feel he's actually with me."

Napoleon grunted. "Will you let me go when my time comes?"

The twenty-first century computer games champion and the eighteenth-century emperor looked at each other.

"Time enough time to make that call. We've a battle to fight first."

*   *   *

For Archie Light, the Battle of Waterloo was proving a miserable experience. Since his Russian adventure as Colonel Swiatto, he had escaped the bear's clutches in pursuit of his errant daughter and followed her into the Belgian campaign. The idea that Cosima might befriend Podric's girlfriend Catherine and attend the Duchess of Richmond's ball had initially surprised him, but on reflection, nothing really did where UAR was concerned. Cosima had been obsessed with experiencing Ultimate Alternative Reality from the moment she knew about it. Given how headstrong she was, Archie knew that this entry would be challenging.

Deciding to participate as part of Wellington's staff (Archie had never been one to opt for lower ranks) he now rode at the duke's side as one of his aides. Dog loped along with them. Wellington, mounted on Copenhagen, seemed oblivious to the early morning rain as the group cantered from the village of Waterloo, south to Mount St. Jean. Inspecting allied positions, the Duke couldn't help noticing Dog.

"What's that animal doing here?"

Stirring from the ranks of aides surrounding Wellington, Archie had to confess the animal was his. Wellington eyed him.

"Light huh? In the 2nd I see. Don't recognise you."

Archie mumbled something about serving on the North American station and being more recently attached to the British diplomatic delegation as a military attaché in Stockholm – theatres he knew Wellington had little knowledge of.

"Fine specimen, damned fine animal. An Irish too. Wouldn't look out of place in Meath. Good luck to you sir!"

Wheeling Copenhagen, Wellington trotted away, his acolytes following in his wake. Holding back, Archie looked down at his wolfhound. Dog's tail wagged and his great jaw panted. Archie took a boot from his stirrup and prodded Dog playfully.

"A day it was when you walked into my life. Guess we'd better find us some action."

The weather began to clear. Viewing the ground from Rossomme farm, Napoleon decided to relinquish much of the battle's management to Marshal Ney, basing himself from La Belle Alliance at the rear of the field.

Fighting began around 11.30am. Batteries of the Comte d'Erlon's Corps commenced firing on Allied positions. The first feint the French made was an attempt to go around Hougomont, but an Allied counter thrust blocked this. Napoleon's next stroke was to get a message to Marshal Grouchy much earlier than he had in the original battle, ordering him to his side before the Prussian's arrived. The emperor also attacked La Haye Sainte earlier than history records and increasing the weight of his thrust on the Allied right, French troops attempted to punch their way through in an aggressive flanking movement.

These attacks expanded the fighting around the Hougomont estate. Several Guards' companies repulsed wave after wave of French attacks. The constant pounding that the château received by French artillery caused fire to break out in a number of farm buildings and despite the previous night's heavy rain, dust, cannon and musket smoke was dense. The fighting intimate and bloody – sabre and bay-onet clashed in fierce hand to hand combat.

Arriving with his Coldstreamers to support the hard-pressed defence, Colonel Woodford was amazed to see an enormous Irish wolfhound running about amidst the chaos and carnage. Peering through the frenzied mayhem, the animal seemed to be in the very epicentre of the action barging all and sundry away from a dragoon captain who was fighting demonically. A wagon had been turned on its side and Woodford squinting into the light, watched as yet anoth-er wave of Cuirassiers was thrown back.

The man and dog epitomized British fighting spirit. The hound particularly inspired soldiers. They yelled huzzahs like banshees at the faltering French who were completely bewildered by the wolfhound's antics. The scene further astonished Woodford as he watched Dog leap on one of the attackers – a French Sous Lieutenant – but rather than attack him, the hound appeared to protect him! Cannon shell exploding on the side of the house temporarily obliterated Wood-ford's vision. When it cleared, the dragoon, dog and young French officer had all disappeared.

In violent struggle behind a burning hayrick, the UAR combat-ants fought like maniacs.

"Nice of you to show up."

Archie parried a French thrust as Podric parried a British one.

"No longer a Pole then."

Archie glanced at Podric briefly.

"I see you've gone Johnny foreigner this time. Thought we were supposed to be playing Boney in the game, rather than taking each other out."

Podric sidestepped an attack.

"That was over in seconds. I moved forces so fast it blew him away."

Dispatching their opponents, they briefly hugged each other much to the amazement of others on their respective sides!

"He's agreed to fight the battle conventionally given he's got the advantage of knowing its previous outcome."

"Trust him, do you?"

British and French troops now converging on Podric and Archie – a particularly vicious lunge on them was thwarted by Corporal Sturridge, serving as a regular in the Grenadiers.

"Wondered where you'd got to?"

Barney was having the time of his life taking on all and sundry.

"Had to be in at the kill sir."

Archie laughed but was hard pressed.

"I can see how well suited you are to all this."

Another lunge, another parry.

"Podric, are you going to wrap this up?"

Not getting a reply, Archie managed a quick glance round but his young business partner was nowhere to be seen.

Standing on a grassy bank near the inn known as la Belle Alliance, Napoleon's Chief of Staff, Marshal Soult surveyed the battlefield. A difficult task through artillery smoke, the marshal didn't like what he saw. His fellow army commander, Ney, had committed several brigades of cavalry that charged the enemy wastefully. Whilst the Prince of Moskowa himself fought with his usual fearlessness, his forces were squandered due to the ill-considered attack.

Scowling, Soult turned to see the emperor's carriage pull up. A hunched Napoleon emerged from its depths. Soult didn't wait for permission to speak.

"Sire, the situation in our centre is precarious."

Napoleon put out a hand. An aide placed a telescope in it. For several seconds Bonaparte scanned the scene.

"I gave no order to attack. This premature movement may lead to fatal results. Wellington is compromising us just as he did at Jena."

An uneasy mood spread amongst the French High Command. Was it really Ney's fault? What had the emperor been doing all this time? Napoleon's customary portable field table was set up and various tactical plans were presented. Bonaparte gave them scant attention.

"Kellermann and Guyot's squadrons must be deployed in order to extricate the situation."

"Is this your command, sire?"

"You question me, marshal?"

Soult bowed, turned away and began conferring with aides. Two were quickly dispatched. Apparently in no further need of communication, Napoleon withdrew into himself. Sitting down at his table, he pressed his right index finger into his left wrist.

Chapter 29

The Final Round

In the evening light, several carriages and broughams had gathered at a clearing beside the Ohain River. Sitting in their conveyances, a number of women recognisable from the Duchess of Richmond's ball watched the battle from their vantage point.

Artillery fire was still intense as fighting continued to rage in the distance. Waves of blue and red were glimpsed through smoke filled haze, and a new colour was gradually discerned – uniforms of grey beginning to enter the field.

An open landau arrived carrying the two young English women who had appeared so enigmatically at the ball. Parked a little distance from the rest, Cosima and Catherine were elegantly dressed and appropriately attired for the outdoors.

Looking through a pair of field glasses, Cosima passed them to Catherine. After the latter had viewed the scene for a moment or two she lowered the binoculars. The two glanced at each other before pressing their right fingers to their left wrists.

Weary beyond belief, the Duke of Wellington rode amongst his men – chivvying them here, berating them there. Moving towards his left flank he approached General Müffling his Prussian liaison officer. Müffling was staring in the direction of the Bois de Ohain and the mass of grey uniforms that had now stopped in front of the woods.

"You seem agitated, General."

Even with the chaos and carnage going on around them, the Prussian general appeared hesitant.

"I am concerned my lord."

Müffling was about to suggest 'muddled orders' but before he could say anything, a cannon exploded nearby. Wheeling their horses, the duke and Müffling galloped off to a safer position.

*   *   *

Sitting in the parlour of a small cottage in the tiny hamlet of Merbe-Braine, a bloodied and dusty Archie Light confronted his elegant daughter.

"What happened to playing Napoleon in the game?"

"Podric advised he wiped him out – a no contest."

"Well, something's gone wrong now. Why don't *you* take Napoleon on and play him?"

Archie looked hesitant. Cosima smiled.

"It's okay dad, I couldn't have done it either. It was all I could do to get here using UAR but when we're done, we've got a whole lot more to learn about this from Podric."

Archie could only grunt in agreement.

"But you've got to advise Zieten otherwise the Prussian intervention won't happen – really!"

Amazed at his daughter's knowledge, Archie looked at her incredulously.

"How do you know so much about Waterloo?"

"You think I was always asleep when you wrote *Napoleonic Wars?* We had nothing else, morning, noon and night for six months!"

Archie stood up and despite his stained tunic, hugged his daughter.

"Still glad you got into this?"

Looking at her father, Cosima's eyes glistened.

"Are you kidding? Ultimate Alternative Reality is the best thing I've ever experienced! My only problem is reality."

Giving him a final squeeze, Cosima stood back.

"Now ride. You were always okay in the saddle."

Archie headed for the door and with a brief wave, went out.

*   *   *

Lieutenant-General von Zieten was worried. Allied ranks breaking in retreat were causing him to temporarily halt the advance of his Prussian 1 Corps. Perhaps he should swing left and head for the main thrust under von Bülow as Blucher had ordered?

Surveying the scene, the general was suddenly aware of a figure riding hard in his direction. His aides closing up to protect Zieten, a cry went up from the rider.

"General Zieten. General Zieten! Weichen Sie nicht – don't deviate!"

Who was this and speaking his own language?

"Light, staff officer 2nd Lancers, general."

"You know me?"

Zieten was stiff.

"Hans Ernst Karl. Born Dechtow, Brandenburg 5th March seventeen seventy. Service in Poland, eminent in the ceasefire at Poishwitz. Subsequently, integral to the withdrawal of allied troops from Bautzen. Today, commanding the Prussian 1 Corps."

"Wellington has remarkably well-informed aides."

Panting from his gallop, Archie's horse bucked.

"Message from Baron von Müffling."

"From Friedrich?"

"Indeed sir, the duke's Prussian advisor."

"I'm aware of the Baron's position!"

Archie reined in his horse.

"It's of the utmost importance you attack immediately, count."

"Count? Count?! What insolence is this?!"

In his excitement, Archie had forgotten the man he was talking to wasn't made Graf von Zieten by Frederick William III of Prussia till 1817!

"Apologies general. The battle, my mind..."

Zieten regarded the lancer. He was probably one of Wellington's insolent staffers, a particular breed and not always diplomatic. On the other hand, the man was au courant.

"Very well. I will delay no longer."

The Prussian general turned to an aide.

"Sound the order to advance."

*   *   *

The game of *Napoleonic Wars* clicked through Options.

French troops under Grouchy attack and make a determined move of strength at the eastern section of the Allied line.

The cursor skimmed about the game.

The French decimate Pack, Best and Kempt's divisions.

Like a possessed man, Napoleon was transfixed. His eyes riveted in the game, a look of arrogant triumph played across his face.

The move renders Wellington's right flank insignificant, French troops pouring into allied positions. A massive artillery bombardment also pounds the British centre utterly demolishing La Haye Sainte and the ridge at Mount St. Jean.

He would show this twenty-first-century boy and his adult accomplice what a person of genius could do in any age.

The Imperial Guard went through the broken gap and began rolling up Wellington's forces. Preparing to manoeuvre light horse artillery into position thereby prohibiting Blucher's Prussian units linking with the British, the French are in a position to seize victory.

There was only one Napoleon – and he would win!

Things were suddenly reversed – French attacks thwarted by counter thrusts at their rear and left.

Napoleon moved his finger across the microchip with ever increasing desperation.

On screen, these lightning tactics crushed the advantages the French had won and they were again vulnerable.

He was being outplayed.

In minutes, it was all over. The Guard was smashed and the French collapsed comprehensively.

In the cellar of a barn at Rossomme, Podric Moon sat opposite Catherine Halliday. He, filthy and battle worn, still in the uniform of a French sous-lieutenant; she, stylish and cool, dressed in ladies' day clothes and cloak.

Podric exited the game and they both stood up. Catherine hugged him. Podric's face was a mixture of sadness and grim satisfaction.

Chapter 30

Farewell

Lying in the South Atlantic, roughly midway between the continents of Africa and South America, the island of St Helena is one of the most remote places on earth. Most of its fifty-square mile coastline is sheer rock and due to its position, the weather experienced renders the western side of the island verdant and tropical whilst the eastern is barren and volcanic. The very severity of this isolated location was a powerful influence when in 1815, Great Britain decided to incarcerate her most dangerous enemy there, dispatching Napoleon to its rocky shores.

Seven years later, Louis Marchand, Napoleon Bonaparte's valet and one of the few remaining members of his entourage, was busy preparing his master's petit dejeuner. To Marchand, the heady days of military campaigns and palace attendances in Paris, Rome and Vienna were a dim and distant past.

The mini court that had accompanied the emperor south on his internment had now largely returned to Europe. All had owed their success to Napoleon, but the entourage had done nothing except bitch and bicker from the moment they set foot on the island, making the emperor's life even more miserable than it already was.

Hearing Napoleon's mutterings in the next room, Marchand briefly left the kitchen and entered the pantry to gather up sweetmeats and the few other little delicacies he was forever trying to forage for his master from his military gaolers.

Looking out of the larder's small window, Marchand saw Company Quartermaster Tweeney at the gate. No doubt Tweeney would be wanting payment for the items Marchand had recently purchased from him at such exorbitant cost. The trouble was there was so little left to barter. Most of Napoleon's personal effects had either already been traded or stolen.

A gig pulled up and a slim young man dressed in civilian clothes stepped out.

"CQMS Ralph Tweeney, so you've pitched up here."

For a second, the slim youth and corpulent quartermaster eyed each other.

"Sir..?"

"Brother of Sergeant Don."

Tweeney took a step backward.

"Sir..?"

Putting on weight since Podric had last seen him, Tweeney's fleshy jowls began to sweat.

"You... know me?"

Opening the gate, Podric Moon didn't immediately reply.

"You were posted here as Quartermaster of Supply having served under Sir Hudson Lowe in earlier campaigns...Yes..?"

"How-?"

"'Fought at the Heights of Toulon in '93 alongside your brother, who was an artilleryman."

Approaching the house, Tweeney was severely shaken. Marchand appeared on the veranda.

"Sergeant Tweeney."

Marchand's high-pitched voice was unwelcoming.

"With a gentleman – a new *young* gentleman."

The valet looked at Podric briefly then back at the quartermaster who was rubbing his forehead as if in a trance.

"You appear somewhat vexed sir. We can have nothing today. The emperor rests."

Longwood not being a large property, Bonaparte's mutterings could be heard coming from an adjacent room.

"Good day to you citizens of King George – the fourth, is it not? Can you English not think of another name for your roi royale?"

Fussing about, Marchand disappeared.

Standing in the sun, Tweeney attempted to pull himself together.

"Forgive me sir... You seem to know so much about me... My service... My brother and me were indeed at Toulon, but you're a young fellow sir. Don was killed nearly thirty years ago."

"You'll have a family – some children."

"Oh don't start again sir, please."

Sweating, Tweeney nodded frantically. Podric handed him a silk handkerchief. Gratefully accepted, the quartermaster wiped his forehead. Podric nodded toward the house.

"What sort of state is he in?"

"Between you and me sir, he's sick, very sick. I wouldn't give him long and when he goes, we can all say goodbye to this accursed isle."

Stepping on to the portico, the house was silent. Quietly opening a door revealed a simple reception room. Podric looked about. Shutters were drawn and though modestly furnished, the effect wasn't unpleasant. Another moan arose from the adjacent room.

Peering into Napoleon's bedchamber, the ex-emperor's appearance shocked Podric. Half-dressed in his old uniform and sitting in a corner chair, Bonaparte was corpulent. With a grey pallor and wracking cough, he looked an ill man. Seeing Podric, Napoleon waved at him through a none too clean towel.

"Ah, mon chéri, you are here at last."

Approaching Napoleon, Podric said nothing.

"Help me up. We will sit on the veranda. At this time of day, it is just bearable."

Podric helped him stand and holding on to his arm, Bonaparte shuffled outside.

Lying on a chaise longue, Napoleon swatted away a fly. Sitting beside him, Podric sipped some coffee Marchand had laid out.

"This island... The weather... The summer, the heat is unpleasant, and the winter it's cold, desolate."

"You cheated on me."

Napoleon waved his hand dismissively.

"Cheated in your game?"

"You said life was one."

"Pchwa. In life victory is everything. I wished to beat you."

"But you lost."

"I was disadvantaged."

Napoleon studied his left wrist. Though faint, the little micro-chip could still be seen below the skin's surface.

"You have timed your arrival well. Today is 21st day of April –the feast of England's St George. Ha, I have just two weeks of life remaining."

Another bout of coughing ensued. Through his wheezing, Napoleon forced a grim smile.

"Of course I went in and saw my end. There's been plenty of time. What else have I had to do these past six years? This villa they put me in – death will be easy."

Napoleon looked as though he might expire at any moment. Turning on his side, he tried to make himself more comfortable.

"Ah, here comes Countess Bertrand and her son Arthur. They've all deserted me – Las Cases, O'Meara, Gourgaud. In marrying her husband, the woman owes everything to him, who in turn owes all his promotions to his emperor, but still she despises me...Madame, join us."

Making an expansive wave, he indicated his welcome. The woman and boy, aged about four, came nearer. Napoleon continued his briefing to Podric as if the newcomers didn't exist.

"Given she and the Count named their eldest son after me, I've wondered at their choice of this one's name. Arthur is your Duke of Wellington's, is it not?"

Arriving at the foot of the steps, the child made a little bow. His mother curtsied perfunctorily. Napoleon smiled at Arthur, who smiled back.

"My husband said you were ill."

"That is nothing new, Countess."

"You are not contagious?"

Napoleon laughed again and managed to stifle a splutter.

"What ails me is a disease of quite a different nature."

As he spoke, Bonaparte rubbed the side of his head as if in pain.

"No, your emperor's ailments are not for catching."

Little Arthur Bertrand stood beside Napoleon's chaise longue. Bonaparte, discovering a sweet in his waistcoat pocket, put it in the boy's hand. After tweaking Arthur's cheek, the ex-emperor looked up at his mother, who sat down on a wicker chair.

"I believe Countess, you regard this island as a place the devil defecated on."

"'Tis a foul rock. You know it, sire!"

"And those of you who've remained await my death to escape the infernal schist. Well it will delight you to know, your sojourn is nearly over. I only have a few days of mortality left."

"You seem remarkably certain as to the timing emperor."

Laughing again, Napoleon winced in pain.

"See Podric, the consideration shown to me by my own people!"

Lying back exhausted, Bonaparte fiddled with a loose button on his jacket.

"If there is nothing else Countess, I will see you and your family again in a day or so."

Napoleon gave Arthur a playful prod and smiled.

Standing, the Countess Bertrand addressed Podric.

"The emperor is renowned for his courtesy."

Watching their departure, Bonaparte appeared in a reverie then suddenly transformed. A fired intensity burned in his eye.

"Marchand!"

The valet appeared.

"Have the carriage brought around."

"Sire – the carriage? You haven't been out, well..."

"I know – ignore my confines. Have it here."

With another Gallic shrug, the servant disappeared. Napoleon felt about his person.

"My snuff box. Could I trouble you to bring it Podric? It'll be beside my cot."

Travelling through the estate, they approached a neatly white-washed cottage.

"That is the little house the Countess, her husband and family reside in."

A horseman was leaving the property as they went by; his eyes studiously avoided them.

"General Montholon. He runs my household. He does not have my favour. The man is an imbecile."

"History wonders if he might have slowly poisoned you. A high level of arsenic is found in your body."

This didn't seem to surprise Napoleon very much.

"With Sir Hudson's approval, no doubt."

Napoleon sat back.

"I welcome death. I have been dying here every day since my arrival – with or without assistance."

The carriage moved along at a pleasant pace in the early after-noon sunshine.

"You know Podric, your youth makes me think of my son His Majesty, the King of Rome. You are only a few years older than he.

"When did you last see him?"

"The times were brief, too brief..."

Bonaparte stared sadly at the passing view.

"Before my exile to Elba. I abdicated in his favour."

Looking at Napoleon, Podric watched him experience another mood change – becoming melancholy and remote.

"Mortality – man's destiny..."

Arriving at the estate entrance, the driver pulled up.

"Why do you stop Archambault?"

"Emperor..."

"Drive on. We visit The Peak."

"But..."

"You will do as you are bid."

The coachman was still hesitant. Opening the carriage door, Na-poleon got out. Stretching his fat legs, he indicated Archambault to approach him.

Standing beside the horse, Napoleon put an arm around the driv-er, who began to sob. After a few moments he put something into the man's hand and parting, patted him on the back. Archambault went down to the gate and communicated with two guards. CQMS Tweeney appeared from a small stone gatehouse and after listening to the discussion, lumbered up to the carriage. Ignoring Napoleon, he addressed Podric.

"Beggin' yer pardon sir, but he's not allowed beyond 'ere. Governor's orders."

"It's alright Quartermaster. General Bonaparte is with me."

"But sir...I can't allow it."

Stepping out of the carriage, Podric took Tweeney aside.

"Sergeant, your prisoner has two weeks to live. Surely for the sake of humanity..."

Tweeney shook his head.

"More than my job's worth."

"Well, that's significant. Supposing you were posted today. How would that suit?"

"Are you serious sir? It can't be done."

"It can sergeant, and it will be. An Indiaman leaves this afternoon. If you go to your quarters now and gather your things, I'll see you're aboard."

Tweeney's eyes narrowed.

"I know you know a lot about me an' all, but what proof have I got this'll happen?"

"May I see you briefly in your office, alone?"

Tweeney shrugged and the two walked down to the gatehouse.

Minutes later, Podric returned to the carriage by himself. Adjusting his sleeve, he touched his left wrist.

"My dignity preserved by a 17-year-old twenty-first-century boy!"

Bonaparte squeezed Podric's arm. The gates swung open and the carriage moved off.

"Why did you do what you did?"

The track they were on was winding its way through lusher, greener countryside.

"Things happened. Toulon – my country – France!"

"But then you became 'First' something or other – then crowned yourself. You didn't have to do that."

"Life does not stand still Podric and a man such as me, cannot. I, a Corsican corporal, could not. When things happen to such a man, you don't stop. Your grip on power rests on activity. But I had such dreams for my country."

"Dreams for yourself..."

"Yes! For myself also – why not?! But I am everything and nothing. I have lived to lead!"

The carriage approached a lovely secluded spot. Napoleon suddenly leaned out of the door and pointed.

"I will be buried here – under those trees!"

Some weeping willows hung over a small stream. The place had a calm, peaceful feel to it.

"In just fourteen days' time... Ha!"

Napoleon fell back.

"Oh, Poderique. To think what could have been and what I have become."

Napoleon was emotional. In front of them the track divided. Archambault guided the horse towards the left fork.

"No Archambault, a deviation – mon promenade!"

"Oui mon empereur. Vive l'empereur!"

Archambault cracked the whip and turned the horse on to the right track. The mood in the carriage became less poignant.

"Your British government put me here in this remote prison, thousands of miles from anywhere. When I first arrived I was tired, so tired – it was tolerable. The man who brought me to my 'île bagne' as governor, Admiral Cockburn, was an intelligent man, a man worthy of Napoleon. But then this vile viper, this cursed Lowe arrives. The little piece of dung with a brain no bigger than a fly..."

Napoleon brushed one from his sleeve before continuing.

"He is awarded the task of guarding the Emperor of France! Such is my treatment. But you know Podric, some would like to see me free – even in England. I know this... Such people still believe in the genius of Napoleon."

They arrived at a cliff top overlooking the sea. Archambault brought the carriage to a halt. With great effort Bonaparte climbed out followed by Podric. Below them a bay was filled with ships – xebecs, barquentines, merchantmen of the East India Company and Navy two-deckers. The predominant flag flown was either a red or white ensign.

Napoleon stood absorbing the scene. Ill, yet defiant in his classic Napoleon stance - one hand inside his coat, he stared out at the maritime activity below.

"I have been to this place many times watching the ships, but I will make a confession to you. In continental war, my victories were unrivalled. I conquered all."

Podric's look was quizzical.

"Russia..?"

"I entered Moscow!"

"But your retreat was a disaster."

"You know little of such things young man."

"I know history."

"Ha! Is that what they say in the future? Yes, I can see it. Anyway, it is not that which destroyed me. We're looking at what destroyed me. Perfidious Albion."

"It took a land battle to finally defeat you."

"That is so, but my nemesis was able to continue its fight against me through all the years of conflict, however many victories I won."

Napoleon kicked a pebble over the edge.

"I was trying to remember. A long time ago a man told me I would fail because of the sea."

"Sounds like Archie. He had a dog."

"Yes. Yes! A dog. I remember your partner - in the garden. Ha!"

Napoleon became reflective again.

"That is where I failed. My navy - the officers... Weak men who promised much but delivered little."

"I told you when we first came into the game, Archie and me, we met Admiral Nelson."

"He is a man I would like to have fought myself. I wish he had been a soldier."

"Wellington..?"

Napoleon laughed.

"So young... I love you Podric because you are 'une original'. At the Belgian battle, I was unwell - and now it is too late. You are going to end this adventure and I am going to die."

Napoleon turned to Podric.

"What is it you English say – 'in at the death'."

They walked a little way along the path.

"Your telling me about finding your father in realité ultime."

Napoleon limped badly and clutched Podric's arm.

"Seeing little of my own boy, I've sometimes felt you were a son to me."

There were tears in Napoleon's eyes. "How small is the time we have to achieve."

Napoleon reached out to Podric, and hugged him. Whilst in the embrace, the boy looked at the ex-emperor's ear. He would leave the little audile membrane where it was. Perhaps posterity would find it one day?

"The reality I've created is a world that never needs to end."

Showing some Napoleonic spirit, Bonaparte had a pinch of snuff.

"You have made me immortal, Podric."

"Give me your wrist."

Napoleon smiled.

"The left one I think."

Producing a small knife, Podric made a tiny incision.

"Have you decided what your next adventures will be?"

Podric didn't reply but neatly removed the microchip, wrapping a piece of fabric around the emperor's wrist.

During this operation Napoleon looked out to sea. For a long while, he continued to gaze at the ocean. When he turned back, he was alone.

The coach climbed away from the cliffs, the hill road twisting and turning upwards into the island's hinterland. Fumbling in his waistcoat pocket, Napoleon took out his snuff box, its coat of arms surrounding an embossed 'N' on the lid. His pudgy fingers opened the silver container. A little piece of metal lay amidst the snuff. Inspecting it, Napoleon couldn't fathom its significance and tossed it away. Gazing back, he saw a youth standing on the promontory.

"Ah, youth éternel."

Envoi

Sitting on the pilot's seat of ZA119 - the Typhoon T3 Podric's father flew and instructed in, Podric felt the full thrust of the two EJ200 engines powering the aeroplane. Bursting through a stratum of cloud into the sunshine above, for a brief second, he looked down at the cumulus below. It was a sensational feeling - one that could go on forever but was dramatically interrupted. The console in front of him flashed a warning 'Combat Imminent - Enemy Attacking. Player 1 Response'.

"Break Podric. Break!"

Sean Moon's voice was urgent, but cool.

A MiG 29 suddenly appeared in Podric's rear view mirror.

"I'm on it Dad!"

The T3 gave a sharp inverse roll, combining the action with jaw-dropping descent. It was a fast manoeuvre. The Typhoon simply disappeared from the MiG's view.

Pulling maximum G, Podric hauled the aeroplane into a tight turn and began a vertical climb. Regaining height at a thousand feet per second, they appeared under the two Russians, shadowing them in a blind spot no more than eighty feet below.

Flipping the Typhoon's missile switches to 'On', Podric throttled back slightly and the millisecond he had the port beam 29 in his sights, released a heat seeking missile. It immediately locked onto the enemy's afterburners. The display flashed 'Target Eradicated'. But quick though he was in attempting to line up on the second MiG, the Russian pulled a similar vanishing manoeuvre to Podric's.

Flying on instinct, the boy spun the Typhoon on its tail.

The 29 pilot was good, very good. The aircraft corkscrewed, climbed, twisted and turned in a series of rivet pulling, eye-bulging weaves and dodges. For a second, Podric thought he had him, but then the Russian evaded his momentary entrapment and the hunt continued its hair-raising chase across the skies.

"Exercises are okay but if you want to make Top Gun Podric, you won't get him like this in combat. Think outside the box."

The son didn't reply to the father's comments but just before entering cloud, Podric appeared to veer away from the MiG in a steep bank.

Inside the whiteness, it was impossible to see what his actions were doing. Only by reading the altimeter, whose needle rotated rapidly, could he know his position. Seconds later and dangerously low, Podric emerged from the cloud right on the tail of the MiG! Activating his missile switch again and depressing the 'fire' button, the 'Target Eradicated' display instantly flashed, followed by 'Combat Concluded: Formulating Score'. He'd outguessed his enemy. Trimming the aircraft, Podric throttled back, easing the control column.

"Where have you been?"

Sean's voice was relaxed.

"Learning some history."

"Good. It's important. I told you – with it, you can get an angle on the present and maybe have a chance dealing with the future."

"I've missed you, dad."

"Me too. But I'm here now – I'll always be here."

"I just don't want to lose you."

"You never will, Podric."

Podric could hear his father's warm chuckle.

"I could fly with you forever."

The console flashed one last time.

'Player 1 wins: Player 1 wins'
'Game Over'.

"Well then, what's to stop us?"

Acknowledgements

The author wishes to thank all those who over the years have given him support and encouragement in his writing endeavours.

Publishing this new edition of *Podric Moon and the Corsican Tyrant* with some flexibility, historical accuracy is generally observed. Special thanks should go to David Percy at Aulis Publishers for his technical preparation of the book, to Kat Patterson at Art of the Possible for web design and Christian Ward at 17 Verde for on-line platform creation.

Finally, the author wishes to thank Seana for putting up with him whilst allowing his imagination to wander in the numerous directions it does.

Where Ultimate Alternative Reality is concerned that can be far-ranging – trying to decipher what's real and what's alternate being of never-ending interest and consuming fascination.

Barney Broom, Blakeney, 2020

Sample extract from

MOON RIVER

Podric Moon's Adventures
in
the American Civil War

Chapter 1

VR versus the ultimate

The Elysian Hall in London's SW3 district was packed. An e-games Star-Pro event in progress, two giant screens were positioned on a raised stage at its centre. The two players wearing VR visors sat at their controls dwarfed by an enormous wall of monitors mirroring their Virtual Reality action two dimensionally.

The game in progress *Civil War* (the American one) the two participants, Michael Allardyce and Podric Moon, had been locked in combat for several hours. Now in its closing stages – in a reversal of history, Podric, fighting the Reb cause had outmanoeuvred Allardyce's Yankee troops, destroying the North's armies and altering the historic results of Shiloh and Antietam. The scene was set for Lee's Army of Virginia to take Washington.

Allardyce boxed in, Podric was bored. As technical head of Pasaro – the world's largest computer games company, Allardyce had been a disappointing player. Podric suspected that although Michael was extremely proficient at analysis and conceptualising games he wasn't a player smart contestant.

Taking his hands from the VR's Xbox controls Podric's right index finger pressed his left wrist activating UAR. A menu appeared at the top of his eyes. Podric moved his finger using it as a cursor and selected the same American Civil War game he was playing in Virtual Reality. It now appeared as Ultimate Alternative Reality.

Highlighting Battles, the first one Podric came across was Bull Run or First Manassas as it was known to the Confederacy. Podric pressed Enter.

*   *   *

The boy - soldier's ragged blue uniform, cap askew and britches mud-splattered, suffered rips and tears as he tumbled over the ridge rolling into the ditch below. Musket fire exploding around him, a panting Podric Moon looked about. Separated from his unit, no other Union soldiers were in sight as the sea of grey uniforms - their 'Stars and Bars' flag fluttering in the Virginian countryside, advanced towards him.

Unlike his UAR partner Dr Archie Light, Podric wasn't concerned about programming himself into a senior position of rank. He was more interested in getting an on the ground feel of things. Experiencing that now, the adrenal rush coursed his veins as he squirmed his way down the gully. Peering through a bush, Henry House Hill was in front of him. Podric didn't know its name or that Confederate general Thomas Jackson would earn his 'Stonewall' sobriquet there fighting his Union counterpart William Tecumseh Sherman - another leader who would rise to fame as the war progressed. But the fighting around the building was fierce.

An explosion erupted and cannon fire deafened Podric covering him with dirt. Two blue clad soldiers jumped down beside him and were immediately set upon by a platoon of Virginians pouring in behind. The two men shot and beaten - Podric unarmed, grabbed the wounded man's musket and swung its stock at the nearest Confederate soldier. The corporal fell back cursing. More men from both sides appeared and more cannon fire exploded. A body flung across Podric felled him. Memories of the Heights of Toulon in *Napoleonic Wars* flashed through his mind. Man was such a violent creature; these historic games highlighted that.

Pushing the dismembered figure away, another Reb screamed into view. Podric ducked behind a tree stump. Bending back its stubby branch he released it into his attacker's guts. The man went down. Podric dragged the comrade he'd been trying to assist along the defile. Reaching a bend, they ran into more grey troopers.

The wounded soldier on Podric's arm drew out a long-bladed knife and hurled it at the nearest enemy. Some ammunition ordnance went off. Obliterating everything, Podric was propelled through the air. Conscious someone was tapping his shoulder, Podric quickly depressed his left wrist.

*   *   *

What was this?

Back in the VR game things had changed dramatically. Podric taking himself off into UAR had allowed Michael Allardyce back into the contest. The Pasaro man was now on the offensive having blocked Podric's Confederate forces in their advance on DC. Gettysburg – the next battle in the time-line – Podric quickly checked data and decided to place 'Jeb' Stuart in command of the South's cavalry. Striking quickly, this move carried the day. Confederate forces took Cemetery Ridge and under Podric's games command, Gettysburg became a Southern victory.

Continuing his momentum Podric began rolling up Allardyce's Union forces. Capitalising on a stronger victory at Second Bull Run and strategically, not allowing other elements that sometimes pressed to deflect him, Lee advanced on Washington. Thus it was that the leader of the Confederate forces reached the capital. Michael Allardyce conceded, and the game was over.

*   *   *

Put up in a London hotel overnight, Podric excused himself from the reception that evening pleading an excess of homework! Retiring to his room, he suddenly felt exhausted as the intensity of the game and his additional adventures, washed over him. Taking some sparkling water from the mini-bar, Podric lay down on the bed.

Whilst acknowledging that diving into UAR in the middle of a VR games tournament was professionally irresponsible Podric didn't worry about it unduly. In spite of his dalliance he'd won the contest and the contrast between VR and UAR - the latter allowing him to apparently *live* the experience - was to his mind, chasmic.

There was some irony that the event had featured the American Civil War. Having had a fix of excitement with his Napoleonic UAR adventures, Podric had been under pressure from his history teacher, Mr Ironside to swat up the US internal conflict for his upcoming GCSE exam. His brief sojourn into it via Ultimate Alternative Reality had shown him the ferocity with which each side fought, though his experiences were a bit too intense and personal for the required essay he was due to write.

Relaxing in his hotel bedroom, Podric activated UAR again. As it loaded up he reflected that he was as bad as his partner. There had been issues between them about alternative reality becoming an escapist drug-of-life preference but in truth he had to acknowledge he was just as keen to escape into UAR as Archie was.

Spooling through *Civil War* Podric checked out the overall structure of the conflict – why it had come about and how the war developed. One figure above all dominated: Abraham Lincoln.

Printed in Great Britain
by Amazon

53648232R00234